CU00731113

WELCOME TO WEAVER STREET

CHRISSIE WALSH

Boldwood

First published in Great Britain in 2022 by Boldwood Books Ltd.

Copyright © Chrissie Walsh, 2022

Cover Design by Colin Thomas

Cover Photography: Colin Thomas

The moral right of Chrissie Walsh to be identified as the author of this work has been asserted in accordance with the Copyright, Designs and Patents Act 1988.

All rights reserved. No part of this book may be reproduced in any form or by any electronic or mechanical means, including information storage and retrieval systems, without written permission from the author, except for the use of brief quotations in a book review.

This book is a work of fiction and, except in the case of historical fact, any resemblance to actual persons, living or dead, is purely coincidental.

Every effort has been made to obtain the necessary permissions with reference to copyright material, both illustrative and quoted. We apologise for any omissions in this respect and will be pleased to make the appropriate acknowledgements in any future edition.

A CIP catalogue record for this book is available from the British Library.

Paperback ISBN 978-1-80280-942-8

Large Print ISBN 978-1-80280-938-1

Hardback ISBN 978-1-80280-937-4

Ebook ISBN 978-1-80280-935-0

Kindle ISBN 978-1-80280-936-7

Audio CD ISBN 978-1-80280-943-5

MP3 CD ISBN 978-1-80280-940-4

Digital audio download ISBN 978-1-80280-934-3

Boldwood Books Ltd
23 Bowerdean Street
London SW6 3TN
www.boldwoodbooks.com

For my family.

The only way to have a friend is to be one.

— RALPH WALDO EMERSON

There is nothing on this earth more to be prized than true friendship

— THOMAS AQUINAS

1

LIVERPOOL, JULY 1916

'Where do we go to now?' Kitty Conlon's luminous hazel eyes anxiously scanned the towering buildings on Liverpool's Albert Dock. The damp, early morning breeze snatched the tendrils of red-gold hair that had escaped from her chignon, scribbling them across her forlorn, pretty face. She peeled them away irritably and breathed a deep sigh, the sharp smell of salt-sea air stinging her pert, little nose. Behind her, the Belfast steam packet was still disgorging passengers who, as they streamed past Kitty, seemed to know exactly where *they* were going.

'The solicitor's office in Portland Street.' Tom Conlon's sharp, blue eyes had been roaming the docks. Now they settled on his wife. He smiled fondly. The voyage had been a nightmare, the steamer buffeted by squalling seas but Kitty still managed to look beautiful, her glorious, tawny hair fanning her cheeks and her diminutive figure shapely in a bottle-green coat with a velvet collar.

Kitty's heavy bag was making her shoulder ache so she dumped it on top of one of the two bulging suitcases Tom had set down. Whichever way they looked, the quayside swarmed with people, lorries and carts. Overhead, gulls swooped and mewed.

'First, we have to find our way off the docks,' Tom said, catching Kitty's elbow and drawing her close as a heavily laden cart trundled past. Kitty pressed her cheek against the sleeve of his rough tweed overcoat, comforted by his nearness. She slipped her arm round his waist, feeling the need to hold on to him, to let the warmth of his body take away the chill that shrouded her own.

Tom lowered his gaze to look at her, and seeing the pallor on her cheeks, he asked, 'Are ye all right?' Kitty heard the concern in his voice as he folded her in his arms. She looked up into his strong, handsome face and saw nothing but love and considerateness. She gave a firm nod and a bright smile. She mustn't let him see how fearful she felt.

'Then we'll make tracks,' he said, releasing his hold on her. Immediately she felt lost and vulnerable but she pushed back her shoulders and lifted her heavy canvas bag that was stuffed to bursting with woollen shawls in case they'd had to sit out on deck, a damp flannel and a brush and comb to tidy themselves up after spending all night at sea, plus a pair of Tom's second best shoes that they hadn't been able to cram into their overloaded suitcases. At the top of the bag were the remains of the sandwiches she had made before they had left Dublin to travel up to Belfast to catch the steam packet. Tom had wanted to throw them to the gulls but Kitty, fearful of going hungry for the rest of the journey, had kept them.

Tom waited while she adjusted the bag, then, pulling the peak of his cap a little lower on his forehead, he lifted the two heavy pieces of luggage that contained the rest of their worldly possessions and set off at a brisk pace.

Kitty hurried alongside, the bag bumping uncomfortably against her hip as she struggled to match his stride, her legs still attuned to the rocking of the boat and the nausea she had suffered on the crossing still gurgling in her stomach. It made her feel unusually fragile. For a few awful moments she wondered if she had fallen victim to whatever ailed the woman who had come to sit next to her on the boat, the scabs round her mouth and eyes and the putrid smell of her indicating she was unwell. Kitty had moved away from the woman as soon as possible in case she might pass on her germs. Even so, she couldn't help feeling as though she had caught something nasty.

'How do we get there – to Portland Street?' she panted.

'I'll ask somebody.' Tom gave her a reassuring smile, and seeing that her cheeks were now red with exertion he slowed his pace.

Weaving their way between large piles of crates and dodging the lorries and carts, they joined the seething, sweaty crush at the port's gate. When it was their turn to pass through the gate, Tom asked the uniformed official for directions to Portland Street.

'It's a fair walk,' the gatekeeper said, glancing at Kitty's strained face and then at her bulging bag and the suitcases. 'You'd be better off taking a cab.' He pointed to where a long queue had formed at the roadside, the people at the head of it boarding the vehicles as one cab after another came chugging down the road.

They joined the tail end of the queue, Kitty relieved that she wasn't faced with a long walk, and Tom quailing inwardly at the thought of the expense; maybe they should walk. He asked the man in front of him if he knew the way to Portland Street, but halfway through the man's *'turn left at this street, right at that one,'* he resigned himself to taking a cab. Kitty, feeling peckish and not wanting to waste the sandwiches, fished them out of her bag and they ate them while they waited their turn.

Once they were seated in the back of the cab, Kitty and Tom smiled at one another, their relief at having made it this far plain on their faces. Tom had stowed the suitcases onto a rack at the rear, but Kitty had held on to her bag, resting it at her feet and liking the feeling of being in control of at least some of their possessions.

As she gazed out of the window at the grand buildings and the crush of people in the busy streets, Tom quizzed the cabbie as to how they should get from Portland Street to Weaver Street in Edge Hill. The cabbie, a mine of information, was able to tell him which tram they needed and where to catch it. Feeling more in control, Tom sat back to enjoy the journey, reasoning that the cab fare was well worth it: Kitty could never have walked the distance.

The cab trundled its way into the centre of Liverpool, stopping and starting in the congested thoroughfares. The streets thronged with people going about their business. Pavements steamed as the early morning sun dried off an earlier shower of rain, and a strong smell of horse dung, oil and pungent unfamiliar smells wafted through the open window. Tom and Kitty peered this way and that, commenting on the vast buildings that towered over dense, sooty rows of shops and houses. Kitty thought it all looked rather dank and depressing, even though they had passed some impressive shops such as Blacklers and Coopers.

'Do ye think we're going to like livin' in Liverpool?' Her voice wobbled plaintively. They hadn't lived in the best part of Dublin, but it had been much pleasanter than anything she had seen so far.

'I've no idea,' Tom replied. 'We'll just have to wait and find out.'

'How long did you say it was since your uncle Seamus had last visited your great-uncle Thomas?' She already knew the answer and it only increased her anxiety but, like the tip of her tongue whenever she had a sore tooth, she felt the need to probe.

'Ah, must be thirty or more years,' Tom said easily.

'That's a long time. Tell me again what Seamus said about it?'

Tom screwed up his face. 'Ach, well, like I already told ye, Seamus went over looking for work but he didn't care for the place and came back home after a month or two. He missed the farm and the wild countryside in Clare, so he said.'

Kitty wondered if she would feel the same. She had grown used to missing her home place in Roscommon and now she worried that she would miss Dublin once she was living in Edge Hill. Home had been a remote smallholding where she had lived with her parents and three brothers. In the same year that she had turned sixteen her parents had died and Shaun, her youngest brother and the one nearest her own age, had left home. After that, things had never been the same.

Her elder brothers, Padraig and Brendan Mulvenny, were ten and more years Kitty's age, and both of them being unmarried, they had expected her to take over her mother's role. Fed up of waiting on them hand and foot and eager to make her own way in the world she had packed her bags and moved to Dublin.

Alone in the big city she had been fortunate enough to get a live-in job as a waitress at the Gresham Hotel. That was where she had met Tom. She'd been bowled over when the handsome man with a roguish smile, flashing blue eyes and black wavy hair had asked her to walk out with him. Her joy hadn't lasted long. When she told him that her brother was a brigade commander in the Irish Republican Army, Tom had been horrified. He told her he wanted no truck with the hotheads ruining the country. All he wanted was to earn his living as a bookmaker, quietly and peaceably, and climb the ladder until one day he had his own business.

'It's fools like them that stop decent fellas like me from making their way. Who cares who governs the country as long as we have money in our pockets and bread in our bellies?' he had argued.

For the next few weeks he had avoided her, but his desire to be with her greater than his abhorrence of her brother's mutinous activities he'd sought her out. 'Promise me ye'll have nothin' to do with your brother or his like,' he'd said. Kitty had promised; she was already head over heels in love. After that, they'd spent every evening together. She had worried over what Shaun would think if he knew she was walking out with a man who didn't support the Republican cause. After all, the Easter Uprising, as people were calling it, had cost many lives and some, like Shaun, were still waiting to learn their fate in an English jail. But when Tom told her he loved her and wanted her to marry him, Kitty had put all other thoughts out of her head.

The wedding had been small, neither Kitty's nor Tom's families making the journey from the west of Ireland to Dublin, but Kitty hadn't expected anything else. She was marrying the handsomest man in Dublin and that was all that had mattered. Her friend, Maureen, from the Gresham Hotel, had been her bridesmaid and a chap from Power's bookmakers had been Tom's best man. During the three months they had been married Kitty and Tom, like two excited children, had sealed their love. Now, in July 1916, she had crossed the Irish Sea and was sitting in a cab to God knows where or what. And had she been able to read Tom's mind she would have learned that his thoughts matched her own: had the decision to come to England been a wise one?

* * *

They had been married just a month when the letter had arrived at the rooming house in Dublin. Kitty would never forget the day. She came home from her job in the Gresham Hotel to find it lying on the little table in the lobby.

No sooner had she lifted it than that old crone, Mary Hannigan, who lived in the bottom half of the house had poked her head out of her door, curiosity burning in her black, currant-bun eyes. 'Yez have a swanky letter wid an Engerlish stamp on it,' she sneered, the derisory expression on her wizened face letting Kitty know just what she thought of anything that came out of England.

As Kitty gazed at the tiny image of King George V, Mary craned her wrinkled neck, peering at the envelope and then at Kitty, her eyes willing Kitty to open it. 'It looks mighty important to me.'

Kitty stared at the envelope, her curiosity mixed with fear. It did look important in an official sort of way, the kind that a court of law might use to issue a summons, she thought. The very sight of it threw her into a tizzy.

'So it does, Mrs Hannigan,' she croaked, hurrying to the foot of the stairs.

'Are yez not goin' to open it?' Mary squawked.

Kitty took the stairs two at a time, Mary's scowl burning holes in her back as she climbed the narrow flight that led up to the two rooms she and Tom thought of as home.

Inside the living room cum kitchen Kitty placed the letter on the table under the window. She gazed at the envelope, her fingers itching to take the knife she used for paring vegetables and slit it open: but it wasn't her letter, and she was unsure how Tom would feel about that. They hadn't been married long enough for her to know such things, and it made her think how little she knew about her husband. Slowly, she unbuttoned her coat. *I've a lot to learn*, she'd told herself, tossing the coat over the back of a chair then smoothing imaginary creases from the crisp white shirt and calf-length black skirt that was her waitress's uniform.

Still feeling hot and bothered, she turned back to study the envelope again. The postmark showed that it had been posted on the fourth of May 1916. That was just three days ago. Kitty neither wrote nor received letters, so she was surprised to learn that one could travel so far in such a short space of time.

The envelope bore the embossed name and address of a solicitor's office in Liverpool, Lancashire, in England. Kitty traced the dark, red lettering with the tip of her finger. Now why would a solicitor in Liverpool – a place she'd only heard tell of – be writing to her Tom? As far as she knew, he'd never been to Liverpool.

Propriety winning over temptation, she set the letter on the mantelpiece. Propped majestically between the chimney breast and a small, lead statue of Our Lady, the thick, cream envelope taunted Kitty as, knife in hand and ears pricked, she began to peel potatoes for the evening meal.

When she heard the thud of feet on the stairs her breath whooshed out. She hadn't been aware of holding it. Almost dizzy with relief she rinsed her hands under the tap and, wiping them dry on her skirt, she ran to open the door.

Tom greeted her with a big smile, his blue eyes dancing as he leaned in from the doorway to kiss her. 'That's a grand welcome for a man to come home to,' he said, pulling off his cap. Locks of wavy black hair fell over his forehead, curled round his ears and at the nape of his neck. Kitty ran her fingers through them as she returned his kiss. Then, words failing her, she wagged a finger in the direction of the mantelpiece. Bemused, Tom looked to where she pointed. Seeing the envelope, he strode over to the fireplace. 'Who's it from?' he asked.

* * *

Seated stiffly upright on the cab's shiny leather seat, too nervous to relax, Tom willed the cab to speed up and get them to the solicitor's office. He would dearly have liked a cigarette. He gazed at the back of the cabbie's head, greying hair straggling over a thick, red neck. If the cabbie lit up then so would he. The cab came to a complete standstill at a busy junction and Tom's hopes rose then fell. Sadly, it seemed the chap was a non-smoker. He felt the warmth of Kitty's thigh next to his own and glanced sideways at her. She looked pensive. He thought he knew exactly how she felt.

In the inside pocket of his best black suit jacket the letter was snug against his chest. With it was another letter in reply to the one Tom had written on the night the first letter had arrived. Had there been some mistake, he had enquired. By return, in grandiose language, Mr James Pennington of Pennington, Pennington and Duckworth had assured him that he was now the rightful owner of number eleven, Weaver Street, Edge Hill, Liverpool, in the county of Lancashire. When he had read it out loud Kitty had burst into tears. Tom still didn't know whether they had been tears of joy or regret.

They had read and reread the letters many times over, gradually unravelling the unfamiliar terms and then digesting the full import of their meaning, all the while barely able to believe what they had read.

'Bequeathed,' Kitty said over and again, tasting the word on her tongue. 'But why did your great-uncle Thomas leave his house to you, Tom?'

Tom had sat back, rubbing his finely sculpted jaw. 'Well, for one, I was named for him, he stood for me at my baptism, and for another, I'm the last of the Conlons in Quilty. What with Da's da being the only brother to marry and have a son, and then my da producing five girls and one son – me – I'm the last of the line to bear the name Conlon. Maybe Great-Uncle Tom hoped I'd be the one to carry it on.' He'd given Kitty a nudge and a suggestive wink.

Kitty had giggled, but her brow had creased as she tried to make sense of it.

Night after night they had talked of little else, and during the day as Kitty served the diners in the Gresham Hotel and Tom took bets behind the counter of Power's bookmakers, the thought of what to do about the house in Edge Hill was never far from their minds. Should they ask Mr Pennington to sell it and send them the proceeds? That seemed to be the simplest answer, Kitty argued. The money would afford them better lodgings in Dublin, maybe even enough to buy their own place.

'I don't know what to think, Tom,' she persisted. 'Will we be safe there? The English are at war with the Germans.'

'Sure, an' aren't we at war with ourselves?' Tom sneered. 'Is Dublin the place where ye want to settle an' raise a family?'

In a quandary, Kitty had given a helpless shrug.

Ever since those dreadful days at Easter, less than two months before, the city had been restless. Neither Tom nor Kitty were involved in the politics of the situation – unlike her brother, Shaun, who was now suffering the consequences – but the dangers could not be ignored. The Irish Republicans still thirsted for Home Rule, and the British Government were still haggling over whether or not they might come to some agreement. Both the British and Irish forces regularly perpetrated terrible deeds, and violence and fear roamed the heart of the city. The more Tom and Kitty had talked, the more convinced Tom was that Ireland was not the place to make his fortune.

'Think on it, Kitty,' he had pleaded. 'A house of our own and jobs aplenty. I know ye're feared by the prospect of a strange place, but Dublin was strange to ye when first ye came from Roscommon. I'm not saying I don't still miss my home in Clare, but I do believe there's so much more opportunity in England. It served Great-Uncle Tom well enough.'

'But I won't know anyone,' Kitty had pleaded. She was gregarious and liked having a circle of friends in a city about which she knew her way. The thought of being uprooted and having to learn about a new place didn't appeal. It had been difficult enough coming from Roscommon to Dublin, but at least the people in Dublin were Irish. What would the English make of her, she wondered.

'Sure, you knew nobody when you first came here, an' look at the friends ye have now. An' it took ye no time at all to learn your way about. Ye'll do the same over there,' Tom had told her confidently.

Kitty had tried to look convinced. Maybe they would be better off living in England. It was true that the shooting in the streets made her nervous. She was frightened of catching a stray bullet as she walked to and from work, or of the Gresham being commandeered by the rebels. The bar staff and waitresses had been told to be vigilant and keep a sharp eye out for strangers who might be carrying guns. The trouble with Dublin was you never knew who was a friend and who was an enemy. But would they be any safer in England? Kitty didn't know what to think. At work she kept her opinions to herself, served at the tables, chatted with Maureen, and each evening she hurried home to the safety of Tom's arms. Tom was so much cleverer than her and knew about these things. She tried to imagine what living in England would be like, and thought about her brother. But Shaun wasn't living a normal life there, so that was no use.

Kitty sought Maureen's advice. 'What do ye think we should do?' Maureen was the under housekeeper at the Gresham. Three years older than Kitty, she seemed to know a lot about everything. 'Better the divil ye know,' she'd replied. 'Ye've not seen the place. It could be a wreck, and Tom might not get work. The English don't like the Irish. An' I'll miss ye if ye go.'

Tom asked the Parish priest. 'England's not the heathen place some think it is,' he had said. 'I was there, in Manchester, as a young curate. If I were you I'd at least go and look at the property if only to assess its value. You wouldn't want the solicitor selling it and telling you one price when he'd got double, now would ye? And ye can always come home.' He gave Tom a benign smile and shook his hand. Tom had seen the wisdom in the old priest's advice and doubled his efforts to persuade Kitty to at least go and look at the house.

* * *

And so – here they were in a cab in Liverpool, Kitty struggling to settle the swarm of butterflies that had invaded her tummy and Tom cogitating on what lay ahead. A punch of fear hit his stomach as he thought of how little they knew about what awaited them.

At last, the cab turned into a street lined with imposing buildings. 'Portland Street,' the cabbie announced. 'Pennington's is the one with the red door.'

Kitty stooped and gathered her bag, her heart pounding. Now they were really going to find out what Tom had inherited. She blinked nervously then smiled at Tom. He looked tense. The cabbie lifted their suitcases from the rack and set them down on the pavement. Then he held out his hand. Tom paid him, begrudgingly adding a sixpenny tip. The cabbie smirked. 'Oh ta, mate, ta very much.' Sarcasm dripped from his tongue, but Tom was past caring. He nodded for Kitty to go to the red door then followed her without looking back.

'Is this the right place?' she asked, her tone a mixture of excitement and fear.

'It says so,' he grunted, his eyes on the gold lettering etched on the window to the side of the door. A brass plaque set into the stone doorpost confirmed it.

He had never been in a solicitor's office and he wondered how to conduct himself. He didn't want to appear to be a gombeen from the bogs. He lifted the brass knocker, which was in the shape of a clenched fist, and rapped it. Then he turned the brass doorknob. The door was locked.

Kitty dithered, the strap on her bag biting into her shoulder. She set it down on the steps then looked expectantly at Tom.

'They're not yet open.' He glanced up and down the street, looking slightly dazed and very apprehensive. 'We're too early.' He stepped away from the door back to where he had left the suitcases.

Kitty also stepped away to lean on Tom. She gazed up into his face enquiringly.

A smartly dressed gentleman approached from behind, muttering an apology and giving a curious look as he sidestepped them and the suitcases. Tom and Kitty jumped apart, embarrassed. The man strutted into the adjacent office and out of sight, but not before Tom had noted his well-cut suit and black Homburg hat. Suddenly he felt gauche and shabby even though he was wearing his good overcoat and best black suit. He pushed his cap to the back of his head then took it off. Folding it, he stuffed it in his pocket. Then he ran his fingers through his hair and straightened his shirt collar. Frowning, he continued fiddling with his attire, unbuttoning his overcoat then buttoning it again.

Kitty saw how unsure he looked and was surprised. As she watched him tidying his clothing she started to do the same. Tom was right as usual. They had to make a good impression, so she pushed stray wisps of hair under her hat and brushed imaginary bits of lint from her green coat. They must have looked an odd pair standing on the pavement, suitcases at their feet and lost expressions on their faces. So odd, that they attracted the attention of an elderly woman coming towards them.

'Are you lost?' Her fleshy face was kind.

Tom scowled. He hated giving the impression that he was out of his depth, so he didn't respond. Kitty, however, seeing the friendly face, said, 'We're just gatherin' ourselves afore goin' in there.' She nodded at the red door.

'You're Irish.' The woman rested her heavy basket on her hip.

'We are,' Kitty agreed, unsure if, in the woman's opinion, that was good or bad.

She beamed at Kitty. 'So was my dear old dad. He came from Cork.'

On friendly ground, Kitty replied, 'Clare for him and

Roscommon for me. We're just after coming off the overnight steam packet.'

'Oh, so you've just arrived in Liverpool?' The woman moved her basket to her other hip, ready for a gossip. Tom slid his eyes to Kitty and gave an imperceptible shake of the head that said: *don't engage her in conversation.* But it was too late.

'I'm surprised at you coming here, 'cos you're not in the war over in Ireland are you? Well, not like we are.' She chuckled. 'You've got your own troubles.' She put the basket down on the pavement and sighed heavily. 'I'm just on me way to me daughter's in Bootle. I go to give her hand wi' me grandchildren. Five of 'em there is, an' her man killed at Ypres so he was.' She pronounced it 'Wipers'. Kitty, none the wiser, murmured her condolences. Tom shuffled his feet irritably.

'It's a proper bad do losing all our lads to the Germans,' the woman continued bitterly, 'and them bombing our ships in the Mersey.' She blew out her cheeks. 'Bloomin' foreigners.' She glanced quickly from Kitty to Tom. 'Present company excepted,' she muttered. As she'd been talking an efficient-looking young woman and a plump, well-dressed man had arrived at the solicitor's office. He unlocked the door and they entered.

'So, whatever brought you to Liverp—'

'We have to go,' Tom barked, cutting the woman off and glowering at Kitty.

'Very nice to meet you,' Kitty blurted, hoisting her bag on her shoulder. The woman looked disappointed and went on her way.

'Ye shouldn't have encouraged her,' Tom snapped.

Kitty was hurt. 'I was just being polite.'

'She was a nosy old besom,' he grunted, mounting the steps to the red door. It just wasn't in his nature to tell everyone his business. Furthermore, he'd reached the stage whereby he himself doubted the wisdom of having made the journey. He turned the doorknob. The door opened. Surprised, he went and snatched up the suitcases and marched inside, Kitty at his heels.

Inside the offices of Pennington, Pennington and Duckworth they were cordially greeted by the efficient young woman and even offered a welcome cup of tea. 'Young Mr Pennington was handling Mr Conlon's affairs but he's gone to join his regiment and do his bit,' the secretary explained as she set down the tray, 'so Mr Duckworth will see you shortly.'

'Everyone seems very friendly,' Kitty whispered, as they sat at a little table in the hallway waiting for Mr Duckworth. She sipped her tea and nibbled a shortbread biscuit. The woman's remarks about the war had unnerved her and the hot, sweet tea was having a calming effect. She patted her hair and yet again smoothed imaginary bits of fluff from her coat. Was she dressed smart enough for a solicitor's office?

Mr Duckworth – plump, pink and balding – ushered them into his office, its walls lined with shelves containing fat, leather-bound books. Once seated behind his desk in a high-backed, leather chair, and with Tom and Kitty perched on two small, spindly chairs in front, the solicitor raced through the details of the last will and testament of Thomas Francis Conlon. Tom did his best to make sense of the legal jargon, but much of it went over his head. Kitty let the solicitor's words wash over her. It was like being at mass when the priest droned on in Latin, and she not understanding a word of it.

'So you see...' Mr Duckworth rested his elbows on the desk and his chins on his steepled fingers. He began speaking very slowly as one might speak to little children. 'Although Mr Conlon left his property to you in its entirety, that being the house and its contents in Weaver Street, he bequeathed his money to the Clan na Gael, a charitable institution with ties to Ireland – a society in which he had an interest.' He sat back to judge their reaction.

The solicitor's condescending attitude irritated Tom, but he silently admitted that he hadn't understood much of what he had heard. Therefore, he was dismayed to hear that his great-uncle had left his money to the Clan na Gael. Tom thought he could have made much better use of it. However, he didn't argue.

Mr Duckworth seemed somewhat puzzled by Tom's acceptance of this fact: he had expected him to quibble. Smiling his relief, he speedily continued with the transaction. After flummoxing them with a stream of legal language and then getting Tom to sign several documents, he handed over a bunch of keys, attached to which was a brown luggage label. On it was written in large black letters: '11, Weaver Street, Edge Hill'. Tom felt a surge of satisfaction as he weighed the keys in the palm of his hand. Then he handed them to Kitty. The moment the cold, hard metal touched her fingers Kitty's heart began to pound and excitement like she had never known before flooded her veins. She gave Tom a triumphant smile and slipped the keys into her pocket.

2

The tram to Edge Hill chugged through streets busy with carts and lorries, every now and then stopping for passengers to board or alight. On the edge of the city centre it picked up speed, leaving behind the large, imposing buildings and rattling along a road lined with rows of small, terraced houses, all built out of rosy-red brick. Kitty read the nameplates fastened to the first house in each row: Dorothy Street; Plimsoll Street; Gladstone Street and so on. She repeated them to Tom. 'That's nice, isn't it?' she said cheerfully.

The rows of shabby, little houses looked drab and impoverished, and although one had been named for a Prime Minister and another after the man who had lent his name to the loading line on a ship, Tom couldn't imagine they had lived in such houses. Their meanness seemed to have escaped Kitty's notice. Tom gazed out at the depressing view veiled in soot and smoke: was Weaver Street a row of houses like these? His spirits drooping, he hoped not.

Before long they came to an area where the houses were not so cramped together. Some of them had gardens. Tom perked up. This was more to his liking. The tram wormed its way past workplaces dwarfed by a huge red-brick building with a towering mill chimney, then a short while later, it juddered to a halt on a wide thorough-fare with shops and offices on either side.

'Your stop, mate,' the tram conductor bawled for Tom and Kitty's benefit. Tom had asked him to let them know when they reached their destination. He worked his way to the back of the tram, Kitty at his heels, and thanking the conductor, he dragged the suitcases from the luggage bay and stepped off the bus. Toting her heavy bag, Kitty jumped down behind him.

'Now to find Weaver Street.' Tom looked from one side of the road to the other. Seeing a street sign on the wall above one of the shops he added, 'We're in Broad Green.'

Kitty spotted a bakery. 'I'll go and ask in there an' buy some bread at the same time. I don't know about ye, but I'm starving.' It was no surprise really because all they had eaten since leaving the ferry was the remains of the sandwiches and the biscuits the solici-tor's receptionist had given them. Leaving Tom on the edge of the pavement with the suitcases, she hurried into the bakery. The tanta-lising smell of freshly baked bread tickled her nose.

'One of those, please.' Kitty pointed to a large, crusty loaf.

'Just out of the oven, love,' the woman behind the counter said.

Kitty paid for the loaf and made her enquiry.

'Weaver Street,' the woman repeated, wrapping the loaf in a sheet of tissue paper. 'It's just round the corner, love. Walk to the end of this row of shops and turn left. You can't miss it. There's a pub at the corner and a church at the top.'

Kitty bounced out of the shop, the bread warm in her hands. She told Tom what the woman had said, and before they left the shops behind she popped into a grocery and bought milk, margarine and ham. At her request, the grocer begrudgingly put them in a large paper bag and she placed the loaf on top. By now, her arms full, she couldn't wait to get to Weaver Street and Tom must have felt the same. Leaving the shops behind then passing an entrance to a wide unpaved lane they made their way as fast as they could to where Weaver Street met Broad Green.

The pub on the corner was called the Weaver's Arms; it made sense. When they reached it they paused. Tom set down the suit-cases, and with Kitty leaning against his side they gazed up Weaver Street to the church at the top.

'They're grand houses,' Tom said, as they set off walking slowly up the street, the heavy bag that Kitty had slung over her shoulder threatening to unbalance her as she grappled with the groceries in her arms. Victorian terraces lined either side of the street. Tom liked the look of their strong, red-brick walls even though they were grimy. Kitty thought about the sandy-coloured buildings in Dublin that looked much cleaner and wondered if the air was dirtier in Edge Hill. Each house had two upstairs windows and below them a bay window to the side of a door that opened straight on to the street. Most of the low steps outside each door were donkey-stoned with white patterns of diamonds and arches, and the doors were painted red, blue or black – some sported gleaming brass knockers.

'It's a lovely street, but Great-Uncle Thomas wasn't very house-proud was he?' Kitty cast a disparaging eye over number eleven's peeling black paintwork and the undecorated step.

'Ye can soon put that right.' Tom dropped the suitcases then rapped the door with the dull brass knocker. It reverberated hollowly. 'Nobody's home,' he quipped, giving Kitty a comical grin.

'Here, hold this.' Kitty shoved the grocery bag at Tom then fished in her pocket for the keys. As she handed them to him he gave her the bag of groceries. He placed the largest of the iron keys in the lock and turned it. It made a creaking, scratchy sound and Tom had to jiggle it before he felt the mechanism shift.

'To say he died but a few weeks ago, ye'd think this door hadn't been opened in years,' he said, pushing the door wide. He lifted the suitcases and stepped inside, leaving them against the wall before relieving Kitty of the groceries then easing the bag from her shoulder.

Kitty had been holding her breath. As she stepped into the long, narrow hallway she released it then drew in the smell of dust and damp. 'Pooh! It's in need of a good airing,' she said, wrinkling her nose. She looked down the passage to the foot of the stairs. Pushing past Tom and the baggage, she arrived at the newel post and stroked its ornate pineapple top. 'That's just grand, isn't it?' She turned to give Tom a delighted smile.

He was admiring the wooden panelling on the lower half of the walls and the heavy Lincrusta wallpaper above it. Its patterned swirls of cream and green reminded him of a stormy sea crashing off the rocks on the shore at Quilty. Had Great-Uncle Tom thought the same?

Against the wall was a tall, narrow hallstand with coat pegs on either side of a mirror. A long, black overcoat hung from one peg and a black trilby hat perched on another. A pair of black leather gloves prayed, palms together, on the lid of the brush and comb box. 'I wasn't expectin' it to be so grand,' Kitty said.

Tom chuckled. 'Ye've seen nothing but a coat stand and a passage,' he scoffed, opening the nearest door and leading Kitty by the hand into a reasonable-sized, square room overlooking the street.

She let out a cry. 'Oh! Oh! By all the saints in heaven what have we come to?' Like an excited child she danced round a sagging, brown leather couch and over to the far wall. 'Look, Tom, did ye ever see the likes of it. A piano!'

She lifted the lid, cautiously pressing one note then another. Then she put the fingers of both hands on several of the keys, the discordant sound making her pull a face. 'Oh, I wish I could play a proper tune!' She closed the lid, rubbing her palms together. 'My goodness, old Tom wasn't one for dusting but he must have been a millionaire to own a grand yoke like this.'

Tom shrugged. 'If he was, he left his millions to charity.' He was bitterly regretting that no money had come their way. 'I know he had a good job in the civil service. An' what with him having no wife and children to keep, he'd have had money to spend on whatever he wanted.'

Kitty inspected the small, iron fireplace and a bookcase in the alcove to the right of it then moved to the window. 'You can see the street from here,' she said, adjusting the folds in the faded, rust velvet curtains and telling herself she'd put a little table by the window with a vase of flowers on it; let the passers-by see what a respectable house she kept. She turned to gaze wide-eyed at Tom. 'I can't believe this is all ours, Tom, I really can't.' Filled with burning curiosity, she grabbed him by the hand. 'Let's find out what else there is.'

A second door in the passage, close to the foot of the stairs, led into a kitchen: a pot sink and cupboards in an alcove to one side of a large, black range with brass knobs. Two shabby armchairs sat on either side of it and against the back wall were a table and four chairs.

The musty smell was even stronger in here, and made Kitty want to open a window and let in some fresh air. But over at the window all thoughts of opening it fled her mind. 'Look, Tom! Look at what we've got!' she squealed. 'A wee garden, and another door to outside.'

At that moment, Kitty believed her world was just perfect.

Tom, who rarely showed his emotions, not even when he was behind the counter in the betting shop and the horse he'd put a shilling on was clearly going to win, stood with his hands in his trouser pockets, assessing his surroundings. Deep inside, his joy matched Kitty's. To think that he now owned all this filled him with elation, not for himself, but for her. He had dreamed of giving her the world, and now it looked as though he had.

He loped over to the window and slipped his arms round her waist. As they gazed out at the neglected garden she leaned back into his embrace. They swayed gently, like lovers dancing to a favourite tune. Kitty felt the steady beat of his heart against her shoulder, and she turned to kiss him. Then, like inquisitive children, they went and opened the back door.

Hand in hand, they walked down the garden path and peered over the gate. A lane ran behind the houses to meet the street they now knew as Broad Green. On the other side was a fairly large plot of land with little sheds and a couple of glasshouses. In the distance, tall sycamore trees stood sentinel on the far edge of the plots.

'That must be a market garden, an' look at the trees,' Tom said, impressed. 'We've got our own wee bit of countryside right on our back doorstep.'

'Maybe you could grow a few greens and potatoes,' Kitty said.

Overwhelmed, they went back inside.

'Let's look upstairs,' said Tom, crossing the kitchen and into the hallway where a steep flight of stairs at the opposite end to the front door led to the upper floor. He mounted them two at a time, Kitty at his heels. At the top, a window gave them another view of the lane, and at the return of the stairs they stepped onto a long, narrow landing that ran from the back of the house to the front. Immediately to the right was a door, and another further down on the left. At the far end were two more doors, one on the right, and one facing them. Kitty and Tom's eyes burning with curiosity they opened the nearest door.

The room contained nothing but a few boxes and a chest of drawers. It smelled unused. The door on the left opened to a narrow flight of stairs leading up to an attic as wide and as long as the house. Lit by a small window in the roof, its sloping ceiling was festooned with cobwebs. Kitty shuddered. 'Good for storage,' Tom said as they clattered back to the landing. Moving further along, he opened the second door on the right. 'This is more like it,' he crowed as they entered a large bedroom.

'It's a big bed,' Kitty commented, thinking of the low, narrow bed they'd shared in the flat in Dublin. She gazed at the ornate, dark oak bed ends and the mattress piled with blankets and quilts. 'He must have felt the cold, poor lamb.'

'He didn't have a wife to keep him warm,' said Tom, playfully pushing her onto the bed and falling on top of her. Kitty saw the look in his eyes and pushed him away.

'Not now, Tom, I'm as hungry as a pauper's child and—' she got to her feet '—I'll need to air the bed before we sleep in it.'

Tom slapped her rump. 'I wasn't thinkin' of sleepin',' he said roguishly.

A grim thought occurred to her. 'D'ye think he died in this bed?' she said, alarmed.

'No, not at all,' Tom was quick to say. 'He most likely died in hospital.' He really had no idea, but they had to sleep somewhere.

Kitty opened the dark oak wardrobe. A black suit hung solemnly and below it a pair of black brogues. 'This suit might fit ye, Tom, an' the shoes.'

'Ye'll not catch me steppin' into a dead man's shoes. Come on now.' Tom led the way out to the landing and opened the final door. 'Oh, jaysus, Kitty,' he cried in wonder, ''tis a bathroom.' He'd been expecting another bedroom.

'Where, where?' Kitty pushed past him into the room. It stank of stale urine but it didn't diminish her joy. Her mouth became a big silent O as she gazed at the white bath with brass taps. Next to it was a washbasin and next to that a lavatory. Skipping over to it, she tugged on the chain. Water whooshed and gurgled. She clapped her hands. What would they say in Roscommon if they saw her now, a woman who had a lavatory that flushed?

Back in the kitchen, Kitty lifted the kettle from the range and filled it at the sink. Then she burst out laughing. How foolish can ye be, Kitty Conlon? Then to Tom, 'I was going to make a pot of tea to wet the sandwiches, but we've no fire to boil the water.'

He was rooting around in the table drawer, looking for a sharp knife to cut the bread. His stomach growled. 'Got one,' he cried, flourishing a serrated edged knife. 'Ye know, Kitty, it seems as though we have everything we need here.'

'Aye, everything but a fire to boil a drop of water an' wet a pot of tea leaves,' she replied tartly.

Abandoning the idea of tea, she wiped the dust from the table with a cloth she found under the sink, then, removing the tissue paper wrapping from the loaf, she smoothed it out to make a temporary tablecloth. She cut the bread into fat, crusty slices then smeared margarine on thick before topping it with the sliced ham, pleased that she'd been astute enough to buy it: it smelled delicious. 'A nice bit o' mustard wouldn't go amiss, but I didn't think to buy any,' she said regretfully. Tom liked mustard.

Tom, who was still investigating cupboards and drawers, danced over to the table flourishing a small jar. 'Madam, your wish is my command,' he said gallantly as he handed her the jar of Colman's Mustard. He sat down at the table. 'There's all manner of packets and tins in the cupboards,' he added, smearing his ham with the stiff, yellow paste.

They ate ravenously, and in between mouthfuls they talked about their new home. 'Here's to many years of happiness.' Tom raised his mug of milk.

Kitty clinked hers against it. 'Oh, we'll have plenty of them to be sure.' She put her mug down and gazed into Tom's eyes. 'When I married ye, Tom Conlon, I never imagined I'd be living in such grand style. In all my dreams I never pictured a home like this.'

'The luck's with us, Kitty,' he gloated, taking a packet of Woodbine out of his jacket pocket. 'I must admit I had me doubts about coming here, but by jaysus it was the right thing for us. All I need to do now is find a job. We've no rent to pay, but we still need to eat.' He lit a cigarette, and puffing out a stream of smoke, he stared pensively into the cloud drifting to the ceiling.

'Sure, with your brains ye'll soon find work, an' so will I.'

'There'll be no need for that if I get the sort of work I'm looking for,' Tom replied confidently. 'In a city like Liverpool there'll be plenty of openings for a fella with my skills – an' I don't just mean as a bookie.'

Kitty stood to clear the remains of the meal. Opening the back door to shake crumbs from the paper for the birds, she called out, 'Where does this door go to?'

'What door?' Tom said, thinking she'd lost her wits. 'It goes into the garden.'

'No, this other door.'

Tom flicked the stub of his cigarette into the empty grate and went to look. In their excitement of discovering they had a back door and a garden they had quite overlooked the plain board door set in the panelling in the small recess. He lifted the latch, expecting to find a cupboard. To his surprise, he saw a flight of stone steps leading down below the house. He peered into the gloom.

'Go to that cupboard above the sink and ye'll find a box of candles,' he said, searching for the box of matches in his trouser pocket.

Holding the lit candle aloft, he descended slowly, the flame flickering and his shadow grotesque against the whitewashed wall. Kitty felt her stomach flutter as he disappeared into the darkness.

When he called up to her, his voice echoed eerily. 'It's a washhouse and a coal cellar. There's a mangle and a tub, an' a heap of coal and sticks.'

Kitty's heart sang. There was no end to the benefits Great-Uncle Tom had left them. Tom filled a bucket with coal and placed a bundle of kindling on top then came back up to the kitchen. 'Now ye can have your cup of tea,' he said.

'I'll take a look for meself whilst ye light the fire,' Kitty said, opening one cupboard then another, making a mental note of what they contained. She was pleased with what she found.

The fire blazing, the kettle boiled and the tea brewed, they sat in the armchairs to drink it.

It wasn't long before Kitty's eyes drooped, but she shook off the urge to doze and wearily got to her feet. 'If we're to sleep in that bed I suppose I should do somethin' about it.'

At the foot of the stairs she paused, afraid to go up alone. 'Tom, come with me. Get the clean bedding out of the suitcase.' Tom stubbed out his cigarette and followed her upstairs.

Kitty stripped the bed whilst he unpacked sheets and pillow-cases. She ran her hands over the mattress. It didn't feel damp, but she wasn't taking any chances.

When Tom flapped a sheet, ready to put it on the bed, Kitty ordered him to fetch up the flat, iron shelves from the range.

'Mind now, they'll be hot. Hold them with a cloth. We'll lay them on the mattress an' drive out the damp.'

'That's a clever idea,' said Tom, marvelling at her thoughtfulness. He was beginning to see Kitty in a new light. In Dublin he'd been the one who led the way, but here, she'd been the one to think of buying bread and milk and ham, and now she was airing the bed so they wouldn't wake up with aching bones.

She's handling all this far better than I am, he thought.

* * *

It was after nine when Tom doused the gaslights in the kitchen. Earlier, he'd lit the one in the hallway and another on the landing and as they climbed the stairs he turned them out. 'Better than candles, eh, Kitty?'

The hot plates had cooled but the bed felt warm and welcoming to the touch. Naked, they climbed in between the fresh sheets and Tom reached for Kitty.

Eagerly, she rolled into his arms.

She had loosened her hair, her tawny curls flaring rebelliously on the pillow. Tom buried his face in them. 'Let's christen the house,' he whispered, moulding his body to hers and caressing her lush breasts.

'Slow down,' Kitty said softly. 'I want this to last.'

Lips found lips and hands found the most secret places as Tom and Kitty moved in perfect harmony, taking them to the brink and then beyond in a glorious rush. Moonlight crept stealthily through the gap in the curtains, its glow reflecting on their naked bodies sleek with sweat.

'The first time in our very own home.' Breathless, Kitty pulled the tossed sheet and quilt up to their chins.

'It won't be the last.' Tom spooned her body into his in much the same way as they had slept since their wedding night.

Tom fell asleep at once but Kitty, cocooned in his arms, stayed awake, listening to the night noises of her new home: a low gurgle in the water pipes, a creak from the stove below as the fire died. She closed her eyes and told herself she was going to be happy in number eleven, Weaver Street.

3

Yesterday and the day before, Kitty had scrubbed and polished until her knuckles were raw and her fingers wrinkling. Dirty and dated though the rooms might be, she got a deep sense of satisfaction from every bucket of mucky water she emptied down the sink.

'Ye've certainly seen off the dirt,' Tom had said, breathing in the fresh smell of soap and bleach on his return from his first fruitless day searching for work. And yesterday he'd told her, 'Ye're a living wonder, Kitty Conlon,' as he'd admired the gleaming range, its brass knobs glinting.

Kitty had asked him the same question that she had asked the previous day. 'Any luck, darlin'? Did ye find something to your liking?'

He'd shrugged his shoulders. 'Ach, ye know how it is. There's jobs to be had but not the sort I'm looking for.' He'd given her a brief smile, trying his best to put on a brave face before adding, 'Sure, it's early days. I'll find something afore long.' Kitty had heard the lack of conviction in his voice and her heart had ached for him. Maybe he'd have better luck today.

And now, with the sun shining and the morning warm enough for her to wear her blue cotton dress and white cardigan – she must look tidy in case she ran into any of her new neighbours – Kitty stepped out of the back door, a basket on her arm. For the past two days she'd concocted meals from things she'd found in the cupboards and now she was going shopping before continuing with her cleaning. She sallied down the garden path, feeling sure that Tom would soon find work.

In the doorway of the house next door a woman was stooping to lift a bottle of milk from the doorstep, her grubby dressing gown flapping open to reveal her bare bosom. Her blonde hair was wound round bright pink curlers. A cigarette drooped from the corner of her mouth.

Kitty paused and smiled. 'Good morning,' she called out, her intention being to ask how to get in touch with the milkman and get her milk delivered too. The woman responded with a bleary stare then went inside, slamming the door.

Oh dear. The neighbour at number nine didn't seem too pleasant. *Perhaps she's had a poor night's sleep,* thought Kitty, willing to forgive her rudeness. Outside number five a woman was tipping ashes into her dustbin. She smiled through the dusty haze as Kitty approached.

'Hello, love, are you the girl that's just moved into number eleven?'

Kitty smiled gratefully. 'That's right. I'm Kitty Conlon. Pleased to meet you.'

'And I'm May Walker. You must be a relative of old Tom's.'

'He was my husband's great-uncle,' Kitty said, 'but I never met him.'

'And he left you his house.' May nodded approvingly. 'That was good of him.' She brushed specks of ash from her flowered apron.

Some twenty years older than Kitty, she had a homely, careworn face but her brown eyes were warm and friendly. 'Are you getting settled then?'

'Yes, the house is grand but it was in sore need of a good clean.'

May grimaced. 'Yeah, I'm sure it was. He wasn't much of a housekeeper was Mr Conlon. He was out at work all day, and when he wasn't he walked that old dog of his miles round the town. I reckon he was lonely.' She gave a sad smile and turned to go. 'Nice to meet you, love, but I have to dash. I do a bit of cleaning for the doctor every morning. Ta-ra.' She hurried indoors.

I've got at least one friendly neighbour, Kitty thought and walked to the end of the lane. Maureen, whom she had worked with in the Gresham, had told her a few scary stories about her cousin who had moved to England and had mud thrown at her and the windows of her house broken because she was Irish. It had worried Kitty, but Tom had said she was just scaremongering. It couldn't be that bad if his great-uncle had stayed for fifty years.

* * *

Kitty was enjoying her shopping. The man in the grocery was sour faced and grumpy, but the butcher was bluff and hearty as he weighed out a half pound of mince, and the nice woman in the bakery remembered her. 'Did you find Weaver Street all right?' she asked.

'We did. We've moved into number eleven,' Kitty replied as she paid for a loaf of bread and two scones.

'In that case, I'll be seeing a lot more of you. I live at number seven. Me name's Connie Longhurst. What's yours?'

Kitty told her and left the bakery to walk back home, feeling rather pleased.

Maureen's cousin must have lived in a horrible part of England, not a bit like Edge Hill. She arrived at her gate at the same time as a man came out of the allotments. He was carrying a cardboard box.

'Hold on a minute,' he called out.

He limped across the lane and dropped four ripe tomatoes from the box into Kitty's basket. 'Here you are, love, a welcome present to Weaver Street. I always grow too much veg so I share it with me neighbours.' He had only one good eye; the other was closed over with a ragged lid.

'That's very kind.' Kitty smiled her thanks, but avoided looking too closely at his disfigurement. He noticed. He'd got used to it.

'I'm Jack Naughton from number seventeen.' He tucked the box under his arm. 'I got this lot at Mons – that's in Belgium, love,' he added pointing to his eye then his leg. 'I was a gunner in the King's Regiment.'

'That's a terrible shame,' Kitty exclaimed, her eyes full of sympathy.

'It could have been worse,' Jack replied stoically, then grinned, 'and it lets me spend all day in me allotment since they pensioned me off. Anytime you want some fresh greens just give me a shout. You know where to find me, missis...'

'Conlon. Kitty Conlon.'

'Then you must be a relative of Tom's.'

'He was my husband's great-uncle,' she said, and went on to tell him where she and Tom had come from.

Jack hobbled off and Kitty went indoors, thrilled to think she had such a kind neighbour. She made a cup of tea and was thinking about changing out of her blue dress and cardigan and into her old skirt and overall when she realised that she'd forgotten to buy washing soda; the hallway had yet to be tackled. She drained her cup and picked up her purse.

In the garden of number seven she saw a small boy, about four years old, making mud pies. A young woman lounged in the doorway. Kitty paused, smiling. 'He looks to be havin' fun!' she said. ''Tis a great day for it.'

The woman looked startled by Kitty's voice, then to Kitty's amazement, she shouted, 'Hey, Irish! Bugger off back where you came from. Filthy bogtrotter. Get back with the pigs in your kitchen.'

Kitty glared at her, then tossing her head, she carried on walking. *Sticks an' stones,* she told herself through gritted teeth. Maureen had been right after all.

She'd gone but a few paces when she felt something thud between her shoulder blades. She stopped short, and glancing behind her, she saw a large sod of earth at her heels. The woman was now standing by her garden gate.

The cheeky gobshite, Kitty fumed, and picking up the sod, she marched back a few paces, her eyes blazing. 'Here, I think this belongs to you,' she shouted, flinging the sod. It landed at the girl's feet. 'An' before ye start insulting me again, I'll have ye know I'm proud to be Irish. What's more, had I been aiming to hit ye with that lump of muck, ye'd have known about it, but I was better reared than that.'

Squaring her shoulders, Kitty glared at the woman. She'd be damned if she was going to let a gobby wagon like that get the better of her. The woman stood gaping, Kitty inwardly gloating at her shocked expression. Then, urging herself not to look back, Kitty set off at a brisk pace down the lane.

Round the corner, she slipped off her cardigan and angrily brushed off bits of soil. In a fine temper she bought the washing soda from Jim Broadhead's hardware store and, feeling as sharp as the crystals in the box, she marched into the bakery.

'Back again,' Connie said, smiling. 'What did you forget?'

'I didn't forget anythin',' Kitty said curtly, 'but somebody at your house forgot their manners. I thought I'd just let ye know.' She gave Connie a challenging look, aware that she now sounded like a gobshite, but she didn't care.

Connie frowned. 'Why? What happened?' She sounded thoroughly bemused.

Kitty told her.

Connie's face fell. 'Aw, that'd be my daughter, Doreen. Ooh, I am sorry.' She began wringing one hand with the other.

A customer came in.

Flustered, Connie said, 'Look, love, let's leave it for now. I'll come round and explain later. I am sorry, believe me.' She looked as though she might cry. 'Our Doreen's had a lot of trouble, like.' The customer coughed impatiently.

Kitty was unwilling to back down. 'She'll have a lot more if she ever speaks to me like that again,' she retorted, turning on her heel and marching out of the shop.

* * *

Down on her knees in the hallway, Kitty dunked her scrubbing brush into the bucket of hot, soapy water. Stretching her right arm to its full length, she created swirling arches of suds on the dirty floorboards, her seething temper adding power to her elbow.

Now, her heels knocking against the front door, she wiped up the suds and got to her feet. She couldn't scrub the last two feet of the passage without turning round. For a split second, she thought she might do that. Then, rejecting the idea of kneeling on the damp floor, she decided to open the door and wash the last bit of the passage and then the front step.

But suppose someone sees me in my old skirt, and in such an ungainly position. She pursed her lips and decided that she had no qualms about letting people know she kept a clean house.

Down on her knees again, her pert behind sticking out through the doorway, she finished the passage floor and moved out onto the step. Out of the corner of her eye she saw a girl of a similar age to herself standing on the step of the house next door: number nine. She recalled the frowsy older woman she had seen earlier that day. The girl looked like her. She must be her daughter.

Kitty leapt to her feet. She felt more in control standing up.

'I was wondering when I'd see you,' the girl said. 'Me ma said she saw you this morning.' Her voice was like gravel over stones and her Liverpool accent thick. Kitty opened her mouth, ready to introduce herself, but before she had a chance to speak, the girl asked, 'Are you Irish an' all?'

The way she said 'Irish' made Kitty's heart flip. She made it sound dirty. *Is this the way it's going to be?* thought Kitty. *Am I going to have to defend meself a dozen times a day?*

'I'm Kitty Conlon. Me an' me husband Tom have just moved in.' She was surprised by how calm she sounded when inside she was raging.

'He were Irish that lived here before you,' the girl said, making it sound as though it was a sin.

Kitty pushed back her shoulders. 'He was my husband's great-uncle,' she said tartly. She wasn't going to let this scruffy-looking girl intimidate her.

'He were a miserable old bugger. Never bothered with anybody in all the years he lived here. It took him all his bloody time to say hello.'

Shocked by the crude description, Kitty drew a sharp breath. 'I wouldn't know. I never met him.'

'Yeah, well, you didn't miss nuthin'.' The girl curled her lip. 'What did you say they call you?'

Kitty swallowed her irritation. 'Kitty Conlon.'

'I'm Maggie Stubbs. Me an' me mother live on this side and them on the other side are old Mr and Mrs Boothroyd. They're miserable sods an' all. You'll get used to 'em if you stay long enough.'

'Oh,' said Kitty, at a loss to continue the conversation.

'Have you any kids?'

'No, we haven't long been married.'

'I'd only been married a week when they sent him off to Egypt. I've not seen him since.' Maggie sounded as though she didn't much care.

'Was that because of the war? Is he a soldier?'

''Course he bloody is. Any fella worth 'is salt's in the army. All the young'uns have joined up. There's hardly a fella under fifty left in Liverpool. Take this street for instance. There's old Walter Garside at number three and Sam, the landlord at the Weaver's – they're both pushing sixty. Young Sammy Walker from number five's in France. May's never done worrying about him. And the Boothroyds lost both their lads.' She sighed. 'And look at the way they sent poor Jack back without his eye and a wonky leg. Bloody rotten war.' Maggie pulled a face. 'I see your chap's still here though – him being Irish.'

Kitty had no answer to that.

Maggie grimaced. 'It doesn't surprise me,' she sneered. 'The Irish can't make up their minds whose side they're on.'

Kitty flushed and thought of her brother Shaun.

'Is yer man at work?'

'Oh, no he's...' Kitty's thoughts still on the war and Shaun, she struggled to gather her wits. 'He's lookin' for something in the city.'

'Have you ever been to Liverpool before?'

'No, never,' Kitty said, recovering from her confusion. She

picked up her bucket. 'It's been nice meetin' ye, Maggie,' she lied, eager to make her escape.

'That church at the top of the street's for your sort.' Maggie volunteered the information in an offhand manner. 'You know what I mean – Catholics.'

'That's good to know,' Kitty murmured.

'Yeah. I'll drop in for a cup o' tea an' a jangle when you're settled.'

Kitty bolted inside and closed the door.

The conversation rumbled round inside her head as she waited for the kettle to boil. She felt in need of a strong cup of tea. *And what was a jangle?* She was just about to sit down when someone knocked at the back door. *Was it that girl, Maggie?*

Connie Longhurst stood on Kitty's back doorstep, her expression penitent. 'Have you a minute, love, so I can explain about what happened this morning?'

Will I keep her on the step or will I ask her to come in? Good manners won over. 'You'd better come in.'

'Thanks, love, it's ever so good of you.' Connie followed Kitty into the kitchen.

'I've just made a pot of tea.' Kitty thought it would be churlish to drink her own cooling tea without offering Connie a cup. 'Sit ye down.' She pointed to a chair at the table. Connie dithered, her lips forming a weak smile as she sat down. Kitty poured the tea and sat facing her, waiting for Connie to speak.

'About our Doreen,' Connie began, 'I'm sorry she did what she did but she had a lot of problems a while back.'

'That doesn't give her the right to throw a lump of muck at me an' insult me because I'm Irish,' Kitty said flatly.

Connie's cup rattled against the saucer. 'I know it doesn't, love,' she pleaded, 'but you see she were let down by an Irish fella and she's never got over it. He was the manager at the hotel she worked at. A right charmer he was, although I only met him the once.' Connie licked her lips as though she tasted something nasty then continued, her voice hardening. 'She thought he loved her, the silly mare, but when he got her pregnant he fired her, left her without a job and a bastard in her belly. That's why she doesn't like the Irish.'

'That's daft, blamin' me just because I'm from Ireland.'

'Yeah, I know it is, love, but our Doreen was hurt badly.' Connie was almost in tears. Kitty felt her heart softening.

'I'm sorry she feels that way, an' I can see how much it upsets you, but names like that hurt when ye've done nothing to deserve them,' Kitty said, feeling less sorry for herself. In fact, the more she thought about Doreen's predicament the more compassionate she felt.

Connie sighed. 'I thought that once she married Idris she'd put it all behind her, 'cos he's ever so good to her and little Eddie. And I'll say this for our Doreen. She loves that little lad more than anything. She never once took it out on him for what his dad did to her.' She rubbed her cheeks with the palms of her hands and then stood. 'I've taken enough of your time. Thanks for hearing me out.'

'I'm glad ye called,' Kitty said, standing and giving Connie a warm smile. 'If it happens again, I'll try an' ignore it 'cos I do understand.'

'That's good of you, love.' Connie managed a smile. 'I've had a word with her, and she's off to live in Wales in a couple of weeks, so it shouldn't happen again.' She paused dejectedly at the door. 'I'll miss her when she goes. Her and me son, Bobby, are all I've got and he's somewhere in France.' Her eyes filled with tears. 'I feel sick every time I think of him in the trenches, dodging bullets in all that mud and never getting a proper bite to eat.'

Kitty's heart went out to Connie. 'I'm sorry to hear your Bobby's in France, and don't let what happened between me an' your

Doreen upset you. It's not important, what with all the real troubles in the world.'

Connie nodded tearfully and said, 'I'll make sure she doesn't do it again.'

'If she does, I'll not blame ye,' Kitty said, relieved to hear that Doreen wouldn't always be around to insult her. 'I'd like us to be friends.'

* * *

Two hours later, Tom came home. She knew by the look on his face that it was unwise to ask if he'd had any success with finding a job. Instead, she told him that the church at the top of the street was Catholic.

When they sat down to eat she said, 'I met some of our neighbours today.' She told him about Jack Naughton and the tomatoes. 'He seems very nice. And the girl next door is called Maggie Stubbs.' Kitty pulled a face. 'She wasn't very pleasant. In fact, she was downright ignorant about your great-uncle. She called him a miserable old bugger. I don't think she likes the Irish.' Kitty's voice rose dramatically. 'An' the girl at number seven chucked a lump of muck at me just because I'm Irish. Then her mam called and apologised. She's the woman in the bakery. I felt sorry for her because she seems ever so nice.'

She sat back, breathless, waiting for Tom's response. He had that look on his face, the one that said, *it's of no interest to me.* 'Ach, take no notice. Ye don't have to neighbour with them if ye don't want,' he growled, scraping back his chair then going to sit by the fire. He lit a cigarette, the subject of their neighbours dismissed.

Kitty's face fell. There were times when Tom seemed very distant, as if the only person of any significance was himself.

'But I'd like to be friends with our neighbours, Tom. That's how it should be,' she insisted, feeling hurt and annoyed. She sensed he wasn't listening, that his thoughts were not of her and her problems. However, she carried on talking, more for her own benefit than his. 'But if most of 'em are as ignorant as Maggie Stubbs an' that cheeky wagon at number seven, I'll not be wanting to know 'em.'

4

Tom didn't like being unemployed. It made him feel disadvantaged in the eyes of his peers. But he wasn't prepared to take any old job. He wanted one befitting the sort of man he considered himself to be. He'd learned early on in life that money talked, and that if you had enough of it, doors opened into places better than the one you were in. Tom craved entry into those places, in the firm belief that that was where he belonged.

He took his role as the breadwinner very seriously, maybe because his father had done the exact opposite, and also because it gave him control over his and Kitty's lives. To that end, finding work was imperative and each day since the day after their arrival in Edge Hill he had plodded round the city, looking for a job of his choosing, and each day he had trudged home, his thoughts black at the indignity he'd suffered.

Tom's knowledge was to do with numbers and calculations. He had worked for Power's bookmakers for seven years after leaving Clare for Dublin when he was sixteen. He was clever at mathematics and could calculate the odds like lightning, as the reference in his jacket pocket stated. It also said he was honest, hard-working and of good character, but it hadn't impressed the managers of several accountancy businesses, or insurance offices, and none of the betting shops were taking on staff now that horse racing had been cancelled because of the war. The Labour Exchange had offered jobs in engineering works, builder's yards and munitions factories but Tom possessed none of the required skills, nor did he want to earn his living from manual labour. Turning his nose up at the offers, he kept on looking.

But the money he had brought with him from Ireland was running low and one afternoon, walking back to Weaver Street, he mentally calculated how much he had left. He reckoned they could survive another two or three weeks at most. Plunging his hands in his trouser pockets, his fingers rubbed against the loose change he'd brought with him that morning.

Outside the Weaver's Arms he halted, and before penury could override rashness, he pushed open the door. He'd go in for a pint, just one, to wash away the despair clogging his throat. It wasn't his first visit. He'd been in before, staying just long enough to drink a pint. The landlord, Sam Bradshaw, had made him welcome. On their first meeting, Sam had asked if he was the young man who had moved into number eleven. *News must travel fast in these parts,* Tom had thought cynically as he'd paid for his pint.

On the second occasion, Sam had asked, 'Where are you working?'

'I'm not,' Tom had said, 'I'm still considering my options.' He hated admitting he was unemployed.

Now, as Tom entered the pub, the men at the bar turned their heads, one or two of them acknowledging his arrival with a nod. He strutted up to the bar and ordered a pint of stout: keeping up appearances was important to Tom. Leaning against the long, oak bar, he swigged a mouthful.

'Ready for that, are you?' The brawny young man at Tom's elbow indicated the pint. He'd clearly had a few already.

'Ye could say that.' Tom took another sip, his terse reply unwelcoming.

'I'm back in Blighty for ten days makin' the most of it. Are you on leave? Me name's Terry Collins, by the way. What's yours?' Terry was clearly looking for a drinking pal.

'Tom Conlon, an' before ye ask, no, I'm not in the forces and yes I'm Irish.' To his own ears he sounded belligerent, but assuming that the fellow was about to be as scathing as the managers in the insurance offices, or as belittling as the accountants, he was on his guard. Then he pasted on a smile to take the heat out of his words. He didn't want any trouble.

'I've nuthin' against the Irish nor anybody else for that matter,' Terry said. 'I've fought alongside some Irish lads an' they were grand.'

Tom forced another smile.

'There was this one big fellow from Cork who was built like a brick shithouse,' Terry continued. 'He had a cracking sense o' humour. He made us laugh even when we wa' shitting us selves and likely to die at any minute.'

Tom relaxed, and feeling in need of male company, he let Terry buy him a pint.

'Whereabouts in Ireland are you from?'

'Dublin.' There was no point in saying Quilty. Nobody had ever heard of it. Furthermore, Tom thought it gave him some prestige to come from a city rather than a tinpot village in the arse end of nowhere.

Terry was off again. 'We have some Dubliners in our regiment, and God, the crack they come out with makes you forget your feet are rotting in your boots and Jerry's waiting over the hill to blow your head off.' He rambled on about fighting in the trenches, then, when his glass was empty, he tapped it on the counter and gave Tom a meaningful look. Against his better judgement Tom bought two more pints.

'What did you work at in Dublin?'

Tom was beginning to find Terry irritating, but encouraged by three pints of stout, before he could stop himself he broke his rule of keeping things to himself and told Terry he had been a clerk for one of the biggest bookmakers in Ireland.

Terry was impressed. 'I'm fond of a gamble, but if you want to lay a proper bet you've to go into the city. We could do with a bookie round here.'

'What's that about a bookies'?' the landlord asked as he wiped the counter in front of them.

'This chap's a bookmaker. I was telling him we don't have one in Edge Hill.'

'Yeah, we could do with one,' Sam said. 'As it is, the lads just bet against one another for a bob or two on local football matches and the like, then fight over who's won. Mind you, what with the proper race meets being cancelled, there's not much call for bookies these days.' He looked sour.

'There's still meets at the Irish racecourses,' Tom cut in.

'And there's allus local stuff like greyhound racing, cock fighting, an' them lads what do the bare-knuckle bouts,' Terry insisted. 'Some lads 'ud bet on two flies climbing up a window.'

'There is that,' Sam said thoughtfully. 'Everybody likes a flutter.'

'You should get Tom to run a book here, Sam.' Terry grinned at Tom. 'He worked for the biggest bookies in Ireland afore he came here,' he added, as though he was providing credentials.

'Did he now,' said Sam.

* * *

An hour and five pints later, Tom walked the few yards to home feeling as though his feet didn't belong to him, partly because of the stout he'd consumed but mostly because of his good fortune. He'd tramped the city looking for work, and now he'd found it right here on his doorstep. No longer dreading the look of disappointment on Kitty's face – for what made him happy also made her happy – he entered the kitchen.

Kitty raised her eyebrows when he burst through the door. Here he was, stinking of strong drink and money tight enough. She eyed him accusingly. Tom held up a staying hand before she had time to rail at him. Then he took her in his arms, swinging her feet off the floor.

'Put me down, ye eejit,' Kitty squealed, 'ye're tipsy! And wherever ye got the notion that spending good money on beer would get ye a job I—'

'But it did, Kitty, it did.' He set her down and kissed her full on the lips.

She pushed him away, wiping her mouth with the back of her hand then giving him a sceptical glare.

'Sit down,' he urged, flopping into an armchair and pulling her onto his knee. 'The landlord at the Weaver's Arms is going to let me open a betting shop in the back of the pub, and a young fella I met is going to show me where they hold the local meets for dog racing an' cock fighting an' such like.' His blue eyes dancing, he went on to explain how it would work.

Kitty's hazel eyes grew round and her mouth dropped open as she listened.

'And do ye think ye can make it work?' she asked anxiously. Personally, she thought a job in a factory would be a surer way of earning money but she hadn't the heart to tell him that. She knew he hated the idea of manual work, and her love for him was so strong she decided to give him the benefit of the doubt. Even so, she didn't like the sound of cock fighting.

'Sure I can. Haven't I been doin' it for seven years? But this time I'll be doin' it for meself, not Mr Dickie Power.'

They talked late into the night, weighing up the pros and cons. When they were in bed, Tom made love to Kitty with the heart of a new man.

5

Kitty sat by the fire, wondering what she could do until Tom came home. As she gazed into the flames she felt a spike of loneliness, so sharp that it brought tears to her eyes. As soon as Tom had left she had done her chores and then wandered from room to room, time hanging heavy on her hands. There wasn't a thing in the house that required her attention. Everywhere was spotless and now she felt like a bird in a gilded cage with no one to sing her song to.

Last week she had written long, newsy letters to Maureen at the Gresham, and to her brothers in Roscommon, making light of the long journey then singing the praises of the house. She thought about writing to Maureen again and telling her about Tom's job, but she might think Kitty was miserable and lonely if she wrote again so soon; and she didn't want that. She would have liked to write to Shaun but she wasn't exactly sure where he was. Ever since she had last heard of his whereabouts she had tried not to think about him, but he kept sidling back into her mind. Brushing away her tears, she got up to fill the kettle. A cup of strong tea was comforting, she told herself, but it always tasted better when shared, particularly with female company.

Her work in the Gresham had afforded her plenty of opportunity to chat. All the waitresses had been her friends, and the regular customers often shared a bit of gossip or told her something about themselves. But here she had no friends that she could call on, and the more she thought about it, the lonelier she felt. The sooner she found a job, the better.

A sharp rap on the back door broke her reverie, and before she could answer it, the door was pushed open. In came Maggie Stubbs.

'I've come for a jangle an' a cup of tea,' she said, walking into the kitchen.

In another mood Kitty might have told her it was rude to walk into someone's house uninvited, but even though she didn't think she much liked Maggie, she was glad to see her. She put the kettle on the hob.

Maggie settled herself on a chair at the table and scanned the kitchen. 'It's not bad, is it?' she said, sounding surprised. 'I thought it'd be a dump, like, what with auld Tom living on his own.'

'It was just in need of a good clean.' Kitty spooned fresh leaves into the teapot. She took another mug out of the cupboard.

'I've never been in before. In fact, I don't know anybody in Weaver Street who has. He kept himself to himself. If he hadn't been taken poorly at work he'd have probably laid here rotting 'cos nobody would have missed him.' Maggie took a packet of Woodbine from her pocket and lit a cigarette. Kitty hurriedly provided an ashtray, shuddering at the thought of Great-Uncle Tom lying dead in the bed she now slept in. Then she wet the tea.

'Milk and sugar?' she asked brightly.

'Yeah, two sugars and just a drop of milk.'

'Have ye always lived in Weaver Street?' Kitty asked, skimping on the sugar, then setting two full mugs and a plate of biscuits on the table. Maggie took a ginger snap, demolishing it in two bites and slurping her tea to wash it down.

'Yeah, I was born next door so—' her eyes narrowed '—there's nuthin' nor nobody I don't know a thing or two about round here.' She lifted another biscuit.

Kitty was unsure what to say next. Tom frequently told her she gave too much of herself away. She dismissed the idea of telling Maggie about the name-calling and the muck-throwing incident in case Maggie took Doreen's side. She couldn't be sure which way the wind blew with Maggie. She topped up her cup.

'How old are you?' Maggie said, crumbs of ginger snap flying from her lips.

Kitty hid a smile. 'Nineteen,' she said. She was getting used to Maggie's blunt manner and the way she switched from one topic to the other.

'Me an' all, and still living with me ma.' Maggie huffed.

'When do you expect your husband home?'

'I haven't a clue,' Maggie hooted, blowing out her cheeks. 'Fred's a regular, you see. He joined up when he was sixteen. It was either that or get sent to one o' them approved schools.' She pulled a face. 'He was a bad lad, my Fred, and he still is.'

'Ye must miss him though, an' worry about him.'

Maggie shrugged. 'I've got used to it. And I don't worry that much. Fred knows what he's doin'. Not like them young'uns who volunteered. They didn't know what they were letting themselves in for, poor sods. Every time I read them bloody awful death columns in the newspaper and see the names of young lads who worked at the mill with me, it breaks my heart.'

'Still, ye must feel very lonely with Fred so far away,' said Kitty, thinking of how she would feel without Tom.

'Oh, I'm not short of company. When the lads come home on leave they're always looking for a bit of home comfort, if you know what I mean. You don't get many of them in the trenches.' Maggie winked as she jauntily dragged on her cigarette.

Kitty was shocked into silence.

'I've seen your chap going in and out but he just nods and says nuthin', just like his uncle did. It must run in the family.' Maggie pulled a face. 'I heard he's opened a betting shop in the Weaver's – that'll make him a fair penny.'

'If he creates the book right it will.' Kitty clapped her hand to her lips, wanting to snatch back the words. Tom had told her if he placed multiple bets for several outcomes it always ensured a profit. If he heard her now, he'd most likely tell her she shouldn't be divulging such information.

Maggie sniffed. 'Me granddad always used to say that bookies robbed the poor to feed the rich.'

Kitty flushed. 'Tom doesn't force men to gamble,' she cried in his defence. 'If he didn't let them place bets with him they'd go somewhere else to do it.'

'Yeah, I suppose you're right. Are you going out to work?'

'I will be,' Kitty said. 'Have you got a job?'

'Yeah, I'm in the weaving shed at Holroyd's. That's that mill at the top of the street. We used to weave twill. Now it's all khaki for the army. It's bloody hard work but the money's not bad. What sort of a job do you want?'

'I was a waitress in a hotel. Silver service, that's what I'm trained for. I worked in one of the best hotels in Dublin.'

'You'd have to go into the city for a job like that. There's no posh hotels round here; in fact, there's bugger all,' she sneered. 'Me mam works evenings in the Wagon an' Horses pub.'

Kitty didn't think she'd fancy travelling into the city every day. 'I could always do housekeeping or shop work, I suppose.'

'Yeah, an' get paid buttons,' Maggie scoffed. 'You should try getting set on at Holroyd's. They're looking for doffers in the spinning shed.'

'I don't even know what that means.'

'Changing empty bobbins for full ones. You'd pick it up in no time.' Maggie pushed her mug across the table. 'Is there another drop of tea?'

* * *

'I had a visitor whilst you were out,' Kitty said, as soon as Tom came through the door that evening.

'Who was that?' he asked curiously.

'Maggie from next door.'

'And...?' He frowned. Kitty understood the look.

'She's not so bad once you get to know her,' she said, bringing the shepherd's pie she had made from the minced beef she'd bought earlier to the table. She was getting used to cooking in the side oven. 'There's cabbage to go with it, an' gravy.' Tom cut a wedge of pie and Kitty spooned cabbage on to his plate. Then she went and got the jug of gravy and sat down.

'What did she say then?' As Tom tucked into the pie, Kitty told him all about Maggie's husband, and her job in the mill.

'She says I might get a job in the spinning shed.' Kitty cut Tom another wedge of pie and popped it on his plate, all the while watching for his reaction.

Tom scowled. 'Mill work's rough. It's not what you're used to.'

'No, but I need to be earning. There's not much left in the pot.' Kitty was referring to the tin in which they kept their household money. Tom glowered.

Kitty, quick to see his disapproval, changed the subject.

'How did ye get on? Was it worth the trip?' she asked. Tom had accompanied Terry on a fact-finding trip, visiting the locations where betting on blood sports such as dog or cock fights and bare-knuckle bouts took place.

'It surely was. It let me see how I can make it work. I even backed a couple of winners.' He put his hand in his trouser pocket then scattered a handful of coins on the table. 'Ye can add that to the pot,' he said sarcastically.

'I do want to go out to work,' Kitty said as she cleared the table. 'If ye're going to be out most of the day I'll be terrible lonely, and it's not as though we don't need the money.'

'Kitty! I'll be the one to provide for us,' Tom said sharply. 'Your job is looking after me.' He lit a cigarette, puffing contentedly whilst Kitty did the washing up. She dabbled her hands in the soapy water, contemplating his words. She didn't really have a plan, all she knew was that something challenging and satisfying was waiting for her to find it, and when she did, she'd make her own success.

6

Kitty's mother had often told her that if you wanted something to happen then you had to make it happen. 'There's no use in ye sitting on your hunkers waiting for some other body to make your life for ye,' she used to say. Kitty had recalled her words as, down in the dank, dimly lit cellar, with the silence of the house oppressive, she turned the mangle. Envisaging the day ahead, and finding no joy in it, she'd dumped the clothes in the wicker basket and was now pegging them out in the back garden.

Leaving the clothes to blow in the warm breeze, she smoothed her apron, patted her hair and went to the house next door. She knew Maggie would be at work but her mother would be at home. Maggie had told her that her mother only worked evenings in the Wagon and Horses pub. Maybe she might know if there were any jobs going in Edge Hill.

On the morning Kitty had seen the woman she took to be Maggie's mother, she had looked old and bedraggled, so she was taken by surprise when a woman looking not much older than Maggie opened the door. Maggie hadn't mentioned a sister. The woman's blonde hair was crimped in deep waves that ended just below her chin and her complexion was smooth and creamy.

'Good morning, I'm Kitty from next door. I thought I'd call and introduce meself to Maggie's mother. Maggie told me she was at home during the day.'

'She is, love. You're looking at her.' She had the same gravelly voice as her daughter and was puffing on a cigarette. The frilly, rather glamorous, dressing gown she was wearing was spoiled by a blob of egg yolk dribbling down the front.

Kitty tried not to look at it.

'Oh, I thought ye must be Maggie's sister,' she said. 'Ye don't look old enough to be her mam.'

A chuckle rattled in the woman's throat then ended in a hacking cough.

'Bloody hell, you must have kissed the Blarney Stone. Come in, love, I'm just about to make a pot of tea.'

The kitchen smelled of stale cigarettes and greasy food. Unwashed dishes filled the sink and the table was cluttered with more dirty dishes and magazines.

'Sit yourself down, love; make yourself at home.'

Thinking she was lucky it wasn't her home, Kitty sat on a chair at the table. Maggie's mother set a cup in front of her.

'Thank ye Mrs...' Kitty realised she didn't know Maggie's mother's name.

'Aw, never mind the missis. Just call me Vi. Everybody else does. Violet Bottomley, that's me, an' I haven't been a missis for years. The arsehole I married left me when our Maggie was a kiddy. He's dead now.'

'I'm sorry to hear that,' Kitty murmured. She sipped her tea. It tasted like perfume. Then she noticed the lipstick smear on the rim of the cup. She turned the cup round to drink from the other side.

'Oh, don't be sorry. I was glad to see the back of him,' Vi said.

Vi continued to denigrate her husband, and Kitty now saw that underneath the thick layers of make-up, Vi was much older than she had first thought.

'So, you've settled in then. I see your husband's running a bookie's shop in the Weaver's. He's a good-looking fella.' Vi rolled her eyes, the lids heavy with blue eye shadow and her lashes spiky with mascara. 'I'll be one of his best customers. I love a flutter.'

'I'm looking to find work,' Kitty said. 'I wondered if you might know of anywhere needin' anybody.'

Vi pursed her lips. 'There's always the mill, and they're always looking for lasses to make munitions.' She pulled a face. 'I can't see you doing that.'

'What's munitions?'

'Making bombs and bullets, love. War stuff. It's mucky work, and dangerous.'

Kitty didn't like the sound of that.

'I'll make enquiries,' she said. 'Thanks for the tea.' Kitty got to her feet. 'It was nice to meet ye.'

'Come anytime you like, love,' said Vi, lighting a cigarette then waving it in an all-encompassing gesture. 'I like a bit of company.'

Kitty went back to her own house, a bit disheartened. Vi hadn't been much help on the job front, and as for making close friends of Vi or Maggie, Kitty found it hard to imagine. It made her all the more determined to find work and widen her circle of acquaintances.

* * *

When Tom came home, she didn't bother to tell him she had visited Maggie's mother. He'd no doubt met her already.

'What do ye say to taking a walk after we've had our dinner?'

Tom took off his jacket and sat down to the hotpot Kitty had dished up.

'I'd love that,' she exclaimed, having been bored and lonely for much of the day. 'I'll get changed as soon as we've finished this.'

A short while later they walked up Weaver Street, Kitty in her green coat with the velvet collar and Tom still wearing the smart, black three-piece suit he wore at work. Kitty thought he looked every inch the businessman. She had always admired his lean, rangy physique and the way his black, wavy hair framed his handsome face. She felt proud to be on his arm.

'Ye look as pretty as a picture,' Tom said, patting the hand linking his arm, 'and once I start making the big money ye can start to dress up.'

'I'm fine as I am,' she protested, thinking that Tom sounded like a braggart with ideas above his station. 'Is the betting going well then?'

Tom's mouth turned down at the corners. 'Ach, it's just tuppeny ha'penny stuff at the moment. Ye know how it is.'

Kitty didn't really know, but she knew that the tin they kept their money in was almost empty. For all Tom's insistence that he would provide for them she worried that the bookmaking business would suddenly come to a sticky end. She felt the urge to argue that she too needed to work, but not wanting to spoil the outing she kept quiet.

It was a glorious evening, the air balmy, and as they approached St Joseph's church a rosy ray of the setting sun struck the spire. 'Oh, look Tom!' Kitty pointed upwards. 'That's a sign of good luck if ever I saw one.'

Tom chuckled. 'Ye're as bad as the old crones back home.' He was referring to the old women who saw signs and superstitions in things that were simply acts of nature. Kitty ignored the jibe.

Neither she nor Tom regularly attended mass; they'd both had enough of it by the time they were teenagers. In the villages they had been reared in you were castigated if you didn't attend, but in Dublin, the people were too busy to notice, and Kitty and Tom had got into the habit of lying in on Sunday mornings.

However, on the first Sunday after their arrival in Edge Hill they had walked to the top of Weaver Street to St Joseph's church to receive communion and give thanks for their good fortune.

Kitty had been pleasantly surprised by how different that end of the street was. At the end nearest to where they lived, the Weaver's Arms and the shops in Broad Green were what you would expect in a busy town, noisy with traffic. The main Liverpool to Manchester railway line ran close by, Edge Hill being the halt before Lime Street Station, its massive archway and tunnels dominating the scene. But up by the church it was like suddenly being in the countryside.

The church stood in its own grounds, surrounded by tall ash and sycamores. Rhododendrons lined a curving path to its main door. At the church gates, Weaver Street turned a corner to the right and led down to the river that ran behind the church. To the left, the road was Mill Lane and ran past Holroyd's Mill.

'Maggie says they're still wanting spinners,' Kitty said, glancing in the direction of the mill. 'Maybe I should call there tomorrow. What do ye think?'

Tom didn't answer but Kitty felt the surge of anger that rippled through him.

They descended the short flight of ancient stone steps that led to the towpath, walking hand in hand by the small river. Neither of them had been this way before. Willow trees trailed their long, leafy fronds in the water, ducks dabbling in the shallows, and the hedgerows bright with wild flowers. They came to a bridge and crossed to the opposite side, both of them of the opinion that they would have to turn back the way they had come. However, rounding a bend in the river they saw another bridge and crossed it. By now, they were further up the towpath, and they turned to walk back to the steps.

'Oh, look!' Kitty cried. 'A café. Let's see if it's still open.' Worry over Tom's stubborn attitude about her finding work and their lack of money had made her throat dry. Throwing caution to the wind she decided they could surely afford a soft drink today, and tomorrow she'd go out and find a job to ease their penury.

They walked the few paces to the pretty, wooden building tucked in between the willows. Painted blue and white, with checked curtains of the same colours at the windows, it looked most inviting. The door was open and they stepped inside.

'You're just in time,' the elderly, red-faced woman behind the counter said. 'I was about to close up. What can I get you?'

'If it's no trouble, I'd like a lemonade,' Kitty replied. Tom said he'd have the same.

They sat at one of the little tables covered with blue and white checked cloths. Seashells decorated the windowsills and pictures of the sea and boats hung on the walls. In one corner there was a model lighthouse. 'It's like being at the seaside,' Kitty remarked.

'It reminds me of home,' the woman said. 'I come from Flamborough.' Seeing their blank expressions, she added, 'That's by the sea.'

'Ye sound as though ye miss it,' said Kitty.

'Oh, I do, even though I've been here forty years. Liverpool was my husband's home, and when he died last year I said I'd pack up and go back to Flamborough, but I've done nothin' about it as yet.'

'Do ye do a good trade?' Tom asked.

'Not as good as it used to be. At weekend I'd get anglers an' bird-watchers an' the cycling clubs, but they were mainly young lads, an' you don't see too many of them about these days. They're all off fighting this blasted war.' The woman shrugged her shoulders and grimaced. 'Still, it could be worse. The lasses come down from t'mill at breakfast and dinner times, an' folks still walk the riverbank of a Sunday.'

They finished their drinks, and as they left Kitty said, 'I'll call with ye again.'

'You're welcome,' the woman replied.

Climbing the stone steps, they walked past the church and down Mill Lane, the towering mill casting a giant shadow that suddenly plunged them in its gloom. 'I don't think I'd want to work in there,' Kitty said, wrinkling her nose at the greasy smell of raw wool.

'I wouldn't want ye to,' Tom growled.

The roads led them back to Broad Green, and they were walking towards home when up ahead of them a man and woman came out of the Wagon and Horses public house. The man had his arm around the woman's waist. She was laughing and leaning into him. He was big and burly with a shock of bright red hair. As Kitty and Tom drew nearer, Kitty saw the man's hand reach down and fondle the woman's backside. She turned her head. Kitty recognised her.

'There's Maggie,' she said, surprised. 'Her husband must be home on leave.' She thought it strange that Vi hadn't mentioned it when she had seen her earlier in the day.

'She's obviously celebrating,' Tom sneered, as Maggie stumbled along, hanging onto the man's arm. He didn't much care for Maggie.

They had almost caught up with them when, unexpectedly, Maggie and the man entered a lodging house halfway along Broad Green. Kitty was puzzled. She had thought they might all walk back to Weaver Street together.

'Why did they go in there, Tom?'

'I haven't a clue, an' what's more, it's none of our business.'

* * *

The next morning, after Kitty and Tom had attended midday mass, Tom went to the Weaver's Arms for a pint. Kitty was preparing the Sunday dinner when Maggie stumbled into the kitchen. 'Give a dying woman a cup of tea,' she groaned. 'Me head's banging, like.'

She certainly looked worse for wear, last night's make-up smudged round her eyes and mouth, and her blonde hair in knots.

'Ye had a good night of it then?' Kitty put on the kettle. 'I didn't know your husband had come home.'

'He hasn't.' Maggie sounded startled. 'I don't know when he'll be back.'

It was on the tip of Kitty's tongue to ask who the red-haired man she'd seen Maggie with the night before was. On second thoughts, she held her tongue.

'What made you think Fred was home?'

Kitty mumbled something about having seen a man outside Maggie's door.

'Coulda been one of me ma's chaps,' Maggie said casually. She swallowed her tea noisily then lit a cigarette.

Kitty told her about the little café. 'It's a lovely wee place.'

'Yeah, it's Gertie Lander's. We all thought she'd close it down when her husband died 'cos she's allus talking about going back to Flamborough.'

'So she told us,' Kitty remarked.

Then, out of the blue, Maggie said, 'Them Zeppelins bombed London again last night. Dozens of houses flattened and people killed. I read it in me ma's newspaper.'

'Oh, that's terrible.' Kitty clapped her hand to her mouth, her eyes wide. When she removed it she said, 'We've been lucky so far. I dread the thought of them bombing Liverpool. Every time I read about those poor souls in London it keeps me waken at night.'

'Yeah, and did you hear about that bomb that went off here on our docks?' Maggie smirked nastily.

Kitty was mystified.

'They're saying it wasn't the Germans, it was the *Irish*.' This time Maggie gave Kitty a spiteful look. 'Who the bloody hell do they think they are, coming over here causing trouble? It's bad enough the bloody Germans dropping bombs on London without the Irish blowing stuff up in Liverpool.'

Kitty's hackles rose. 'We're not all like that,' she snapped, and thought of Shaun. She didn't think he had ever been responsible for any of the targets in London that the Irish Republican Army had bombed, but she knew he was involved with the men who had carried out the explosions. It broke her heart to think that he was now in jail, but at least he couldn't be blamed for the bomb on the docks, if indeed it was the Irish. She only wished she knew which jail he was in. Then she could write and comfort him.

'Everybody knows the Irish want to get their own back on the British,' Maggie persisted. 'They—'

Kitty cut her off short. 'Aye, they do,' she retaliated heatedly, 'but it's only because of the way they treated us for hundreds of years, stealing our land an' starving our people. Ye know nothing about it, Maggie.' She jumped to her feet, her hazel eyes flashing as she cleared the cups from the table.

'All right! Keep your hair on, I was just saying. You never know who you can trust these days.' Maggie stood up. 'I'll get off now. Oh, an' before I go can you lend me a cup of sugar.'

Kitty didn't know what to make of Maggie. One minute she was pleasant and the next she was making cruel jibes about the Irish.

'I think she just says whatever comes into her head without engagin' her brain,' she said to Tom later that evening.

'I don't know why ye bother with her,' he replied. She heard the disinterest in his voice and would have liked to rip the *Sporting*

Times that he was studying out of his hands. She wanted to scream that she bothered with Maggie because even though Maggie might not be to his or her liking, Maggie was all she'd got.

It's all right for you, Tom, she thought angrily, *you have lots of company all day, and every time I mention going out to work I feel as though my words are knocking against a brick wall.*

* * *

The next day, Monday, and every day after that for the entire week, Kitty dressed carefully in her smartest blouse, skirt and jacket, and hopeful of creating a good impression, she called at all the nearby shops and the restaurant on Broad Green then further afield on Edge Lane. None of them were hiring assistants. By midday on Friday she had given up hope and walked back to Weaver Street feeling utterly disconsolate and in desperate need of something to lighten her misery. When she arrived at the back lane, instead of walking up it she carried on to the front of the street, striding past her own front door and up to the church.

Inside, on her knees, she bowed her head, and breathing in the sweet smell of incense, she asked Our Lady to find her a job. Feeling somewhat consoled, she decided to revisit the blue and white café, just as she had said she would. Tom had gone to a dog fight in Kirby early that morning, and wouldn't be back until late that night. Kitty detested the idea of him taking bets on such a cruel sport. She hadn't objected to his work before – she thought there was something noble about horse racing – but there was nothing decent about watching dogs tear one another to pieces. She shuddered as she made her way down to the riverbank.

The café was busy when she arrived. Mill workers whose dinnertime was between twelve and one o'clock came in and out, ordering hot pies, sandwiches and scones. Most of the tables were occupied and the woman she now knew as Gertie Lander was rushed off her feet.

Kitty found an empty chair, and when Gertie eventually came to take her order she said, 'Oh, I remember you. You're the girl who said it was like being at the seaside. What can I get you?'

Kitty ordered a cup of tea. It was a long time coming, and she felt sorry for the woman who seemed to be serving a dozen people at once. Stout, and probably in her sixties, she was red in the face and flustered, and as she shuffled from behind the counter to clear used crockery from a table, Kitty noticed that her ankles were badly swollen.

Four young women came and sat at the table next to Kitty. They chatted for a moment or two then one of them shouted, 'Hey! Is there any chance of getting served?' and another called out, 'An' this table needs clearing.'

'With you in a minute,' Gertie panted as she threaded her way between the tables carrying a loaded tray. She looked thoroughly fed up. A seed of an idea worked its way into Kitty's mind.

'Well, don't take all day, Gertie,' the young woman retorted.

Kitty got to her feet, and in a most professional manner, she stacked the dirty crockery that was on the table where the young women were sitting and then, carrying it to the counter, she stepped behind it and put the crockery in the sink.

Gertie's jaw dropped. 'You're busy, so I'll give ye a hand,' said Kitty. She whipped off her jacket and then hurried to clear two more tables. Back at the counter she said, 'Who needs serving next?'

'Them in the far corner.' Gertie's expression was a mixture of amazement and relief as she handed over a tray of tea and sandwiches.

'Your new assistant's better looking than the last one, Gertie,' a cheeky, young lad called out as Kitty served his hot pie and peas.

Young men were so scarce these days that he almost looked out of place amongst all the women. Then Kitty noticed his thick-soled boot. The poor lad had a club foot, one leg shorter than the other. She gave him a warm smile. *An impediment it might be, but at least it's saved you from the carnage in France,* she thought as she hurried back to the counter.

'You keep your hands and eyes off her, Mickey Briggs,' Gertie shouted at the lad. 'She's an angel in disguise.'

The mill workers returned to work, leaving the café with only three customers. Gertie plumped down on a stool and raised one leg, rubbing at her puffy ankle. 'My, but you're a godsend,' she said, wiping perspiration from her plump cheeks. 'The way you had them orders delivered and the tables cleared, you'd think you'd been doing it all your life.'

Kitty laughed. 'I have – or at least for the past four years. I used to be a silver service waitress in the Gresham Hotel in Dublin. I've had plenty of practice.'

'You can say that again. It's nothing short of a miracle you turning up today. The girl that usually helps me's gone to be a VAD – you know – the Voluntary Aid Detachment or whatever they call it – an' just when me legs are playing up.' Wincing, Gertie propped both feet up on a stool and beamed at Kitty. 'I don't know what I'd have done without you. Sit yourself down and have a cup of tea.'

Kitty was in bed when Tom arrived back from Kirby, but she wasn't sleeping. He undressed and slipped in beside her. She cuddled up to him. He felt cold.

'I got meself a job today,' she said. She felt his body stiffen. Kitty pulled away from him. Propping her elbow on the pillow, she looked down at him, her hazel eyes glinting. 'Tom, we need the money. It's no use pretending we don't. I can't sit about the house all day, just to satisfy your manly pride.'

Tom jutted his lip like a petulant schoolboy. 'But—'

'But nothin', Tom,' Kitty continued. 'I know ye are doin' your best, but your business has yet to take off. We'll have bills to pay afore long for gas an' coal. We have to have money put by to meet them. Ye didn't object to me working in the Gresham, so why do ye object to me working here?'

'It's not fitting for a man in my position,' he huffed.

'Would ye listen to yourself, Tom Conlon? Who do ye think ye are?' Kitty said, turning away from him.

Tom closed his eyes, recalling the independent, vibrant girl with a fiery mass of curly hair and eyes that were flecked with gold that he had fallen for one rainy afternoon in Dublin. He'd been standing at the bar in the hotel, watching her swish from table to table taking and serving orders, her black dress and white apron showing off her pert figure. She'd seemed very much in charge of herself, and he'd liked that. Then he remembered the way she'd had the foresight to buy groceries as soon as they arrived in Edge Hill, and the way she'd organised the house whilst he was job hunting. He'd loved her free spirit and the manner in which she just got on with things. She was right, as usual.

He rolled over and took her in his arms, feeling the tension ease from her body as he gently asked, 'Now, tell me. What kind of work is it?'

He laughed when Kitty told him about what she'd done in the busy café. Even so, she sensed that his pride was hurt. 'My wages'll help us out till you find your feet, an' it'll not interfere with me looking after ye an' the house,' she said, her tone begging him not to argue.

'Aye, they will so,' he said unenthusiastically. In her excitement, Kitty didn't hear the disappointment in his reply.

Her heart soared.

'But—' his voice took on a serious tone '—when you're talking to people, it's best if you don't mention anything about my business – or Shaun. There's them who think the bookies are always out to cheat 'em so don't be gossiping about things I've told ye. Like the way I fix the odds an' so on.' He turned his back to her. 'An' as for that brother of yours. I can't afford to be associated with jailbird rebel, so say nothing.'

'As if I would,' Kitty said, her heart plummeting to the pit of her stomach.

7

Kitty turned up early for her first day's work in the café. She was wearing her black skirt and a freshly ironed white blouse, and she'd fastened her hair back in a neat chignon. However, she never quite managed to prevent silky little tendrils escaping and enhancing her pretty face. Flecks of gold shone in her hazel eyes as, bubbling with anticipation and excitement, she greeted Gertie.

'My, you're keen,' Gertie said, glancing at the clock. 'The other lass I employed was always ten minutes late an' more.' Her eyes appraised Kitty. 'And you look ever so smart. I'll have to put me prices up to match the service.'

Kitty giggled. 'I wore this when I worked in the Gresham. It's one of the best hotels in Dublin.'

'An' this is the best café on the towpath – on account of it being the only one,' Gertie replied drolly, 'but between you an' me we can make it even better, so let's get started.' She clapped her hands.

* * *

By the end of September, Kitty felt as though she had worked in Lander's Café for years instead of just weeks. The customers, most of them from the mill, called her by name and had a bit of banter with her as she served them. In between waiting on tables she made sandwiches and warmed pies and made pots of tea, getting to know the customers' likes and dislikes.

'No mustard for you, Jim,' she said, handing the elderly loom tuner his potted meat sandwich.

'Jim's hot enough, aren't ya, Jim?' shouted one of the raucous girls at the next table. She cackled lewdly and winked at him. He ignored her.

'Leave the poor old bugger alone,' a big, beefy lad called out.

'Why? Are you jealous, Danny? Sally from spinnin' told me your willy wa' as limp as wet lettuce. A bit o' mustard might stiffen it up.'

The big lad's face turned red, and Gertie shouted, 'Now, now. Less o' that.'

Kitty glanced over at the girl sitting in the corner by the window. *What does she make of all this risqué talk?* she wondered. She seemed very prim and proper, and dressed rather sedately for a girl of her age. Kitty thought she'd seen her somewhere before but couldn't recall where. She cut a lonely figure as she nibbled her sandwich and gazed out at the river or read her book. She sat by herself and Kitty wondered if she chose to do so because of the crude banter. She walked over to the table. 'Can I get ye anything else?'

'No thank you.' The girl smiled shyly but the smile didn't reach her pale grey eyes. Kitty thought she looked sad.

'Excuse me for being nosy,' she said, 'but why don't ye ever sit with the others?'

'They wouldn't want me to. I'm not one of them. They work in the weaving and spinning sheds. I work in the office.' She gave a deprecating shrug.

Kitty didn't know what to say to that so she said, 'I'm Kitty Conlon. I'm from Ireland. I've come to live in Weaver Street.'

The girl smiled. 'I know. I'm Beth Garside, and I also live in Weaver Street.'

'I knew I'd seen ye before somewhere. Ye live at number three, don't ye?' All at once Kitty remembered the pale, miserable face she'd seen gazing out of the window overlooking the back lane.

'That's right. I live there with my dad. He's a manager in the mill in charge of the weaving and spinning sheds.' She looked downcast as she said this, and Kitty understood why the other girls might not want her company. She was the boss's daughter.

'I can't think why I haven't met ye before,' Kitty said, 'but now we know we live in the same street we can call with one another for a cup of tea and a chat.' Beth seemed like a nice girl and she thought she'd like her for a friend.

Beth looked doubtful. Then she smiled. 'I'd like that,' she said.

* * *

'How's the job going?' Tom asked one evening as they sat down to dinner. It was the first time he'd shown any interest.

'It's grand. I'm getting to meet all sorts of people.' Kitty told him about Beth Garside. 'She works in the mill office and her dad's a manager there.'

Tom perked up. 'That's the sort of people ye should be making friends with,' he effused, his tone implying that he didn't consider Maggie suitable.

'Aye, Beth's very proper. She's not rough like Maggie, although I don't mind her now I've got used to her. She makes me laugh.'

'She's like her ma. She keeps the fellas in the bar amused – in more ways than one,' he said disapprovingly. 'She's a fly one is Vi.'

A stab of jealousy pierced Kitty's chest. She didn't like to think of women hanging round him at work. They hadn't when he'd worked in Dublin. Decent women there didn't go to betting shops or into pubs without their husbands, but over here was different. 'Do a lot of women gamble with ye, Tom?' she asked.

Tom heard the sharpness in her voice and looked up from his plate. 'Ach, don't fash yourself, Kitty. Ye don't have to worry about me.' He gave her his most charming smile. 'I only have eyes for you, me darlin' girl.'

* * *

On a late Saturday afternoon on a blustery day at the end of October, Kitty was on her way home from the café and doing some last minute shopping when Maggie came walking towards her on the arm of a skinny, little man in uniform. He was almost a head shorter than her. The wind tugged at his sparse, mousy hair. His bristly, little moustache and protruding front teeth had Kitty thinking he looked a bit like a weasel.

'Hiya, Kitty!' Maggie's smile didn't quite reach her eyes. 'This is Fred.' She flicked her thumb at him. 'He got a forty-eight-hour pass.' She didn't sound too happy about it. Fred gave Kitty a disinterested smile.

'Pleased to meet you, Fred.' She stuck out her hand but Fred didn't appear to notice. He seemed to want to keep moving.

'He's itching to get to the pub,' Maggie said. 'He'll not sober up till he has to go back.'

Fred gave her a dirty look. 'You'd do the same if you'd been where I've been.'

'Where was that then, Fred?' Kitty asked in an attempt to defuse the animosity that bristled between Maggie and her husband.

'Egypt. Keeping Jerry and them barmy Turks away from the Suez Canal.' He scowled. 'There wa' sand an' flies in every bloody thing we ate, an' the heat would have killed you, never mind the Germans.'

'Oh, that sounds terrible, Fred.' Kitty's tone oozed with sympathy.

'Yeah, it was. Me throat's been parched for months.' He tugged Maggie's arm.

'I won't keep you then,' said Kitty, and let them go on their way. Maggie didn't seem at all pleased that Fred was home and Kitty wondered why. Surely, if she'd loved him enough to marry him, she should be thrilled to have him back.

Tom was getting ready to go to the Weaver's Arms when Kitty got back to the house. 'He's not a bit like the kind of fella ye'd think Maggie would go for,' she exclaimed, telling Tom how she'd met them in Broad Green.

'I don't think Maggie has a type. She'd go for anything in trousers.'

'That's an awful thing to say, Tom Conlon.'

'I'll be off,' he said, kissing her and then lifting his briefcase. He wouldn't upset Kitty by telling her that Maggie, along with several of the other mill girls who came into the pub, had given him the glad eye more than once. Not that he was interested. The women he fancied were much classier than that.

Kitty waved him off at the front door, just as a hearse passed slowly by on its way to St Joseph's. She blessed herself and was saying a prayer for the repose of the dead person's soul when she heard someone knocking on her back door. She hurried through into the kitchen.

'I hope it's convenient... but... there's a funeral... and my dad's gone so I...' Overcome with embarrassment, Beth Garside's words petered out.

'Come in, come in,' Kitty said, somewhat mystified yet pleased to see her. It was more than a week since she had issued the invitation and although she had seen Beth in the café she had made no mention of calling.

'Sit ye down. I'll make some tea.' She pulled out a chair at the table and Beth sat down, looking shyly around her as Kitty set the kettle to boil and took out her best cups – white china with gold bands round the rims; something else they had inherited from Great-Uncle Tom.

Kitty could tell that the poor girl was nervous, and wanting to put her at ease and keep the conversation going she said, 'I saw a hearse going up the street. I wondered if the poor soul in the coffin had been fightin' in France. So many young men have lost their lives there. It's terrible, isn't it?'

Beth leapt on the subject. 'I know. It's awful, isn't it? He used to work in the dye house at the mill. He was only eighteen. My dad always attends the funerals of the workers who've been killed. That's why I could come,' she gabbled.

Bemused, Kitty raised her eyebrows.

'I mean... I...' Beth took a deep breath. 'Dad disapproves of me going into other people's houses in the street,' she said, her cheeks flushing, 'but... but because he's at the funeral... and afterwards he's going to a meeting at the Conservative Club... I thought I'd...'

'Come an' visit me,' Kitty concluded brightly. She sat down at the table and poured tea. Then she began talking about the weather, and when she saw that Beth was more at ease she said, 'Tell me this. Why does your dad not let ye visit with people?'

Beth sighed. 'It's silly really. He has this bee in his bonnet that people want to be friendly only so that they can learn your business and then gossip about you. He doesn't have a very good opinion of our neighbours. Actually, he's a bit of a snob.' She essayed a smile. 'He's always been like that, even before Mam died.'

'I'm sorry to hear that,' Kitty said, pushing a plate of biscuits towards Beth. 'When did ye lose her?'

'Thirteen years ago, when I was seven,' Beth said, her expression woebegone. She accepted a biscuit and nibbled on it.

'So it's just been the two of ye since then.' Kitty sipped her tea, thoughtful. 'Mebbe I can understand why he'd want to keep ye close, but—' she weighed her words carefully '—ye shouldn't let him bully ye. Ye have a right to have friends and go where ye please.'

Beth's face crumpled. 'Dad doesn't seem to think so,' she mumbled, her hand shaking as she lifted her cup.

Kitty could see that the conversation was making Beth sad, so she changed the subject. She told her about Ireland and the long journey to Liverpool. Beth cheered up, and before long they were chatting happily about hairstyles and clothes and other things young women talk about. They discovered that they both liked the countryside and knitting and reading magazines.

When it was time for Beth to go, she said, 'It's been lovely sitting here talking to you but I'd appreciate it if you don't call at my house. I'd like to invite you back, but Dad would only kick up a fuss.'

'Think nothin' of it. Ye're always welcome here.'

'Thanks. I'll call again when I get the chance. I've really enjoyed it.'

* * *

Later that same evening, as Kitty and Tom were drinking cups of cocoa before retiring for the night, they were startled by screaming and shouting outside their back door. Tom leapt to his feet and yanked it opened, Kitty peering round him to see who was making such a racket.

Fred stood swaying on the steps, Maggie clutching at the tail of his jacket and bawling, 'It's the wrong house, you daft bugger. We live next door.'

Drunk as a skunk, Fred collapsed in a heap on the step. Maggie gave him a kick before looking apologetically up at Tom and Kitty. 'I tried to stop him,' she cried, 'but he's that far gone he doesn't know where he is.' She bent down to pull him up, but she couldn't shift him.

Tom stepped over Fred, dragged him to his feet, then threw him over his shoulder as if he were a sack of potatoes. Maggie staggered to her own back door, Tom behind her. When she opened it he dumped Fred inside.

'Ye had a good night of it then,' Tom said, wiping his palms on his trousers.

Maggie glared. ''Course we bloody didn't. He never stays sober long enough to make anything good – but ta, Tom.' She leaned forward to kiss him, her beery breath wafting an inch from his face.

Tom took two quick steps back. 'No bother, Maggie,' he said, turning hastily and hurrying back to his own house.

'Did she try to kiss you?' Kitty had been watching the whole time. 'She's as drunk as he is.' They went inside and closed the door. 'Still, it must be hard for her, him coming home after so long away and then getting absolutely blootered. They should be kissin' an' cuddlin' an' makin' up for lost time, not fightin' in the street.'

'They're both as bad as one another.' Tom doused one gas mantle, an indication that Kitty should go to the foot of the stairs before he doused the other. 'An' her mother's not much better. Tarts, the pair of 'em.' He climbed the stairs, Kitty in front of him, hurrying to the bedroom before he doused the gas mantle on the landing.

Kitty felt annoyed at his censorial remarks. Fred was to blame, not poor Maggie. 'Ye're awful hard on Maggie,' she said, thinking that she'd never known him judge people as harshly as he did Maggie and Vi. But then, she'd noticed a change in him since he'd started running the betting shop. It seemed to her that he was getting uppity now that he was his own boss. Though boss of what? she mused, for Tom's business had yet to make any decent money, and if it wasn't for her wages from the café she didn't know how they would manage.

Tom undressed and climbed into bed. He appeared to have dismissed the ugly scene they had just witnessed completely from his mind, but as Kitty sat at the dressing table taking pins out of her chignon, she tried to make sense of it. To be honest, she didn't much care for Maggie's drinking and going out with other men whilst Fred was away – she was fairly sure that's what she did – but they had grown close and she felt something akin to pity for her friend. She began to brush her hair. As her curls untangled she reached the conclusion that Maggie had never known what it was like to be loved and wanted, and truly in love.

Kitty had never doubted her own mother's affection for her, but she couldn't imagine Vi giving Maggie the unconditional love that she had received as a child. Vi acted more like a big sister or a pal than she did a mother. As for Maggie and Fred's marriage, she didn't know what to make of it. Here was she, secure in the knowledge that the love she felt for Tom was wholly reciprocated, and all poor Maggie had was a husband who was absent for most of the time and when he was present he got so stinking drunk that he couldn't possibly make Maggie feel loved and wanted. *We might be as poor as crows*, she thought, *but at least we have our love for each other*. On that pleasant thought she turned out the light.

'I'm lucky to have you,' she said, climbing in beside Tom. She was going to tell him why she thought that, but Tom was asleep.

* * *

The next day, Tom at the Weaver's for his Sunday pint and Kitty alone in the kitchen, Maggie crept in, her shoulders slumped and her head covered by a closely tied scarf that almost hid her face.

'I'm sorry about last night,' she mumbled, flopping into the nearest chair then pulling off the scarf.

Kitty stopped whisking the batter she was making and cried, 'Who in God's name gave ye that?' Then without giving Maggie time to answer she sneered, 'As if I need ask.'

Maggie's left eye was puffed and purple and her top lip swollen. She took a cigarette from its packet, her hands shaking as she attempted to light it. When at last it ignited, she puffed on it furiously. Kitty's kind heart went out to her.

'Ach, Maggie love, why did ye let him do that to ye?' Tom had never raised his hand to her, nor for that matter had anyone else. She put an ashtray on the table.

'I was sleeping. He did it this in the morning before he left,' Maggie said brokenly, then cynically added, 'You don't think I asked him to hit me, do you?'

'By all the saints, Maggie, that's terrible. What sort of a man is he?'

'A rotten, drunken pig,' she snarled. 'I never should have married him.'

'Then why did ye?' Kitty forgot about the batter and sat down.

'Because I thought I had to,' Maggie said despairingly.

'What do ye mean ye had to? Were you...?'

'I thought I was pregnant, so I got him to marry me,' Maggie said hollowly. Then she burst into hysterical laughter. 'It turned out to be a bloody cyst.'

'A cyst,' Kitty echoed, not sure what a cyst was.

'Yeah, there was no baby,' Maggie said bitterly, 'so I needn't have bothered me arse. And now I'm stuck with him.' She lit another cigarette.

'Ye don't have to be,' Kitty said. 'Just tell him to go an' never come back.'

Maggie sniggered. 'Do you think it's that easy? The nasty sod seems to think I'm his property an' that he can turn up whenever he pleases.'

'Did ye ever love him?' Kitty asked softly, her heart aching to think that Maggie's hopes and dreams had been shattered by Fred's disgusting behaviour.

'Nah, I just wanted the kid to have a father. Round here they look at you like muck if you're not married and have a kid.'

'It's the same in Ireland,' said Kitty. 'Girls have to go into hiding or leave home if they fall for a baby and them not married. I had a friend at the Gresham who got pregnant by a travelling salesman. She never saw him again, an' they packed her off to the Magdalene's.'

'What's the Magdalene's when they're at home?'

'Nuns who take unmarried mothers in an' then treat 'em like slaves. An' when the babies are born the nuns take 'em away for adoption. Some people say they sell them to rich Americans. Poor Sheila never even saw her baby before they took it away. She doesn't even know if it was a girl or a boy.' Kitty's voice had gone up an octave and her eyes had widened in disgust.

'God Almighty! I thought nuns were supposed to be kind and Christian.'

'There's good an' bad in all people, even nuns.' Kitty retrieved the bowl of batter and whisked furiously. Tom would be home for dinner soon. 'Would ye have liked a baby if ye'd been having one?' she asked, at the same time thinking that she might like one of her own.

Maggie frowned. 'I dunno. I suppose if I had a husband like your Tom I'd want kids. You don't know how lucky you are.'

'Oh, but I do,' said Kitty, pouring the batter into a pudding tray.

8

It was a cold, grey morning at the end of November. When Kitty heard the letterbox rattle she went to the front door and picked up the long, brown envelope. Back in the kitchen she handed it to Tom.

'Bloody bejaysus! Holy Mother of God!' Tom threw the letter down on the table amongst the breakfast dishes. His face was dark with rage.

Startled, Kitty dropped the porridge pan she was scouring into the sink. Water splashed onto her apron. She was more surprised by Tom's choice of words than anything else. Just lately he'd taken to speaking 'awfully Anglified' as she termed it. Sometimes he said 'you' instead of 'ye' in his attempt to sound English and now, to hear him cursing in the old Irish way, let her know that whatever was in the letter must be serious.

'What is it?' She dried her hands and hurried to the table. 'Is it bad?'

'Bad enough,' Tom growled. 'I've been conscripted into the navy. I've to report to Derby House for enlistment the day after tomorrow.' He ran his fingers through his hair, almost tugging it out by the roots.

Kitty felt a knot of panic form in her stomach. 'But why you, Tom?' She flung her arms around him, cradling his head to her breast. Her heart was racing and she felt sure he must have heard it drumming in his ear. She wanted to cry out that she wouldn't let them take him. Instead, the lump in her throat almost choking her, she croaked, 'Sure, an' ye knowing nothin' about sailin'. Why ever would they want ye?'

'They don't want me to sail the bloody ship,' he snarled, pulling away from her. 'They want me to be feckin' cannon fodder.' He buried his head in his hands. Kitty patted his shoulder ineffectually and tried to make sense of it all. She conjured up a picture of him on the deck of one of the battleships she'd seen in the docks. Swirling black water, guns blazing, and her poor Tom clinging on for dear life as German ships bombarded it with shot and shell.

'Oh, Tom,' she wailed, clasping him to her breast again. This time Tom didn't pull away and they rocked back and forth for a long moment, each contemplating his fate. Then, in an attempt to bring reason to bear she said, 'I suppose it's only to be expected. You're livin' in their country.' She still thought of England as not being *their* country.

Tom raised his head, his eyes dark as he gazed at her beseechingly. 'What am I to do, Kitty?' His voice wobbled. 'I don't want to go an' fight.'

'I don't think ye have much choice, Tom,' she said, her voice hollow. Yet again, the full impact of what was about to happen punched her chest. She began to tremble. Tom would go and leave her all alone. He might be killed. She pictured the hearses that regularly passed by her front door. Would one of them be carrying her Tom one day soon? She picked up the letter and stared at it through her tears. Plip! Plop! They fell, unchecked, blurring the ink.

Their perfect lives had been changed by a few typed words on a sheet of thick, cream paper, and Kitty wasn't sure what to do next.

* * *

'Tom's been conscripted,' Kitty told Gertie when she arrived at the café. 'He doesn't want to be called up, and I don't want him to go.' She bit down on her lip to stem her tears.

Gertie heard the desolation in Kitty's voice. She stopped slicing bread and said, 'Ooh, that's shocking! But it's not unexpected. My cousin in Flamborough has five lads an' they're all in France, even though one of 'em tried to claim exemption.'

'What's that?'

'Tried to get out o' going by sayin' his job as an electrician was too important. You see, in t'first round-up you could be made exempt if you worked at something really necessary, but then they changed the law 'cos they're that desperate for men, what wi' so many being killed already, an' this time he's been forced to go.'

'He could allus be a conchie if he wanted to get out of it bad enough.' Willie Taylor, a wizened old chap who worked in the dyeing shed at the mill, butted in.

'What's a conchie?' Kitty saw a glimmer of hope for Tom.

'Conscientious objector,' Willie sneered. 'Them what don't agree wi' fightin' an' killin'. Bloody cowards the lot of 'em. Kill or be killed is what I say – an' hurry up wi' that bloody sandwich, Gertie, I'm fair clemmed.'

Gertie smeared margarine then meat paste on the bread, slapped the slices together and handed them over. 'I don't think your Tom'd want to be a conchie. They either send 'em to prison or down t'coal mines. He'd be better off in t'navy. He'd look nice in a uniform would your Tom.'

Kitty had to agree with that but her throat tightened as she thought of him in jail or underground, digging coal in the dark. It was bad enough Shaun being locked up. She didn't want her husband to go to prison. For the rest of her shift, she served at the tables, made sandwiches and heated up pies, all the while making a feeble attempt to join in the banter, but her heart wasn't in it.

'Try not to worry, love,' Gertie said as Kitty put on her coat ready to go home. 'He might not be away that long. This war can't go on forever.' She didn't really believe that, but she liked Kitty and was downhearted to see her so miserable. Then, before she could prevent herself from ruining the comfort she'd just given, she thought of her own problems. 'An' if it does go on much longer I'll shut up shop 'cos I'm havin' a hell of a job gettin' flour to bake me baps, an' margarine's been scarce this while back. If it wasn't for the stuff me sister's husband slips me off the docks I don't know how we'd go on.'

It was a well-known fact that the stevedores unloading cargo from the ships helped themselves to whatever they could get away with.

Kitty's spirits sank further. 'Oh, don't say that, Gertie. I love working here.' *And I need the money*, she silently added as she thought of their almost empty money tin. Tom's bookmaking business showed no sign of improving.

Willie cut in again. 'Aye, if they keep sinkin' ships afore they reach the docks we'll all starve. On'y last week three of our ships never made it back to Liverpool. My neighbour's lad wa' on one of 'em. Sunk with all hands.' Willie shook his head despairingly. 'Kaiser Wilhelm said he'd sink all our ships an' he's makin' a bloody good job of it,' he concluded gloomily.

Kitty couldn't bear to hear any more.

She understood very little about the war. To be honest, she didn't want to know. As yet, the impact it made on her life had been slight. Yes, there was a scarcity of food in the shops, with sugar, butter and cheese all in short supply, but she and Tom had grown used to making do.

She also knew how important the docks in Liverpool were, and that they were heavily guarded against attack from the Germans, but the distance between them and Weaver Street was enough for her not to worry. Even the threat of Zeppelin raids didn't cost her much thought. As yet, no bombs had been dropped on Liverpool. If there was a warning, she and Tom went into the cellar to sit it out on the blankets and cushions she'd taken down. She held the same opinion about the trains that thundered up and down the Liverpool to Manchester line carrying troops and weapons and other war supplies, and about the ships that sailed in and out of the docks. Nobody she knew was on a train or a ship so it hadn't seemed to matter until now. Suddenly, the war felt very close at hand. One day soon, a ship would sail out of Liverpool with her lovely Tom on it. Kitty wept as she walked back to Weaver Street.

'Gertie says you can tell them that your job is too important, or that you can be a conscientious objector to get out of going,' Kitty told Tom as she served up a shepherdess pie and cabbage with Bisto gravy.

'I hardly think a bookie is what you'd call essential,' Tom growled, 'and I'll not be labelled a coward. There'll be no white feathers for me.' Tom understood about all these things. He'd heard talk in the bookie's shop as he took the bets.

'I'll go an' be damned with it.'

That same night, in bed, Kitty lay awake, pressed against Tom's warm body, tormented by the horrors that he was about to face.

What if he didn't come back? Her skin turned clammy, her fears for him making her heart race. When she could bear it no longer she wakened him, needing his kisses to quell her fears.

9

December brought with it the first flurry of snow. Tom had reported to Derby House and been ordered to start his training on the thirteenth. *He won't even be here to celebrate our first Christmas in our own home,* Kitty thought despondently, banking up the fire before putting on her coat ready to go to work. They could have at least let him stay home till then. What sort of men were they that they'd send a man off to fight at this time of year? Christmas was the time families should be together. Then she thought of all the soldiers and sailors who wouldn't be with their loved ones, some of them never again. She silently chastised herself for being selfish, but with less than two weeks to Tom's impending departure she couldn't help but feel hard done by.

She had barely slept again and her head ached. Tom seemed to have accepted his fate but there was hardly a moment in which Kitty didn't feel rising panic for his safety. She had thought that their first Christmas in their new home would be a joyous affair. Now, the pleasure of that had been taken away from her. Life just wasn't fair. Living in Weaver Street had proved to be all she had hoped it would be, but soon she'd be here without Tom and she didn't like the thought of that.

In a futile attempt to take her mind elsewhere, she had begun frantically knitting socks for Tom and gifts for her friends, the simple repetition of knit and purl bringing with it an air of normality, but each stitch accompanied by a prayer.

Now, she walked down the lane with her wool and needles in her bag. If the café wasn't busy she might get a chance to finish the gloves she was knitting for Maggie.

* * *

Kitty was sitting down to a cup of tea when Beth popped in. 'You're home early. Have you had a good day?'

'Much the same as usual,' Kitty replied.

'Me too. Now I'm taking the opportunity to have a natter seeing as my dad's working overtime.' Beth frequently took advantage to call with Kitty when her father was otherwise occupied. Kitty was amused by the reasons she gave such as *he's having a bath* or *he has a migraine so he's gone to lie down*. Kitty laughed at her excuses, but was irked to think that Beth couldn't visit as and when she pleased. When Beth joined in the laughter there was still sadness in her eyes and the wariness of a person who carried a heavy burden.

On Beth's last visit, Kitty had given her a good talking to. 'Stand up to him,' she'd told her, 'otherwise ye'll regret it. My brothers dictated to me after my parents died an' at first I put up with it. I was afraid to do anything else. Then they started makin' a slave of me so I upped an' packed me bags an' left for Dublin. That soon wiped the smile off their faces, I can tell ye.'

Beth had paled. 'Oh, I wouldn't want to have to leave home to prove a point,' she'd gasped, 'I couldn't leave Dad on his own. He's useless at looking after himself.'

'Ye won't have to if ye stick to your guns an' not let him walk all over ye.' Kitty had given Beth an encouraging grin. Beth had responded with a wan smile, but today her eyes were sparkling, and as they sat over the tea Kitty said, 'Tom's going to Bootle on Saturday an' I'll be on me own till late. We could go an' see Douglas Fairbanks in *Flirting With Fate* at the picture house if you want.'

Beth smiled. 'I'd love to,' she said. 'I took your advice and told Dad I had a right to visit whom I pleased. He isn't happy about it, but like you said, I have my own life to lead, and at my age I should get on with it.'

'So ye should,' Kitty said, delighted that Beth had heeded her advice. 'See ye on Saturday then.'

* * *

On Saturday morning, Kitty arrived at the café with her bag filled with teacakes she'd bought at the bakery. Gertie usually baked her own and she grimaced as Kitty set them on the counter saying, 'They're not half as good as your own.'

'Aye, you're right,' Gertie huffed, 'but flour's that scarce I couldn't buy any this week, and I'll not use that ground turnip that the gover'ment's telling us to use. If things get any worse, I'll shut up shop.'

Kitty flinched. Each time Gertie threatened to close the café her spirits sank, but Gertie soon had her laughing. Throughout the day she kept up a lively stream of chatter and made droll remarks about the clientele.

'Look out! Here comes half-price Arthur,' Gertie chortled as they were getting ready to close the café. She had nicknames for several of her regulars.

Arthur shuffled up to the counter. 'Have you got owt that you want rid of?' he asked craftily. Gertie pointed to two cold pies on the counter. 'I'll not want to pay full price for 'em if they're yesterday's,' he said.

'You never do,' Gertie scoffed, wrapping the pies and taking his money. Arthur scuttled out, clutching them to his chest. Gertie grimaced. 'Between him an' Percy-Pay-You-Later, it's a wonder I make any profit. The trouble wi' Percy is he never told me how much later.'

'Your problem is ye're too big hearted,' Kitty said as she wiped down the tables.

'An' I'm not the only one,' Gertie affirmed. 'Every time you walk through that door you take the weight off my shoulders – an' me feet. You've a knack for making people happy, Kitty. When I said you were an angel in disguise I wasn't wrong.' Her plump cheeks wobbled.

Kitty tossed her dishcloth at Gertie. 'Ach, away out o' that! Ye'll have me canonised afore long. St Kitty of the café,' she said, laughing.

'But it's true,' Gertie remonstrated. 'I've seen the way you make Beth Garside smile. She was a lonely little thing until you came along.'

'I like Beth. She's good company once ye get to know her.' Kitty went back behind the counter and rinsed out her cloth.

'Aye, the poor lass's not had much of a life since her mam died.' Gertie pulled a face. 'The trouble wi' Walter Garside is he thinks he's a cut above everybody else because he's a manager. He'll ruin that girl's life if he gets chance – just like he ruined her mother's. He'll not let Beth go because he needs somebody to cook an' clean for him, an' he's too mean to pay for it.'

'I think we've made a start in addressing that problem.' Kitty put on her coat ready to go home. 'Beth's told him she'll lead her own life from now on.'

Gertie grinned. 'An' I'll bet it was you encouraged her to do that.'

'I might have had a word or two,' Kitty said modestly.

'Oh, I'll bet it was more than two words, knowing you,' Gertie chuckled, 'but well done, Kitty. You're a good-hearted lass.'

* * *

On her way home from the café, Kitty walked down Weaver Street, and passing by her own front door, she walked round the end of the street and into the back lane. She'd noticed that most of her neighbours rarely used their front doors and she was doing the same. As she approached number five she saw that May Walker was pegging washing on the line.

'Hello, Mrs Walker, busy as usual.'

'Yeah, but when I've finished pegging this lot I'm putting the kettle on. Why don't you come in for a cuppa?'

'Thank ye. I will.' Kitty walked into May's garden and helped her peg the rest of the washing before following her indoors.

May's kitchen was shabby but spotlessly clean. As she made the tea, Kitty talked about the café and about being a waitress in Dublin.

'You're making yourself at home then,' May said.

'I might as well if I'm going to live here,' Kitty laughed, her smile slipping as she added, 'Though how I'll feel when Tom's away I don't know.'

'Away? Why, where's he going? He's just started up a business here.'

'He's been conscripted into the navy. He had to go to Derby House to sign on. He leaves at the end of next week.' Kitty sounded as though she was announcing the end of the world.

'Oh, I am sorry, love. I know how you feel. I've hardly slept a wink since my eldest lad, our Sammy, joined up.' May sniffed back impending tears. 'He's in France, up to his knees in mud,' she continued, her voice wobbling. 'He says his feet are rotten and that there's rats as big as cats in the trenches.' She shuddered. 'In his last letter he told me that two of his best mates had been killed.' Her tears spilled over. 'I don't know what I'd do if that happened to our Sammy.'

Kitty searched for comforting words. 'Try not to think like that, May. I don't know just where your Sammy is but I did read that our forces had beaten the Germans at Ancre. With a bit of luck it'll all soon be over.'

'Mebbe it will, love,' May said wearily, 'but there's nowhere safe these days. Not even here.' She poured two cups of tea and sat down. 'I haven't forgotten when them German ships bombed Scarborough back at the start of the war. They killed over a hundred people – some of 'em were on their holidays, bless 'em.'

She gave a wistful little smile. 'Me and Bill took our lads there once for a long weekend. It's only sixty miles away. We stayed in a caravan right near the beach.' She shook her head. 'And look what they're doin' to Sheffield, bombing the steelworks. It's all too close for my liking. We're all in danger, love.'

'Aye, these days we never know the minute,' Kitty agreed. ''Tis them Zeppelins that has me afraid. They bombed Sheffield and somewhere near Leeds. Ye never know when they're coming or where they'll drop their bombs.'

'I know what you mean, love. Where is it they're sending your Tom?'

'I don't know as yet,' Kitty said dismally, unwilling to think of him in danger.

The miserable conversation was curtailed as May's back door rattled open and two of her sons burst in. They stopped short when they saw Kitty.

'This is our Joey and our Ronnie,' May said, pride colouring her words. The boys blushed and shuffled their feet. 'Our Ronnie leaves school next Easter, and our Joey's twelve. They're both good lads, and if you ever want any errands running they'll be more than happy to oblige.'

Kitty gave each of them a smile. 'That's good to know,' she said.

'Where's our Steven?' May was frowning.

'He stayed to play footie,' Joey said. 'He got picked for the school team.'

May shook her head. 'Lads, who'd have 'em?' she groaned, but Kitty could see that she adored her sons. She left May's house feeling as though she was making her presence known in Weaver Street and she liked that feeling.

She'd no sooner arrived back in her own house than Maggie dropped in. 'Fred's back again,' she announced, her face as black as thunder. 'He's gonna be based in Chester driving a captain round. That's too bloody near for my liking. He'll never be off the flaming doorstep. You'd think with a war on that they'd find something better for him to do.'

'I'd like to think they'll give Tom a job that'll let him come home as often,' Kitty said, shaking potatoes into the sink to wash, and thinking it would seem strange when she was cooking a dinner for one instead of two.

'Yeah, well, your Tom's different,' Maggie groused. 'I'd best get back an' feed the bugger before he starts kicking off. Ta-ra, love.' She banged out of the house. Kitty boiled the potatoes ready for when Tom arrived home. Saturday was his busy day and he wouldn't be back until late but he might want feeding. Then, making do with a tomato and spam sandwich for her own meal, she got ready for her evening out with Beth.

* * *

Kitty and Beth had just arrived back from the cinema and were sitting over a cup of tea in Kitty's house when Maggie walked in.

'Oh, I didn't know you had company,' she said crossly.

Kitty got to her feet and fetched another cup to the table. 'We're just back from seeing *Flirting With Fate*. It was grand. Douglas Fairbanks is a real heart-throb, but he's not as handsome as my Tom.'

Maggie scowled. 'I wouldn't have minded seeing it meself if you'd bothered to ask me,' she groused.

'Sorry, Maggie, I thought ye'd be out with Fred.' Kitty poured her a cup of tea.

Maggie accepted it ungraciously. 'We had a big row an' he buggered off back to camp.' She blew out a stream of smoke from the cigarette she had just lit.

'Couldn't you live with Fred on the camp? Don't they have married quarters?' Beth spoke tentatively, believing that if Maggie and Fred saw one another more often they might get on better.

Maggie sneered. 'They do, an' when I married him I thought he'd take me with him, but he prefers living in the barracks with the men. An' I wouldn't go with him now even if he begged me.' She stubbed out her cigarette, grinding it into the ashtray. After draining her cup, she said, 'Any road, I'm off. Ta-ra.' Both Kitty and Beth exchanged glances.

As soon as she was out of earshot, Kitty said, 'I wish I'd known Fred had gone back. I'd have asked her to come with us. She'd have enjoyed it, an' she's so unhappy at the moment it might have taken her mind off things.'

'I've never had much to do with her,' Beth said. 'We were in the same class in junior school, but I went on to the grammar and Maggie stayed in the board school. We've never really been friends.' She giggled behind her hand. 'To be honest, I've always been a bit scared of her.'

'I can well imagine why,' said Kitty, and grinned. 'She can be a bit rough at times, but I've got to like her. I think her bark's worse than her bite.'

On Sunday, after Tom had had his lunchtime pint in the Weaver's Arms, Kitty brought up the subject of having a farewell party. She dearly wanted his leaving to end on a happy note; a pleasant memory for him to carry with him wherever they sent him.

'Do ye think we should invite a few friends in for a drink and a bite to eat?' She set the jug of gravy at Tom's elbow then took her place at the table, her enquiring expression hopeful.

'Why would you want to do that?' Tom smothered his potatoes with gravy.

'I've been thinking, Tom, an' it's like this,' Kitty said. 'I work at the top of the street and ye at the bottom, and I'd like to invite people into our house now that we're part of Weaver Street. Give ye a good send off.'

Tom's disinterested shrug and his silence letting her know he didn't think much of the idea, she let it go for the time being.

10

The nearer it got to Tom's departure date, the more Kitty's emotions see-sawed. One minute she was close to tears at the thought of losing him, and the next she was excited about holding a party. At the start of the week, after working in the café, she had called with an invitation for Connie and had been pleasantly surprised to see that Connie's son, Bobby, was home on leave. 'Ye can come as well, Bobby,' she'd said.

'Why not?' he'd replied. 'I might as well get into the way of having a bit of fun again. You don't get much of that in the trenches.'

Now, as she made her way up the back lane, instead of going into her own house she went next door to number thirteen where the elderly couple Mr and Mrs Boothroyd lived. Up until today she had only exchanged pleasantries with them over the garden wall but now she was intending to invite them to her party.

Margery Boothroyd answered the door. She looked rather taken aback when she saw Kitty, but quickly remembering her manners she invited her into the kitchen. Dan Boothroyd glanced up from his newspaper and smiled.

'This is a surprise,' Margery said, 'what can we do for you?'

'Tom and I would like ye to come to a wee gathering in our house this Saturday before he goes off to join the navy. It'll be just for friends and neighbours, nothing grand, but it'll be our way of thanking ye for us making us welcome in Weaver Street, an' it'll mean Tom can leave on a happy note.' Kitty flushed and twisted her hands together, hoping she didn't sound presumptuous.

Margery's eyes widened and she covered her mouth with her hand. 'Oh, how thoughtful of you,' she gasped. 'Dan, did you hear that? Mr and Mrs Conlon are asking us to a party.' In a complete tizzy she clasped Kitty's arm. 'Oh dear, where are my manners? Please sit down. Can I offer you a cup of tea?' She led Kitty to the sofa.

'That's very kind of you,' Dan said, putting aside his newspaper and turning to face Kitty. 'We don't get many invitations these days, do we, Marge?'

His wife was rattling cups onto a tray. She was a plump, homely body in her flowered apron and carpet slippers. Her cheeks were like two little, red apples and her white hair was neatly curled. Kitty thought she looked very motherly as she mashed the tea and arranged a plate of biscuits on the tray covered with a prettily embroidered cloth.

'There now,' Margery puffed, placing the tray on a little table between the sofa and Dan's chair. 'Do help yourself to milk and sugar.'

Kitty had let her gaze roam round the kitchen and noted how neat it was. The patina on the old-fashioned sideboard gleamed and there were beautifully embroidered cushions in the corners of the sofa. She also noticed that there were several photographs of two young boys and two young men in uniform, on the mantelpiece and sideboard.

'Thank ye,' she said, pouring milk into her tea then taking a biscuit and placing it on the pretty side-plate that matched her cup: white china decorated with pink roses. 'This is lovely. I'm ready for a cup. I came straight from the café.'

'You like working for Gertie then,' Dan said, reaching for a biscuit.

'I do. I'm thoroughly enjoying it. I'm not used with sitting at home all day.' She told them about her work in the Gresham and about Tom being a bookmaker and how they had come to be living in Weaver Street.

'We liked Mr Conlon, didn't we, Dan?' Margery said. Dan agreed.

Kitty's curiosity was aroused. 'Did ye know him well?'

Margery frowned. 'We lived next door to him for thirty years, but I wouldn't say we knew him well. I don't think anybody in the street did. He was a very solitary man. He seemed to require no company.'

'He was very good to us when we lost...' Dan's eyes misting, he gestured to the photographs on the mantelpiece. 'He'd come in and light the fire and see that we were all right without making any fuss about it. You see, Marge and me could barely function when it happened.' Dan's long, lean face puckered and he wiped his eyes with the back of his hand. Kitty felt her heart melt as she recalled Maggie telling her that their two sons had been killed in the war.

'Are they...?' She nodded at the photographs.

Margery drew a deep breath. 'They are our sons, Peter and Phillip; we lost them both.' Tears sprang to her eyes. 'Peter in December 1914 and Phillip in January 1915.' She gazed vacantly into space as if she had suddenly lost sense of reality.

'I'm so sorry,' Kitty gasped, 'I didn't mean to upset ye.'

Dan reached out and patted her hand. 'It's all right, love,' he said softly. 'You weren't to know. We've never been the same since it happened, have we, Marge?'

'They're handsome boys,' Kitty said, dabbing at her eyes.

'Have you lost anybody in the war?' Margery asked, her voice hollow.

Kitty hesitated and thought of Shaun. 'In a way,' she murmured and thought, *but not your war.*

Lost for a moment in the grief of their memories, Margery and Dan didn't press her to explain what she meant by that. They went on to tell her that they had a daughter who lived in Southport, and how Peter had been killed outright in the battle for Mons, and that Phillip had been injured at Ypres and died of his wounds in a field station. They spoke about their dead sons sadly and proudly.

Kitty came away feeling older and wiser. Rather than finding them to be the grumpy, old miseries that Maggie had described, she thought the Boothroyds were perfectly charming. She was glad she had taken the trouble to call on them.

She told Tom all about them when he came home.

'An' who else will you invite?' Tom's blue eyes twinkled. He'd decided he quite liked the idea of a party held in his honour.

Kitty pursed her lips and held up her hand. 'Gertie, Maggie and Vi, and Beth and her dad – if he'll come – and the Boothroyds. Then there's Connie and Bobby,' she said, ticking them off on her fingers. 'Is there anyone ye'd like to ask?'

Tom's brow creased. 'I could ask Sam and Cora,' he said, 'although they won't get here until after they've closed the pub.'

'That'd be grand,' said Kitty, totting up on her fingers. Her face fell. 'Ooh, that's thirteen counting us, Tom. I don't want it to be like the Last Supper. Who else can we invite?'

Tom grimaced. 'I'm sure you'll come up with somebody,' he said.

* * *

'It smells like Christmas in here,' Kitty said, sniffing the air appreciatively. It was the morning of the day of the party.

'That's 'cos I've made mince pies.' Gertie put a tray piled high with the small, lidded tarts on the counter.

'They look delicious,' Kitty said, admiring the golden pastry dusted with icing sugar. 'I'll buy some to take home for the party.'

'No need for that,' chirped Gertie. 'I've made another batch especially for you.'

Kitty gave Gertie a quick hug. 'Ye are good to me.'

'And you to me, love.' Gertie returned the hug. 'You've made my life a lot easier. If you hadn't come along when you did I'd have packed it in and gone back to Flamborough.' She began cutting slices of bread, preparing for the lunchtime rush. Kitty put salt and pepper pots and bottles of Heinz ketchup on the tables then made sure the tea urn was ready to supply the dozens of cups of tea she'd soon be serving. For the next twenty minutes she and Gertie worked and chatted, Kitty thinking what a good team they made.

It being a Saturday, the customers were mainly hikers, anglers and bird watchers, most of them elderly, for the younger generation was involved in entirely different pursuits fighting a war, and Tom would soon be joining them. Although she wasn't rushed off her feet Kitty was relieved when her shift ended.

'That's it then,' she said, wiping her hands and getting ready to put on her coat. 'I've lots to do to get ready for tonight so I'll get straight off.' She lifted her cotton shopping bag and took out a small package. 'Oh, by the way, I knitted ye a wee gift. Ye're always complaining that your feet are cold now that ye have nobody to warm them on in bed.'

Gertie's eyes moistened as she held up the pair of cosy pink bed socks. 'Ah, thanks, love,' she cried, her voice ragged. 'You're such a thoughtful girl.' She pecked Kitty's cheek. They smiled at one another, the bond that had formed between them during these past few months plain to see.

'I'll see you later then, Kitty. Have you everything you need for the party?'

'More than enough,' Kitty said, lifting the box of mince pies. She slid them carefully into her bag. 'I'm going to pick some holly and ivy on my way home to decorate the house. I know Christmas is still two weeks off but seeing as Tom won't be here for it I'm doing it early. I'm even going to do us a Christmas dinner tomorrow. I want it to be special seeing as it should be our first Christmas in the house.' Having voiced that made her feel sad and she visibly drooped.

'Come on, love, be brave about it.' Gertie patted Kitty's shoulder comfortingly.

'I'm tryin' to,' Kitty hiccupped, 'but it's awful hard.'

* * *

Along the riverbank, Kitty broke off trailers of ivy and sprigs of holly, wincing and crying 'Ouch!' when the needle-sharp leaves pricked her fingers. With her arms full, she made her way back to Weaver Street. She was almost level with her own front door when she saw Mavis Robson coming towards her. Mavis lived two doors up from Kitty, and other than passing the time of day with her she knew little about her except that she lived alone. Kitty waited at her gate for Mavis to draw nearer.

'Hello, Miss Robson, chilly today, isn't it?'

Mavis drew to a halt. 'Very, but only to be expected at this time of year.' She bobbed her small, neat head, the cherries on her hat bouncing as she flicked the tails of a long, bright red scarf over her narrow shoulders. She reminded Kitty of a Christmas robin. 'That's a lovely bunch of holly,' Mavis continued perkily, 'the berries are just like jewels, don't you think?'

'I'm to decorate the house with it. I'm having a party,' Kitty said, and on an impulse she added, 'would ye like to come?'

Mavis flushed prettily, her beady eyes sparkling. 'Why, thank you, that's most kind. I love a party.'

Kitty gave her the details. Mavis responded by telling her that she had once worked as a pastry cook in the Adelphi, a hotel in the city centre, and that she'd bring some to the party. When Kitty heard that, she said, 'I used to work as waitress in the Gresham Hotel in Dublin. It's one of the best hotels in the city.' Mavis then told her she now worked in munitions. 'It's so much more worthwhile to help the war effort,' she said. They chatted for a while about hotel work and how different it was making shells and bullets. Kitty thought Mavis was very brave. Just before they parted Mavis said, 'Do you mind if I bring Jack?'

Kitty had no objections. Mavis went home with a broad smile on her face and Kitty felt pleased she'd added to her guest list.

* * *

The sprigs of holly intertwined with ivy glistened beautifully on the front room mantelpiece and the polished floorboards and the piano gleamed in the firelight. Kitty had made four red cushions to hide the shabbiness of the couch. 'Ye could invite the Queen of Sheba in here it's that grand,' she said to Tom that evening.

She was feeling rather pleased and proud of herself. Yesterday, to make sure they arrived in time for Christmas, she had posted cards and socks to her brothers in Roscommon, and a lovely green and gold scarf to Maureen at the Gresham. She would dearly have liked to send a card and a gift to Shaun but she didn't know where to send them; and if she had it would have made Tom angry. Nearer the time she'd deliver cards to her neighbours, along with a tin of Crawford's assorted biscuits for Margery and Dan. Flushed with the thrill of giving, she had knitted gloves for Maggie and a scarf for Vi. Beth had told her that she liked reading so Kitty had gone to the quaint second-hand bookshop in Mill Street and bought her a copy of a book called *Zuleika Dobson*. She didn't know much about books but she'd been attracted by the funny name. It had cost only a shilling, and the man in the shop had said it was about a woman.

Now, all she had to do was wrap Tom's present. She had deliberated long and hard over what to buy for him and had finally settled on the pair of expanding silver armbands that she had seen in the pawnbroker's window. Tom usually worked in his shirtsleeves as he took the bets, and his cotton-covered elastic armbands were frayed. She knew he wouldn't be able to use them for some time, but splashing out money she could barely afford to purchase them seemed like an omen telling her they would guarantee his safe return. Kitty was delighted with them. They looked just like new, and the pawnbroker had assured her they had belonged to a gentleman. Carrying out these pleasurable activities helped take her mind off the loneliness she would inevitably feel when Tom went away.

Tom was busy, the punters in a betting mood. Saturday was always a good day for business. As he was chalking the odds for the Irish horse races he overheard one of his customers saying, 'Do you want to know what I'm gettin' for Christmas for me wife?'

When his mate asked what, the man said, 'A barrel of ale. It's a bloody good swap, ain't it?' He burst out laughing and his mate joined in.

Jaysus! Tom cursed under his breath. What with thinking about little else but his future in the navy, and trying to keep the business going to the bitter end, he hadn't given a thought to Christmas presents – but he was sure that Kitty had. He couldn't leave the betting shop just now to go shopping and tomorrow was Sunday, no shops open. Then, on Monday morning he had to report to Derby House for enlistment. Damn an' blast it!

Thinking on his feet, he dashed into the bar. 'Cora,' he said, to the landlord's wife, 'would you ever nip out and buy a present for Kitty?' He shoved money across the counter. 'I want to get her a wee bit of something before I go seeing as I won't be here on Christmas Day.' He gave Cora a rueful smile, his blue eyes pleading and hoping for her sympathy now he'd been called up.

Cora raised her eyebrows. 'You men are all the same,' she said, pumping stout into a pint glass. 'What do you want me to get? What does she like?'

'Some wee thing for the house,' he said, hurrying back to take more bets.

Later that same evening, at Tom's suggestion, he and Kitty went to the Weaver's Arms for a drink before the party started. Kitty had dressed carefully in her best green wool dress and loosened her hair, clouds of red-gold curls caressing her shoulders and kissing her cheeks to which she had applied a smidgen of rouge. Soft orange lipstick added a final touch.

The bar was packed with rowdy merrymakers, drinking and singing and making the most of the weekend. Tom found a seat for Kitty in a corner away from the bar. As he made his way to the counter for drinks he was stopped by person after person clapping him on the back or exchanging a few words. They all knew Tom. It took him a long time to reach the bar, and even longer to be served.

Kitty began to feel foolish, sitting on her own for so long. She waved across the room to some of the mill girls who were there with their husbands or boyfriends, then glanced over at the bar. Tom was deep in conversation with a fat, balding man. He seemed to have forgotten about her.

Cora Bradshaw broke off pulling pints, long enough to see Kitty sitting with a long face all by herself. She thought about the present Tom had asked her to buy. She'd been in a rush and chosen the first thing she'd laid eyes on; now she was having doubts. She looked at Tom. He was laughing at something the man was telling him, the drinks Sam had served him several minutes before still sitting on the counter. Cora frowned. He was neglecting his wife and she didn't like it.

'Oi! Tom Conlon,' she cried, moving down the counter to face him. 'Have you forgotten you have a wife?'

Tom grinned and winked. Picking up the pint of stout and the gin and orange he made his way back to Kitty, lingering again to banter with his customers.

'Ye took your time,' she said, feeling righteously disgruntled.

'Ach, ye know how it is,' said Tom, handing her the gin and orange, 'at times like this, everybody wants a piece of ye. A few drinks inside them an' they only remember the days when ye brought them in a winner at ten to one. They forget ye fleeced them only last week.' He sat down beside her.

Kitty flinched at his comments. He sounded hard and brazen.

'Do ye fleece them, Tom?' she asked, uncomfortable to think that some poor family was going without because her husband had taken a father's last penny.

'Doesn't every bookie?' Tom took a swig of his pint.

Kitty sipped her drink. She was trying hard to feel in a party mood but instead she felt a moment of violent loneliness. Tom had barely spoken to her all evening, preferring instead to engage in chatter with whoever stopped by. Not for the first time, Kitty thought about how much he had changed since they had come to England.

Kitty didn't often accompany Tom to the pub but with it being the last time they'd go together before he went away, she hadn't liked to refuse. He deserved to have his own way, and she desperately wanted to please him, for goodness knew when she'd get the chance to do so again. Tonight she'd looked on it as a special occasion, but the longer she'd sat on her own the more miserable she'd begun to feel. Their time together was precious and now that it was so short she thought he should want to spend every minute of it with her.

In less than fifteen minutes Tom had finished the last of his pint and was off again. Kitty seethed as she drained her glass of gin and orange and sipped the second one that Sam had brought over to their table. Tom, on his way back from the gents, was now talking and laughing with a pretty young woman. Kitty felt her temper rising and was in two minds to go home and leave him to it.

The crowd started a singsong, taking it in turn to sing their favourites. When it came to Kitty she got to her feet. *If you can't beat 'em, then join 'em,* she thought, bursting into a lusty rendition of 'The Golden Jubilee'.

> 'Put on your old knee-britches
> and your coat of emerald green
> Put on your hat me darlin' Pat,
> put on your old cobeen
> For we're going to a wedding,
> an' I want ye all to know
> How it was when we were wed,
> fifty years ago.'

Jigging from foot to foot and lifting her skirt, her high, sweet voice brought the house down. As the crowd roared and clapped, Tom looked over at her, his eyebrows raised disapprovingly. Kitty flashed him a defiant smile. *There ye are, Tom Conlon. Ye're married to me, an' that's just a reminder.*

11

'My dad's not coming,' Beth said, putting the apple tart she had made for the party on Kitty's kitchen table. She was the first to arrive.

Kitty now regretted letting Tom persuade her to go to the pub. She had hurried home at half past eight, leaving him there.

'I didn't think he would.' Kitty frowned and continued making potted meat sandwiches. In the first flush of deciding to hold a party she had failed to consider the expense of providing enough food and drink. Now, as she looked at the meagre fare she groaned out loud.

'Are you feeling unwell? You don't look yourself.' Beth was concerned.

'Just anxious,' Kitty said, forcing a smile. 'I hope this party goes well.'

'It will,' Beth assured. 'Everybody will do their best to see that Tom gets a good send off.'

'I hope you're right,' Kitty replied gloomily. Her nerves were getting the better of her. She gazed at the plates filled with sandwiches and the scones she had made, then at Gertie's mince pies and Beth's apple tart. 'Will this be enough?' she asked anxiously.

'Of course it will. They'll not expect a feast. It's more about being together and giving Tom a good time to remember.'

She had no sooner spoken than Mavis and Jack arrived at the door, Mavis proffering a tray of iced buns and Jack a bottle of elderflower wine. Minutes later, May Walker came in. 'Bill's not coming. He's drunk already,' she huffed, plonking a plate of sliced spam on the table. Kitty's spirits rose; it was going to be all right.

Tom and most of the guests arrived back from the pub, bringing with them crates of bottled beer for the men and bottles of sherry and gin for the ladies. Kitty began to relax, and before long the party was going full swing. To her delight Dan Boothroyd could play the piano. Margery, May, Mavis and Jack sang tunefully, and as one old favourite after another livened up the guests, Kitty and Beth kept the drinks and food flowing. Then Sam and Cora Bradshaw arrived, bringing yet more strong drink, and accompanied by their friend, John Sykes.

Vi, her faded blonde hair caught up at the side with a glittery comb and the neckline of her dress too low, was dancing with Sam. Vi wiggled provocatively and Sam squirmed with embarrassment. Maggie kept making a play for Tom, her huge silver earrings swinging from her earlobes as she cavorted in front of him. Kitty smiled, pleased that Tom appeared indifferent to Maggie's charms.

Tonight, Tom was playing the part of loving husband, genial host and the hero about to go to war. He had helped Kitty attend to their guests, and when that wasn't needed he danced with her or stood with his arm draped about her shoulder. Having finally heeded Cora's words, he was paying more attention to his wife than the mix of people in the room. Not that he thought they were worthy of his attention; he wished they were more like the wealthy punters he'd met at the racetracks in Ireland, and the toffs at the blood sports meets. Those were the people he'd have liked to be mixing with, for none of this lot, other than Sam, were of any advantage to him.

At one point, Tom caught Cora eyeing him cynically. He made his way over to her and, keeping his voice low, he said, 'Did you get that present for Kitty?'

'It's in me bag. I'll give it you later.'

'What did you get?'

'Six teaspoons in a box.'

Tom was aghast. 'Teaspoons! What the hell were you thinking? Teaspoons for Christ's sake.' He'd been expecting a bit of cheap jewellery.

'You said to get her something for the house,' Cora replied tartly.

Tom remembered; he had said that. 'Sorry, Cora, my fault.'

'It is, and if you spent more time with your wife and bought your own presents you wouldn't be snapping at me.' She handed him her empty glass. 'Now bugger off and get me another drink.'

Tom swallowed his anger and as he went to refill Cora's glass he told himself that he'd make it up to Kitty when he came home on leave. He'd buy her a nice brooch. After giving Cora her fresh drink, he went and danced with Kitty, holding her lovingly, dropping kisses on her brow and lips and trying not to feel guilty.

He saw Cora watching them, a smile twitching the corners of her mouth. She raised her glass to him as if to say, *That's right. Show her you love her*. He grinned and winked. Tom was silently congratulating himself at the show he was putting on for the benefit of his guests: the successful businessman with a lovely home and a beautiful wife, the intrepid sailor, hero of the hour, going off to do his duty.

Dan began to play 'My Wild Irish Rose'. Taking advantage of Tom being out of the room, John Sykes asked Kitty to dance. Sam had introduced him as an old friend who happened to have called at the pub that night. He apologised to Kitty for coming uninvited, Kitty telling him he was more than welcome. As he and Kitty moved around the room, her hand on his shoulder and his gently pressing the small of her back, he had to suppress the urge to hold her closer: Kitty Conlon was a girl to be desired. She smiled up at him, her hazel eyes full of fun, and John's heart missed a beat. The music faded and reluctantly he let her go.

Kitty was in the hallway on her way to fetch Margery a cup of tea when there was a knock at her front door. Tom answered it, coming back into the room with Jim and Phyllis Dawson and Flo and Janet Johnson, workers at Holroyd's and regulars in the café.

'We were on our way home when we heard the racket from your place so we've come to make a bit more,' Flo said.

Kitty went off to fetch drinks for her newly arrived guests, giggling at her own foolishness. *There's me worrying about tonight not being a success and now there's near a score of people in my front room all having a good time, and all because I decided to have a little party.*

When she returned she saw Bobby dancing with Janet. They seemed to be getting on like a house on fire. Kitty couldn't have felt happier.

Long after midnight, Dan thumped out 'Pack Up Your Troubles' on the piano and everyone joined in. Margery and Dan declared it the best night they'd had for years, and Sam and Cora said they wouldn't have missed it for the world. John Sykes gazed deeply into Kitty's eyes and told her he looked forward to meeting her again. Then, with everyone wishing Tom a safe voyage, they went back to their own homes. Tom and Kitty began to clear up.

'Throwing a party was a great idea, darlin',' he said, as he placed glasses on the draining board for Kitty to wash. He put his arms round her waist and she leaned back into his embrace. 'Sometimes,' he said against her hair, 'I think I'm guilty of underestimating you. You have a great capacity for doing the right thing.'

Kitty turned and kissed him full on the mouth.

* * *

The next morning, Sunday, Kitty and Tom slept in, and when they woke he made love to her. Kitty's pulse quickened as the familiar feelings flooded her body. She arched her back, riding with him and at the same time wondering when they might do this again. Sensing that Tom was thinking the same thing, she matched his urgency with her own, seeking out the special things that gave pleasure to them both. Sated, she lay entwined in his arms and gave way to her tears. Tom kissed them away, telling her she need not be afraid. Then they made love again.

By mid-afternoon, Kitty had made a Christmas dinner: stewed rabbit, roasted potatoes, sprouts and apple pudding. When they had finished eating she went to the cupboard and took out a package. She handed it to Tom.

'It's our Christmas Day, Tom. Here's your present,' she said, her face wreathed in smiles as she anticipated his pleasure.

Tom's eyes lit up when he saw the armbands. 'God, Kitty, they're beautiful.' He expanded one and slipped it up his white shirt's sleeve and then did the same with the other. 'They're just what I wanted.' He stood and tenderly kissed her.

Then, feeling choked with guilt, he went over to the sideboard where he had hidden the gift that Cora had bought. He took out the small flat box. He had no idea what the contents looked like, he'd simply taken the box from Cora's hand, and as the shopkeeper had wrapped it neatly he had left it unopened.

'For you, darlin',' he said, handing Kitty the box and sending up a silent prayer that the teaspoons were not the usual sort; that they were decorated with hearts or butterflies or some such pretty thing that defined them from being ordinary.

Kitty held the box reverently, judging by its flat shape that it must contain a necklace. She flushed with pleasure and beamed at Tom, grateful for his thoughtfulness. Her fingers trembled as she carefully undid the fancy wrapping.

'Teaspoons,' Kitty said hollowly, unable to disguise her disappointment. 'They're... they're... lovely... thank ye, Tom.' She set the box on the table. The six ordinary teaspoons embedded in a casing of white satin stared up at her, their unexciting, sunken faces mirroring her own.

Tom glowered. The pleasure was taken out of the day, and in the hours that followed the atmosphere was strained, Kitty struggling to conceal her disappointment, and Tom annoyed by his thoughtlessness.

Towards bedtime the tension eased as they talked about what Kitty should do whilst Tom was away. 'You will take care of yourself when I'm gone, won't you, Kitty?' he asked, his eyes dark with sadness.

'And you,' she said, more worried for his safety than her own.

They went upstairs so that Kitty could check he had packed all that he needed. Tom carried the briefcase in which he kept his bookmaking details. He had closed the bookmaker's business for now but he definitely intended to open it again on his return. He hoped that would be soon.

'These are the books I keep on the betting.' Tom stowed the briefcase in the bottom of the wardrobe then turned to give Kitty a stern look. 'Don't hand them over to anybody who comes asking,' he said, making it sound more like a threat. 'There's some very private stuff in there.' He was referring to the bare-knuckle fighters he'd paid to throw a match, and the dogs he knew had been doped to the eyeballs to make them more ferocious, or win the race. But he voiced none of this; Kitty didn't need to know.

Kitty paused midway between packing extra socks into his case. Here she was, her heart breaking at the thought of being without him, and he was discussing business. It felt wrong. The uneasy feelings she had been harbouring for much of the day crept back, unbidden. It shouldn't be like this, she thought, not on our last night together. She rushed across the room and threw herself at him, clinging on and pushing the unwelcome thoughts from her mind. Nothing else mattered.

'Oh, Tom,' she sobbed, 'what am I going to do without ye?'

Her impassioned cry made Tom realise that all too soon he'd be parted from her, and his chest ached as though he'd been kicked. He wrapped his arms around her and they fell on to the bed, Kitty breathing in his cologne, Tom the scent of her hair, as hungry fingers traced faces and limbs and lips sought lips as if to imprint the taste, touch and smell of each other into the deepest parts of their hearts and minds. Then they talked in whispers of how their love would carry them through their time apart, neither of them daring to voice their worst thoughts.

Tom fell asleep but Kitty stayed awake. Much as she wanted to believe that their love for one another would sustain them once they were apart, and that he would come to no harm and miss her just as much as she would miss him, she couldn't dispel the niggling doubts that had plagued her during the past two days. Abandoning all thoughts of sleeping, she crept downstairs.

As she waited for the milk to boil to make a cup of cocoa, she stared at the teaspoons on the table, couldn't look away even when the milk spilled over on the hob. Tomorrow he'd be gone, leaving her with no time to put right the things that she felt were wrong with her marriage.

Did a man who loved his wife and thought about her happiness buy her teaspoons? she wondered. And last night in the pub he hadn't given a thought to her enjoyment. He'd been far more concerned with his own importance, the great Tom Conlon, the most popular man in the bar, lapping up the approval of the men and the adulation of the women. He wasn't her Tom any more. She felt such a profound sense of loss that it made her breath catch in her throat, and deep inside something told her that nothing in her life would ever be the same again.

12

Kitty celebrated the New Year, 1917, in the Weaver's Arms at a party that Sam and Cora held for their friends and neighbours. As the church bells rang out the old year and welcomed in the new, and the clock behind the bar chimed midnight, she joined the circle, hands crossed with a man on her right and a woman on her left. They were lustily singing 'Auld Lang Syne' but Kitty simply mouthed the words. *Tom should be here*, she thought, the aching loneliness that had filled the days since his departure clutching at her insides, making her feel utterly bereft.

One brief letter had told her he was training aboard a ship but he wasn't allowed to say where, and that she could send her letters to Derby House and they would send them on to him. He'd finished off the letter with a few brief loving sentiments. Kitty had never before received a letter from him, nor had she ever been the recipient of a love letter, yet somehow Tom's had left her feeling terribly disappointed.

'Happy New Year.' The man on her right held out his hand.

Kitty shook it and accepted a fleeting kiss on her cheek. 'An' a Happy New Year to you,' she said, recognising him as the man who had come to Tom's leaving party with Cora and Sam. He smiled warmly at her.

'Oh, I remember ye now,' she said. 'It's John, isn't it?'

'That's right. John Sykes. You may recall we shared a dance.' His dark brown eyes twinkled. He found seats for them and bought Kitty a port and lemon. Still feeling miserable, she stayed to talk with him rather than go home to an empty house. He really was engaging company, and she enjoyed hearing him tell her about his love of the countryside and his native Lancashire after she had answered his questions about her home place in Ireland.

When it came for the time to go home he saw her to her own front door. 'I hope we meet again soon,' he said before striding off into the darkness. Kitty stood inside the doorway of the silent, darkened house, gazing up at the brittle stars in the purple sky and silently asking them: *What are you doing now, Tom?*

As the words flitted through her mind she felt a dim uneasiness like something you see but don't see out of the corner your eye. Would she ever recapture the happiness she seemed to have lost?

That night, in bed, she prayed with all her might that she would.

* * *

Kitty knocked the snow off her boots on the top step outside her back door and stepped inside. For the past six weeks the weather had been awful. If it wasn't snowing it was raining, the freezing cold nights forming thick crusts of ice or compacted snow. The pavements were treacherous, Kitty slipping and sliding as she'd made her way back home from the café.

She had banked the fire before going to work, and the first thing she did after taking off her coat and scarf was to poke the cinders until they blazed into life. Feeling the need for a hot drink she was making a cup of tea when Maggie came in through the back door. She looked weary, the skin beneath her eyes puffed and purple. Sighing noisily, she sat down at the table.

'Are ye not well, Maggie?' Kitty asked, surprised to see her at this time of day.

Maggie shook her head. 'I was as sick as a dog this morning so I didn't go to work. I'm still feeling lousy.' She lit a cigarette.

Kitty put two mugs on the table and sat down. 'Ye were sick a couple of days ago as I recall. Maybe ye should see the doctor.'

'He'd be no use,' Maggie said bitterly. 'I don't need to pay him to tell me what I already know.' She sipped her tea and then gagged. 'See, I can't even enjoy a cup of tea.'

'Are ye...?' Kitty's eyes widened.

Maggie didn't let her finish. 'Yeah. I'm friggin' pregnant!'

'And do ye not want to be?' Kitty asked innocently. 'It's not as if ye aren't married, and maybe Fred'll be a bit more caring if he knows he's going to be a father.' Her face lit up. 'I once worked with a right tearaway of a fella who changed into an angel when his wife gave him a son.'

'The things is,' Maggie said grimly, 'it's not Fred's baby.'

Shocked, Kitty squealed, 'Not Fred's baby!' She gave Maggie a puzzled look.

Maggie sighed. 'No, it's a chap I was doing a line with at the back end of last year. He allus used one o' them thingumabobs so I don't know how it happened.'

'Oh,' said Kitty, recalling the day she and Tom had seen Maggie going into a lodging house with the big man with flaming red hair. Was he the father?

'So there you have it,' Maggie sneered, grinding her cigarette in the ashtray.

Kitty did a quick mental calculation. 'But it could be Fred's. He was home about that time,' she said hopefully.

'No, it couldn't. That last time he was home he was always drunk and I wouldn't let him near me. That's why he gave me a black eye an' a bust lip.'

'Oh,' Kitty repeated, at a loss how to deal with the situation. She topped up her own and Maggie's cup. Maggie lit another cigarette, and each of them lost in their own thoughts, they drank their tea. It was Kitty who broke the silence. 'Maybe Fred won't remember. Perhaps he won't know it's not his,' she hazarded.

'He will if he can count,' moaned Maggie. 'He might not be the sharpest knife in the box, but he's not that bloody stupid.' She sighed heavily, cigarette smoke streaming from her nostrils.

Kitty grappled for something positive to say. 'What does your mother have to say about it?'

Maggie smothered a bitter laugh. 'Me mother! That selfish mare! All she thinks about is herself,' she sneered. 'You should have heard her,' and adopting Vi's whining voice she mimicked, 'Who'll keep us when you have to give up work? And what if Fred withdraws your separation money when he knows it's not his?' Her shoulders slumped and she scrabbled for another cigarette from her packet on the table.

Kitty was desperate to help Maggie, and even though she thought it was a bad idea, she said, 'Ye could carry on working if your mam looked after the baby. That way, ye wouldn't go short.'

'You must be joking,' Maggie hooted. 'She's not fit to look after a dog. She never looked after me.' Her eyes clouded and she clamped her lips round her cigarette and puffed furiously.

'Then it's well you have me to rely on. Nobody should be on their own at a time like this. I'll stand by ye every step of the way. That's what friends do.'

Maggie's eyes filled with tears. 'Do you mean that, Kitty?'

''Course I do. Ye might pretend to have a tough shell, Maggie

Stubbs, but I know ye better than that. Ye've lightened my day for many an' hour, an I'll do the same for ye. We're in this together.'

Maggie gulped, and her voice thick with emotion she mumbled, 'Ta, Kitty. You're a smashing friend.' She wiped her eyes on the back of her hand and giggled. 'I'm not sure I'll know what to do with it when it comes though.'

'It's a baby, Maggie. Ye'll love it once it's born no matter who its father is.'

'Will I?' Maggie said hollowly.

'Ye'll have to, because who else will if ye don't?' Kitty said sagely.

13

The success of Kitty's party had brought the neighbours in Weaver Street closer together. When Jack went down with bronchitis, Mavis, who had danced several times that night with him, made Jack nourishing soups and cured him. And when Bill Walker, tipsy, slipped on the ice outside the Weaver's and broke his hip, the neighbours provided hot casseroles, bread and coal to eke out May's meagre earnings. Jack kept Bill company playing cards, and Kitty and Beth knitted jumpers for the boys. Furthermore, Bobby Longhurst and Janet Johnson had fallen for each other, and with Bobby back in France, love letters were flying back and forth. Kitty was thrilled for them. With everyone pulling together, and romance in the air, it made the long winter and the deprivations that a country at war had to suffer, easier to bear.

However, there were things beyond their control going on in the wider world and no matter how brave a face the inhabitants of Weaver Street presented, there were some things that brought them close to breaking point.

'A four pound loaf's gone up to eight pence,' Gertie complained as she sliced into one to make sandwiches in the café on a Friday morning in late February. 'I could put me prices up again but trade's not what it was an' it'll only get worse if them from t'mill stop buying 'em. I'm thinkin' it's time to call it a day.'

Whenever Gertie threatened to close down the café, Kitty's heart always plummeted. While she often had Beth and Maggie's company in the evenings, the house was empty without Tom, and working in the café was the highlight of her day. Also, what she earned added nicely to Tom's navy allowance so she didn't have to scrimp and scrape.

Kitty smeared margarine on the bread Gertie had sliced. 'Will we use the pilchards Mickey brought off the docks? They'll make a welcome change from meat paste an' spam,' she said, thinking that if the customers were offered something tasty it might boost trade.

'Aye, why not,' Gertie puffed, her florid face breaking into a smile.

* * *

On a Saturday afternoon in March, Kitty came home early from the café. 'There's not enough custom to keep the two of us here. You get off,' Gertie had said, her usual jolly face despondent at the lack of trade. Kitty had reluctantly agreed.

She had almost reached her own back door when Maggie burst out of hers, her face wreathed in smiles. She'd been pretty miserable since she'd found out she was pregnant and Kitty was pleased to see her looking a bit brighter.

'I saw you through the window. You're home early.'

Kitty told her why. 'I've got an awful feeling Gertie'll close it down altogether.' She gave a forlorn little shrug.

'You need cheering up. Let's go up town this avvy,' Maggie said chirpily. 'We got a bonus this week for all the khaki we've turned out and I want to buy sumthin' to wear.' She patted her belly. 'Me skirts are getting tight round me middle.'

Ten minutes later they were standing at the tram stop ready to catch the tram into the city centre. A long line of army lorries passed by on their way to the railway line at Edge Hill. A soldier sitting at the rear of one of the lorries waved at the girls and gave them a rueful smile.

'You can't get away from it,' complained Maggie as she and Kitty waved back at the convoy. 'Everywhere you look there's sumthin' to remind you there's a war on. I wonder where them poor blighters are off to.'

The tram came, and as it trundled along, Kitty thought of Tom. His last letter had sounded quite cheery. He'd written that now he'd finished his training he was what they called an 'ordinary seaman' and worked on deck on a ship that was sailing to... the next bit had been blacked out by the censor. He told her he'd made some good friends, the food wasn't bad, and that he loved and missed her. Even so, Kitty had had many sleepless nights imagining him on storm-tossed seas under enemy fire. She'd wake suddenly, her skin clammy and her heart pounding; she didn't even know if Tom could swim. But then where would he swim to? At times like those she missed him more than ever.

'Let's go to Woolies first,' Maggie suggested. Kitty, unfamiliar with the city, let her lead the way to Church Street. As they walked along the busy pavements they passed lots of men in khaki and some in naval uniform. Outside Woolworths a tall, dark-haired lad wearing a navy blouson with a white striped collar lounged against the entrance, his cap at a jaunty angle. *That's what Tom must look like,* Kitty thought, feeling rather proud.

In the crowded store they bought pick'n'mix and some broken biscuits. Maggie chose a skirt in brown tweed and a fussy blouse in a horrible shade of mauve. Kitty wondered if she was colour blind and tried unsuccessfully to persuade her to take it in cream. After that they strolled down Bold Street, gaping in awe at the expensive silk dresses, fur coats and fancy hats in Cripps' window display. Maggie lit a cigarette.

'Who the hell can afford stuff like that? Don't they know there's a war on?' she exclaimed. She blew out a stream of smoke to show her disgust.

'The rich man at his castle and the poor man at his gate.' Kitty had read that somewhere. Maggie gave her a funny look. She wasn't a reader.

'There'll always be them that can afford whatever they want,' Kitty said by way of explanation. ''Tis the way of the world, an' the poor will always be with us.' This encouraged another funny look.

'And we're the poor buggers who can only afford to look,' Maggie growled.

On their way back to the tram stop they came to a burnt-out shop, its timbers still smouldering and the wreckage of what had been living quarters sagging on charred rafters. A man stood gazing at it, his face dark with rage.

'What happened here?' Maggie, nosy as usual, addressed the man.

'Murder, that's what happened,' he grunted, twisting his cap in his hands. 'They might have been Germans but they were grand people. They'd been here for years but some miserable bastards decided to burn 'em out.'

'Holy Mother of God!' Kitty exclaimed. 'I thought it was the Germans that had done it.' She gazed pityingly at the remains of a burnt bed balanced precariously on what remained of the upper floor.

They walked on to the tram stop, both in their own way sobered by man's inhumanity to man. Back at Edge Hill, as they turned into the back lane behind Weaver Street, a telegram boy on his bike whizzed past them.

Kitty's heart lurched. The sight of a lad on a bike in a navy blue uniform with a brown leather pouch across his shoulder was enough to put fear and dread into anyone.

Kitty gasped and looked at Maggie. Maggie looked back, her eyes questioning.

'Ye... don't think he... called at my house... an' me not there?' Kitty could hardly get the words out.

'It could have been mine,' Maggie said flatly.

They continued up the lane, Kitty feeling as though she was treading on eggshells. As they came level with the Walkers' house they heard the shrieking. Kitty's shoulders relaxed, but only for a second. She clamped her hand to her mouth, spluttering through her fingers, 'Oh, dear God! Poor May.'

14

The death of young Sammy Walker plunged the neighbours in Weaver Street into a deep gloom. When Kitty called in with May she could find no words to comfort her. And anyway, she thought, words are meaningless at times like this. Instead, she turned to practicalities, tidying the cluttered kitchen and making a stew to cook slowly on the hob.

'I knew it! I knew it!' May sobbed into her folded arms resting on the table. 'When he was in Catterick I knew he was safe, but the minute they sent him to France I knew I'd never set eyes on him again.'

May's cries tore at Kitty's heart. She wiped the draining board, thinking that what May had once said had come true. Nowhere was safe these days. Was Tom in a dangerous place? she wondered. Of course he was, she told herself sadly.

Bill Walker, sober for once, sat by the fire with a stunned expression on his whiskery face. His bloodshot eyes followed Kitty as she moved about the room then, giving a sob that seemed to come from his boots, he got up and shambled out of the house. May watched him go.

'He'll have gone for a couple of pints,' she said bleakly. She had aged ten years in one day. 'And my poor Sammy'll never have a pint in his life.' Tears coursed down her ravaged cheeks.

Kitty went to sit beside her, cradling her like a child, and wondering if May would do the same for her if Tom were killed. Before she could prevent them, her tears matched May's and they clung together, trying to find strength in one another.

* * *

When Kitty arrived at the café on Monday morning she found Gertie in tears behind the counter. In front of it an irate woman was shouting the odds.

'I had to get the doctor he was that bad,' she bawled. 'He was never off the lavvy all Sat'day an' Sunday. You an' your bloody pilchards.' She turned as Kitty came up behind her. 'You've not heard the last of it,' she threatened. 'He's not the only one. The doctor says it's food poisoning. You're bloody lucky nobody's died – well, as yet they haven't.' Waving her fist in Kitty's face, she stormed out.

'That's it,' Gertie cried, wiping her cheeks and pushing back her frazzled hair, 'I've had all I can take. Lock that door. I'm closing down for good.'

'But how can she be sure it was our pilchards?'

'She's the fourth person this morning tellin' me that sumb'dy belongin' 'em wa' taken badly an' that the doctor said they'd got fish poisoning. They all had pilchards on Friday. I'm shuttin' up shop before the authorities come callin'. Mickey could lose his job on the docks over this.'

'I'm so sorry, Gertie.' Kitty felt like weeping. 'Ye worked so hard to make a success of the café. What will ye do now?'

'I'll go to me sister in Flamborough. I should have done that before now,' Gertie said stoutly. 'Now you help me clear this place up. I don't want rats getting in. Take what you want in the food line, and chuck them damned pilchards. I want to leave it tidy. I'll most likely put it on the market an' sell it.'

For the rest of the day and the morning after, Kitty cleaned and packed things into boxes with a heavy heart, and when everything was ready for Gertie's brother-in-law to come with his van, she hugged Gertie, thanking her for being such a good friend.

'I'll keep in touch,' Gertie said, choking back her tears. 'I'll send you a postcard of Flamborough.'

* * *

'I've lost me job,' Kitty told Maggie and Beth later that night as she related the story of the pilchards. They both offered their commiserations – they knew she'd loved working in the café – but, as usual, Maggie saw the funny side of it.

'I'm not surprised,' she hooted. 'I heard tell that some of 'em had rings round their arses they were on the lavvy that long.'

Beth looked shocked at Maggie's language, but even she couldn't resist adding to the humour. 'I'm just glad I stuck with the potted meat,' she murmured.

'I'll have to find something else,' Kitty said. 'I can't sit here all day doing nothing. I'd go out of my mind.'

When first Jack called with a bunch of spring greens, shortly followed by Mavis, they too offered their sympathy. Kitty reiterated her need to find another job. 'The trouble is, I'm not trained for anything but waiting on tables. What I'd like to do is something to aid the war effort, anything useful that'll bring this rotten war to an end.'

Mavis nodded. 'They might be looking for girls at the tobacco factory. I've heard they're very busy—' she gave a prim little smile

'—you know, smokes for the troops. Then there's Tate's sugar refinery, you could try there or Dobson's sweets. Or you could join me at the munitions factory. It's very dangerous work,' she warned, 'but it's the most necessary in this day and age.'

'Aye, it's not really a job for women. But like Mavis says, it needs to be done if we're going to beat Jerry at his own game,' Jack agreed.

'There's lots of women doing men's jobs, Jack,' Maggie reminded him tartly, 'and they do 'em just as well as the fellas. Two lasses that worked with me in the mill are driving trams, and another one's a porter on Lime Street Station.'

'Yes. Look at all the girls who've joined the Land Army. They're farming to keep us in food,' Beth said.

'We', what's it to be, Kitty?' Mavis asked. 'Cigarettes, sweets, tram driving, digging for victory, or munitions?'

Kitty's eyes lit up. Munitions. Making the bombs and the bullets that would put paid to the Germans. 'Munitions it is,' she said firmly.

* * *

On deck, aboard HMS *Result*, just off the southern coast of Ireland, Tom took a deep breath of salty, morning air. Last night had been one he wouldn't easily forget. They had been patrolling the English Channel on the hunt for U-boats, the *Result* pitching and rolling viciously. Tom considered bad weather to be as great an enemy as the Germans, and he struggled to keep his dinner down and his feet under him as grey-green water sloshed over slippery steel. Then the night watch had spotted a U-boat's conning tower. Tom's innards had turned to tripe as he crouched in the gun turret waiting for the order to fire and listening for the hissing wake of an enemy torpedo; a terrifying sound he knew he'd never get used to. The battle had been short and sharp, the

U-boat despatched, and as Tom went about his duties he felt glad to be alive.

He finished coiling a heaving rope and turned to his mate, Harry Webster. 'Do you remember the way Ally Sloper came in two lengths ahead of the track at the Grand National in 1915? That was a great day for anybody who had money on him. He came in at a 100/8, a rank outsider. An' it was a good day for the bookie seeing as not many had bet on him.'

Harry grimaced. 'I didn't put a penny on him, but I'll bet you did.'

Tom gave him a wolfish smile and nodded.

Tom and Harry had forged a friendship through their love of horse racing, and much of their conversation was about horses, jockeys and trainers. Tom was considered to be a racing pundit by many of the crew who also had an interest in gambling. It made him feel a cut above, and he liked airing his superior knowledge. He got on well with his shipmates and had easily adapted to life on board. He discovered he had good sea legs and being young, fit and healthy, the drills and the duties weren't half as onerous as he had thought they might be.

After training aboard HMS *Eaglet* he had been deployed to a Q-ship, an armed merchant ship with hidden guns. Their purpose was to act as a decoy to attract the German U-boats to surface by appearing unarmed. Then, when the U-boat surfaced to attack, the apparently defenceless ship revealed its guns and fired.

'They must be bloody crazy wanting us to attract U-boats,' Tom had grumbled when he'd first heard of the order, but after a few successful sorties, he'd begun to enjoy the rush of adrenaline and subsequent sense of victory. He took a personal pride in the fact that the British ships' gun power was far superior to the Germans', who didn't care for open warfare at sea.

Now, as he stood on deck, a bracing sea breeze blowing in his face, he gazed across the distance to Ireland's southern coastline. 'If anybody had told me I'd end up defending the shores of my own country, I wouldn't have believed 'em,' he'd remarked when he learned that HMS *Result*'s task was to patrol the waters between the English and St George's Channels.

That morning he had received a letter from Kitty. He'd laughed about the pilchards' incident, and was saddened to hear of Sammy Walker's death, but life was all about immediacy for Tom: Weaver Street and its inhabitants might never have existed. Of course, he thought about Kitty, particularly in his bunk at night. He missed their lovemaking and her soft, warm body against his as he fell asleep. Kitty's letters were full of loving words and he tried to reciprocate, but with Tom, for the majority of the time, it was a case of out of sight out of mind.

* * *

As Tom stood on deck aboard HMS *Result*, breathing in salt-laden air, Kitty was breathing in the unfamiliar stink of the munitions factory. She had taken Mavis's advice and was now being inducted to the work of a munitionette.

'No metal objects, no hairpins, no jewellery, no matches to be carried on your person once you leave the changing room and enter the cleanway,' the instructor warned in a strict no-nonsense way. 'The cleanway is where the bombs and bullets are manufactured. You must wear your uniform and must not carry any of the forbidden items. Anyone breaking the rules could be sent to prison.'

The instructor followed this with more horrifying cautions and reasons for obeying them. 'Never forget to wear your cap. A girl caught her hair in a drill and had her scalp peeled off. Do not put in or take out a shell while the machine is in motion. Otherwise you'll blow us all to kingdom come.'

'Holy Mother of God, what are we letting ourselves in for?' Kitty whispered to the girl standing next to her. Like Kitty, she was wearing a baggy pair of overalls, buttoned across the front and tight round the cuffs and ankles. A tight-fitting mob-cap covered her hair. Kitty thought she looked rather ridiculous and presumed that she looked the same. She giggled.

* * *

'It's the most unglamorous thing I've ever worn, but it's all to do with safety,' she told Maggie at the end of her first day. 'I just thank God Tom can't see me dressed like that. I even have a tag with a number on it so they can identify my body if I get blown up,' she continued, her voice rising at the idea.

'Charming, I'm sure,' Maggie replied drolly.

* * *

At half past five, Kitty closed the front door behind her and smiled up at the pale bands of yellow early morning light streaking the sky above Weaver Street. She had grown used to rising in the dark to go to her twelve-hour shift in the factory but now that spring was in full swing it was a more pleasant task. Still smiling, she briskly walked the few paces to Mavis's door and rapped it smartly. Mavis answered almost immediately, her currant-bun eyes twinkling as she said, 'Just on time.' Arms linked, they began the short walk to work.

'I had a letter from Tom yesterday,' Kitty said.

'That's nice,' replied Mavis, giving Kitty's arm a little squeeze. 'What did he have to say?'

'Much the same as always, and that he's finding things easier now the winter storms are over.' Kitty refrained from telling Mavis that Tom's letters disappointed her. He'd never had cause to write to her before he went away and although she was eternally grateful that he was still alive and able to write, his letters failed to convey the words she wanted to hear. Pies that didn't taste as good as hers, foul weather and wet socks left her feeling somewhat cheated even though he always signed off with how much he loved and missed her.

'I think spring always brings new hope with it. Let's hope it brings an end to this rotten war,' said Mavis as they turned into Edge Lane and met with more women on their way to the factory. 'Morning, Jessie, Pat, Sarah,' she called out cheerily. Kitty echoed the greeting then gave Jessie an admiring grin.

'Oooh, Jessie! Ye've done your hair like Mary Pickford's this morning. It looks lovely,' she complimented. Jessie patted the deep waves in her chestnut hair.

'It'll not stay long like that,' Pat said sourly. 'Them bloody mob-caps make your head sweat and make your hair go all frizzy.' The women agreed.

'Mine's gone yellow at the ends,' Pat moaned, flicking the tails of her mousy hair. She was one of the women whose job it was to pour trinitrotoluene – TNT – into the empty shell cases, a dangerous task that turned their hair and skin yellow. They were known as the 'Canary Girls'. Kitty felt sorry for them.

Gossiping convivially, they passed through the factory gates and straight to the changing rooms. It was fair to say that Kitty had been rather overwhelmed by her introduction to making munitions, but now she'd got used to the overpowering smell of TNT and the noise of the machinery, the grinding roar and buzz almost deafening, and the hazards that the work presented terrifying. She routinely accepted and obeyed all the rules and no longer felt ridiculous in her cumbersome uniform. She actually enjoyed her work, even though standing for twelve hours at her bench wadding potentially lethal shells was back breaking, and she liked to think that the shells she tamped during her shift were helping Tom to fight the war. He was never far away from Kitty's thoughts. And now, as she walked down the cleanway with her workmates, she was ready to start another gruelling day's labour. The jobs they were doing were the only way they could secure the safe return of their husbands, fathers, sons and brothers, and the women worked willingly. Kitty wondered if the shells she handled eventually ended up in Tom's hands. She liked to think they might.

At her bench lined with shell cases waiting to be tamped, Kitty set to work, taking great care not to trigger the detonator and blow them all sky high as she joined in the gossip.

'My Bert's got ten days' leave. He's arriving tomorrow,' the recently married girl working next to Kitty said breathlessly.

'Oh, that's grand. I'm made up for ye, love,' Kitty replied, feeling an aching regret that the exchange wasn't the other way round. Her hand hovered over a shell and she felt such an aching need to see Tom again that it hurt.

'When my old man came home last week he couldn't hear a thing I said,' an older woman interjected. 'He blamed the bombs, said they'd made him deaf.'

'More like an excuse so that he didn't have to listen to you, Sally.' Jessie laughed as she spoke then asked, 'Anybody seen *The Poor Little Rich Girl*? I'm thinking of going tonight.'

'That's Mary Pickford, isn't it?' the excited girl asked. 'I love the way she does her hair.'

'Jessie's giving her a run for her money,' Kitty chipped in, 'though you can't tell with her cap on.' Jessie acknowledged the compliment with a wink.

'I like the musicals best,' Sally said, then burst into song. Kitty and the rest of the women joined in, singing about a yellow tulip and a big red rose. Songs and chatter made the day go quicker.

Kitty carefully tamped another shell and thought of Tom. She missed him dreadfully, and his joining the navy had brought the war right to her doorstep. Although she was happy at work, at night in bed she felt an enormous sense of restlessness and loss, and she craved for the day when things would be as they had been before the war.

Maggie hitched up her skirt and sat on the wall outside Kitty's back door, her bare legs dangling. Kitty handed her the cups of tea. Then, sitting down beside her, she swung her aching legs up on to the wall's broad top and retrieved her own cup. It was pleasant to sit out in the warmth of the May evening after the heat and noise of the factory.

'Can't hide this any longer,' Maggie groused, patting her belly.

Kitty made a sympathetic noise. She felt sorry for Maggie. Expecting a baby should be a joyous time in your life, something to share with your husband, but not for poor Maggie. She didn't know where the father of her baby was, and she was unsure that Fred would accept it as his when she gave him the news. He was still stationed in England and she was expecting him home at the end of the month for two weeks' leave.

'Have ye thought about what you're going to tell Fred?' Kitty wasn't sure Maggie would welcome the question.

'I did think about writing him a letter, but I changed me mind.'

'You should have done it.'

'I know, 'cos I'll have to tell him sometime,' Maggie moaned. 'I can hardly pass it off as wind.' She began chewing on her fingernail.

Kitty set her cup on the wall. 'If I were ye I'd just let him think the baby's his.'

Maggie stopped chewing but she kept her finger on her lips ready to gnaw at it again. 'I've been thinking that meself,' she mumbled. 'The old bags in this street 'ud have a field day gossiping about me if they knew the truth. They don't think much of me as it is.'

'Oh, Maggie, don't be so hard on yourself. They're all fond of ye. An' if they're not, I am.'

'That's because you're a good mate with a big heart.' Maggie's tone softened. 'Don't let on to Beth about it not being Fred's, will you? I don't want Walter Garside slagging me off like he did Doreen when she was having Eddie. She couldn't go by but he called her filthy names, telling her no daughter of his would behave in such a disgraceful fashion.'

'I don't suppose Beth would,' said Kitty. 'She'd be too afraid.'

'Yeah, she used to be scared to death of him when she were a kid. If he caught her playing out with us she'd shake like jelly.' Maggie pulled a face. 'Mind you, I don't think she's that frightened of him now. Not since she started chumming with you.'

'An' rightly so. No child should ever be afraid of its parents.' Kitty patted Maggie's tummy. 'Ye just make sure this little one is loved to the moon an' back.'

15

It was shortly after six o'clock on a glorious morning in July, when, walking to the factory, Kitty thought about the café by the river. Working there had been a pleasure on days like this and just for a moment she was tempted to keep on walking. But duty called.

When she arrived at the munitions factory she changed into her uniform, ready to go to her station for another long day of wadding shells. Threading her arms into the thick twill sleeves of her overalls, she remarked: 'Today's going to be a scorcher. I'll be sweating cobs before this shift's over.' Next to her was a girl she hadn't seen before. She was fumbling her way into her overalls, all fingers and thumbs. Kitty could tell she was nervous and gave her a warm smile. 'Are ye new?'

The girl nodded sullenly.

'Well, I'm Kitty Conlon. Pleased to meet ye. What's your name?'

'Rosie Smith.' The girl raised her right hand to tuck her hair under her cap, the broad gold ring on her middle finger catching Kitty's attention.

'Well, Rosie, ye'd best take that off.' Kitty spoke kindly as she pointed at the ring. 'Ye can't wear anything metal in the cleanway.'

The girl glared. 'They made me take it off when I was training but I allus wear it,' she snapped. 'It was me dead mam's. It brings me luck.'

'No matter, love, it's dangerous to keep it on, an' it's against the rules.' Kitty spoke firmly then patted Rosie's arm. 'An' I'm sorry about your mam. What have they got ye doing?'

'Using a lathe to do the openings on friggin' hand grenades,' Rosie groused.

'All the more reason to take that ring off,' Kitty advised. 'It'll not bring ye luck in the cleanway so—'

'Oi, Kitty! Some of us are going to the pictures tonight. Do you want to come?' Jessie shouted for Kitty's attention. Kitty told her she'd think about it. When she turned back, Rosie Smith had left the changing room.

Towards the end of the afternoon Kitty was still deliberating whether or not to go to the cinema when a sudden rush of hot, sulphurous air whirled through the workshop, swiftly followed by a massive explosion in the adjoining room. The ground beneath Kitty's feet shook, and the assembly line of shells clinked and clattered threateningly. Rooted to the spot, her heart racing, she eyed them nervously. Another explosion had her gathering her wits.

'Everybody out!' she screamed at the top of her lungs.

'Oh my God! Let me get out of here,' Jessie shrieked, knocking Kitty aside as she stumbled the length of the bench. Kitty ran after her, half-blinded by the dust that swirled through the shed as someone pushed open the doors.

The klaxon blared, its eerie wail signalling for everyone to evacuate.

'Don't panic, don't push,' Kitty yelled as a stream of screaming women rushed to the doors, trying to get through them all at once and out to safety. Her cries went unheard. Falling over one another, they piled out into the yard, casting wild glances at the devastation before running to the designated assembly point.

Smoke belched out of the doors and flames shot through a hole in the roof of the workshop next to theirs. Screams could be heard above the crackling and hissing.

Kitty slowed her pace and blinked to clear the dust from her eyes. 'Come on, Kitty, come on,' Mavis shouted, clutching at her sleeve then letting go and running with the other women.

Kitty's first instinct was to follow Mavis, but halfway across the yard she came to a sudden halt, her heart pounding and her ears incapable of ignoring the frenzied screams and shouts coming from the burning shed. She turned tail, racing in their direction, and rushed straight into the wrecked workshop.

Red-hot chunks of debris littered the floor, igniting anything combustible. Sparks flew and flames licked hungrily at whatever was in their path. It looked like a scene from hell.

'Come on, darlin', let's get ye out of here.' Kitty placed her hands under the armpits of an elderly woman lying just inside the doorway. Blood seeped from a ragged tear in her scalp. Kitty dragged her as gently and quickly as she could out into the open as, bells ringing and engines revving, the rescue team arrived.

'Here, see to her,' Kitty shouted to one of the wardens before hurtling back into the shed. The firemen unreeled their hosepipes. Peering through the dust, her cheeks stinging from the heat, Kitty spotted a screaming girl lumbering amongst the debris, her arms outstretched. One look at her badly burnt face let Kitty know she had been blinded. After hopping over fallen spars, she grabbed her and, dodging the streaming jets of water now dousing the blazing debris, she led her to safety. Then, sure she had seen a body lying beside a piece of machinery, she ducked back into the workshop and was making her way towards it when she heard someone roaring her name.

'Kitty! Kitty Conlon! Get out of here and stay out!'

Kitty whirled round. John Sykes was charging through the debris towards her. The angry, dark eyes in a face livid with rage bore little resemblance to the handsome face and gentle brown eyes she remembered from the night he had danced with her at Tom's going away party, or when he'd kept her company on New Year's Eve. She was as much shocked to see him there as she was by his outrage, and when he bundled her in his arms, sweeping her off her feet, she did not resist. He had no sooner set off running than another massive explosion tore through the workshop, the sheer force of it hurtling them out into the yard. Sprawled amidst the ash and debris, they lay side by side, stunned into silence. He still had hold of her, and Kitty gazed into his tormented eyes, horrified.

John struggled to his feet and pulled Kitty to hers. He held her close. Through the thick twill of her overall she felt his heart thudding against her own. 'You foolish girl! What on earth were you thinking?' he cried. 'I couldn't bear it if you...' Tenderness mingled with anguish as Kitty looked up at him. Then, shaking her by the shoulders like a naughty child he barked, 'Go to the assembly point this minute, you silly girl – and stay there!'

Shaken by his obvious concern for her, and even more so by having been thrown to the ground and then reprimanded, Kitty overlooked his harsh manner of speaking, although his words stung. 'I couldn't just leave 'em when I could hear 'em crying for help,' she mumbled.

When he gave her a gentle shove she indignantly stalked off to join the other women. 'Oh, Kitty! Thank goodness you're safe.' Mavis hugged her, and huddled together at the assembly point, they watched as firemen, volunteer wardens and ambulance men carried out their grizzly tasks.

Tongues wagged like a murmuration of starlings.

'Has anybody been killed?'

'You were daft going in there, Kitty.'

'I thought she was brave.'

'Who wa' that lass wi' the burnt face?'

'It puts you in mind of that explosion in Essex a few weeks ago. Seventy-three killed! We must be crackers working here.'

Kitty heard the voices as though from a distance. A chill of horror ran down her spine. Swaying dizzily, she put her hand to her clammy forehead, suddenly aware of her own mortality. A few seconds later and John might not have saved her. She began to shake uncontrollably. Mavis put her arms round her.

The supervisor hurried over, and full of his own importance he dashed off the roll, one voice after another affirming they were alive and uninjured. 'Two killed, twenty-three injured,' he reported, and in case any of the dead or injured were related to the women he reeled off a list of names. One of them was Rosie Smith. Was it her ring that had caused the explosion? Kitty wondered. Then the supervisor told them to go home. 'I'm going with Mrs Harper to the hospital,' Mavis said. 'Her daughter's one of the injured. Are you coming?'

Kitty shook her head. She just wanted to go home. On feet that felt like lead, Kitty trudged to the factory gate. Heavy footsteps thudded behind her. John appeared at her side and caught hold of her arm.

'Are you all right, Kitty?' he cried, his concern so apparent that she began to tremble again. She had been reckless. She looked away, embarrassed.

He placed a finger under her chin, turning her head so that he could look into her face. 'Oh, Kitty,' he said softly. The tenderness in his voice and his warm, brown eyes made her want to collapse into his arms. Blood rushed to her cheeks. She pulled away quickly, and ignoring John's cries, she hurried to the gate. She plodded along

Edge Lane on legs that felt quite insubstantial, struggling to hold back tears.

She'd walked a hundred yards or so before she realised she was still wearing her bloodstained, filthy overall. She felt rather embarrassed walking the streets looking so disreputable. When a sleek, black car drew alongside her and John Sykes offered her a lift, she was mortified. However, she felt exhausted and climbed in.

'Sorry for bawling you out back there,' he said, setting the car in motion.

'I know ye were only thinking of my safety. It's me who might have been sorry had ye not come along,' she mumbled.

'I'm just glad I did.' He was so kind and understanding she felt close to tears.

He drove her to her front door. 'Take care, Kitty. I wouldn't want anything bad to happen to you,' he said, his words ringing with sincerity.

'I will,' she replied wearily.

16

Beth burst into Kitty's kitchen, her cheeks blooming with barely suppressed rage. 'It's my dad. He gets worse,' Beth confided, as Kitty invited her to sit down. 'I don't think I can bear it for much longer, but I can't afford to move out.'

'Just try an' keep out of his way,' Kitty said. 'Ye know you're always welcome here. An' now Tom's out of the house, I'm glad to see ye coming.'

Beth smiled gratefully. 'But all I do is moan when I'm here,' she said ruefully.

'Moan all ye like. Get it off your chest.'

'He's just so obnoxious,' Beth grumbled. 'He rants and raves about my friends, saying he didn't send me to the grammar school and get me a job in the mill office for me to mix with people he doesn't approve of, and then there's the house. It's so rundown I hate living in it. I'm so fed up I feel like screaming...' She stopped talking and clapped her hands to her cheeks.

'Oh, Kitty, I'm so sorry. Whatever must you think of me? I'm so wrapped up in my own problems I forgot all about the explosion.' She looked truly penitent as she asked, 'How are you feeling? It must have been terrifying. I heard there were more than twenty injured and two killed.'

Kitty grimaced. 'There might have been one more if it hadn't been for John Sykes. Do you remember him? He came to my party with Sam and Cora. I don't know why he was at the factory.'

Beth did remember him. 'Why? What did he do?'

'He most likely saved my life,' said Kitty. She let the words hang in the air.

Beth's cheeks blanched and her jaw dropped as Kitty told her the full story.

'Oh, Kitty, you are brave,' Beth exclaimed.

Kitty shook her head. 'No, I'm just daft. I did it without thinking.'

'Well, I think you're brave. I'd never have the courage to do anything like that.' Beth gave a helpless shrug. 'Look at me. I can't even stand up to my dad. I'm a virtual prisoner in my own home – the shabbiest house in the street. Dad won't part with a shilling, and I can't afford to do it up on my own.'

'Ye shouldn't have to,' Kitty expostulated. 'It's about time that dad of yours faced up to his responsibilities. Ye let him off with far too much.'

Beth gave a pathetic shrug. 'Talking of responsibilities,' she said, reluctant to dwell any longer on her own problems, 'does Fred know he's going to be a father? Has Maggie let him know?' By now, all the neighbours knew that Maggie was expecting even though she'd tried to hide it.

'She's telling him tomorrow when he comes home.' Kitty grimaced comically. 'So ye'll find me hiding in the cellar when she does. There's always ructions when those two get together.'

'He should be pleased,' said Beth, unaware that he was not the father.

'He might well be,' Kitty agreed. She wasn't about to divulge Maggie's secret.

* * *

The next day, Maggie strutted into Kitty's kitchen, grinning like a cat that had found the cream. 'Fred's home an' I've told him!' she crowed.

'An' he accepted it just like that?' Kitty said, clicking her fingers when she saw how delighted Maggie looked.

'He did,' Maggie said, her amazement plain to hear. 'He even said he was dead sorry for blacking me eye last time he was home.'

'He might black it again if he finds out the truth,' Kitty said grimly.

Maggie's face fell. 'Aw, Kitty! I thought you'd be made up for me.'

'I am, love. I was just saying...'

'Well I'll not be telling him, an' I hope you won't,' Maggie said vehemently.

'I'll not breathe a word,' said Kitty, blessing herself for compounding the lie.

'He seems to like the idea of being a father.' Maggie looked rather bemused. 'He's been ever so nice to me since I told him.'

'There ye are then.' Kitty smiled smugly. 'Didn't I tell ye that it can make an awful change in some men?'

'I'd best get back. Keep him in a good mood. He's taking me out tomorrow to buy me some new clothes. Ta-ra.' For the first time in ages, Maggie looked happy, and Kitty was pleased for her. She just hoped that Fred wouldn't put on his thinking cap and do some counting when the baby finally arrived.

* * *

In the weeks following the explosion, life went on in much the same way. Spring edged its way towards summer and each weekday Kitty made munitions for a war that seemed as though it would never end. In the evenings, with more time on her hands now that she had only herself to care for, she began knitting tiny cardigans, bootees and bonnets for Maggie's baby, and when she tired of that she paid a visit to the second-hand shop and bought a Singer sewing machine. She put it in the front room.

'You'll be able to make me some nightdresses and cot covers,' Maggie said, when she saw it. 'I'll buy some off-cuts from the market. It'll be cheaper than buying stuff from the shops.'

Kitty grinned. It was typical of Maggie to presume that Kitty would do the sewing in the same way Maggie expected to borrow a cup of sugar or a drop of milk without ever returning them. Kitty didn't object, but she couldn't help thinking that Maggie had the neck of a brass monkey.

'Oh, an' by the way,' Maggie continued, 'I've changed me job. I'll have to give up weaving once it's born, so I'm learning to be a mender. I can do that at home. Holroyd's'll set me up with a frame. I'll put it in the front room.' She lit a cigarette, beaming through the cloud of smoke she blew out.

'Oh, I'm glad for ye. I worried as to how ye'd manage once the baby came.' Kitty had dreaded the idea of Maggie leaving her baby for Vi to look after; she'd probably suffocate it with cigarette smoke or leave it to starve to death. 'I'd have offered to have it meself if things had been different,' she said, 'but I don't want to give up me work in munitions. If the only way to end this war is by making enough shells and bullets to kill off the Germans then I think it's worthwhile.'

'Too friggin' right,' Maggie hooted, 'keep 'em coming, girl.' She patted the top of the sewing machine. 'Eh, what do you say to going to the Saturday market and gettin' some stuff to make things for the baby?'

'Why not,' said Kitty.

* * *

On Saturday morning after Kitty had done her washing she called for Maggie. 'Are ye ready to go to the market?' she asked, ''cos if ye are we'll be just in time to catch the next tram.' Maggie pulled on a baggy cardigan and they hurried down the lane, catching the tram by the skin of their teeth.

At the market they joined the crowds hovering round the stalls on the lookout for bargains. Maggie bought soft, white cotton lawn and fluffy blanket cloth. 'I like that blue but ye can't buy that in case it's a girl,' Kitty said, wishing it was her baby they were shopping for before wistfully adding, 'Tom'd want a boy.'

'Just because he thinks the sun shines out of his own arse doesn't mean he can pick an' choose,' Maggie scoffed.

'He would if he could,' Kitty grunted. On the rare occasions they had discussed starting a family, Tom hadn't shown much interest, but his use of the terms 'he' and 'him' had made her extremely conscious of how disappointed he would be if she gave birth to a girl.

Arm in arm, Kitty and Maggie sauntered round the stalls, Maggie's bump leading the way. 'I'm as fat as a bladder of lard,' she moaned, easing her fingers into her waistband.

'Wait till ye're as fat as a barrel. Then ye'll have something to complain about.'

'You'll not be so friggin' cheeky when it's your turn,' Maggie retorted.

They stopped by the second-hand furniture and bric-a-brac

stall. Maggie had bought a second-hand pram from the stall the week before, and now she was on the lookout for a cot.

'Ooh look!' She pointed to a wooden cot, its paintwork chipped and stained.

'It's not in very good condition, an' it's pink. What if ye have a boy?' Kitty said.

'The baby won't know what colour it is,' Maggie scoffed. 'They don't know their colours till they're about three. Anyway, I can paint it whatever colour I fancy.' She pulled the cot from where it was crammed in between an old chair and a fireguard. It wobbled dangerously. Maggie's hard shell suddenly crumbled. 'Aw, Kitty,' she said despairingly, 'I wish I could buy everything brand new. I want my kid to have the best in the world, 'cos I never did.' Her eyes moistened and she bit down on her lip to stem the tears.

Instinctively, Kitty hugged her. 'It'll have your love, Maggie,' she said urgently, 'an' that's the most important thing. Love an' care is all a baby needs.'

Maggie swallowed her tears. 'Yeah, you're right. And I will love it, Kitty.' She shoved the cot away, and adopting her usual tough demeanour, she snapped, 'And I'll not be buying that thing.'

'I wouldn't put a monkey in it, let alone a baby,' Kitty said, giggling.

Maggie snorted. 'I'm not havin' a monkey – but it'd be easier if I was. I could sell it to a zoo.'

Kitty raised her eyes in despair. 'Ye're the craziest woman I ever met, an' before ye have any more daft notions, let's go home. We'll have a bit of tea then I'll make a start on these,' she said, patting the parcel of material.

Maggie stayed until after ten, gossiping and smoking, and Kitty cut out the sheets and blankets. After she'd seen Maggie to the door Kitty returned to the front room. She had long since reached the conclusion that the only way to dispel the emptiness she felt whenever she was in the house alone, and fill the void left by Tom's absence, was to keep busy. So, in order to get a good night's sleep she sat down at her machine to stretch the hour before she went to her half-empty bed.

She was just finishing off a cot sheet when above the clacking and whirring of the treadle and the wheel she heard a hammering on her back door. She rushed to answer it.

Dan Boothroyd was standing there, panic-stricken. 'It's Margery,' he blurted, 'she can barely get a breath and she's burning up.' Kitty closed the door behind her and together they ran next door.

Margery was in bed, her usually neat hair plastered to her forehead and a slick sheen of perspiration covering her pallid cheeks. Her eyes were glazed and there was a bluish tinge to her lips. Her breath came in gasps and gurgles, the nasty bubbling sound in Margery's chest alarming Kitty.

'Have you sent for the doctor?' she cried.

'No,' said Dan. 'When she woke up this morning she was complaining of a pain in her back so she stayed in bed. I kept looking in on her but she wouldn't have anything to eat. She said she just wanted to sleep, and just now when I brought her up a cup of tea I found her like this.'

'Go and get him,' Kitty ordered.

Dan hared from the room, surprisingly agile for a man of his years, and Kitty asked the Virgin Mary to let the doctor be at home and not at the Conservative Club. It was common knowledge that he spent his leisure time there.

Desperate as to what she should do, Kitty dampened a flannel in the bathroom and bathed Margery's face to lower the fever but there was nothing she could do to alleviate her tortured breathing. Barely conscious, Margery seemed unaware of Kitty's presence. Wracking her brains as to what she might do next, Kitty remembered how her mam had propped her granda up on his pillows to help him breathe when his bronchitis was troubling him.

Her hands shook as she eased Margery's plump body off the bed and then rammed Dan's pillow on top of Margery's own. Margery lay back, and for a moment the gurgling ceased only to be replaced by a terrible rasping. Kitty broke out in a sweat. Had she done more harm than good? The minutes ticked by and she began to panic. Her chest tightened as she drew in the room's fuggy air.

Where were Dan and Dr Metcalfe?

Just as Kitty had feared, when they entered the bedroom Dan gasped, 'I had to go all the way to the Con Club.'

Looking none too pleased, the doctor gave Margery a cursory examination.

'Pneumonia,' he said. Kitty smelled the whiskey on his breath. 'I'll leave these for you to administer.' He fished in his bag. 'Two pills every two hours with plenty of fluids. Open the windows to let in the fresh air. I'll call again in the morning.'

'Do ye not think she should be in hospital?' Kitty's voice was high with anxiety as she followed him downstairs to the front door.

The doctor paused on the bottom step and turned to face Kitty, a sympathetic expression on his florid face. 'Mrs Boothroyd's heart and lungs have been severely damaged for some time, Mrs Conlon. I doubt she'll see tomorrow, otherwise I would have sent her to hospital.' He shrugged then made his way to the door. 'Better to let her die in her own bed,' he said, matter of fact. He drove away in his big, black car, Kitty thinking he'd most likely forget all about poor Margery before he reached the bottom of the street.

After she had urged Margery to swallow two of the pills, Kitty sat at the opposite side of the bed to Dan, listening to Margery's ragged breathing. She decided not to tell Dan what the doctor had said. Time would tell.

'I'll just pop back home and put the lights out an' lock the door,' she said. 'I'll be back shortly.' She wouldn't leave poor Dan to sit through the night, alone.

She returned ten minutes later, praying as she climbed the stairs that Margery's fever had broken and that she was breathing more easily. Dan was sitting by the bed, holding Margery's limp hand. 'No change,' he said brokenly.

'The pills take time to work,' she said, sitting down and desperately wishing she could find something more comforting to say. Not that Dan was listening. He was oblivious to everything other than Margery. Kitty felt her eyes drooping. Fighting sleep, she went downstairs to make a pot of tea. The kettle seemed to take forever to boil and she bounced on her heels and wrung her hands.

'No! No! Oh Madge!'

Dan's plaintive cry echoed through the house. Kitty rushed up to the bedroom. He was cradling his wife in his arms, his shoulders heaving. When Kitty whispered his name, he turned his tearstained face to her.

'She's gone,' he said bleakly, 'my Margery's gone.' Great gulping sobs escaped his throat as he mourned his loss.

Kitty slowly approached the bed. She was relieved to find that Margery's eyes were closed. Her face was a strange greyish-blue, but other than that she looked as though she was sleeping peacefully. She knelt by the bed and intoned the prayers for the repose of Margery's soul.

Leaving Dan to grieve, she went back down the kitchen and brewed the tea. Then, hunting in Margery's tidy cupboards she found a small bottle of spirits. She mounted the stairs with the loaded tray: strong, sweet tea, the panacea for all ills, and brandy to dull the pain.

She sat with Dan, sipping her tea and half-listening as he recounted his life with Margery. He talked of how they had met, and how they had fallen in love at first sight, and their joy in raising two sons and a daughter. He seemed barely conscious of what he was saying, his voice barely above a whisper. Kitty let him talk without interruption, knowing that his beautiful memories would sustain him during the long, dark days ahead.

Dawn was breaking, pale bands of yellow light streaking the sky as Kitty went to notify the doctor. At the bottom of Dan's garden path, she paused, staring out over the allotments to the sycamore trees, now in full leaf. In Jack Naughton's patch, bright green cabbages and rows of beans and peas were flourishing. A multi-coloured row of tall gladioli caught the early morning light. *Life goes on*, mused Kitty. *Everything has its own season*. Poor Margery had had hers. As Kitty walked down the lane she consoled herself that at last Margery was with her sons in heaven.

* * *

On the day of the funeral, Kitty and Beth made sandwiches and tea for the small reception in Dan's house. Although his daughter, Pauline, had attended the funeral service with her husband and son, she refused to mingle with the neighbours. She disappeared upstairs leaving everyone to wonder why.

'If she were my daughter I'd make sure she did as she was told,' Walter Garside blustered to Nellie Haigh and Gertie Lander. 'It's a disgrace leaving a stranger to organise the refreshments.'

'I'm not a stranger, Mr Garside, I'm a good friend and neigh-bour,' Kitty said tartly, 'an' I consider it a privilege to give Margery a good wake.'

'Wake! What on earth are you talking about?' Walter snapped.

'In Ireland we wake the dead to celebrate their life,' Kitty explained.

'Pshaw! Irish nonsense.'

'What's Dad giving off about now?' Beth whispered as she came from across the room. She had been sitting with Dan and Margery's brother and his wife.

'He's just after calling me a stranger an' saying that if Pauline was his daughter he'd have insisted she served the tea,' Kitty said loudly.

Walter's jaw dropped and he stared, shocked by her audacity.

'Take no notice of him,' Beth said, emboldened by Kitty's defiant grin. 'Dad likes to think he rules the world, and that everybody in it should do as he says.'

Walter looked fit to explode.

Kitty and Beth were still giggling as they helped Dan clear up after everyone else had left. 'Did ye see his face?' Kitty chortled. 'I thought his eyes were going to pop right eyes of his head.'

'He's not used to being spoken to like that.' Beth laughed. 'In future I'll take a leaf out of your book and stick up for myself a bit more.'

'Ye've not been doing too badly just lately. Ye put your foot down about coming to my house and he's had to accept that whether he likes it or not.'

Dan smiled as he listened to the two young women at the sink. He didn't know what he would have done without Kitty these past few days. He was going to miss her. 'Put the kettle on, Kitty, I've something to say to you,' he said.

They sat at the table to drink their tea. 'I've been talking with Pauline and Robert, and they want me to go and live with them in Southport. I don't want to stay here now Margery's gone so that's what I'm going to do.'

Kitty's face crumpled. 'Oh, Dan! I'll miss ye. We all will.' Beth echoed Kitty's words.

'I think I'm doing the right thing,' Dan said, 'I've missed our Pauline something shocking. My only regret is that Margery never saw where our lads are buried. We always talked about going to

France and laying flowers on their graves, and now it's too late.' He shook his head despairingly. Kitty placed her hand on his and squeezed it tightly. He gazed into the face he had grown fond of and said, 'Think on, you young'uns, don't ever let things pass you by. If there's something you want to do then make sure you do it while you have the chance.'

Kitty and Beth nodded solemnly.

17

The morning after the funeral, Kitty sat down to write to Tom. These days his letters were few and far between, and when they did arrive they told Kitty very little. Hers, on the other hand, told him all the latest home news – Margery's sudden death and Maggie's advancing pregnancy – and always how much she loved and missed him. She liked writing her letters; it made her feel closer to him. However, she hadn't told him about her narrow escape in the explosion. In one of his letters he'd strongly objected to her working in the factory, stating that it was only rough, common women that undertook such work. Besides, she didn't want to worry him. She did enough worrying for both of them.

She had just put the letter in an envelope ready to post when Maggie dropped in. It was a scorching hot Sunday at the beginning of August and after Kitty had made a pot of tea they went and sat out on two kitchen chairs in Kitty's back garden. Maggie rolled up her skirt, her pale, plump legs sticking out from under her distended belly. She was huge and, much to her disgust, she waddled when she walked. She looked rather woeful as she sipped her tea then lit a cigarette.

'Will you keep an eye on me when the time comes?' Maggie spoke with none of her usual cockiness. 'You know what I mean like. Keep popping in and out to see if I'm all right.'

'Sure an' ye know I will.' Kitty patted Maggie's bare leg, sounding far more confident than she felt.

'Do you think you'd like to be there when I have it?' Maggie pressed, her voice high with anxiety.

'If ye want me to be.' Kitty was somewhat surprised that bold, hard-bitten Maggie was afraid. 'But you'll have the midwife with ye, and your mam.'

Maggie snorted. 'Me mam! She'll not be within a mile if I know her. She can't stand babies and blood.'

Kitty quailed at the thought of blood. She pondered on whether or not watching Maggie give birth would help when her own time came to have a baby. The only births she'd attended were those of lambs on the farm in Roscommon, and if she were perfectly honest, she had little or no idea of what took place with humans. She imagined that when the baby was ready it just slipped out; although how it got through such a tiny space was a mystery.

'Do you think ye'll know what to do when the time comes?' Kitty screwed her face in puzzlement.

'I suppose so,' said Maggie, offhandedly, 'it can't be all that hard. Thousands of women do it every day.'

'Well, the midwife will know what she's doing,' Kitty said confidently.

'I can't stand her,' Maggie groused, 'poking her nose into everything, asking where's the father, an' have I got enough nappies. An' if that's not bad enough she's peering at me private bits as though it were a bloody peep show.'

Kitty exploded with laughter. 'She'll be doing more than peeping before it's all over,' she squealed, waving her fingers suggestively at Maggie's crotch.

Renee Spivey, the midwife, had called with Maggie the previous afternoon, and Kitty had been keeping her company as she worked at her mending. 'Walking and fresh air are good for you and the baby,' Renee had said. 'Plenty of exercise will speed things along. You're three or four days overdue to my reckoning.'

With that in mind, when they'd finished their tea Kitty suggested they go for a walk. Maggie snorted at the idea. 'She wants to try dodging between two looms all day catching loose ends. That'd show her what real work is.'

'But ye don't do that any more. You're sitting all day,' Kitty reminded her as she chivvied her up off the chair. 'Come on, I'll post my letter on the way then we'll walk up to the towpath.'

'I feel as though I've been blown up and stuffed,' Maggie groaned, as she and Kitty walked up Weaver Street.

'A bit of exercise might make you feel better.' Kitty linked Maggie's arm in hers.

'I don't think I'll make it to the top of the street without collapsing,' Maggie moaned, deliberately dragging her feet.

'Just take it steady,' Kitty advised.

Maggie tugged at the front of the blue and white checked maternity dress she had bought in Woolworth's. It was stretched taut over her belly and kept riding up. 'I can't wait to get out of these bloody awful smocks and back into normal clothes,' she grumbled. 'I feel about as a glamorous as an elephant.'

'I don't mind takin' an elephant for a walk,' Kitty quipped, trying to keep a steady pace. She herself was wearing a pale green cotton frock she had just finished making the night before, the cap-sleeved, loose tunic style in the new shorter length deliciously cool in the heat of the afternoon.

They hadn't gone far when they met Mavis Robson. Neat and prim in her starched white blouse and grey skirt and looking as cool as a cucumber she contrasted sharply with Maggie who by now was puffing and panting and sweating profusely. 'Lovely day for a walk,' Mavis said cheerily. 'You're positively blooming, Maggie.'

'Blooming! I'm blooming fed up, if that's what you mean.'

'You can't have long to go now.' Mavis eyed the mound of Maggie's blue and white checked belly.

'Any day now, an' I can't wait to get it over with,' Maggie moaned. 'In fact, I might just have it here the way I feel.' She burped loudly. 'I'm crippled with wind.' She rubbed her chest then let out a ripping fart. 'Sorry about that.' She grimaced. 'Better out than in.'

Mavis's eyebrows, having shot up into her hairline, resumed their normal position. 'Indeed. Whatever makes you feel comfortable,' she twittered.

Slightly alarmed, Kitty said she thought they ought to turn back even though they had walked less than five hundred yards from Maggie's door. However, Mavis delayed them, wanting to gossip. 'Where were you going?'

'We were heading for the towpath on the river but I don't think we should go that far now,' replied Kitty.

'Oh, that's a lovely walk on a grand day like this,' Mavis gushed.

'It is,' Kitty agreed, 'although the towpath's not the same without the café.' Crestfallen, she recalled the happy days she had worked there.

'An' I won't be the same if I don't get back home,' Maggie groused, shuffling her swollen feet. 'There's sumthin' funny going on in here—' she patted her bump '—an' I think I know what it is.'

Really alarmed this time, Kitty took Maggie's arm. 'We'll be seein' ye, Mavis,' she said, propelling Maggie back the way they had come, Kitty moving as fast as she was able with Maggie waddling alongside.

Kitty pushed the door of number nine open with her foot and

blundered into the kitchen, trailing Maggie behind her. Vi was doing her make-up in the mirror over the sideboard ready for going out. Kitty shouted for her to lend a hand as, crossing the room, she bundled Maggie up the stairs into her bedroom.

'What's the rush?' Vi shouted. 'What's wrong with her?'

'I think she's having the baby,' Kitty bawled back, panic-stricken. 'Go and get Renee Spivey. Tell her to come at once.'

'Who?'

'The midwife,' Kitty screeched, wanting to wring Vi's selfish neck.

'I'll go as soon as I've put me face on,' Vi replied, not sounding in the least fussed. 'I can't go out looking like this.'

Maggie struggled on to the bed, her face growing steadily paler. Kitty dashed into the messy bathroom to wash her hands. She thought she might be using them any minute now to do something she didn't want to do and she didn't want any germs to harm the baby.

'Kitty,' Maggie wailed, 'I've peed meself. The bed's all wet.'

Kitty ran back into the bedroom. 'It's your waters. They've broken. The baby must be on its way.' She ran to get towels and a sheet from the airing cupboard.

'Put these underneath ye,' she panted. 'Put your knees up – and breathe.'

'I am breathing,' Maggie gasped. 'If I wasn't I'd be dead.'

Downstairs, the door slammed. 'Your mam's gone for Renee,' Kitty said, hoping it was true.

Maggie grunted and then let out piercing wail. 'Don't push,' Kitty cried. 'Wait for Renee. Take deep breaths and keep calm.'

'Oh... oh... oh...' Maggie moaned. 'I can feel it coming.'

Kitty rolled up her sleeves.

* * *

'You did well, Kitty,' Renee praised, as they sat beside Maggie's bed, cups of tea in hand. Maggie lay back on the pillow, flushed with triumph, her daughter at her breast. Kitty had knelt on the bed at Maggie's feet, amazed and afraid as the baby's head had appeared. She had cupped her hands underneath it, urging herself not to pull. Back in Roscommon she'd heard that the girl with the funny-shaped head was like that because the midwife had pulled her out too quick.

Kitty raised her cup to her lips, her hands still trembling from her ordeal. She could still feel the fragile shape of the head against her palms, and as she sipped she was barely able to believe that less than half an hour ago these same hands that held the cup had held a newborn baby as it slithered into the world. She was just glad that Renee had arrived in time to take charge and cut the cord. Kitty didn't think she could have managed that.

'I'll be off,' said Renee, putting down her cup and picking up her bag. 'I'll be back after six. Keep on with the feeding.'

Mesmerised, Kitty listened to the suck and slurp as the baby took her fill. 'What are ye going to call her?' She peered at the little pale face under a wispy straggle of bright red hair.

'Lily. I think it sounds nice an' ladylike.'

'It's a lovely name, an' she's a lovely baby. Seeing her being born was one of the best things I've ever seen, although I have to admit I was scared stiff I'd do something wrong.'

Maggie smiled at Kitty, her face glowing with gratitude. 'You were bloody marvellous! I don't know what I'd have done without you.' She chuckled. 'If you hadn't been here I'd have had to cross me legs an' hope she stayed where she was.' Maggie gazed fondly at Lily and then at Kitty. 'I never thought I'd have a friend like you,' she said, her eyes moist and her voice thick with tenderness.

Kitty blinked back tears. 'Ye'd have done the same for me,' she said.

18

Kitty stripped off her overalls ready to leave the factory. It was shortly after midday on a Friday in November, and she was taking one of her half-days leave. The fog that had all but blinded her on her walk to the factory had lifted but it was still bitingly cold. *Not long till Christmas.* Would this be another without Tom, she wondered as she made her way back to Weaver Street.

At the back of the Weaver's Arms, Cora Bradshaw was putting out the empties ready for the draymen to collect the crates of empty bottles when they delivered the kegs. A loud wolf whistle pierced the air and when Cora looked round she saw Tom Conlon swaggering towards her. Devastatingly handsome in his navy uniform, his greatcoat lying open and the white stripes on his sailor's collar matching his even white teeth, he flashed her a cocksure smile.

'My, aren't you just the bee's knees,' Cora said admiringly.

Tom saluted. 'You're not looking so bad yourself, Cora.'

'Thanks.' The tart reply was replaced by a puzzled frown. 'I saw Kitty yesterday. She never mentioned you were coming home on leave.'

'That's because she doesn't know,' he said, tapping the side of his nose. 'I copped a forty-eight-hour pass and here I am.'

'Well, it's good to see you. Enjoy your leave.' Cora headed for the pub's open back door.

'I intend to, and I'll start by having a pint of your best stout,' he said. Cora looked surprised as he followed her inside. Kitty had just reached the corner of Weaver Street. She had missed seeing him by a matter of seconds.

Kitty carried on up the lane. After she'd washed off the stink of TNT and changed her dress she went straight into Maggie's. Most of her free time these days was spent helping care for baby Lily. Maggie's love for her daughter was plain to see, but the everyday chores of motherhood were a foreign country as far as Maggie was concerned and Kitty sometimes wondered how little Lily would have survived over the past three months had she not called each day to make sure she was clean and dry and fed.

Checking in on Lily and Maggie only took a few minutes and soon Kitty was back home. She was going into the front room to do some sewing when someone rapped on the front door. Unlocking it, she pulled the door wide, her delighted squeals echoing from one end of Weaver Street to the other. In her excitement, she flung her arms round Tom with such force that they almost toppled over.

'Tom! Tom!' she cried, clinging to him and dropping kisses on his smiling face.

'You're pleased to see me then?' He laughed, and pushing her back into the hallway and kicking the door shut with his heel, his hungry lips found hers.

'Oh, Tom! Why didn't ye let me know ye were coming?' she gasped when the kiss ended. She couldn't help feeling a twinge of disappointment at tasting stout on his lips. He must have stopped off to have a pint before coming home.

'No time,' he replied. 'I only got to know at the last minute.' He kissed her again, stroking his hands over her curves and enjoying the soft warm feel and taste of her. She smelled of soap and lavender, and he realised just how much he had missed her. He shrugged out of his greatcoat. Kitty's heart swelled with pride as she drank in how handsome he looked in his uniform.

'Come in, come in.' Tugging at his arm, she led him into the kitchen, gabbling, 'What can I get ye? A bite to eat? A cup of tea?' She could hardly believe that he was really here.

Laughing, Tom sat down in his chair, and to Kitty the room suddenly looked perfect again. He was back where he belonged. He lit a cigarette. She couldn't take her eyes off him. If only she had known he was coming she'd have worn something more attractive, she thought, as she clumsily filled the kettle. Water splashed over the sink. He stubbed out his cigarette, and coming up behind her, he embraced her trembling body. The kettle clanked into the sink as she leaned back into his arms. Now she was where she belonged.

'The only thing I want is you,' he whispered against her hair. Then, taking her hand, he led her up the stairs and into bed.

* * *

Forty-eight hours – well, not even that considering he'd had to travel home and had to get back to his ship in that time – but Kitty was intent on making the most of it. When she woke the next morning and felt Tom's lean, hard body next to her, she shivered with delight. It hadn't been a dream after all. She rolled over, and with the tip of her tongue she licked the shell of his ear. He woke with a start. Then, little by little in the magic moments that followed they lay separated only by their skin as they made sweet, languid love. Oh, the joy of no longer feeling that half the bed was empty.

Up and about, they recaptured the ordinary things they had

done before he went away, Tom popping out to the pub and Kitty doing her chores then nipping in to see Maggie and Lily. She felt guilty at neglecting little Lily but Tom came first. Sadly, Maggie found it hard to hide her jealousy.

'Off you go, back to Mr Kiss My Arse it's Made of Treacle,' she'd sneered when Kitty said she had to get back to make Tom's dinner.

Kitty wanted everything to be perfect, but behind every silver lining there had to be a cloud and she sensed there was one that she couldn't quite fathom. While Tom had praised her cooking, told her she was wonderful, and made love to her, she couldn't help feeling that it lacked real depth. It was as if Tom was merely passing the time in a distracted kind of way: a man on leave taking the pleasures on offer before he returned to his ship. He appeared to have no qualms at leaving her again and that left her feeling as though something very important was missing from their relationship. She tried not to dwell on it, and putting it down to her silly, superstitious nature, she kept a brave smile on her face.

On Saturday night they went to the Weaver's Arms where Tom was welcomed like a returning hero. Afterwards, at home by the fire, Tom in his chair and Kitty on the rug with her arms about his knees and her head resting in his lap she insisted that he tell her what his life was like aboard HMS *Result*.

'It's the same thing day after day,' he said, lighting a cigarette and puffing contentedly. 'We plough the English Channel guarding the convoys taking supplies to France and watch out for Jerry's U-boats so that we can get them before they get us.' He made it sound so ordinary but the thought of German submarines sneaking up on Tom's ship made Kitty shudder.

'Do ye not feel afraid?' she asked, her voice wobbling as she gazed up at him.

'No point,' he said, flicking ash into the hearth. 'The lads are a great bunch and we all look out for one another.' He then went on to tell her about how he ran a book on board, the crew betting on cockroach races and the like. He was happy to talk about that.

'That sounds like you're enjoying it,' she replied, sliding up to sit on his lap then hugging him, 'but I do worry about ye. I hate to think of you in danger.' She kissed his brow, and unwilling to let her fears overtake her, she sat up straight and forced a giggle. 'When I'm at my bench in the factory filling shells I pretend I'm doing it so that ye can fire them at the Germans,' she said, her impish smile fading as she felt him stiffen, and his sullen expression letting her know she'd been wrong to mention her work in munitions.

She got to her feet to face him. 'I know ye don't like me working there, Tom, but it's what we women have to do if we're going to beat 'em.' His stony silence told her he didn't agree. Saddened that she'd spoiled the evening and desperate to recapture the joy of having him home, she reached for his hand. 'Let's go to bed,' she said.

By the time the clock on the dressing table showed midnight Kitty and Tom's disappointment in each other had been forgotten. The euphoria of their lovemaking stayed with them throughout the next morning. After a long lie-in Tom lit the fire whilst Kitty made breakfast, their chores interrupted by hugs and kisses and fond words. Memories of the first few months of marriage in the little flat in Dublin filled Kitty's mind and although deep inside she dreaded Tom's departure, for their last few hours together she couldn't have been happier.

* * *

Come Sunday afternoon, Kitty's bubble burst. As she stood on the docks with Tom about to re-join his ship, she gazed into the distance through eyes blurred with tears, picking out the Liver Building, the Cunard headquarters and the Mersey Docks and Harbour Building – the Three Graces. But she felt there was little grace in saying goodbye. Tom on the other hand seemed eager to be aboard. She was determined not to cry; Tom would be embarrassed. So she clung to his arm until the last minute, imprinting her body with the feel and scent of him. One final kiss and he was gone. On her way back to Weaver Street she cursed the rotten war, the Kaiser and all the Germans. Would it be another year before she would see Tom again?

* * *

Later that evening, Kitty sat in Tom's chair with her knitting, savouring the lingering smell of his cologne and tobacco. The house felt empty and seemed twice as lonely, so she was glad when there was a knock at the door and Beth came in.

'Did you and Tom have a lovely weekend?' She sat down in Kitty's chair.

'We did,' Kitty said wistfully, 'an' it's left me feelin' down in the dumps now that he's not here.' She gave a brief account of events, and as she talked she couldn't help noticing that Beth seemed to be positively glowing. Curious, she asked, 'And ye. What have ye been up to?'

Beth took a deep breath. 'I went out with a man from the mill,' she said. 'He's called Blair Forsythe. He comes from Scotland and...' She paused before dreamily adding, 'Oh Kitty, he's absolutely wonderful.' She then went on to tell how Blair had kept popping into her office on any excuse and that he had eventually asked her out, that he had floppy fair hair and kind grey eyes, and that they shared the same interests. Kitty could tell that she was enjoying talking about him. She nodded for Beth to continue.

'And...?' she said.

Beth smiled dreamily. 'We walked in the Botanic Gardens. He held my hand. It made my blood tingle, Kitty. He speaks with a lovely Scottish burr, and we found so much to talk about I didn't want the evening to come to an end.' She paused and gave a satisfied sigh. 'He wants to take me out again.'

'Ye sly, little madam,' Kitty giggled. 'Why did ye not mention him before?'

Beth blushed. 'I didn't want to get my hopes up. I thought nothing would come of it, that he might not even turn up but—' her face lit up with a rapturous smile '—he did, Kitty, and it was wonderful.'

Kitty smiled fondly at Beth's enthusiasm. 'Is he the first fella ye've ever been out with?' she asked, although she thought she already knew the answer.

'He is. And I will go out with him again.' Her face lost its glow. 'Of course, I haven't mentioned it to Dad. I told Blair not to show me any special attention at work in case he got to hear of it. I'd rather he didn't know until I'm sure how things will turn out.'

'Maybe that's for the best,' Kitty agreed. 'No sense in looking for trouble.'

'Was Tom your first boyfriend?' Beth asked, her thoughts on romance.

Kitty grimaced. 'I dallied with one or two before Tom, but nothin' serious. Then, when I met Tom I knew he was the only man for me.' She paused, a sad and thoughtful look darkening her pretty face. 'The funny thing is, when we got married we really didn't know one another at all. We've been married for nigh on two years now, an' I still don't think I know who Tom really is.' She thought back to the way in which he had parted so easily from her on the docks when her own heart had been breaking.

'But you still love one another,' Beth said anxiously.

'We do.' Kitty said the words firmly and wished that she could believe them as fervently as she had said them.

19

Another Christmas without Tom came and went. January brought snow, sleet and thick fog, making Kitty's journey to and from the factory hazardous. The snow turned to slush, the fog lifted, and throughout all that time Kitty was nursing the most wonderful secret of her life.

One morning she'd been walking to the factory, thanking God that the pavements were clean and dry, and thinking that if winter was on the wane then spring couldn't be far behind. Suddenly, for no reason at all except that that particular season always reminded her of the earth's promise to bring new life, she started counting the days since she had last had her monthly show. Her footsteps had slowed, and twice as slowly she'd counted back the weeks since Tom's leave. Then she had come to a sudden halt. She had missed her period more than a week ago. A fizz of excitement coupled with disbelief had her counting again.

Each morning after that she had woken and waited for the usual cramps that always preceded the flow of blood, but none came. She itched to tell Tom, and Maggie and Beth, but not wanting to be proved wrong she had waited. At the beginning of

February, she was sure she was pregnant. An appointment with the doctor confirmed it. She walked back home on air. She was going to be a mother.

* * *

In the pitch-black, wet and windy night, HMS *Result* was luring a U-boat in the murky, choppy waters of the English Channel. Tom was standing on deck, his arms clasped across his chest in an attempt to stave off the freezing cold. Off to starboard he could see the faint winking navigation light of a cargo ship. The wind blew strongly in his face and he shivered uncontrollably.

'I'd give a king's ransom for a seat by a roaring fire,' he muttered to Harry.

'An' a nice hot toddy in your hand,' Harry replied, his teeth chattering.

Out in the dark, a swirl of water heaved and the sea slewed in a welter of seething foam.

'Hands to panic station,' came the order from the bridge.

Tom and Harry leapt into action, their task being to let the U-boat think that the crew were panicking and preparing to abandon ship. Swiftly they began lowering a lifeboat, giving time for the hidden gunners on deck to open fire. The U-boat, confident of attacking an unarmed vessel, closed in. The guns opened fire with a crashing roar that reverberated in Tom's ears. The first salvo took out the U-boat's conning tower.

'We've got the bugger!' Tom's triumphant shout was drowned by a massive, sickening thud, his elation turning to fear as the deck beneath his feet shuddered violently then split apart. He felt himself falling and his stomach turned over in shock. Above his head he could hear screams and shouts, and a succession of dull, heavy rumblings below. He felt a hot wetness creeping up inside his trouser legs. He wondered if it was his own blood.

We've been torpedoed, he thought as the oily, black water came up to meet him.

* * *

'It must be catching. First me, and now you,' Maggie said, dumping Lily into her pram and then lighting a cigarette, ready to walk to the market. 'Weaver Street's gonna be full of screaming brats.'

'She's not a brat, Maggie. Ye shouldn't call her that,' Kitty said hotly. She looked into the pram at Lily. She was sleeping, golden lashes fanning her chubby cheeks, her bonny face framed by a halo of bright red curls.

'I know she's not,' Maggie said, gazing fondly at her daughter, 'but she can be sometimes. The little mare had me up at five this morning.' She yawned noisily, the yawn ending in a disgruntled sigh. 'I got a letter from Fred this morning,' she said irritably, her ill temper quickening her pace as they walked down the lane. 'He wants to know why she has red hair. In his last letter he asked me what she looked like, so me, like a daft sod, wrote back and told him. I wish I hadn't bothered. The cheeky bugger had the nerve to ask me if I've been playing away,' she snorted, yanking the pram to a halt at the edge of the road.

Kitty had difficulty hiding a smile. They crossed over and when they were safely on the pavement Maggie gave her a sideways glance. 'What do you think Tom'll say when he gets your letter?'

'He'll be over the moon,' said Kitty, and could have bitten her tongue. If Fred was having doubts about having fathered Lily, it didn't seem fair to crow about her own good fortune so as they made their way between the market stalls she changed the subject and told Maggie about Beth's night out with her young man.

'Good for her,' Maggie grunted as she picked over a pile of wilted cabbage. 'Knowing Beth Garside, her kind of fella will be a damned sight better than mine.'

Dreamily, Kitty eyed the stall selling baby clothes, resisting the temptation to make a purchase. It was too soon.

* * *

Too wrapped up in her own wonderful condition, Kitty paid little heed to Maggie's problems. Every day she hurried home from the factory, hopeful that the postman had delivered Tom's reply. When at last a letter did arrive it wasn't the one she was expecting.

'Tom's coming home,' she cried, rushing into Maggie's kitchen and almost shoving the long, brown envelope into Maggie's face. Her own face was crumpled and tearstained, and she sounded close to hysteria.

Maggie gave her a bemused look, but before she could speak Kitty began to wail. 'His ship was blown up! He's in a hospital in Plymouth! Oh, Maggie, what if he was badly injured? It doesn't say.'

Maggie took the envelope from Kitty's trembling hand then scanned the letter. 'They're sending him home,' she said. 'He can't be that bad if they're letting him come home.' She pulled Kitty into her arms. 'Come on, love, just be thankful he's alive an' that you'll have him back for a bit.'

Kitty saw the reason in that, and after a strong cup of tea she even managed to giggle when Maggie gave a throaty chuckle and said, 'Look, if your Tom fell in a barrel of shit he'd come up smelling of roses.'

However, the shock was such that Kitty felt as though she was living in purgatory. At night she tossed and turned, imagining him thrashing about in dark, stormy waters, bleeding and broken. She dozed and woke up sweating, panic clutching her heart and making it thud as she pictured his beautiful body missing a limb, or his handsome face gashed and scarred. Throughout the day she relived the nightmare and felt so unsure of her actions that she didn't go to the factory. Her hands weren't steady enough to wad lethal shells.

* * *

Tom arrived home in a cab. Kitty had rushed to answer the door just in time to see it driving away. Looking pale and drawn, Tom mounted the steps into her waiting arms. She held him close, her breath gushing from her. Miraculously, he was all in one piece, no limbs missing, no obvious scars or injuries. He looked just like her Tom, despite his pallor. Even so, she led him to his chair by the hearth as if he were frail and ancient.

'I'm all right. Don't fuss,' he growled shrugging her away and sitting down.

Kitty hovered over him. 'Oh, Tom, tell me what happened,' she pleaded, reaching out and stroking a livid bruise on the back of his hand as she choked back tears. 'Have ye injuries that I can't see? Was it terrible, darlin'?' Her voice high with anxiety, she knelt at his feet, and taking his hands in hers, she squeezed them comfortingly.

Tom shrugged. 'It was bad enough,' he said, his tone matter of fact. 'You know, the blackness... the icy water... and the hissing of the torpedo... then that bloody awful thud.' He pulled his hands free and lit a cigarette.

Kitty lurched to her feet. 'Oh, my poor, poor love,' she crooned, cradling his head to her breast and stroking his hair. Tom lolled against her. 'But ye're safe now, darlin. Ye're home with me.' She let go of him to ask, 'How did they save ye?'

Tom sat back. 'I don't know. The first thing I knew was when I woke up in hospital. After a few days they told me I was unfit for duty. A wee Scots doctor told me to "gae hame and take a wee rest for the time being",' he mimicked, then gave Kitty a lopsided grin.

'For the time being,' Kitty said hollowly, those four small words sending her joy at seeing him unharmed crashing down round her ears. 'When will they send ye back?'

Tom didn't answer immediately. He gave a grim smile. 'Never. I'm not going back,' he said, his expression sneering and resolute. 'I've no intentions of that happening – ever!'

Kitty was puzzled. 'But won't they make you—'

'Shut up, Kitty! I don't want to talk about it any more,' Tom snarled.

Shocked by the ferocity of his sudden change of mood, Kitty fought back tears. At a loss what to do next, she went over to the sink and gazed out of the window.

Tom had been home for less than an hour and already things had gone terribly wrong. Disappointment curdled her insides. He hadn't asked about the baby. Had he not received her letter? She glanced over her shoulder at him. Was he sorry for his outburst?

Tom sat slumped in his chair by the fire, lighting one cigarette off the other. When Kitty broke the ugly silence in the room by asking, 'Did you get my letter telling you...?' he leapt to his feet growling, 'I'm going to lie down.' He shambled to the door and clumped upstairs. Kitty dithered, aching to follow him then deciding against it.

Instead, she made a pie with the last of her flour and the mince she'd managed to get the day before. Tom liked pies. Impatiently, she waited for him to come downstairs, every now and then glancing at the pie in the oven and the potatoes in the pot. When the crust was browning and drying up she took the pie out, placed a plate over it then wrapped it in a tea towel to keep it warm. The potatoes had gone mushy and the cabbage limp by the time Tom appeared, and Kitty's euphoria at his homecoming had utterly evaporated.

She filled their plates and then sat at the table, her appetite gone. Tom tucked in, but where once he would have exclaimed his delight, this time he said nothing about the pie. Kitty pushed hers listlessly around her plate, and then, unable to maintain the silence any longer, she clattered her cutlery onto her plate and took a deep breath.

'Did ye get my letter tellin' ye I'm havin' a baby, Tom?'

Tom raised his eyes from his plate and stared at her, his mouth hanging open and his blue eyes unfathomable. 'Oh, aye, the baby,' he said.

Kitty thought she might as well have told him it was raining. She clenched her teeth, her stomach tightening and her heart hammering. Did their baby mean nothing to him? Swallowing tears, she said, 'Aye, we're having a baby, Tom.'

Then, looking as though he'd been suddenly wakened from a deep sleep, Tom leapt to his feet, his chair falling over backwards as he reached for her. 'Oh, my darlin' girl,' he cried, lifting her out of her chair and crushing her to his chest. She felt the thud of his heart beneath his shirt and her own thudded in tandem as he covered her face with butterfly kisses.

'Ye are pleased then,' she said, relief washing over her.

Tom laughed. 'Pleased? Oh, my clever Kitty. What an amazing girl ye are. Ye've made a baby.'

She felt as though her insides were melting as she gazed into his flashing blue eyes. He'd come back to her. He was hers again. 'Aye, Tom, we made a baby,' she cried. 'Ye did your bit, now I'm doing mine. Come August we'll be parents.'

20

Out of sight of Derby House, Tom's faltering steps changed to a jaunty swagger. It was a warm, sunny day in mid-July and he quickened his pace, eager to get back to Weaver Street and the Weaver's Arms. He was going to open up his betting shop again, and this time he was intent on making a killing.

Twice now, he'd managed to fool the examining doctors in Derby House that he was still traumatised. He'd shuffled in, mumbled his replies and made sure to keep the nervous tic in his right eye and cheek twitching. Feeling rather pleased with his performance, he caught the tram back to Edge Hill.

He went straight to the pub, called a pint then went into the back room. Tomorrow he'd be back in business. He stayed there for the rest of the afternoon.

* * *

On her way home from work, Beth called in with Kitty. 'How are you today? You're not still feeling sick, are you?'

Kitty grimaced. She'd had several bouts of nausea in the past few months but she put it down to the anxiety Tom's uncaring attitude towards her was causing, and nothing to do with her pregnancy. Still, she wasn't going to tell Beth that.

'It's not as bad as it was, but I can't stand the smell of fried bacon. Not that ye can get much of that these days. I hate this rationing malarkey. Me belly's yearning for a taste of steak and kidney.'

'Don't talk to me about rationing,' Beth said. 'My dad blames me, not the government, if I don't get meat for his dinner every day. I've told him time and again that the butcher's only allowed to sell it on three days a week. As for butter and sugar, he still wants his bread coated, and three spoonfuls in his tea.' She raised her eyes in despair.

'It's the endless queuing for stuff that gets to me,' Kitty said, 'an' when ye get to be served, the things that ye wanted are all sold out.'

'Even so, you look positively blooming,' Beth said, accepting the cup of tea Kitty had just brewed.

'Well, apart from the odd bout of sickness I had early on I feel grand.' She sat down, her expression clouding. 'In fact, I should still be working at the factory,' she said irritably. 'I hate sitting about doing nothing.'

'I must say I was surprised when you gave up the munitions so soon, but I thought it was because you were staying home to nurse Tom.'

'Tom didn't need any nursing,' Kitty replied darkly, 'but it was because of him I gave it up. He didn't like me working there.'

'Why?' Beth was confused, not so much at Tom's demands but at Kitty's compliance. She wasn't one to be bullied into anything.

'It doesn't agree with his manly pride,' Kitty said, reflecting on the arguments they'd had. 'He doesn't think I should work at all, but we need the money. Tom's navy pay doesn't go far, and I'd like to have a bit extra for when the baby comes.'

She sipped her tea, thinking how sad it was that after Tom's initial display of joy he hadn't chosen to mention the baby again. He seemed to be living inside his head – a place to which she didn't have access – and she'd grown weary of his distraction and his sulky moods. She didn't know what he was thinking, but it certainly wasn't about her or his home life.

Beth, having enquired after Kitty's health and listened to her problems, now felt ready to air her own. Her pretty face puckered and she began wringing one hand with the other. 'I'm having trouble with my dad over Blair. I really don't know what to do about it.'

Kitty shifted her swollen ankles from one place to another on the footstool, trying to find a more comfortable position. For two weeks now she had been suffering with excess fluid in her limbs, her feet puffed up like rising dough and her ankles twice their normal size. Sticking out in front was bad enough without having legs and feet that resembled a baby elephant's. She felt ugly, and she knew that that was how Tom saw her. He averted his eyes when she undressed, and a few days ago he had told her to stay indoors not, she knew, because he was concerned for her health but because he didn't want people to see her looking like this. Then, she had felt like crying and now, still feeling abject and uncomfortable, she struggled to worry about Beth's problems; she had enough of her own.

However, being the good friend that she was, she pushed aside her own discomfort and said, 'Beth, you've got to stop letting your father dominate your life. If ye love Blair and want to be with him then ye have to stop hiding. Tell your dad before someone else does.'

Beth nodded, her newly bobbed, glossy brown hair brushing her cheeks. Kitty had noticed that since Beth had fallen in love she was taking much more care with her appearance, and now she gazed almost enviously at Beth's neat figure in a soft grey wool dress that hugged her slender hips.

'I know you're right in what you say,' said Beth, 'but I'm afraid of the trouble Dad might cause. He could cost Blair his job and I wouldn't want that.'

'Is your dad so important at Holroyd's that he could do that?' Kitty's surprise showed. She didn't think Whingeing Walter, as she thought of him, had that kind of power. She could well imagine that he was an obsequious boot-licker, always looking to curry favour with his bosses, but she didn't see him having any real clout when it came to hiring or firing mill personnel.

Beth looked anguished. 'He did it before,' she said tearfully. 'I made friends with a boy who worked there. He really needed the job to support his widowed mother and five younger brothers and sisters. It was nothing serious. We just liked one another. We went for walks at lunchtime, and swapped books. When Dad found out he started spreading malicious gossip about him, then he accused him of stealing. He'll do the same to Blair if he finds out about us.' She shook her head despairingly.

'Your dad's just being wicked. He doesn't want ye to get married and leave him because you're a free housekeeper,' Kitty said disparagingly. 'He knows that if he lets ye go he'll have to fend for himself. An' hell slap it into him if ye did.' She struggled to her feet, aware that it was time to start making the dinner for Tom coming home. 'It's down to ye, Beth, if ye want Blair then ye've got to make a stand.'

Beth stood. 'I'll think about it,' she said uncertainly, 'but I can't see a happy ending.' Disconsolate, she let herself out.

Kitty began to peel potatoes at the sink. It made her feel miserable to think that she hadn't solved Beth's problems for her, but what could she do? Until this baby came she could barely put two thoughts together. It wasn't so much anxiety over giving birth –

after all, Maggie had done it easily – it was Tom's behaviour that clouded her thoughts. He spent every waking hour in the betting shop or at the race meets, obsessed by making money. When Kitty complained he gruffly told her she should be glad. Whilst she understood his need to earn a living she thought there was something disturbing in the way he was going about it. He paid scant attention to her or their home life, and although he might be pleasant at one minute, in the next he could be cold and resentful. These days she never knew what to expect. Was it what had happened to him in the war that had left him so unpredictable? Outwardly, he seemed fit and healthy. Yet, each time he visited Derby House they declared him unfit for duty. God knows, she didn't want them to return him to his ship – that didn't bear thinking about – yet she was puzzled as to why they hadn't. What was it that she wasn't seeing?

When he went out he solicitously told her to take care of herself and when he came back in he politely asked her how she'd been, but he no longer kissed her or held her like he used to, and because they could no longer make love he fell asleep as soon as they were in bed. As for the baby, he acted as though it was nothing to do with him. He didn't want to talk about it, and took no pleasure in feeling it move when Kitty urged him to feel the little kicks or wriggles. Disconsolately, she put the pan of potatoes on the range. Perhaps things would be different after the baby was born.

* * *

Tom Conlon sauntered across the bar room floor in the Weaver's Arm's, his thumb hooked in the loop of his suit jacket so that it swung nonchalantly behind his broad shoulders. His waistcoat was buttoned tight, showing off his muscular chest and slender waist, and the silver armbands secured the sleeves of his white shirt. He looked every inch the successful bookmaker. Nodding and smiling at the customers sitting over their drinks, he walked out of the pub.

Out on the street he dropped his carefree pose, and putting on his jacket, he trudged up Weaver Street, his hands plunged deep in his trouser pockets. He felt bored and dissatisfied, but he wasn't about to let his acquaintances know that; he had to keep up appearances. He didn't particularly want to go home but he didn't want to stay in the pub either. He craved the excitement of the blood sport meets and the company he kept. Mixing with men with money was just as thrilling as seeing the dog or the bare-knuckle fighter he had backed win at twenty to one. But the meetings were few and far between, and he was stuck with the humdrum sameness of every day.

He paused to light a cigarette, the smoke he puffed out vaporising in the chill night air. He gazed into the misty cloud until it evaporated, his thoughts black. He supposed he shouldn't really complain about business, it was steady enough. But that was the trouble; it was too steady. Horse racing still took place on the Irish racetracks and he encouraged his customers to place their bets there, but many of them looked on Ireland as a foreign country: the Curragh and Leopardstown didn't have the same pull as Aintree and Haydock Park had had before the war. He was making decent money now, but it didn't satisfy his lust for more.

He yearned to be in with the big spenders: wealthy gambling men who had frequented the racetracks before the war put a stop to horse racing. One night he'd told Kitty about them, his blue eyes flashing with admiration as he urged her to be as ambitious for him as he was for himself. 'They own racehorses, and they wear suits that cost more than I earn in a month. They wager huge sums of cash as though there were no tomorrow and stroll about the tracks with glamorous women on their arms.' She'd spoiled it by saying, 'Ye sound awful envious, Tom.'

Now, as he envisaged those women his thoughts turned to Kitty, her shapely figure now swollen and distorted and her slender ankles as thick as a navvy's forearm. It pained him to look at her. Even the feel of her in bed had him moving to the edge of the mattress and feigning sleep when she caressed him. He didn't want to feel this way, he just couldn't help it. He forced a smile as he entered the kitchen.

Kitty crossed the room to greet him, her lips puckered to exchange a kiss. He pecked her cheek, stepping back quickly as her bulk brushed against his middle.

Tears stung her eyes. She bit down on her bottom lip to stem the tide. Over at the range she concentrated on dishing up the dinner. Tom hooked the toe of his boot under the rung of a chair and pulled it out from the table. He sat down heavily.

'Did ye have a good day?' Kitty set the plates on the table.

'So-so,' he replied, looking at her from under his eyes as she squeezed into the opposite chair. His lip curled.

'Ye don't seem too happy,' she said, taking a mouthful of stew. She swallowed. The hot stew hit her stomach and the baby gave a sharp kick. Kitty's hand flew to her belly. 'Ye'd think this babby wants to kick its way out,' she giggled, 'it's like a wee hallion—' She got no further.

'For God's sake, Kitty!' Tom roared. 'Do you ever listen to yourself? Whining on about the baby and talking like a woman from the bog – ye this and ye that. Say *you*, Kitty, if *you* want me to listen to *you*.'

Kitty blinked, her eyes widening and her jaw dropping as she stared at him. The stare became a glare. Warm hazel irises darkened, golden flecks glinting.

'Oh, so it's not just the way I look that pains *you*, Tom, it's the way I speak an' all,' she said, her tone dripping with sarcasm. 'I don't *just* offend your eyes. I offend your ears as well.' She took a deep breath. 'Well, let me tell ye this, Tom Conlon. I can't help the way I look but I'll talk how I bloody well please – an' I'll also tell ye this. Ye think that having your own business makes ye a gentleman but all it does is make ye a jumped-up, arse-licking, uncaring bastard.'

Her dinner forgotten, she stormed from the room and stamped upstairs. Fuming, she undressed and threw herself into bed. It was still early and she didn't think she would sleep, but anger mixed with hunger had tired her out. Gently running her hands over her bump she began saying her prayers, the ritual learned at her mother's knee having a hypnotic effect on her troubled soul and lulling her into sleep.

When she woke the next morning, Tom had already left the house.

21

'Hello, Kitty, I haven't seen you for some time. How are you?'

Kitty was still feeling bruised from Tom's rejection of her and the warmth in John Sykes's soft, brown eyes and the way they crinkled at the corners when he smiled at her made it all the more poignant. She gave a sad, little smile.

'Oh, hello, John – and in answer to your question – I'm just waiting for the day.' She patted her bump.

John's glance followed her hand to her distended belly. 'I take it you've given up working in munitions then.'

Kitty cheeks reddened. 'Aye. Ye'll not be called on to save me life again.' She gave a penitent, impish grin.

'Think nothing of it. I'd do it again. Anything for you, Kitty.' He eyed her fondly. 'You look positively blooming. Motherhood suits you.'

For some reason she couldn't pinpoint, Kitty was glad she was wearing her best, pale green linen maternity dress. *At least someone thinks I look nice*, she thought, but the pleasure was fleeting. The compliment reminded her of Tom's hurtful glances.

'Why, thank ye, John, it's kind of ye to say so,' she replied, fighting back tears. She mustn't start crying in front of this lovely, well-meaning man.

'Tom's a lucky fellow,' he said, at the same time thinking that Tom didn't know how lucky. He'd liked Tom when first they met, but of late he'd formed the opinion that pleasant company though he was, Tom Conlon thought only of himself. He'd heard nasty rumours about Tom's dealings on the gambling circuit.

He no longer trusted him.

'And what about yourself, John?' Kitty felt the need to prolong the pleasant conversation and take away the hurt she felt. 'Have ye been anywhere interesting or done anything exciting lately?'

John's face broke into a wide grin. 'As a matter of fact I have. I try to make the most of it when I'm on leave.'

Oh, so that's why she didn't see him very often, Kitty thought. He was in the services. She was about to ask whether he was in the army or the navy but John, keen to hold her attention, stole the opportunity.

'I saw a brilliant variety show in the Adelphi last week,' he continued, 'and a couple of days ago I was in Kirby at a fundraiser for the troops. That was fun. I was invited to help judge the events – you know – dog races, and prizes for the biggest or smallest, or best dressed dog. A poodle dressed as a ballet dancer won.' He laughed. 'You'd be surprised what I get up to.'

Kitty giggled. 'Ye do get about,' she said rather enviously, and anxious to know more about him she added, 'an' is there a lucky lady to share these outings with ye?'

John grinned ruefully. 'Not as yet. I'm waiting for the right girl to come along.' He gazed deeply into Kitty's hazel eyes, sorely tempted to tuck back a silky red-gold lock of hair that had escaped from under her straw boater. He shoved his hand in his trouser pocket.

'Well, when she does she'll be fortunate to have such a grand man as ye, John. I'm pleased I met ye because I was feeling down in the dumps, but you've cheered me up no end.'

'Glad to hear it,' said John, thinking that was the least he wanted to do.

Something in the way he was looking at her made Kitty realise he was reluctant to let her go, and the tiny flutter in her insides caused her to feel slightly uncomfortable.

'I'd best get to the bakery before they sell out,' Kitty blurted, and giving him the sweetest smile, she went on her way thinking what a lovely man he was. Just a kind friend, she reminded herself, but one who made her feel good.

Sadly, the feeling didn't last. Back in the house, the silence oppressive and her feet and legs aching, she once again felt the sting of Tom's rejection. She flopped into the armchair by the hearth and lifted her knitting. He'd never before criticised the way she spoke, but the more she thought about it, the more it made her aware of how he had taken to speaking just lately. At first she hadn't paid much heed to it, but now, mulling it over – and dropping stitches – she heard his voice inside her head. *He sounds like a posh Dubliner instead of a man from Clare. Ye'd hardly know he was an Irishman.*

The back door opened. Startled from her reverie, Kitty dropped a few more stitches. Leaving the spoiled knitting aside, she struggled to her feet.

'Here, you take her.' Maggie shoved little Lily Stubbs into Kitty's arms. 'She kept me awake all night,' she grumbled as she lit a cigarette.

Kitty wrinkled her nose. 'Pooh! When did ye last change her?'

'This morning after I fed her.' Maggie was clearly bursting to impart something of far more interest. 'Jack Naughton's just after tellin' me that the Russians murdered their royal family – all of 'em – him an' the wife an' all the kids, the evil buggers.'

'That's Tsar Nicholas an' his family,' Kitty said. 'I read about it in the paper not long after it happened.'

'Well, you didn't tell me.' Maggie was offended to think that her news was old news. 'Nobody tells me anything,' she moaned, taking a seat at the table.

'I had other things on my mind,' Kitty said, sitting back down with Lily on her lap. 'But it's terrible, isn't it? Why are people so cruel these days?'

'I suppose it's 'cos the poor Russians got fed up of having nothing and the what-you-called-him having all the money, but even so, it's downright wicked killing little kids that haven't done anythin' wrong. If anybody tried that with my Lily I'd kill 'em first.' Maggie widened her eyes. 'Do you think same thing could happen to our lot? They've got all them palaces and stuff.'

As Kitty listened to Maggie rattling on, she suddenly felt weary and sick of all the awful things that were happening in the world and in her own life. A dam burst inside her. 'Don't be so ridiculous,' she snapped, getting to her feet and shoving Lily back into her mother's arms. 'Here, take her home. She stinks.'

'But I just got here,' Maggie wailed. 'I thought you could get a bit of practice minding Lily while I had a cup of tea an' a bit of peace.'

'Well ye thought wrong, Maggie. I'm feeling absolutely rotten. An' whilst you're changing her nappy, change her dress. It's crusted in sour milk.' '

'That's because she keeps spewing,' Maggie retorted, jiggling Lily in her arms. 'Yours'll do the same, so don't be so bloody high an' mighty, you mardy-arsed cow.' She slammed out of the house. Kitty felt awful. She didn't want to fall out with Maggie but her nerves were raw and her head and her heart ached.

Sorely needing something to lighten her mood, she decided to go for a walk. She smoothed her green linen dress with her hands, the fact that her bump made it wrinkle only increasing her irritation. Her tawny hair was the only thing that was still lovely, she thought miserably, jamming on the straw boater then securing it with a hatpin.

She walked up the street, and when she reached the steps leading down to the riverbank she descended them carefully. The café's boarded-up windows did little to lighten her mood. Sadly, she recalled happier days. Gertie had sent her a postcard of Flamborough Head, the vast cliff bleak and forbidding, and Gertie's news no cheerier. She had no intention of returning to Liverpool and reopening the café. She'd wished Kitty well for the baby.

As Kitty gazed at the blue and white peeling paintwork the baby jiggled, and glancing down, she quite clearly saw the shape of a little foot pressing through the fabric of her dress. Her mouth formed the shape of an O but no sound came out. Holding her breath, she placed a gentle hand on the protrusion. The little foot wiggled then subsided. Her heart racing, Kitty walked as swiftly as she could back to Weaver Street. The walk had done nothing for her appearance, and she was aware that her cheeks were red and that perspiration lined her top lip, so she felt rather embarrassed when a young man standing at Dan Boothroyd's gate gave her a friendly smile and said hello.

Dan's house had stayed empty since his departure. Kitty and Maggie had speculated more than once as to who might come to live there. Now, Kitty returned the smile and hurried up her own path to the safety of her own home. The sight of the little foot had quite unnerved her and she felt an urgent need to sit down and dwell on the miracle that was growing inside her. Oh, but she'd love this baby with all her heart. She'd never let anyone or anything harm it. And in return it would love her. It wouldn't be offended by the way she looked or spoke. Their love would be unconditional.

She dozed and dreamed, but when she woke, she couldn't recall what the dream had been, only that it had left her feeling strangely calm and at peace. She stretched lazily, her peace shattered as Maggie bustled in with Lily in her arms. She dumped the baby on Kitty's lap.

'Nurse her for me an' let me have a fag.' She filched her Woodbines out of her apron pocket and lit up. 'It's a bugger when you don't even have time for a decent smoke,' she whined, flopping into the armchair.

Kitty told her about the little foot. 'It was perfectly shaped,' she said, 'I could see a little heel and the toes.' Her eyes were wide as she spoke.

'He must be fighting his way out – or she is. Though it seems like the sort of thing a lad would do,' Maggie said sagely.

'I don't care what it is as long as it comes soon.'

Next door, in number thirteen, Blair Forsythe was walking from room to room, imagining how they might look when he and Beth moved in. He hadn't told her he was coming to view the empty house, and he was still questioning the wisdom of living so near to her father, but he knew she wouldn't settle if she totally abandoned him.

He had written home to tell his parents he had met the most wonderful girl and was going to ask her to marry him. He'd not only received their blessing and hearty congratulation, but a nice sum of money from his paternal grandfather. *Here's your inheritance now; no point in waiting till I leave this mortal coil,* his grandfather's scribbled note had said. Blair had been overwhelmed. Now all he needed to do was ask for Beth's hand, and whether or not Walter Garside consented, he was fairly certain that Beth would accept his proposal.

Congratulating himself on how his plans were coming together, Blair went out by the back door and walked down the lane. Maggie saw him pass by Kitty's kitchen window. 'Who's that?' she said, craning her neck.

Kitty, at the sink filling the kettle, also saw him. 'He was just going into Dan's house when I came back from my walk,' she said. 'I don't know who he is, but I suppose he must be looking to buy it.'

The days dragged by, the sultry weather making Kitty lethargic. The baby was due any day now. Since Beth had introduced Kitty to reading novels, she spent long hours engrossed in books and when Tom came home one night, very late, she was sitting reading *A Room with a View*. She had already worked her way through *Zuleika Dobson*. Beth had told her what a brilliant story it was, and although the lives of both heroines were far removed from Kitty's own, she was intrigued by their romances; something that was sadly lacking for her.

Kitty's new interest in reading rather amused Tom. He had never thought of her as scholarly. She was, or had once been, his pretty, little Kitty with her head full of quaint ideas, a barrel of fun to be with. Now, looking at her puffy features and swollen body he was repulsed as Kitty struggled to her feet to greet him. Seeking to avoid the feel of her body against his own he backed away, flinching at the disloyal thoughts running through his mind as he made a show of divesting his jacket then hanging it in the hallway.

After Tom had eaten the spam and chips Kitty had made for

him, he sat at the hearth smoking. An uncomfortable silence reigned, neither of them willing to break it.

Kitty put aside her knitting. 'I'm going up to bed,' she murmured.

Tom nodded then lit another cigarette.

* * *

Rain was battering against the windowpanes when Kitty woke up. Instinctively, she knew that something had wakened her. Yesterday evening, the heat of the day had resulted in a thunderstorm, flashes of light and loud rumbles splitting the sky. Presuming it had returned, she closed her eyes ready to go back to sleep.

Then she felt it: a warm oozing sensation between her thighs that spread under her back and down to her knees. Her hands explored the bed sheet; it felt hot, and was soaking wet.

This is it, she thought, *it's started*. For a moment she lay perfectly still, listening to Tom's steady breathing and the downpour as it gurgled in the gutters. Then she felt a tightening in her womb and a cramping sensation that moved down to her inner thighs. Cautiously, Kitty rolled onto her side, the pain in her lower back increasing with every second. She felt a desperate need to go to the lavatory. As she attempted to sit up, a violent contraction almost lifted her off the bed.

'Tom! Tom!' She shook him furiously. 'Tom! The baby's coming.'

* * *

Upstairs, Renee Spivey and Dr Metcalfe were doing what they had so often done before. Down below in the sitting room, soaked to the skin, Tom was pacing the floor, lighting one cigarette off another. He could hear their feet cross the floor, the creak of the boards, and Kitty's cries piercing the night. He'd dashed through the pouring rain to the midwife's house at the top of Weaver Street, and then leaving her at his door he had raced along Broad Green to fetch Dr Metcalfe. Renee had told him it wasn't really necessary, but Tom's guilty feelings drove him on: he at least owed Kitty the very best attention he could afford.

He hadn't given any particular thought to the birth and now that he did his heart twisted with love and regret. An agonised scream had him clasping his hands to his ears, and he vowed to mend his ways. He would forget about the high life and devote himself to his wife and child from now on. He had once upon a time loved Kitty with a passion, he reminded himself, and he would again.

The screaming had stopped, and now a deathly hush hung above his head, a silence so deep that he felt paralysed. Then, as though from a great distance, he heard the sound of hurrying feet and the gush of water. The inside of his mouth felt thick and furry and his chest felt tight.

'You can come up now, Mr Conlon.'

Tom's heart jumped up into his throat at the sound of Dr Metcalfe's voice. He stubbed out his cigarette and mounted the stairs two at a time.

Renee met him on the landing. She was carrying a bloodstained bundle.

Tom paled. Was he being punished for his wickedness?

Kitty was floating in a dream-like state, the only reality the tiny warm body nestled against her breast. She gazed down at the little puckered face, mouth like a rosebud and oily black hair caressing a high forehead. This was her daughter, she marvelled, still finding it hard to believe she wasn't dreaming.

'You have a daughter, Mr Conlon.' Dr Metcalfe stuck out his

hand. Tom grasped it, more to keep himself upright than to receive congratulations.

Then he looked at Kitty. Her glorious hair fanned the pillow, damp red-gold tendrils scribbling her flushed cheeks. His heart swelled. How beautiful she looked. He tiptoed forward and peered at the baby in her arms.

22

Margaret Mary Conlon was a beautiful, placid baby. They had agreed to name her after her maternal and paternal grandmothers; had she been a boy she would have been called Patrick after her grandfathers. Her mother adored her and her father, apparently not in the least disappointed that she wasn't a son, seemed delighted with his little princess, as he called her. Kitty called her Molly.

The time-consuming chores of motherhood took Kitty by surprise. She had never realised how demanding a new baby could be, even one as sweet natured as Molly. 'I'm blessed that she's not like your Lily,' she told Maggie, for Lily seemed to do nothing but cry.

'Don't tell me,' Maggie snorted, 'I'm the one that has to listen to her morning, noon and night.' Maggie popped in frequently and whilst she would make a cup of tea for Kitty and herself she didn't offer any practical help.

May Walker, on the other hand, called in three times during the first week and while she was there she washed a few nappies and tidied the house. Kitty could have hugged her. Mavis also visited, bringing casseroles and pastries, and Jack dropped in once or twice with lettuce and tomatoes. Whenever Beth called, she brought books or the latest magazines insisting that Kitty put her feet up and read and that she, Beth, would see to Molly. She fussed over her like a child with a new doll, but Kitty didn't object: she enjoyed these brief respites.

Even so, she felt more tired than she thought it possible to be. Her breasts were tender and every time she went for a pee it stung and made her feel as though she was falling apart. Being responsible for keeping this precious little bundle alive and well, a bundle that felt so soft and malleable in her clumsy hands, was nothing like she had thought it would be. For the first few days and nights she barely slept – even when Molly was sleeping, Kitty stayed awake, watching the rise and fall of her tiny chest to make sure she was still breathing. And in between feeding and nursing and doing twice as much laundering, there were all the other household jobs to see to. Tom turned a blind eye to the chores, and nursed his daughter when it suited him.

'She's so tiny,' Kitty said one morning as she walked in on Tom in the bathroom. She'd barely slept, and she felt wretched.

'She'll grow,' Tom replied, more interested in shaving under his chin. Kitty stood there, Molly in her arms, and watched him slide the razor up over his jaw and cheeks in swift, sure strokes. Even with his face coated in lather he still managed to look attractive, whereas she felt like a crumpled bag of rags. *And I probably look like one too*, she thought miserably, pulling at the front of her milk-stained dressing gown. The smell of regurgitated milk hit her nose.

What Kitty desperately wanted was for Tom to take her in his arms and tell her she was doing a wonderful job, or even offer to lend a hand now and then and show some interest in and responsibility for their daughter. But Tom seemed oblivious.

His face cleanly shaven, he pushed past her and went into the bedroom to dress. Feeling bereft of any support, Kitty went down to the kitchen and put Molly in her pram. She put two rashers of bacon into the frying pan on the stove then hurried out to the clothesline to peg a basket full of baby clothes that she'd washed the night before. It was a warm, sunny morning and she was glad of it; the clothes would dry in no time. It had rained on and off for the past weeks, and Kitty preferred to dry her washing in the clean, fresh air rather than on the clotheshorse round the fire.

Fluffy white clouds hovered above the sycamore trees in the allotments. Kitty gazed into the distance, the sunshine making her feel invigorated. She decided it was a pleasant day for a walk. The pouring rain had kept Molly indoors and this concerned Kitty. She had a vague memory of newly born babies in Roscommon spending most of the day out in God's good air.

Tom was sitting at the table reading the *Sporting Times* when Kitty went back inside. 'Are ye studying form for today's bets?' she asked brightly. Tom merely nodded. *So much for conversation,* she thought irritably as she lifted the sizzling bacon from the pan then set the plate in front of him.

She stayed standing to eat her own sandwich and drink a cup of tea, then whilst Tom was eating and reading, she dressed Molly in a pink dress and cardigan. Molly Conlon at six weeks old had a larger wardrobe than her mother had ever owned in her entire life, most of it knitted by Kitty or Mavis.

As Kitty pushed little arms and legs that felt as though they might break at any moment into sleeves and socks, Molly gripped her finger. Kitty looked down at the tiny hand with its perfectly formed pink and white nails. Molly's grip tightened and Kitty felt her heart almost explode with love. It was moments like these that made all the effort seem worthwhile, and she hugged and kissed her daughter: she wouldn't be without her for the world. The love she felt for Molly was like no other. Suddenly, Kitty felt brave and strong, and no matter how difficult things were, she knew she was capable of dealing with them.

'I'm going to take Molly for a walk whilst the sun's shining,' she announced, putting Molly into the pram that filled an entire corner of the kitchen. She went into the hallway and pinned on her hat. Shortly after the birth she'd had her long locks cut into a fashionable bob that reached just below her chin and the green band on her boater enhanced the colour of her hair and her creamy complexion.

'Hold on and I'll come with ye,' said Tom, folding the paper then slipping it into the pocket of his overcoat that he'd left hanging on a chair back. Startled, Kitty fumbled with the sleeves of the white cardigan she was putting on over a new green and white striped blouse she'd ran up for when she lost her excess weight. It fitted neatly with her long, narrow grey skirt.

When she walked back into the kitchen Tom gave her an admiring smile, and she knew that it pleased him now that she had almost regained her trim figure. As she tied a pretty pink and white cotton bonnet under Molly's chin, Kitty recalled the time when he could barely look at her, let alone touch her. She remembered the nights when he had kept to the edge of the bed, flinching if her swollen body connected with his. She watched him thoughtfully as he slipped his black jacket over the crisp, white shirt she had ironed late last night, her back aching with weariness and she longing for her bed. When he put on his overcoat and trilby hat she thought how dashing he looked. *It's all right for you, Tom Conlon. You'll never lose your figure unless you eat too much.*

Tom drew the line at pushing the pram and walked alongside, proudly accepting the compliments of his customers that they happened to meet as they paused to admire his daughter and the pram. Tom had insisted on buying a Silver Cross pram: nothing but the best for his little princess. Four large, sprung wheels supported a gleaming white body and navy blue hood. Shiny chrome fixtures winked and glinted in the sunlight. The first time Kitty and Maggie had taken their daughters out together, Kitty had felt rather embarrassed as she pushed it alongside Maggie's second-hand pram with its little wheels and scuffed black canvas covering. She'd have preferred something far less showy, and thought it an extravagant waste, but Tom had told her the business was doing well and that they could afford it.

They walked round the Botanic Gardens and then back to the Weaver's Arms.

Tom went inside, leaving Kitty to take Molly back home. Kitty had been touched by his offer to accompany them, as much as she had welcomed his smiles and kisses now that she looked like 'his Kitty' again. However, she couldn't suppress a niggling irritation. She thought he should love her no matter what, just as she would love him even if he went bald or developed a paunch.

She hadn't been at home long when Maggie trailed in with Lily grizzling in her arms. 'She's been like this all morning an' I'm fed up to the back teeth of her,' she moaned, shifting Lily from one hip to the other.

'Give her here.' Kitty held out her arms. Molly was asleep in her pram after her walk in the fresh air. Maggie passed Lily over then searched her pockets for her Woodbines. She lit up and sat down at the table, puffing contentedly.

Kitty set Lily down on her feet, and holding both of her hands, she began walking backwards slowly across the floor. At just turned one, Lily was taking her first steps. Kitty let go and Lily wobbled then tottered back into Kitty's arms. 'Good girl, Lily,' Kitty praised. 'Did ye see that, Maggie?'

'Yeah, she's been doing that a lot this past couple of days,' Maggie said, her face flushed with pride. 'She's gonna be a quick learner like me.' She held out her hands to Lily. 'Come to your ma, love.' Lily did so, her mother scooping her up and smothering her face in kisses.

Kitty laughed. 'I can never make ye out, Maggie Stubbs. Ye do nothin' but complain about her yet ye love her to bits.'

''Course I do,' Maggie hooted. 'I just like complaining. That way you get folks to listen to you.' She jiggled Lily on her knee, making her laugh. 'Eh! Guess what. Ronnie Walker's gone an' joined up. May's in bits.'

'Oh, poor May,' Kitty gasped. 'I'm sure she is after what happened to her Sammy. It near broke her heart.'

'Yeah. It was dead rotten him being killed like that.'

'Ronnie's only just had his sixteenth birthday,' Kitty commented. 'I would have thought he'd have waited until they called him up instead of rushing into it. He's too young to put himself in danger.'

'He told me he's doing it to get his own back on the Germans for what they did to their Sammy.'

'It'll take a lot more than Ronnie Walker before we get our own back, Maggie,' Kitty said dismally. 'Though they do say that this new offensive that all the allies are in on has pushed the Germans to the limits. Jack Naughton says he thinks it could be over before the end of the year.'

'Hoo-bloody-ray to that,' Maggie cheered.

'Aye, it can't come soon enough,' Kitty agreed. 'All that loss of life an' men away from their families for years on end.'

'I'm surprised they've never sent your Tom back to his ship.'

Kitty flinched. 'They say he's not fit for duty,' she muttered, feeling as though she was telling a lie.

'He looks fit enough to me.' Maggie gave a naughty wink. 'Still, you wouldn't want 'em to take him back, would you?'

'Indeed I would not! He's done his bit an' near lost his life doing it,'

Kitty said defensively, at the same time suppressing the urge to confide in Maggie and air her suspicions that his not being returned to duty was in some way connected to his odd behaviour. 'Have ye heard from Fred lately?' she asked, keen to deflect the conversation away from Tom.

'He's still somewhere in England driving that captain up and down, and he's still making threats about Lily's red hair and what he'll do if he finds out I've been unfaithful.' Maggie didn't sound too concerned.

'Well, if ye hadn't been, ye'd have nothing to worry about would ye?'

Maggie burst out laughing. 'You know what? You're a right cheeky bitch when you want to be even though you're me best mate.' Still laughing, she lifted Lily and went back to her own house.

Molly wakened and gurgled sweetly. Kitty lifted her from the pram, and back in the armchair she unbuttoned her blouse. Molly sucked ravenously, the soft slurp music to Kitty's ears. At times like these, her worry over Tom came second place to her love for her daughter.

* * *

Summer dwindled into autumn. The flowers in Kitty's back garden withered and clumps of burnished leaves blown from the sycamores in the allotment took their place. The world was changing – and fast. So was the war in Europe. The allies were winning, and the Germans on the run.

'The German navy have mutinied,' Kitty told Tom, one morning at the start of November. 'They're refusing to go to sea.'

'Can't say I blame them. I'd do the same,' was Tom's laconic reply.

But Kitty was excited. During the next few days she avidly followed the news.

'The German army's retreating,' she said to Maggie. 'They've run out of food an' weapons. It'll not be long afore it's all over.'

'I'll not hold me breath,' Maggie said cynically, but when she and Kitty went shopping the words on everyone's lips were that the war would soon be over. So, like the rest of the world, the two friends held their breaths and waited. Less than a week later, Kaiser Wilhelm was forced to abdicate.

The eleventh of November started with mizzling rain, but by eleven o'clock a watery sun was breaking through. Come midday, Kitty was pushing Molly in her pram along Broad Green when she heard the news. Jim Broadhead from the hardware store came rushing out to the pavement.

'The war's over!' he shouted at the top of his lungs. 'I've just heard it on me wireless. They've declared peace.'

Kitty raced back home to share the news with Maggie.

The war was over. Then the celebrations began. Like every street in Liverpool, Weaver Street came alive with bunting and flags. Kitty, Maggie and Mavis organised a street party: eating, singing and dancing into the early hours. May Walker, still numb from the loss of her beloved son, Sammy, couldn't bring herself to join in, but for everyone else it was their way of shedding the trappings of war that, for so many, had become a way of life.

On Armistice night Kitty stood with Tom, watching Maggie lead a conga line up and down the back lane. Fred, being a regular, had yet to come home, and Maggie was making the most of his absence. Although Tom's arm was round her shoulders, Kitty couldn't help sensing that he'd rather be somewhere else. Her heart ached at the thought of it.

23

Kitty propped the little Christmas tree on the pram's apron, careful to ensure the branches weren't invading Molly's space. She was tucked under the waterproof cover, well wrapped up against any lingering flu germs and the chill December wind gusting down the alleyways in the market. Canvas awnings slapped and creaked as last minute shoppers searched the stalls for Christmas Eve bargains. Kitty, not in the best of tempers, was tempted to use the pram as a battering ram as she dodged through the crowds. She was grieved that Tom had refused to accompany her.

'But it's Molly's first Christmas,' she'd pleaded. 'We have to trim the house for her.'

'Molly doesn't know it's Christmas, Kitty, she's barely four months old,' he had replied, his face closed and his thoughts else-where. He had met her suggestion to hold a party with the same dismissive attitude. 'It isn't up to you to entertain the entire street,' he had said, 'and it isn't sensible with a young child in the house.'

However, Kitty was partly ignoring his lack of Christmas spirit.

On her way home from the market she caught up with May Walker, also making her way back to Weaver Street.

'I see somebody's going to deck the halls,' May remarked, nodding at the tree. 'I'll not be celebrating. I can't bring meself to do anything like that since our Sammy was killed.' She drew a sharp breath as if in pain. 'And what with our Ronnie still somewhere in Italy, I'll leave it up to other folks to make merry.'

'Aye, but they're repatriating them as quick as they can. With a bit of luck you might have him home for New Year.'

'You could be right, lass,' May agreed, sounding a bit cheerier. 'Are you having a party?'

'Not this time,' Kitty said, and found herself giving Tom's reason as an excuse.

'It's maybe as well,' said May, 'You don't want a crowd of people in the house with a new baby. You just need the three of you to be happy.'

Kitty clenched her teeth, not at all happy. She was sad for May, and poor dead Sammy, but she was more annoyed with herself for bending to Tom's will. *What's got into me?* she asked herself. *Getting pregnant and having a baby must have softened my wits. What's become of the girl who, once upon a time, wouldn't have let anyone dictate to her?*

By now, they had arrived at May's house. 'Ye must drop in for a cuppa over Christmas if ye feel up to it, May,' Kitty offered, knowing full well that May wouldn't accept the invitation. She rarely neighboured with anyone these days.

'Ta, love. You have a merry Christmas with your hubby and that lovely little lass of yours.' May trudged up the path to her door and Kitty went up the lane.

On an impulse she walked up to Maggie's door, and lifting Molly out of her pram, she knocked and went in. She didn't drop in often because there was little pleasure in sitting in the messy kitchen in a fug of cigarette smoke and the smell of yesterday's chips. She far preferred Maggie to come to hers. There was no sign of Christmas in Vi's house, just the usual clutter of unwashed dishes and chairs strewn with cast-off clothes.

'She's in the front room,' Vi said, waving her cigarette without stirring from her chair by the fire. 'She has to finish a piece before the lorry comes to collect it.'

Vi was still in her dressing gown, her hair in curlers that made her head look like a spiky, metal helmet. Kitty noticed how haggard she looked without the layers of make-up she'd thicken on before going off to serve behind the bar in the Wagon and Horses. She hid a smile and wondered what the customers would think if they saw Vi without her war paint.

Kitty carried Molly into the front room. Maggie was bent over a long piece of cloth stretched over the mending frame and Lily was sitting in her pram, chewing on an old magazine. 'Take that out of your mouth, Lily, it's dirty,' Kitty cried.

'It's keepin' her quiet,' Maggie grunted without looking up from the frame.

'It's making her as black as the ace of spades,' said Kitty, removing a wad of chewed-up paper from Lily's hands. 'She's covered in ink.'

'She'll have to stay that way till I get this finished.' Maggie deftly snipped a knot from the fabric then inserted her needle and mended the flaw. Kitty went and peered over Maggie's shoulder. Several bright yellow chalk marks indicated where the worsted was flawed.

'Do you have to get all them done today?'

'If I don't go blind in the attempt,' Maggie retorted. 'I've got to get it done or I'll not get me Christmas bonus. And listening to her's not helping.' Deprived of the paper, Lily had started to wail.

'Where's Fred?' Kitty asked, thinking that he should be helping mind Lily.

'Out boozing,' Maggie sneered. 'I thought when he came back

he'd have some brass and we'd be all right for Christmas, but he says he's skint.'

'He can't be that hard-up if he can buy drink.'

'You don't have to tell me that,' Maggie cried, 'but look, Kitty, I have to get on with this.' She bent over the frame.

'I'll take Lily round to mine,' Kitty said, hearing the desperation in Maggie's voice and thinking how lucky she herself was; Tom's business was flourishing and he was more than generous with the housekeeping money. *Here's poor Maggie, working against the clock to make a living, when I've no money worries and no jobs that need urgent attention.* 'I'll just nip an' put Molly in her pram then I'll be back for Lily.'

'You're a godsend,' Maggie cried, as Kitty came back and lifted Lily.

'Give us a shout when you want her back.'

'When she's fourteen.'

* * *

Kitty covered a stout cardboard box with red crepe paper and set it in a corner of the kitchen. She placed the little tree on top then decorated it with sparkling baubles and tinsel. There was little point in putting the tree in the front room; they rarely sat in there, and if they weren't having a party then she and Molly would be the only ones to admire it. Topping the tree with a white crepe paper angel she lifted Molly from her pram then sat down on her knees with Molly on her lap. 'Look at the pretty baubles, Molly.' She pointed at each one. 'Red, blue, green and gold... and an angel to watch over us.'

Molly stared, but her placid expression didn't light up and Kitty felt somewhat cheated. *Never mind, next Christmas will be different*, she consoled herself. She did, however, feel better about having helped Maggie out; that's what Christmas was all about, goodwill to all men and all that. Maggie had been cock-a-hoop when she came to collect Lily. She'd finished her piece, got her money and was going for a night out to the pub with the girls from the mill. Flo's younger sister was babysitting Lily in her own house, leaving Maggie as free as a bird. Kitty envied her. She'd even felt jealous when Maggie had told her that she and Vi were going to Vi's sister for their Christmas Day dinner. 'There'll be a houseful. It'll be a right drunken do,' Maggie had said. Kitty formed a mental image of her and Tom in their house and thought: *What fun will that be?*

It was past midnight when Tom came home. Kitty was in bed. As he climbed in beside her she smelled the reek of whiskey on his breath. He reached for her, but feigning sleep, she didn't respond. He continued to paw her, and she turned on him angrily. 'Leave me alone, Tom Conlon. I'm not your puppet,' she snapped. When he tried to roll her over she cried, 'I said leave me alone!' Then, laughing bitterly, she added, 'But that's foolish of me because ye do, don't ye, Tom?'

* * *

Tom stayed home on Christmas Day but the house was fraught with tension. He was restless and bored, but Kitty pretended not to notice as she made a great show of giving Molly her gifts.

'Look what Father Christmas brought ye, Molly,' she cooed, holding out a soft teddy bear. Molly grasped an arm and put it to her mouth, Kitty crying, 'No! No! Ye don't eat him.' Molly rested her chin on the bear's head, her bright blue eyes so like her father's staring fixedly as Kitty waved the rattle from Maggie then pressed the squeaking ball Beth had bought.

'Oh, for jaysus sake, leave her be. Those things mean nothing to her,' Tom barked. He had been imagining what it would be like to celebrate Christmas with the wealthy punters he met at the race-tracks. He paced to the window, gazing out as though he longed to escape.

'Of course they mean something, Tom. That's how babies learn what things are.' Kitty's hot-tempered response caused Molly to screw up her face and wail. Kitty felt like crying too. For the rest of the day she and Tom barely exchanged a word, Kitty relieved when bedtime came, so they could get the miserable day over and done with.

On Boxing Day, Kitty had been up and about with Molly for more than two hours before Tom came downstairs. He lifted Molly from her pram and danced around the kitchen with her in his arms. Kitty smiled as she stirred the porridge. He was in a better mood. Maybe they could spend a happy day together.

'I'm going off for the day,' Tom announced over breakfast. 'There's racing at Aintree. Don't wait up for me.'

Kitty didn't know whether to cry or cheer. She decided on the latter, glad to see the back of him. 'Aye, off ye go an' enjoy yourself,' she said brightly.

He went upstairs, and when he came back down dressed in his good black suit she couldn't help thinking how handsome he looked. He was smiling, but she knew the smile wasn't meant for her, or Molly. He leaned into the pram and plopped a kiss on Molly's cheek. 'Be a good girl for your mammy,' he said, before turning and kissing Kitty full on the mouth. She breathed in the smell of his cologne, sad that the kiss was his way of thanking her for not raising any objections, and not because he would miss her whilst he was away.

In the early afternoon Maggie knocked the door, hopeful that Kitty would answer it and not Tom. When Kitty opened the door, Maggie whispered, 'Is he in?' Kitty beckoned her inside. They both knew that had he been there he would have objected to Maggie calling.

'He's gone to Aintree, or so he says,' Kitty said sourly, 'an' to be honest I don't know whether I'm mad or glad. Sometimes I think I'd be happier living on me own. At least I'd know where I stood.'

'Me an' all,' Maggie moaned. 'Fred's lying flat out on the couch. He hasn't been sober since Christmas Eve. At least your Tom's not raving drunk all the time, he's just a selfish bastard.'

'Yes, he is,' Kitty agreed fervently, 'an' do ye know something? It's taken me this long to realise that. He's like a wee boy wanting all his own way an' to hell with everybody else. I used to think he was the kindest, gentlest soul on earth but I've had my eyes opened this last while back, and let me tell ye this, I'll be making some serious changes come this next year. I've got me head screwed back on like it used to be.'

Maggie gasped. 'You're not thinking of leaving him are you?'

'God no! Why would I leave all this? It's my home, an' me friends are here. But from now on ye'll not find me dancing attendance on Mr Tom Conlon.' Kitty's hazel eyes flashed defiantly. 'I'll be putting me an' Molly first, see if I don't.'

24

Beth was walking briskly down the back lane as Kitty was hurrying up it. Kitty had been to the tobacconist's shop on Broad Green, and was seething at her own weakness for having run the errand when she should have put her foot down and told Tom to go and fetch his own cigarettes. *So much for my brave words on Boxing Day,* she fumed, shivering in the icy gusts nipping at her nose and ankles. He had come in from work, and giving her his most charming smile, he'd said, 'Off ye go and get me a packet of Player's while I have a cuddle with my princess.' He'd taken off his coat, and without thinking for one moment that Kitty would refuse he'd lifted Molly from her pram. 'An' like a fool I fell for it,' she hissed, her breath clouding and evaporating in the cold air and Kitty thinking how much better things would be if she could make her problems disappear as quickly.

'Hello, Kitty,' Beth said. 'It's freezing, isn't it?'

'It is, but we can't expect anything else in January, can we?' Kitty pulled her scarf closer round her head.

It had just turned seven o'clock and the wind was funnelling down the lane, the sky black and threatening rain. 'Where are ye off to?' Kitty asked, curious as to why anyone would want to be out on a cold, dark night like this.

'I'm meeting Blair.' Instead of seeming happy, Beth looked and sounded rather miserable. 'This weather's not kind to courting couples like us,' she said, giving a helpless shrug. 'We can't go to the cinema *every* night or sit in a café drinking endless cups of tea so I'm meeting him in the Botanic Gardens. We'll probably freeze to death or—' she glanced up at the angry sky '—get soaked through.' She giggled to take the sting out of her words, but Kitty could tell she wasn't relishing walking round the park even though she'd be with the man she loved.

Kitty's kind heart went out to her. 'Ye can sit in my front room if you like. Tom and me always sit in the kitchen. The fire's set, ye'll just have to put a match to it. It'll be preferable to catching pneumonia in the gardens.'

'Could we?' Beth gasped. 'You don't mind if I bring him back to your house?'

'If I did, I wouldn't have offered,' Kitty said warmly.

'That's awfully kind of you. I should be able to take him to my own house but Dad would go spare. He hates the idea of me going out with Blair. And Blair's landlady doesn't allow her lodgers to take anyone in, well, certainly not women.'

'Go an' meet him an' bring him back. Come to the front door an' I'll let ye in.'

Kitty ran on, shivering from having stood too long in the cold.

'You took your time,' Tom said, handing Molly to her and taking the cigarettes in one easy move.

'A "thank you" wouldn't go amiss,' Kitty said tersely, nuzzling her lips into Molly's sweet-smelling neck to calm her anger.

A short while later the knock came at the front door. Kitty jumped up and ran to answer it. Beth and Blair looked rather embarrassed as Kitty ushered them in but she immediately put them at their ease. 'The room's all yours. Just put a match to the fire,' she said, opening the sitting room door then leaving them to it.

'Who was that?' Tom asked. She told him. He widened his eyes. 'Really, Kitty! What next? Now you're turning my home into a refuge for waifs and strays.'

'It's my home as well,' she snapped. 'An' Beth an' Blair are not waifs and strays. They're a young couple madly in love that have nowhere else to go. I'm just helping them out. Don't be so unfeeling, Tom.'

She fed and changed Molly and put her down to sleep in the pram. Then, as Tom sat sulking and ignoring her attempts to make conversation, Kitty washed the dishes and attended to a dozen small jobs before sitting down to knit.

An hour or so later there was a gentle tap on the kitchen door. Tom raised his eyebrows. 'They're no doubt looking for tea and biscuits,' he said sarcastically.

Kitty tossed her head and went to open the door into the hallway. Beth's face was wreathed in smiles, her eyes dancing. She beckoned for Kitty to step into the hall out of Tom's hearing. 'Blair's asked me to marry him,' she gushed, 'and guess what? We're going to live next door in Dan's house. I'll tell you all about it tomorrow.' She sounded like a little girl whose birthdays had all come at once.

Kitty offered her congratulations, Blair thanking her profusely as she let them out into the cold night air. Standing in the hallway, thinking about life and the way in which it made unexpected changes to the most perfect situations, she prayed that their happiness would last.

'Beth and Blair are getting married,' she said when she went back into the kitchen. 'He's just after proposing to her.'

'Ah, so, 'tis a matchmaker ye are now,' Tom said, sneeringly exaggerating his Irish accent. 'It seems there's no end to your talents.' He got to his feet. 'I'm away to bed. Don't be long now.'

A short while later, Kitty climbed the stairs, cradling her sleeping daughter in her arms. She placed Molly in the crib at the side of the bed and then, stealthily undressing, she slipped into bed beside Tom. He turned, pulling her into his arms and burying his face into her hair. He felt the pulse in her neck like a captive bird fluttering and flapping, and the urge to make swift, passionate love to her had him covering her body with his own. Exhausted though she was, Kitty moved with him until they both climaxed in a flurry of tangled limbs, hot kisses and cries of delight, but for all she enjoyed their lovemaking she couldn't prevent herself from thinking that relenting to his demands was another sign of her weakness. *Although he thinks me foolish at times and treats me with cold disdain he must still love me*, she thought sleepily.

Kitty was dreaming. She was back in Ireland, on Howth Head, the sun high in the sky and the sea below a calm, glassy blue. The tall, darkly handsome man at her side was about to tell her something of great importance and she turned to face him eagerly. But instead of seeing Tom's face as she had expected, she was looking up into the face of her brother, Shaun. He was crying, tears coursing his swarthy cheeks, but his cries were not those of a man but a wailing baby.

Shocked, Kitty wakened instantly. A sharp elbow was nudging her ribs.

'Your baby's crying,' Tom mumbled, nudging her again.

Kitty's thoughts tumbled and clashed inside her head, fear mixing with anger. Why did Tom have to say 'your baby' when Molly was his just as much as she was hers? Not once in the six months since she had been born had he taken a turn at comforting her when she wakened in the night. She climbed out of bed,

Shaun's sad face still printed on her eyeballs as she tottered across the room and lit the gas mantle. It plopped into life, too bright, and she turned it down low, its eerie glow casting grim shadows that made Kitty puzzle all the more as to why she had dreamed of her brother. The last time had been at Christmas, when she was feeling sad at not being able to send him a gift or a card. Was the dream his way of sending her a message? Was he in danger? She shuddered at the thought.

Molly's wails bringing her back to the present, Kitty lifted her from the crib. The bedroom plunged into sudden silence. Seated on the nursing chair by the window, Kitty unbuttoned her nightdress and Molly latched on to her nipple. Tired though she was, Kitty relished these moments in the wee, small hours, listening to her baby's snuffling breath and feeling the heat from her tiny body warming her own cold fingers. She propped Molly up to her shoulder. Molly nuzzled her lips into Kitty's neck, breathing damply in her ear, and as Kitty cuddled her daughter she thought about Beth, and then about her own marriage. Tom had changed; she had no doubts about that. There had been a time when she firmly believed that she meant the world to him, that their life together raising a family, having a comfortable home and a profitable business would be enough for him. But now she sensed that he craved something else. Try as she might, she couldn't figure out what more he could want, but deep in her heart she knew that the life they shared no longer satisfied his needs. *And if I'm being perfectly honest, it no longer satisfies mine,* she told herself. *I need to make somethin' of meself, be my own person and do somethin' more than just being Tom's wife.*

'Men are strange creatures, Molly,' she whispered into her daughter's hair. 'I didn't know your daddy too well when I married him, and after all this time I still don't understand him.' She put the sleeping baby into her crib and then back in bed she lay with her eyes open, puzzling as to why she should feel so desolate.

* * *

The next afternoon, Beth was bubbling with excitement as she entered Kitty's kitchen. Kitty's eyes sparkled with affection and curiosity. 'Come, sit ye down an' tell me all about it.'

'I'm still finding it hard to believe,' Beth gasped, and then breathily continued, 'I knew the moment I met Blair that we were meant for each other, but I didn't dare to think that anything could come of it, what with my dad being the way he is. I could scarcely believe what I was hearing when Blair told me that he had spoken with Joseph Holroyd about my father's unreasonable attitude. Wasn't that extremely brave of him?'

As Beth talked, Kitty thought it was like listening to a fairy tale where the benighted lovers seek the help of the good fairy to overcome the wicked king, although Joseph Holroyd was hardly a fairy godmother and Walter Garside certainly wasn't a king. 'An what did Mr Holroyd say?' she asked out loud.

'He laughed. He said that Dad had always been an old curmudgeon, and that whilst he was good at his job he was never happy unless he was making somebody else miserable.' Beth paused for breath and grimaced. 'He obviously knows him well.'

'An' what was that about ye coming to live next door?' Kitty asked.

'Blair's bought the house with money his grandfather gave him. We'll move in as soon as we're married. Isn't that just marvellous?'

'I'll love having ye for a neighbour,' Kitty paused, 'but isn't it a bit near to your dad? Are ye not afraid he'll come causing trouble?'

Beth shook her head. 'I did at first, and then I realised how handy it would be. I'll be near enough to pop in and make him his meals and clean the house. He won't have time to miss me.' She seemed so happy with this solution that Kitty couldn't find it in her heart to disillusion her.

'When's the wedding then?' she said enthusiastically.

'Easter. Blair wants us to redecorate every room before we move in, and April's a lovely month for a wedding. I wouldn't want to get married on a cold, miserable day. I want the sun to be shining and the birds to be singing.' Beth's eyes gleamed with the wonder of it all.

'An' long may the sun shine on the both of ye,' Kitty said warmly.

* * *

'I can't see Walter Garside letting her go that easy,' Maggie said dourly as she sat down, dandling Lily on her knee as Kitty told her Beth's news. 'He'll never be off her bloody doorstep ranting and raving that she's not doing enough for him. If I were her I'd move to the moon.'

'Ah, but you're not Beth. She has a kind heart,' Kitty mocked, 'an' bad an' all as her dad is, she still feels for him.' She put Molly in the pram and then put on the kettle. 'I think she'd be crippled with guilt if she left him to fend for himself. She's taken her mother's place for so long that she can't let go.'

Maggie snorted. 'Me mam says Walter drove Alice Garside to an early grave he was that horrible to her. He didn't allow her to go any further than the shops on Broad Green, an' he threw a fit if he found out she'd been neighbouring. Me mam says she died in self-defence.'

'The poor woman – an' poor Beth,' Kitty said, pouring boiling water over the leaves in the teapot. 'Maybe Blair'll be fit for him an' tell him where to get off.' She took two mugs from the cupboard.

'I'll look forward to the ructions.' Maggie's tone dripped sarcasm as, getting to her feet, she set Lily on the hearthrug. Back at the table she sat down and lit a cigarette. 'I've had a letter from

Fred. He's coming home for good at the end of the week.' She didn't sound remotely thrilled at the prospect. 'He's done his nine years an' he can choose to come out if he wants.'

'Nine years is a long time,' Kitty said, thinking of Shaun. How many years had the British Government sentenced him to, and how long would it be before she saw him again if she ever did, she pondered, gazing into space and distractedly sipping her tea.

'Penny for 'em,' Maggie said, puffing out a stream of smoke and making Kitty jump. 'What were you thinking of? You were miles away.'

'Oh nothing,' Kitty said, flustered. 'I was... I was... just wondering what Fred'll do now he's home for good. What did he work at before he joined the army?'

'Nuthin'. He was only sixteen. He's never had a proper job so God knows what he's capable of. He's a useless bugger at best.'

'Well, at least Lily will have her daddy.' Kitty clapped a hand over her mouth when she realised what she'd said.

'Don't you be saying anything,' Maggie said darkly. 'He thinks she's his an' I'm letting him.' She lit another cigarette. 'I wonder if anybody in his family had ginger hair. Nobody in ours did, as far as I know.'

'Lots of people have ginger hair. An' Lily's hair is more auburn than ginger. Ye'd not call her a carrot top,' Kitty said, in order to make amends.

Her remark seemed to please Maggie, and they went back to talking about Beth's forthcoming wedding.

* * *

As Kitty stepped out of her back door to put rubbish in the dustbin, she was slightly alarmed to hear angry voices outside number thirteen. Curious as to what was going on she dawdled over the task.

Walter Garside and Blair Forsythe were arguing heatedly. Blair stood tall and straight, his grey eyes glinting like steel behind his glasses.

Walter was the first to drop his gaze. 'I'll do no such thing,' he growled, taking a step back. 'I'll not give permission for her to marry someone she knows nowt about.'

'Beth does know me, sir, and I'm only asking you for her hand as a matter of courtesy,' Blair said calmly. 'We'll marry with or without your permission.'

Kitty cheered inwardly.

'I'll have you run out of town, back to where you came from,' Walter blustered. 'She'll not want you when you've no job – and I can soon arrange that.'

Blair smiled at Walter's threat. 'I've already spoken with Mr Holroyd about my intentions to marry Beth, and he gave us his blessing.'

Walter paled. 'What do you mean spoken with—'

Blair didn't let him finish. 'I told him I thought you might try to cause trouble for me so I took preventative measures, Mr Garside. As I've already said, nothing will stop me marrying Beth.'

Walter, lost for words, spun on his heels and marched out of the garden and down the lane.

'Good on ye, Blair,' Kitty called out, waving the brush triumphantly.

Blair gave her a wide grin and made the thumbs up sign.

25

Kitty could barely conceal a satisfied smirk as she watched Tom plunge his hand inside one of his best, black boots, a grim smile hovering on his lips as he vigorously swept the blacking brush to and fro over its upper. Kitty had caught him by surprise. When he'd asked if she had cleaned his boots, Kitty had told him firmly where he could find the brushes and the polish. For some time now she no longer waited on him hand and foot, but his stubbornness wouldn't allow him to let her see that it bothered him, although on one occasion he had accused her of being childish. Childish or not, Kitty was sticking to her resolution.

Still smiling, she ran hot water into the washing up bowl, feeling not in the least guilty at making him do a job that she had always done. *He comes and goes as he pleases, forever expecting me to be on hand to attend to his needs, and shows little respect for mine,* she told herself as she clattered plates into the bowl. At first, it had pained her to take this stance and she dearly wished they could go back to the way things used to be, but if this marriage was to be an equal partnership then Tom had to stop treating her like a servant.

She blamed Tom's job for the way things were, but deep inside she knew there was more to it than that. He could, if he wanted, spend far more time with her and Molly rather than the hours he spent in the Weaver's Arms sitting with his cronies long after the betting shop closed. Or like today, he'd be gone until late, swanking around Aintree like the big I am, she thought bitterly. She wasn't sure how much longer she could sustain this line of resistance – it certainly wasn't having the desired effect – but if she was to keep the promise she had made at the beginning of the year then she had to persist; things had to change.

Of course, not all days were as fraught as this one was turning out to be. For much of the time nothing seemed to have changed. Tom was never blatantly unkind. He paid attention to Molly when it pleased him and he regularly made love to Kitty, but for all that, there was still an undercurrent of discontent that cast a shadow over their lives.

Tom laced his boots, and crossing the kitchen, he reached round Kitty at the sink and washed his hands in the bowl of soapy water. She automatically leaned back into his embrace and he kissed the nape of her neck before turning her round. She felt his wet hands soaking through her blouse, and as he kissed her lips she wanted to cry for all that they had lost.

'I'll be off then,' he said, striding into the hallway for his overcoat. 'It's a big day today. It's the Grand National. One of the big-time owners, Nigel Hutchinson, has invited me to share his box. Wish me luck.' The front door slammed behind him.

Kitty finished her chores and then went upstairs. It was a bright, breezy day and the sun was shining, the month of March having come in like a lion and now settling to go out like a lamb.

Feeling in need of cheering up, she put on her new dress with a pleated skirt and over it a knitted jacket she had made herself, the green dress enhancing the colour of her eyes and the cream jacket highlighting her tawny hair. She posed in the mirror, pleased with what she saw, her pleasure fading when she thought how sad it was that Tom no longer seemed to admire the way she looked. She wondered what the ladies attending the Grand National would be wearing, her musings interrupted by a pitiful wail from the kitchen. Kitty hurried downstairs to the one person she was sure loved her.

Molly's cries ceased as soon as she saw her mother. She gave her a gummy smile. Kitty's spirits lifted. Molly was still at the stage where she slept for much of the time, but hardly a day went by that Kitty didn't notice something new in her development. Recently she'd begun to follow Kitty's movements with her eyes and to recognise her name. Now, Molly babbled something that Kitty was sure sounded like 'mama', and as she dressed her in warm leggings and a knitted coat and bonnet, Molly grabbed her fingers and said it again.

'Hey, Miss Busybody, let Mammy do your buttons,' Kitty said, delighted by her daughter's first word and her interfering hands.

She put Molly in her pram and pushed the cumbersome vehicle carefully down the steps and out into the lane, wishing she had a smaller, less ostentatious mode of transport for her daughter. Molly sat propped up on her pillow, her dark blue eyes drinking in her surroundings. At almost eight months old, she was a robust, bonny child with a creamy complexion, her mop of black curls peeping delightfully from under her cream bonnet.

Kitty paused outside Maggie's gate, about to call and see if Maggie wanted her to take Lily with her: the pram was big enough to hold both girls. But realising it was far too early for Maggie to be up and dressed, she abandoned the idea and carried on down the lane. She had barely gone a couple of yards before Jack Naughton stopped her.

'Let's be having a look at her,' he said, peering round the hood of the pram. To his delight Molly blew a bubble. 'Eeh! Isn't she bonny? I'll be bringing her some strawberries later on in t'year. I'm just off into me allotment to do a bit of digging ready for getting me veg in. I'll see to it that you get some, Mrs Conlon.'

'That's very kind of ye, Mr Naughton. I'll look forward to that.'

Jack hobbled off, and Kitty went on her way only to be hailed by May Walker.

'How's she doin'?' May called from over her garden wall. Kitty halted, and May hurried out into the lane. 'Ooh, you do have her nice,' she said, admiring Molly's bonnet. 'I allus wanted a little girl to dress up. Keep her warm now, this wind's still a bit nippy.' She clutched her baggy cardigan round her and went back into her garden.

Molly's like a magnet, Kitty thought as she pushed the pram to the end of the lane. It was the same wherever she went, people stopping to enquire after her daughter's health. It made Kitty feel that they really belonged here in Edge Hill, a place she had grown to love even though, like today, she had some regrets. Perhaps if she and Tom had stayed in Dublin he would still be the man she had fallen so madly in love with and not the distracted, dissatisfied man who had gone to Aintree for the day. As she rounded the corner into Broad Green she bumped into Cora Bradshaw.

'I see he didn't take you with him then,' Cora said. 'I did offer to have Molly for the day, and he said he'd think about it. You'd have enjoyed a day out at Aintree.'

Kitty leaned into the pram to hide her humiliation. Tom had never mentioned Cora's offer. She fiddled with Molly's bonnet. 'That was very kind of ye, Cora, but I didn't fancy taking Molly all that way on the train.'

'They've gone in Sam's car.' Cora seemed surprised that Kitty didn't know this. 'I told him that if he wanted to take both of you that I'd get that little pushchair out of the loft so you could push Molly about in it. It's what I used when our Sarah and Paul were babies, and I've kept it all these years.' She was clearly annoyed that Tom hadn't conveyed any of this to Kitty.

'Ah, well, maybe another year,' Kitty said.

'It's a grand day out is the National,' Cora said wistfully. 'I'd go meself if I didn't have a pub to run. And Tom's left that young lad, Rodney Hill, in charge of taking the bets. I know he's been training him up, but there's allus trouble when he's left on his own. He can't stand up to them that claim they laid out more than what's written on the docket. He's not like Tom.' She gave what Kitty interpreted as a menacing look. 'They don't dare do that when he's in charge.'

Kitty was somewhat taken aback, not only by Cora's expression but also by the fact that Tom had an apprentice; yet another thing he'd failed to mention.

Cora continued to rant about the woes of running a public house that had a betting shop on the premises, and as Kitty listened, she realised how little she knew about Tom's business. She'd never given much thought to who ran the book when Tom went off to the races. Furthermore, she hadn't liked Cora's tone of voice when she had said that the punters didn't dare question Tom. She made him sound like a man you'd be a fool to cross.

'Well, thanks again for the offer, Cora,' said Kitty, feeling a little light-headed after listening to Cora's harangue. 'I'll not keep ye, I'm sure you have lots to do.'

'You're not kidding,' Cora groaned. 'Ta-ra, love. Sorry about today.'

Kitty went to the bakery, the butcher's and the newspaper shop but her mind wasn't on her purchases, it was on Tom and the way in which he kept so much of his life secret from her.

Kitty put her shopping away, and after feeding and changing Molly, she put her down to sleep. Then she sat down to read the newspaper.

She turned the pages, her attention caught by an article on the conflict between Ireland and the British Government. She knew from what she had previously read that the troubles still persisted, and that the Irish Republican movement had formed their own breakaway government, the Dáil Éireann. She'd read hair-raising stories about the killing of both soldiers and civilians, and the reign of terror that was being inflicted on her native country. Kitty was glad that Shaun was no longer free to fight alongside his compatriots in the Irish Republican Army.

Maureen, her friend from the Gresham, had written telling her how lucky she was not to be living in Dublin, that unruly mobs of murderers prowled the street, putting the fear of God into anyone who fell foul of them. Kitty had shuddered when she'd read the letter and would have liked to discuss the problems in Ireland with Tom – he being the only person that she could talk to about such things – but he flatly refused to talk about the past, as he called it. Now, as she read on, her heart leapt. The article talked of a truce between the British and the Irish that might lead to there being peace in Ireland. Kitty wondered what this might mean for Shaun.

* * *

Next door, as Kitty read her newspaper and thought about her brother, Vi was sitting with her feet up and her face lathered in Pond's cold cream. Lily was in her pushchair, screeching.

'For Christ's sake will you shut that bleedin' mare up,' Vi roared. 'This house hasn't known a minute's peace since she was born. And if Fred Stubbs comes back in today full of drink and looking for a fight you're out, the lot of you.'

Maggie stubbed out her cigarette and went to lift Lily. She knew that her mother's patience was wearing thin and that she should keep on the right side of her if they were to remain living with her. Fred had still to find work – not that he was looking too hard – and until he did they couldn't afford to rent a house of their own so she had to keep her mother sweet.

'I'll take her out,' she said, patting Lily's back to quieten her. Lily hiccupped. Maggie shoved her roughly into a romper suit and sat her back in the pushchair. Then, her face grim, she trundled it across the kitchen and out through the back door. Leaving it at the foot of the steps, she went back inside and got her coat, the nippy March breeze letting her know she'd need one if she were to stay outside any length of time. She wheeled the pushchair down her own garden path and then up to Kitty's back door. Lily was wailing fit to be tied.

'I'm taking Lily for a walk,' Maggie called out, pushing open Kitty's door. 'Do you want to come?'

Kitty folded the newspaper and got to her feet. 'Aye, just give me a minute.' A walk would take her mind off things. She went to get her coat then pushed Molly's pram to the door.

'What's the matter with Lily?' she asked, hearing her pitiful cries.

Maggie lifted Lily, kissed her snotty little face then set her on her feet. Lily sniffed back her tears and hid her face in her mother's skirt.

'It's me ma's fault. She's been shouting all morning, and it upsets you doesn't it, love?' said Maggie, lifting Lily up and stroking her hair. Lily jutted her lip and nodded. 'She's threatening to chuck us out. She says she's had enough of the carry-on between me and Fred. Him coming in drunk, and me having a go at him.'

'Oh, Maggie! That's awful. Ye'll have to get that sorted out – an' quick. Vi's not an innocent party in all this, what with all the complainin' she does, an' she'd not manage without ye. How would she afford the rent? 'Tis ye that keeps her.'

'You try telling the ungrateful sod that.'

'Aye, she's that all right,' Kitty agreed as she pushed Molly's pram down the steps and out into the lane. Maggie followed, with Lily back in her pushchair. Unfortunately, she had neglected to strap Lily in and as they reached the end of the lane the pram's front wheels hit a deep rut. Lily tumbled out, landing on her knees. She let out a scream.

Kitty whirled round then rushed to lift her. 'My God, Maggie. Ye could have killed her,' she cried, brushing the dirt of Lily's knees then kissing them better. She handed her to Maggie who went through the same motions until Lily stopped crying. She strapped her into the pushchair.

'A bit late for that,' Kitty snapped.

'I know – I know,' Maggie groaned. 'What with all this carry-on with me ma, I just wasn't thinking.'

'That's the trouble with ye, Maggie. Ye don't think,' said Kitty, the shock of what could have resulted in a nasty injury making her cross. 'She could have landed on her face. Ye need to take more care. You've had her all this time an' ye still haven't learned.'

'Learned what?' Beth came up behind them.

'How to be a better mother,' Maggie hooted, not in the least offended by Kitty's chastisement.

Kitty laughed too. 'You're a hopeless case, Maggie Stubbs, but I still love ye.'

The three girls walked down the lane, Beth pushing Lily's pram so that Maggie could have a cigarette. 'I'd love a baby,' Beth said, beaming at Lily who was now happily drumming her feet on the pushchair's footrest.

'You would if you had one like little Miss Goodie-Two-Shoes,' said Maggie, pointing at Molly, 'but if you had one like Lily, you'd soon send her back.'

'Maggie Stubbs! Ye don't mean that,' Kitty cried.

'No, I don't. I love her to bits really – even if I don't know how to look after her.' Maggie smirked at Kitty, the silly smile falling away as she added, 'I only wish Fred did. When he thought he it 'ud be a boy he was all smiles, but he doesn't love Lily.' Maggie looked sad. Kitty wondered if Fred had put on his thinking cap and done some counting? She didn't voice her thoughts because Beth still didn't know that Fred wasn't Lily's father.

They turned the corner and walked up Weaver Street, Beth telling them about the decorating she and Blair were doing. At the top of the street they turned and went down to the towpath. The river was in full spate, the water high up the banks and tall reeds swaying in the breeze. A mother duck was leading her brood of ducklings in the shelter of the water's edge. The girls stopped to watch them, Kitty saying, 'Look, Molly. Look, Lily. Little duckies, see them swimming.'

Molly pointed a chubby finger and gurgled delightfully. Lily leaned forward in her pushchair. 'Duck-ducks,' she crowed.

'You see,' Maggie said, 'that's the difference between me an' Kitty. I'd never have thought to tell Lily to look at the ducks – and you can see she likes 'em. She can even say their names, can't you, love?' She beamed proudly at her daughter.

When they came to the neglected cabin that had once been Lander's Café, Kitty gazed at it with longing, remembering the days when she had whisked between the tables, serving meals to the rowdy mill workers and laughing at Gertie's witty remarks. What fun they had been. Now, it looked sad, its windows boarded up and its blue and white paint faded to a murky grey.

'Do ye remember the first day we met, Beth?' she said.

Beth smiled. 'I do, and I'm glad we did. You turned out to be a smashing friend.' She turned to Maggie. 'She even lets me and Blair use her front room on nights when the weather's lousy and we've nowhere else to go.'

'Yeah, so I heard. She's a heart as big as China, has Kitty Conlon.' She gave Kitty a sincere smile. 'I knew she was the best mate I'd ever have when she delivered my Lily. You can't get better than that, can you?'

Kitty blushed. 'Ach, stop it! Ye'll have me in tears.' She was already feeling emotional about the café, and her friends' praises tugged at her heart. 'Ye know what?' She looked directly at Maggie and Beth. 'One of these days I'm going to do sumthin' about this place. I'll not stand by an' see it rot,' she said, her voice high and her eyes dancing. 'I'll open it up as a tea room an' call it Kitty's Café.'

Maggie and Beth giggled at her enthusiasm. 'She probably will an' all,' Maggie said. 'She seems to have a knack for getting stuff done.'

'It's a lovely idea,' said Beth, 'but I don't think it would pay.'

'I'd make sure it did,' Kitty said, marching ahead with her pram like a tank commander going into battle.

* * *

Tom Conlon threaded his way through the crowds at Aintree racetrack, a smile on his face. He'd just collected his winnings on the previous race, and the big race had yet to be run. Tom was fast becoming a popular figure on the racing circuit. As he made his way back to the private box he'd been invited to share, several people acknowledged the charming Irishman with a knack for picking a winner.

'What did you get back?' Nigel Hutchinson asked as Tom entered the box. Tom told him. The wealthy horse owner and trainer whistled appreciatively. 'I now wish I'd taken your advice,' he said.

'I told you, Daddy, you should always listen to Tom.' Priscilla Hutchinson slotted her arm through Tom's and gazed up at him with lust and longing as she purred, 'Tom knows what's what, don't you, darling?'

Tom smiled down at her, his eyes dark and enigmatic. His friendship with the Hutchinsons was progressing nicely. Not only did it raise his profile, it put him where he wanted to be: in with the big players. Now, as he listened to Priscilla's husky upper-class voice singing his praises he couldn't have wished for more. This was where he belonged.

A frisson of excitement rippled through the crowd as over the tannoy a crackling voice announced the big race of the day: the Grand National. Nigel's private box had a perfect view of the parade ring and the track, and Tom focused his attention on three particular mounts as the horses and riders made their way towards the starting line.

'What's your money on?' Nigel gestured with his cigar as the horses passed by.

'The favourite, Poethlyn,' Tom replied. 'I like Ernie Piggot's style. He knows how to get the best out of a horse.' He didn't divulge the side bets he placed on two outsiders. 'What about you, Nigel?'

'I'm going with Bob Chadwick on All White and a couple of others. Prissy fancies Ballyboggan, don't you, darling?'

Priscilla smiled, all teeth. 'Ballyboggan is one of Ireland's entrants and I have a thing about handsome Irish animals. Did you know that, Tom?' She fluttered her eyelashes suggestively.

Tom had known from the first time they'd met that she was his for the asking but he was treading carefully, playing a long game. He'd never strayed before – well, not if you discounted the fumble with Flo Wainwright in the back of the Weaver's Arms after he'd had a few whiskeys too many. Cora had eyed him suspiciously that night. But Cora was a long way from here, and as Priscilla's perfume wafted under his nose and her hot body pressed against his, he allowed himself a moment to contemplate what the future might hold.

'They're off!' The roar went up from the crowd and Tom came

back to reality. He raised his binoculars as the horses thundered down the track, two fallers at the first fence, more at Beecher's Brook and then The Chair. Acting on impulse he'd also put money on an outsider called Shaun Spadah. He hated Kitty's brother and forbade her to mention his name, but somehow, today, the name seemed like an omen.

The horses thundered round the track, the jockeys urging their mounts into the second circuit and the crowd going wild as horse after horse fell at the fences. Poethlyn took first place. Shaun Spadah wasn't placed, and in Tom's weird logic that meant his feelings for Priscilla were not misplaced, and that his life could only get better with Kitty and her brother out of the running.

He let out a mighty whoop.

Nigel turned to look at him, his eyebrows raised. 'Am I to take it that you put big money on the winner?'

'Of course he did, Daddy. How many times do I have to tell you to listen to Tom?' Priscilla twined her arms round Tom's neck and kissed his cheek. 'Congratulations, darling.'

Tom's wallet was bulging when he came back from the tote. Swaggering into the box, he ordered champagne for everyone.

'We must celebrate,' Priscilla twittered, clutching at his arm. 'We're staying at the Adelphi tonight, join us and make a night of it?' She turned to her father. 'Tom can come too, can't he, Daddy?' Tom looked at her shapely legs, the left one raised as she put her arms around her father's neck. Her blue silk dress in the new short style had ridden above her knees, exposing the pretty dimples behind them. Tom felt a twitching in his groin.

'Daddy says you must come.' Priscilla possessively hooked her arm into Tom's. Tom glanced at Sam Bradshaw, who shook his head. Tom excused himself from Priscilla's clutches and went over to him.

'What do you say, Sam?' Tom flashed the landlord a roguish smile.

'I'm going straight back home,' Sam declared. 'Cora 'ud have a fit if I stayed out all night. If you want a lift you'd better come now.'

Tom looked at Nigel and then at Priscilla. She smiled, her green eyes flashing and the chin-length flicks of her blonde hair – sharply cut in the latest style – swinging against her creamy cheeks as she beckoned him with a tilt of her head.

'You go on, I'll make my own way back,' Tom said, ignoring the dirty look Sam fired at him.

26

Kitty wakened to Molly's cries, surprised that she had slept at all. She had finally gone to bed at almost two in the morning and Tom still not back from his day out at the Grand National. However, it wasn't just his lateness that had kept her so late, it was the idea she'd had on the towpath that afternoon.

After putting Molly down for the night, she had taken out a notebook and under the heading 'KITTY'S CAFÉ' she had jotted down what turning the notion into a reality entailed: pay rent to Gertie, repaint the building, purchase new stock. She'd quailed at the expense. Each week for more than a year she'd salted away what was left over from the housekeeping money but it wasn't enough to make a start. She wouldn't ask for Tom's help because she knew he would refuse. Eventually, the flush of excitement fading, she had climbed the stairs to bed.

Now, a glimmer of daylight shining through the curtains, she was shocked to find that Tom wasn't lying beside her. Panicking, she jumped out of bed then lifted Molly. Hurrying downstairs, she wondered if he and Sam had met with an accident whilst driving back. Surely if they had she'd have heard something by now.

Forcing herself to keep calm, she fed and changed Molly, the simple actions soothing and bringing reason to bear. As she raked the embers in the fire she consoled herself that more than likely Sam had taken too many drinks the night before and they'd stayed over in Aintree. She'd call at the pub and see what Cora had to say, but first she had to dress Molly and herself. Maybe Tom would be back by the time she'd done that.

On her way to the Weaver's Arms she saw John Sykes's car parked outside the shops. He was just climbing out as she approached. When he saw Kitty his eyes lit up and he smiled. 'You're out bright and early, Mrs Conlon,' he said, falling into step with her.

'Did ye go to the National with Tom and Sam yesterday?' Kitty asked as they walked towards the Weaver's Arms.

'No, I had business in Newcastle.'

If Sam's car wasn't in its usual spot she'd know he and Tom had stayed in Aintree. Her face fell when she saw Sam's Austin. 'Oh,' she gasped, unable to conceal her dismay.

'What is it?' John said, concerned. 'Is something wrong?'

'I don't know. I need to see Sam. Goodbye, John.' She quickened her pace, the pram careering over the pavement as she dashed towards the Weaver's Arms, annoyed that John was still at her side. She didn't want him to know that her husband had stayed out all night without letting her know that he had intended to do so.

Inside the pub, Sam was filling the optics behind the bar. He turned as Kitty burst through the door, frowning when he saw her.

'Did Tom not come back with ye last night, Sam?' she blurted.

Sam's eyes slid to John's then back to Kitty's, his cheeks colouring as he said, 'Er... no... he didn't. He said he had some business to attend to that couldn't wait.' Bristling visibly, he growled, 'I did offer to bring him back.'

Kitty could see that he was annoyed and that there was something he wasn't telling her. Quick to hide her humiliation, she swung the pram round and with a curt, 'Ta, Sam. I'm sure he'll be back some time,' she made to leave.

'Wait, Kitty!' John placed a restraining hand on her arm, and pained by her obvious distress, he longed to comfort her. She shook him off, charging for the door, her back ramrod straight and her head high.

John watched her go then turned to Sam. 'What was all that about?'

* * *

Tom arrived back shortly after midday. He was in a filthy temper, the entire business of staying overnight in the most expensive hotel in Liverpool an absolute waste of time and money. Once they had arrived at the Adelphi, Nigel had ditched Tom for a group of wealthy owners and trainers, Tom hovering on the edge in the hope of being drawn into such an illustrious circle. When that hadn't happened he'd had to make do with Priscilla who, halfway through the evening, having drunk too much champagne, had had to be carted off to her room by two of the trainers' wives.

Thoroughly disgruntled, he let himself in through his own front door.

Kitty looked at him accusingly as he entered the kitchen. 'Ye might have let me know,' she said softly, the words more biting than if she had raved and shouted.

Tom shrugged off his overcoat and gave her a self-deprecating smile. A wave of relief flooded his veins. At least, he hadn't betrayed her with Priscilla. It made it so much easier to meet those disappointed hazel eyes looking into his own.

'Sorry, darlin', but Sam celebrated a bit too much on his winnings and didn't want to drive home.' He smiled again, this time a devil-may-care smile. 'You know what we men get like when we're let loose.'

Kitty felt her heart breaking into tiny little pieces.

'Don't lie to me, Tom. Please don't lie,' she said, her voice barely above a whisper. 'Sam came home last night. I went to the pub first thing this morning. I was worried that ye might have had an accident.' Her face crumpled and she pressed the palms of her hands against her cheeks to hide the pain.

A cold hand clutched at Tom's heart. He hung his head. 'I... I... got caught up in something,' he mumbled. 'When I went looking for Sam he'd gone without me. I knew you'd worry, but it was too late to do anything about it.'

Kitty knew that he was lying, but his deceit was tearing her to pieces and she didn't have the strength to argue. 'Well, you're home now,' she said, turning her back on him and blinking away tears that she didn't want him to see.

* * *

'Blair has the key for next door,' Beth said when she called later. 'Would you like to come in with us and see what needs doing? I'm sure it's plenty.' Her eyes were shining and she didn't seem at all daunted by the task, for all her words.

'I'd love to,' Kitty gushed, desperately in need of something to banish the hurt that Tom's lies had caused. 'Just let me put Molly's romper on. We'll be with ye in two ticks. Tom's in bed after a hard night, so I've all the time in the world.'

She was just doing up Molly's buttons when Maggie came in with Lily. 'Where are you off to?' she asked, sounding a little peevish. She was inclined to be jealous of Beth and liked to think she came first in Kitty's affections.

'Next door, Blair's in there now,' Beth replied excitedly. 'We're going to see what needs doing. Are you coming?'

'Try and stop me.' Maggie hoisted Lily up to her shoulder. 'I love nosying round other people's houses.'

Kitty shivered as she stepped into what had been Margery and Dan's house. It seemed strange to think that they were no longer there. She recalled the last time she had seen Margery alive, and how she'd sat through the night with Dan as he wept for the loss of his beloved wife.

They entered by the back door into the kitchen. Without the Boothroyds' cosy furniture it looked cold and unloved, the mantelpiece bare now the photographs of their dead sons had been removed. Kitty thought how sad it was that Margery had been denied the opportunity to visit their graves in France.

Blair came clattering down the stairs and greeted them heartily. 'I hope you're going to give Beth a hand with the scrubbing and polishing,' he said.

'That's what we're here for,' chirped Maggie. 'We're sizing up the job so we know how much to charge. We get paid by the hour.'

Blair frowned, but Beth and Kitty roared with laughter.

'Nobody in their right mind would pay ye to clean for them, Maggie.' Kitty gave her a friendly nudge.

Maggie pretended to be offended. 'I'll have you know I'm a bloody good scrubber. Ask any of the chaps at Holroyd's Mill.' She glanced at Blair and mumbled, 'Present company not included.'

Kitty was mystified. 'How would they know?'

Maggie gave a raucous laugh. 'They don't, you daft ha'porth. A scrubber's what they call lasses who let 'em have it for free. I was joking.'

'Oh,' said Kitty. 'In Ireland we call 'em doxies or floosies.'

Blair gave an embarrassed cough then said, 'Shall we make the grand tour?'

They went from room to room discussing colours of paint and necessary repairs. In the bedroom that had been Margery's, Kitty breathed in the sweet scent of lavender: Margery's smell still lingered. Tears sprang to her eyes.

Back downstairs they gathered in the front room, Blair announcing that he would strip off the old wallpaper in each room and sand down the paintwork before they undertook any serious cleaning.

'We'll help with that, won't we, Maggie?' said Kitty. 'And when I repaper my front room ye can give me hand, Blair, in return for my services.'

Blair laughingly agreed. Then, Kitty welcoming the diversion, they all trooped back to her house for a cup of tea. It delayed having to think about how she and Tom might deal with their current unhappy situation.

* * *

'I've cleaned out the range and lit the fire,' Tom said the next morning when Kitty arrived downstairs with Molly in her arms. Kitty blinked her surprise; he'd never done that before.

'That's grand.' Her smile fleeting, Kitty turned to the task of feeding Molly. She didn't want him thinking that she could be so easily appeased. When he left for work he kissed her, and again when he arrived home much earlier than usual. He did the same the following day and for the rest of that week.

'Go easy on the coal,' Kitty advised him. 'The miners are talking about striking.'

'Don't worry, darlin'. You've got me to keep you warm.' He winked roguishly. Kitty wondered how long he would keep up his charm offensive. She knew this was his way of making amends, and though she accepted his efforts she still mistrusted him.

For the next two weeks he was sweetly attentive and unusually helpful. One day he suggested she ask Beth to babysit so that they could go to the cinema. That evening they went to see *Here Comes the Bride,* laughing at the exploits of a young man without means chasing after a wealthy girl – and Tom silently drawing comparisons – as though neither of them had a care in the world. But Kitty was uneasy. She still wanted to be his wife but she mustn't let him think that a few kisses and help with the chores or a night out at the cinema would inveigle her into sliding back into the way things had been. She wanted more than that. She wanted loyalty and respect.

Her mother had often told her that respect had to be earned, and each day as she went about her chores, Kitty pondered on how to gain Tom's respect without losing her own. Deep down, she felt that she and Tom were only playing at being a happy couple, and that the dissatisfaction they both felt still lurked underneath all the pleasantries. She hadn't yet fathomed what it was that Tom was looking for to make him completely satisfied but Kitty knew in her heart and her head that she was a pale shadow of the person she wanted to be, and that if she was to be completely happy then she needed to make something for herself. She couldn't continue to be just an appendage to Tom's busy life.

She thought of the café. The brave announcement she'd made to Maggie and Beth that day they'd walked on the towpath had never been far from her mind. She knew she could make the cafe successful again, and if she did then maybe Tom would see her in a different light: not just as a housewife and mother but a person with drive and ambition, more like the people he met at the tracks, the 'big-timers', as he called them, people he admired. And she knew in her heart that she wouldn't just be doing it to heal the rift in their marriage, she would be doing it for her own self-respect. She knew her own worth. She decided to ask Tom to help her finance the venture. Surely, he couldn't refuse.

* * *

'An' how are my beautiful girls?' Tom asked as he came through the door one evening in mid-April.

'One of us has just filled her nappy and the other one has just cleaned up the mess.' Kitty was sitting with Molly across her knee as she pinned the clean nappy in place. 'Your dinner's warming in the oven if ye want to lift it.'

'Finish what you're doing,' Tom said, and making no move to help himself, he sat down in the armchair and crossed his legs. He lit a cigarette, drawing on it lazily as he waited for her to serve up his dinner.

Ah, so you think you've exonerated yourself, Tom Conlon. You think two weeks of coming home early and sweet-talking me puts everything right. Kitty eased a pair of rubberised knickers up Molly's chubby legs then put on her nightgown. She got to her feet. 'She's all yours,' she said, holding Molly out for Tom to take. He flicked his cigarette stub into the fire.

'Come to Daddy, my little princess.' Tom cradled Molly against his chest. She closed her dark blue eyes, so like his own, and snuffled gently. At nine months old, she not only had his eyes, she also had his black hair and high cheekbones. In fact, her looks so favoured her father's that Kitty was tempted to think that was the one of the reasons he found his daughter so delightful.

Kitty took the plate from the oven and set it on the table. Tom handed Molly over to her then sat down to eat. Kitty went and sat by the fire with Molly on her lap. She felt unusually weary, and the cramps she had felt in her tummy for the past two mornings returned, making her feel queasy. She thought she could be sickening for something. She hoped it wasn't the Spanish flu. It still flared up every now and then.

'Is there any mustard?' Tom poked at the slices of spam.

Kitty bit her tongue. She dearly wanted to say, '*You know where it is. Get it yourself,*' but she didn't want to annoy him because after he had eaten she intended to tell him about her plans to reopen the café. If he agreed to help her she'd write to Gertie, telling her that she had Tom's backing. That way Gertie would be assured of her rent. She might even suggest he lend a hand with the repainting. If they did it themselves, it would work out cheaper.

Kitty waited for Tom to leave the table, ideas of what she was about to say bubbling in her head. The cramping sensation worsened and she put it down to butterflies in her tummy. At last, Tom came to sit by the fire. He opened up the *Sporting Life* and Kitty put Molly into her pram, hoping she'd go to sleep. She didn't want any distractions interrupting what she was about to do.

Kitty sat down again. 'Tom... I'd like to talk to ye about an idea I have.'

'What idea?' he asked from behind the paper. Kitty suppressed her irritation.

'Ye know the café on the towpath...' she began. 'Well... I've been thinking I could...' Tom twitched the paper irritably and Kitty lost her patience. 'Tom Conlon,' she yelled, 'would ye ever put that blasted newspaper down an' pay me the respect of listenin' to me?'

Tom dropped the paper. 'Stop shouting, Kitty. You'll upset Molly.' He glared at her. Kitty glared back, but when she started to speak again she kept her voice low. Out tumbled all that she had planned to say, her tone urgent and her eyes begging him to agree. Tom listened, a sneer forming on his lips.

'Don't be so ridiculous,' he scoffed as Kitty ran out of words. 'It wouldn't pay, and furthermore, you don't need to run a café. You have enough responsibility looking after Molly and me.' He picked up the paper.

'But that's just it, Tom,' Kitty cried, 'it's not enough to satisfy me. I want something for myself, something that I can get my teeth in, make a success of and feel that I'm more than just a wife and a mother.'

Tom gave her a disparaging look. 'But that's what you are, Kitty, a wife and a mother. Be satisfied with that, and let's have no more of your crazy ideas.' He got to his feet. 'I'm away for a pint,' he said, walking into the hallway to get his coat.

'Aye, off ye go, Tom. Run away. Do what ye want to do, an' to hell with everyone else!'

27

'There, Beth Garside – soon to be Forsythe – that's your front room scrubbed and polished till me arms have near dropped off.' Kitty danced into the kitchen at number thirteen and clanked her bucket on the bare floorboards.

Beth broke off hanging curtains at the kitchen window to run and look. 'It's lovely, Kitty. Thanks ever so much,' she said, coming back into the kitchen. 'Blair and I can't thank you enough for all your help.'

'It's what we do in Weaver Street,' Maggie said, getting up off her knees and waving the cloth she was using to polish the hearth. 'You couldn't ask for a better neighbour than Kitty – an' me an' all. I'm the Virgin Mary in disguise.' She struck a holier-than-thou pose and Kitty and Beth fell about laughing.

'Virgin my backside,' Kitty hooted. 'Put the kettle on, Beth, an' let's have a cup of tea.' She suddenly felt weary and wondered why it was that she kept having these lapses of energy. She flopped into a chair, watching as Lily built a tower of coloured bricks and Molly knocked them down. The girls enjoyed playing together as long as Molly let Lily be the boss.

Beth filled the shiny, new kettle and set it on the stove, then proudly took three mugs from her cupboards filled with new crockery.

Maggie lit a cigarette and then pointed it at Beth. 'This time next Saturday you'll be Mrs Blair Forsythe.'

Beth cheeks pinked. 'I know, I still can't believe it. I feel as though I'm dancing on a cloud,' she said, her eyes sparkling as she brewed the tea.

Kitty and Maggie exchanged meaningful glances, Maggie thinking of her own disastrous marriage to Fred, and Kitty thinking that she had once felt just like Beth. Then, she had thought she was the happiest woman in the world.

'Is Tom working late tonight?' Maggie asked Kitty as they sipped their tea.

'He is,' said Kitty, resigned to the fact that now the racing season was in full swing she would see even less of her husband in daylight hours. Tom had reverted to coming and going as he pleased, with little thought for her feelings and she had given up hoping they could recapture the love they had once had. In the house they were always civil with one another, even sharing a moment of laughter now and then, but as far as Kitty was concerned he was still pretending to enjoy married life and she was still yearning for something more.

'Then let's take the girls an' go to the chippy for us tea,' Maggie suggested.

Kitty gladly agreed, thinking how fortunate she was to have her friends. 'What about ye, Beth,' she said, 'are ye coming?'

'No thanks, Blair and I are having our tea with my dad.' She grimaced. 'I'm trying to keep him sweet between now and next Saturday. I don't want him spoiling my big day.'

* * *

Tom took the last bets of the day and began to tally the book. Saturdays were always good for business, but he wasn't happy. Rodney had let Syd Moorhouse run up a large debt, and now Syd was steering clear of the Weaver's Arms to avoid paying up. Tom's lip curled as he looked at the amount and a surge of anger ran through his veins. *Syd should know that nobody takes Tom Conlon for a fool,* he thought, calling to his assistant, 'Finish up in here, Rodney. I've something to sort out.' He pushed back his chair and strode into the bar.

John Sykes greeted him, but Tom more or less ignored him as he walked over to two burly fellows standing at the end of the counter. John watched as Tom spoke urgently and then handed money over. The thugs grinned and strutted out of the pub. Tom called for two pints of stout and went to stand next to John.

John's estimation of Tom had lowered the more he'd got to know him. He'd heard the gossip about Tom's dealings with unsavoury characters that hung around the tracks and the way he ingratiated himself into the company of the wealthier racing fraternity. It made John uneasy and he no longer thought of him as a friend. Yet another reason was the way John felt about Kitty.

'Did you have a good day?' John asked.

'It'll get a whole lot better before it's over,' Tom replied, giving a nasty grin. He raised his glass and clinked it against John's. 'Cheers,' he said cockily.

* * *

'That'll be two shillings, May,' Kitty said, handing over the two pairs of trousers that she had altered to fit May's boys.

May held them up for inspection. 'You've made a lovely job of 'em, Kitty. Nobody 'ud guess they were off Lizzie Booth's second-hand stall. I'll look out for a pair for our Ronnie next week. Now he's out of the army he's working in John Lewis's. He needs to look smart,' she said proudly.

'Things must be easier for ye with another worker in the house,' Kitty said warmly. What with Bill being a boozer and a poor provider, she knew how hard May struggled to clothe her three sons.

May smiled and then sighed. 'It's sad that all the suits Lizzie sells are dead men's suits, an' all of 'em men bigger than my lads. Still beggars can't be choosers. Do you think you could alter a jacket for our Ronnie if I get one?'

'I can try. We can't have your Ronnie looking scruffy when he's selling John Lewis's grand furniture.' She pocketed the two shillings and hurried back home. She had a pair of curtains to finish for Beth and a dress to shorten for Vi, and only yesterday she had delivered two skirts to Connie for which she'd been paid two shillings and sixpence.

Her sewing business had come about quite by accident some weeks earlier. She had been pushing the pram up the street when Connie stopped her to admire Molly. 'She's a beauty,' she had said. 'She takes after her dad though, not you.' Then, realising her faux pas, she'd quickly added, 'Not that you aren't bonny, and I must say you look nice today. That's a lovely skirt you're wearing.'

Amused by Connie's blunder, Kitty had swallowed her giggles. 'Thank you,' she'd said, 'I made it meself out of a fent I bought on the market. It had a damage right down the middle but I managed to cut round it.'

Connie had looked the skirt up and down. 'You made a lovely job of it. Can you make one for me?' she'd then asked.

And that had been the start of it.

Once word got round that Kitty had a sewing machine and was a dab hand at using it, the requests had flooded in. With the country still reeling from the war, everybody was still taking the government's advice to make do and mend and Kitty readily turned sheets into dresses and altered outdated costumes. She took pride in putting the skills her mother and grandmother had taught her to use, and furthermore, the money she earned was making her dream of the café a reality.

She was still feeling hurt and angry at Tom's dismissal of her idea to reopen it but she hadn't abandoned it. She had written to Gertie, and Gertie had written back saying she was willing to lease the premises. Better still, the rent she required was ridiculously low. As Kitty walked away with two more shillings to add to her nest egg she felt both pleased and proud of her achievements.

* * *

The sun was shining and the birds were singing on Beth's wedding day. Kitty had been flattered when Beth asked her to be her matron of honour and now, at five minutes to eleven, she stood on the steps of the Methodist chapel in Mill Lane, awaiting the bride's arrival. Passers-by might have mistaken her for the bride, for Kitty was a vision of loveliness in her pale blue satin dress. Her tawny hair was caught up in a circlet of cream roses that matched the posy she held in her right hand, and there was a special bloom about her creamy complexion.

'You look so beautiful I want to marry you all over again,' Tom had said before they left the house. Kitty had wanted to believe him.

She glanced up at the clock above the door of the austere building, wondering what was keeping Beth, and at the same time thinking that St Joseph's church at the top of Weaver Street was a much prettier place for a wedding. The minute hand juddered to the hour and there was still no sign of Beth and her father.

Vi and Maggie came puffing and panting down Mill Lane. 'It

hasn't started then?' Maggie called out when she saw Kitty. 'We thought we were late.'

Lily was bawling, her little face as fiery as her hair. Maggie lifted her out of the pushchair and fluffed out the pretty, pink cotton frock Kitty had made. 'She looks lovely, dun't she,' Maggie boasted.

'She would if she stopped crying,' Vi grumbled, tugging at her garish flowered dress. Too tight and too short, it showed every lump and bump of her ageing figure. 'I'm off inside.' On heels too high she tottered into the chapel.

'Beth should be here by now,' Kitty said anxiously.

'Maybe that miserable bugger's locked her in to stop her getting married,' Maggie said dramatically. 'I wouldn't put it past him.' She struck a pose and asked, 'Do I look all right? You look absolutely bloody gorgeous.'

'So do ye.' Kitty meant it. Maggie had brushed back her hair and fastened it with a lemon ribbon to match her bright lemon dress and jacket. She'd also toned down her make-up and looked young and fresh. 'Your hair suits you like that. It makes ye look really pretty.'

Maggie flushed with pleasure.

A big, black car with ribbons on it glided down the street. 'She's here,' Kitty exclaimed. Maggie ducked inside the chapel with Lily squawking in her arms. Kitty hurried forward to meet the car.

Beth climbed out, her blue eyes like delphiniums after a shower of rain. Kitty could tell she had been crying. She took her in her arms, careful not to crease the smooth white satin. 'What's the matter, Beth?'

'It's him. He kicked up a fuss just as we were about to leave. He tried to stop me coming.'

Walter stood by the car, his sullen face speaking a thousand words. Kitty marched up to him. 'Mr Garside, this is Beth's big day and I'll not have ye spoil it for her any more than ye have done already,' she snapped. 'If ye don't want to walk her down the aisle an' give her away then I'll do it meself.'

Walter's jaw dropped and his cheeks blazed. He shuffled his feet and looked down at the ground. Through her tears, Beth managed to smile; Kitty's Irish accent was always more pronounced when she was angry.

'Now, take Beth's arm an' get in there,' Kitty continued, 'an' be proud to be giving away such a beautiful daughter.' She turned to Beth. 'Are ye all right?'

'I am now,' Beth sighed, linking her arm through Walter's as he shuffled to her side. He gave her something resembling a smile, and then, head held high, he marched her into the chapel. Kitty walked behind, smiling serenely.

* * *

'Was it him that kept her late?' Maggie asked as she and Kitty sat drinking tea at the small reception Beth had organised in the chapel's community hall.

'Ye might know it was.' Kitty pulled face. 'He had the poor wee soul in tears before they set off. I gave him a piece of my mind.'

'But look at 'em now. Her an' Blair make a smashing couple.' Maggie sounded wistful.

Just then, Tom sauntered over. 'Can I have the pleasure of this dance?' He gazed deeply into Kitty's eyes. Her heart fluttered.

'I'm dancing with the most beautiful girl in the room,' Tom whispered against Kitty's hair. She felt the heat of his body, smelled his cologne and wanted to believe him but she knew it was all a game: the loving husband doing what the people in the room expected of him. *Never let it be said that Tom Conlon didn't put on a good show,* she thought sadly as the music faded.

28

Kitty heard her back door open then footsteps making their way towards her front room where she was bent over her sewing machine. She stilled the treadle and glanced at the door expectantly. Maggie and Beth walked in looking like a deputation from the city council.

'I told you this was where we'd find her,' Maggie said. 'She does nothing but sew. If I call in for a cuppa she can't wait to get rid of me.'

Kitty looked abashed. 'Oh, don't be like that, Maggie. I know I've not been neighbourly just lately, but I've loads of work on.' She waved at the pile of garments on the chair waiting to be altered then got to her feet, glancing into the pram where Molly was sleeping. 'The whirring of the machine works like a charm,' she said with a grin. 'I'll go an' put the kettle on.'

The women trooped into the kitchen. Beth and Maggie sat at the table and Kitty prepared the tea.

'Do you not think you're taking too much on?' Beth asked as they waited for the kettle to boil.

Kitty leaned back against the sink and sighed. 'It's the only way I know of making enough money to get what I want.'

Maggie and Beth looked at her then at one another with puzzled expressions.

Kitty turned her back to pour water into the teapot, then, going and placing it on the table, she took a deep breath and gabbled, 'Do you remember me telling you I wanted to reopen Gertie's café? Well, I've been saving all the money I earn from me sewing to do just that.' She gave them a challenging smile and hardened her tone. 'I want a business – to make something of meself and show what I can do.' She sat down and poured tea into the cups. 'I've got nearly enough money to make a start. I know I can make it work,' she said, pushing the cups in Maggie and Beth's direction.

'Get away,' Maggie gasped. 'I didn't believe you that day on the towpath, I thought it was just daft talk.'

'You're really serious about this, aren't you?' Beth said.

Kitty nodded and grinned. 'Deadly serious,' she said. 'An' don't go thinking I don't want your company just 'cos I don't have as much time on me hands as I used to. Ye are the best friends I could ever have, an' don't ye forget it.'

'Yeah, well don't go killing yourself over it,' Maggie said cynically.

Down on her knees, Kitty riddled the cinders she'd taken out of the range. She wasn't usually so careful, but coal was scarce and she was saving what she could to burn again. Only yesterday she'd had to lend May Walker a bucketful. May had been red with embarrassment when she had asked for it. 'It's just that I thought you might have some to spare what with your Tom doing so well in the bookies,' she'd said. The Conlons' newfound affluence hadn't escaped the notice of their neighbours. *Not that any of it's coming my way to open the café,* Kitty had thought as she went down the cellar to fill May's bucket. Still, she wouldn't see her friend go without a fire.

'I'll let you have it back the day after tomorrow, Queen,' May had told her. 'The coalman says he's expecting a delivery at his yard then.'

'That'll be grand, May,' Kitty had replied, knowing May would keep her word, but her own coal cellar was looking bare and she hoped that the coalman would call soon. He'd missed the week before last due to having run out of coal.

'Ta, love. You're a pal.'

May went off, Kitty calling after her, 'Think nothing of it. At least we're not as badly off as the poor miners.'

Coal pits throughout the country had been shut down, the miners striking in the hope that the pit owners would meet their demands for better pay and safer working conditions. Heart-breaking stories of children going hungry and their fathers beaten on the picket lines filled the newspapers. Kitty had shed tears for the miners and their families as she read about the plight. The stories reminded her of Ireland and her country's fight for independence. This of course had made her think of Shaun.

He'd been fighting for better conditions for the Irish. Like many of the young men in Roscommon, he had been reared on bitter stories of English oppression; they had stolen the land that he considered was his by birthright and installed their absentee land-lords whose only desire was profit, and when the potato blight had robbed the Irish of their main source of sustenance, they had let them starve. Even though that was seventy and more years ago, it still burned in the memory, fuelling the minds of young men like Shaun. Kitty had feared for him when he'd left home to join the Roscommon Brigade, a wing of the Republican Army, and cried bitter tears when he had been captured and imprisoned in an English jail.

I should have tried harder to find out where he is and keep in touch, she berated herself, as she pictured her much-loved brother languishing in a prison cell, *and I would have done had I not heeded Tom.* Ever since then she had been consumed with guilt, hiding her thoughts and feelings for her brother from her husband and despising herself for her weakness. But she still lived in hope that one day they would be reunited.

More recently she had read about an Anglo-Irish Treaty. It suggested there might soon be a peaceful settlement and if an agreement between the British and the Irish could be reached there would be a reprieve for those who had fought against British rule. She wondered how this would affect Shaun. Would they set him free from wherever it was they had him incarcerated?

Or was it just talk? she asked herself, as she mixed the cinders with coal and shovelled them into the grate. The poor miners had won nothing in the end. Betrayed by their unions and the government they had been forced to return to work or starve. It seemed to Kitty that almost everywhere she looked there were people whose lives were governed by powers beyond their control.

Even me, she thought, getting to her feet and going to wash her hands. She'd had such high hopes of reopening the café before the summer ended, but now she knew for certain she would have to wait. For weeks she had tried to ignore the unexpected tiredness that suddenly crept over her, but now she thought she knew the cause of her symptoms.

* * *

'I'd no idea,' Kitty said to Maggie as they sat on the garden wall with cups of tea. 'My monthlies have been all over the place since I had

Molly so I haven't been counting the days.' She gave a bemused smile. 'I don't know how it happened.'

'Hang on a minute,' Maggie exhorted. 'You mean you an' Tom haven't...' Her eyes boggled mischievously. 'Are you telling me this is a virgin birth?'

Kitty gave an exasperated chuckle. 'No! I just didn't think I could get pregnant again so soon after Molly.'

'*I* never thought *I'd* get pregnant,' Maggie groaned, 'but I did. An' there's the proof of it.' She pointed to Lily sitting on a blanket on the patch of grass with Molly beside her. The two girls were pulling at the arms and legs of Molly's teddy bear, both of them declaring ownership by squealing, 'Mine! No! Mine.'

'I don't feel at all like I did last time,' Kitty continued. 'My breasts aren't tender and I haven't had morning sickness, but I did feel tired and not meself. I thought it might be somethin' terrible so I took meself off to the doctor this morning. Dr Metcalfe seems sure I'm pregnant.'

'You'll know for certain in about seven months' time,' Maggie said dryly. 'Then you'll have two bundles of joy to keep you awake at night.' She made it sound like a death sentence.

If Kitty was completely honest, she too considered her pregnancy a drawback. Her first thoughts had been about the café. Suddenly, it seemed as though her life had been put on hold, that all she had planned and hoped for had been pushed into the background by circumstances beyond her control. These thoughts made her feel guilty; the baby in her belly hadn't asked to be conceived and she shouldn't hold anything against it.

'Do you want any more, Maggie?' she asked, struggling to quell her guilt.

'Not with Fred, I don't. I don't even want him,' Maggie said vehemently. 'I keep hoping he'll bugger off an' never come back, but he knows that living with me an' me mam's a cheap billet so I suppose

I'm stuck with him. He's been sacked from that job in the scrapyard, and he's back on the drink. I haven't had a penny off him in two weeks.' She sounded thoroughly disgusted.

'Ye should chuck him,' Kitty snarled. 'Just pack his bags an' show him the door.'

'If it was that easy I'd have done it ages ago.' Maggie heaved a sigh that seemed to come up from her toes.

Kitty sipped her tea. *Neither of us has a happy marriage*, she thought. *Poor Maggie's saddled with a lazy boozer who fails to support her, and me who has no real money worries has a husband who chooses to exclude her from the life he leads. What a sorry pair we are.* Still, it wasn't all doom and gloom. She placed a hand on her tummy and thought of the new baby. Then, her eyes clouding, she thought about what Tom would say when she told him.

'Do ye think it might be a boy this time, or will I have another girl?' she asked, picturing a little boy with black hair and blue eyes: that might please Tom.

'It'll be one or the other,' Maggie drawled. 'You don't have a lot of options.'

Kitty giggled, and jumping from the wall, she lifted Molly with one hand and Lily with the other. 'But look what we've got already,' she said, jigging the girls round. 'Two of the most beautiful daughters in the world.'

* * *

'Another baby!' Tom felt the beer souring in his gut and his words hung like dead crows on barbed wire as he calculated the effect another child would have on his life. Children bound you even tighter to the woman you had married, and Tom didn't want to be tied down. He wanted to be free to plough his own furrow without being made to look a complete bastard when he brought in his harvest. Miss Priscilla Hutchinson was ripening nicely. Leaving Kitty, as he soon planned to do, would be hard enough, but to walk out on her when she was pregnant would make people think he was an absolute blackguard. He didn't find the thought appealing.

'That's grand,' he said without the enthusiasm he had shown when she was expecting Molly.

Kitty wanted to cry but she stayed calm and in control. If this was the way things were going to be from now on, so be it.

However, Tom's obvious disinterest in her and their family fired her determination to make something for herself and her children. Once the new baby was born she would open the café. She didn't see staying with Tom and putting up with the life she had as a weakness; she saw it as common sense, even though in the cold light of day she felt cruelly disappointed. It would benefit neither her nor their children to let anger and heartache rule her head.

Had Kitty been able to look into Tom's heart and mind she would have learned that his disinterest in his family was due partly to problems at the racetrack and mainly to Priscilla Hutchinson. His greed had led him to become involved in some shady dealings, and his heart to become more involved with Priscilla. On the same day that Kitty had told him about the baby, he'd received an invitation to the Hutchinsons' home in York to celebrate Priscilla's birthday. Whilst Kitty had been talking about the new life they had created, he had been contemplating the weekend ahead. To be invited to rub shoulders with the elite of the racing fraternity surely meant that they accepted him as a member of their circle. He was more absorbed in his immediate future and the benefits this party could offer than an event that was months away, an eventuality that wouldn't particularly fill him with joy.

29

Kitty pushed Molly's pushchair along the towpath, stopping every now and then to point out the butterflies resting on the nettles or the glorious buttercups and red campions. 'Look, Molly,' she said, breaking the stem of a giant buttercup. 'This colour is called yellow, and this flower will let me know if ye like butter.' Molly stuck out a pudgy hand to grab the buttercup as Kitty held it under her chin. 'Oh, ye love butter, Molly, and so do I.'

'Me too, I love butter.' Kitty turned round to see John Sykes smiling at her. 'And so does this fellow,' he added, flicking the lead of the beautiful golden retriever at his heels.

Kitty chuckled as she patted the dog. 'Doggie, Molly,' she said, 'big doggie.'

Suddenly, the emptiness she had been feeling was filled with pleasure. Tom had left early that morning, his excuses for having to stay away for the weekend still echoing inside her head. 'How nice to see you,' she said, smiling warmly at John.

'The pleasure's all mine. Do you mind if we walk along with you? Goldie loves company, and so do I.'

The way he said it made Kitty blush. She bobbed a mock curtsey. 'We'd be delighted, wouldn't we, Molly?' They continued on along the towpath.

'Look at him,' John urged as a flurry of iridescent blue wings swooped low across the water.

'Oh, isn't he just marvellous? What kind of bird is he?'

'A kingfisher,' John told her, tightening his grip on Goldie's lead as she made a sudden lunge towards the water. Kitty gasped, her hands flying to her face like two little brown birds. John looked into her dancing eyes, thinking that the bird wasn't the only marvellous thing on the riverbank that afternoon.

The kingfisher flew into the willows that swept the river's edge and perched arrogantly on an overhanging branch, his beady eyes scanning the water. 'He looks just like a king, wearing all his finery to impress the other birds,' Kitty remarked. 'I'll bet the wee sparrows are afraid of him.'

'They need to be. He's a bird of prey. He prefers fish but he eats small birds as well. Watch him now,' he whispered as a flurry of ripples appeared on the river's surface. The kingfisher dived then soared upwards.

'Oh, the poor wee fish,' Kitty cried, seeing it flapping pathetically.

'His beak's like a dagger. One stab and the fish doesn't stand a chance. But that's nature for you, Kitty. If one species is to survive, another one has to suffer.' Kitty thought of Tom.

'Tom's gone to York,' she said. 'He has to attend business meetings with an important man called Hutchinson. He'll have to stay overnight.' She didn't really want to talk about Tom, but he was lurking in the back of her mind, unbidden.

'That'll be Nigel Hutchinson,' John said. 'He breeds and trains racehorses. I've met him once or twice at Aintree. He's big time in racing circles.'

John silently recalled other race meets where he'd seen Tom

and Priscilla Hutchinson together. He suspected that it wasn't just Nigel that Tom had gone to meet. His thoughts turned sour. He couldn't understand the man. He had a beautiful wife and child, and that should be more than any man could wish for. 'He's a busy man is Tom,' he muttered. Then pushing him from his mind he concentrated on Kitty and Molly, and the delights of the riverbank.

'Ye must be friends with Mother Nature,' Kitty giggled, thinking what a lovely man he was to be with as John showed her a grebe's nest, a badger's set and other secrets of the hedgerows.

Goldie was keeping Molly highly entertained. The big, friendly dog seemed fascinated by the little girl and was plodding alongside the pushchair, every wag of her tail making Molly giggle. As for Kitty, she was enjoying herself immensely even though there were moments tinged with sadness. It reminded her of walking down the country lanes in Roscommon with her brother, Shaun. He knew a lot about wildlife.

They came to the sad, neglected building that had once been Gertie's café.

'It's a shame this place closed down,' John commented. 'I remember coming here after me and my dad had been fishing. He'd buy me an ice cream. A real treat for the little lad I was then.'

Kitty smiled, picturing John as a small boy, his floppy brown hair falling into his big brown eyes as he sat waiting to catch a fish. 'Were ye close to your dad?' she asked. If the child she was carrying were a boy she couldn't imagine Tom bringing him fishing.

'He was a grand man,' John said wistfully. 'I always think of him when I pass this place.'

'I'm thinking of opening it up again,' Kitty said.

John looked at her, surprised. 'You? Running a café? But why?'

'It's what I want to do. I want to have something for meself.'

'And what does Tom think?'

'It doesn't matter what Tom thinks. I've already arranged things with Gertie.' She paused. 'Of course, I can't do it until after this baby's born, but I'll go ahead as soon as I can.' She sounded very businesslike.

A baby? John felt his heart tighten and a plummeting in the pit of his stomach. *Your errant husband still manages to find time to make love to you then,* he thought, jealousy flooding his chest. But for Kitty's sake he banished the feeling. 'So you're having another baby? That's... that's wonderful.'

Kitty heard the insincerity in his tone and changed the subject. 'Tell me about what the café was like when you were young,' she said, grasping the pram's handle to resume walking.

John fell into step, recalling the busy weekends in summer, families taking a walk on the towpath then stopping for tea and cakes.

'That's why I'll do just Thursday to Sunday for a start. See how it goes,' said Kitty. 'But first I'll have to carry out repairs and freshen up the paint.'

'I see you've thought it all out.' John was impressed.

'I was thinking of little else, until I found out I was pregnant again.' She chuckled then, sounding very determined. 'An' even though I'll have to put it on the long finger, I've not given up. I rather fancy being independent and in charge of something that's all mine.' She looked directly into John's eyes as he helped her lift the pram up the towpath steps. 'Do ye think that sounds daft?'

'Not at all,' he said, setting the pram on the road. They walked on in silence, Kitty thinking about the café and John mulling over what he knew about Tom. No matter how charming Tom Conlon was, he wasn't good enough for Kitty. He recalled the incident in the pub. A man who hired thugs to do his dirty work was beneath contempt. Syd Moorhouse had been so badly beaten he was lucky to be alive. And rumour had it that another heavy gambler had left Edge Hill in fear of his life, after falling foul of Tom. Was Kitty aware of his shady dealings, John wondered, and did she know about his dalliance with Priscilla Hutchinson? If so, was having her own business Kitty's way of preparing for a future without Tom?

'I really enjoyed our walk,' Kitty said as they reached the top of Weaver Street.

'So did I,' John replied. 'I must look out for you again. Me and Goldie walk the towpath most Saturday afternoons.' He gave her a meaningful look, hoping she'd get the message.

To his dismay, Kitty appeared oblivious to the gentle hint, her mind elsewhere. When they came to where Kitty would turn off to go home she laid her hand on John's arm. 'Don't be saying anything about the café just yet,' she said. 'Let it be our secret for now.'

John grinned. 'Cross my heart and hope to die.' He made the sign on his broad chest. 'And when you do get round to it I'll give you hand with the repairs and the painting.'

'That'll be just grand,' she said, bestowing him a grateful smile.

* * *

On Sunday afternoon, Tom still not back from York and Kitty catching up with her sewing whilst Molly had her afternoon nap, Beth called round. She looked utterly dejected. Kitty suspected that Walter was to blame; not a day went by without the man pestering his daughter

'Come and sit down, love, and tell me what's wrong.'

Beth slumped onto a chair next to the sewing machine and began to cry. 'It's my dad,' she said brokenly. 'I do as much as I can for him yet he's never satisfied and Blair's losing his patience. I don't want us to quarrel, not when we should be so happy. We've never argued,' she said desolately, 'but now Blair's losing patience. He called Dad an ingrate and a bully. He says his demands are excessive and that he's not prepared to let him treat me that way.'

Kitty swivelled on her chair and took Beth's trembling hands in her own. 'An' rightly so,' she said. 'I can't say I didn't have me doubts when ye took next door, it being so close, an' I don't know what ye can do to prevent him pestering when it's so easy for him to just march up the street to your door. What I do know is, ye mustn't let him come between ye an' Blair. Marriage is hard enough without interference.' She thought of how Tom's job interfered with the happiness of her own.

'I know, I know,' Beth cried, 'but when Dad comes complaining about the meals I make for him and demands his shirts ironing, I just give into him.' She gulped back a sob. 'I love Blair, but I can't help feeling responsible for Dad.' She raised her tearstained face, imploring, 'What am I to do, Kitty?'

'Ye'll just have to put your foot down, an' by that I mean you, Beth. Not Blair. It's *your* dad that's the problem, an' it's *ye* that has to deal with it. If ye leave it to Blair ye'll end up falling out with him and blaming him for your troubles. So get down there an' read your dad the riot act. Tell him any more of that carry-on, an' ye'll never go near him again.'

Beth blinked away her tears. 'I will,' she said unsteadily. 'I have to, don't I?'

Beth went home, and Kitty carried on sewing and mulling over Beth's problems and her own. If Beth took her advice she might solve her troubles, but Kitty was damned if she could think of a solution for her own.

Tom arrived home a few hours later. He seemed awfully pleased with himself, and after cuddling Molly and giving Kitty a warm embrace and a brief kiss he told her that his business meeting had been successful. What he was really saying was that Nigel had offered to let him into the racing syndicate, and that Priscilla had been exciting in bed.

30

Kitty put flour and yeast and dried fruit into a bag, and carrying Molly in her arms, she hurried up the lane to Mavis's house. Rather than allow her idea for the café to lie fallow, Kitty was taking lessons in pastry and cake making. If she was to make the café profitable then her pies and confectionery had to be the best, and she needed to improve her baking skills before she opened. She hadn't mentioned any of this to Tom.

'Is it convenient for another lesson?' she asked when Mavis answered the door.

'More than,' Mavis replied, taking Kitty's bag and ushering her into the kitchen. 'I'm always glad of the company now that I'm only working part-time. I miss the chat in the hotel, but I don't miss the long hours.' She gave Kitty a rueful smile. 'Remember all those hours we worked in munitions? I didn't know what work was until I went there. Thank goodness we don't have to do that any more.'

'Aye, I know what ye mean. Aching backs an' aching feet, an' scared to death ye'd be blown to pieces,' Kitty agreed, cushioning Molly into an armchair. 'Still, I miss the company. They were a great bunch of women.'

'And not one of them will ever think that it was their efforts that helped us win the war,' Mavis said. 'We women are like that. We just get on with what needs to be done and we don't expect any medals.'

Kitty weighed the fruit and flour and they began mixing scones. At her first lesson, Mavis had taught Kitty the importance of weighing and measuring the ingredients. 'It pays to make them exactly the same each time,' she had said, 'and it also helps you to calculate the cost. You lose profit if you don't know how much you've spent making things.' Kitty had seen the wisdom in this and was glad she'd asked for Mavis's advice.

'She is a good little thing.' Mavis nodded bird-like at Molly who was playing with her teddy bear and watching the women work.

'She's a wee dream,' Kitty agreed as she dusted the dried fruit lightly with flour to stop it sinking to the bottom of the scones; yet another trick Mavis had taught her. 'I just hope this next one will be as easy.'

Mavis smiled wistfully. 'I'd have liked to have children.'

Kitty was surprised. She had presumed the bright, little spinster was single and childless by choice.

Now, as she heard the yearning in Mavis's remark, she asked, 'Did ye never think of marrying, Mavis?'

'Oh, yes! I dearly wanted to be married.' The baking tray she was greasing rattled onto the table. 'I was engaged to be married before war broke out. When Robbie was called up we talked about bringing the wedding forward but everybody said the war would be over by Christmas so we left things as they were. We'd planned to marry in spring.' Her eyes misted, and her voice dropped to a whisper. 'Then in February... on Valentine's Day 1915... Robbie was killed in Liège.' She blinked rapidly then lifted the tray and rubbed it with the greasy blob of paper screwed tight in her hand. 'That's in

Belgium,' she said, sniffing as she struggled to regain her composure.

The flour sifter fell from Kitty's hand. 'Oh, I'm so sorry, darlin'. Me an' my nosy questions. I didn't mean to upset ye.'

'You weren't to know,' Mavis murmured. 'But that's why I don't have children. I couldn't imagine marrying anyone other than Robbie.' She drew back her shoulders, her bird-like, dark eyes brightening. 'But don't go pitying me. I've a job I love, good neighbours like you, and the sweetest of memories. Now, let's get these scones made and then we'll use that yeast and I'll show you how to make tea cakes and fruit scones.'

They continued mixing and kneading and shaping and rolling, Kitty paying close attention to Mavis's instructions, and at the same time pondering on how she might have coped had she lost Tom in the same way as Mavis had lost Robbie. *But I have lost him*, she thought sadly, her heart aching for herself as much as it ached for her friend.

* * *

Later, back in her own kitchen, Kitty found the time to open the newspaper she'd bought the day before. She skimmed through an article on the race riots in Liverpool: white workers refusing to work alongside the black seafarers who had settled in the port after the war ended. She'd had a taste of not being accepted because she wasn't English, though she hadn't known these levels, and a burning rage crackled inside her at the unfair treatment of the black workers. She was flicking through the pages when Molly, on the hearthrug, let out a piercing wail. Flipping the newspaper over, Kitty jumped to her feet.

'There, there,' she cooed, kissing the finger that Molly had nipped in the lid of her Jack-in-a-Box. It did the trick and Kitty returned to the table.

The newspaper was face down. Kitty never read to the end of the paper where the sporting news was reported, but unthinkingly, she now turned the back page. Inside, a familiar face stared out at her from a large photograph. Her breath caught in her throat. She peered more closely to make sure she hadn't made a mistake. For a second or two her brain refused to function and she felt paralysed, unable to breathe, like a fish flapping in the bottom of a boat. She slumped into a chair and read the caption.

One of racing's beautiful couples celebrate their winnings.

Then she read the small print below.

Irish landowner Mr Tom Conlon and Miss Priscilla Hutchinson, daughter of Mr Nigel...

A couple! The newspaper referred to them as a couple. Stunned, Kitty stared at the photograph. And landowner? What land? What lies had Tom been telling?

Tom's arm was draped round the shoulders of a beautiful girl. She was pressed into his side, her smiling face tilted as though she was waiting to be kissed. Although Tom was smiling into the camera there was something about his smile that told Kitty his thoughts were not on his winnings but much more to do with the girl. Kitty knew that look.

It had once belonged to her.

Hot tears and heartache turned to cold fury as she studied the girl. Her slinky dress was in the latest style, the neckline and hem encrusted with dangling beads. Her hair was held in place with a broad bandeau decorated with a glittering brooch and her long, slender legs ended in strappy, high-heeled shoes. *She looks expensive and she no doubt smells it,* Kitty thought bitterly. She closed the newspaper, feeling as though the bottom had dropped out of her world.

Listlessly, she began to prepare the evening meal for Tom coming home. *Although why I should feed him is beyond me*, she thought angrily as she hacked skins off potatoes. Then, she suddenly stiffened as an awful thought occurred to her. The knife clattered into the sink. How many other people had seen the photograph? Were Cora and Sam, and all the customers in the Weaver's Arms gossiping about it and laughing at her behind her back? Silly, innocent little Kitty, stuck at home while her husband played the field with the daughter of a wealthy horse breeder. Almost choking with humiliation she marched over to the table and folded the newspaper so that the photograph was visible. Then she placed it where Tom always sat to take his dinner.

She was nursing Molly when Tom came home. 'How's my two best girls?' he said, shrugging off his coat and giving Kitty a charming smile. Kitty didn't reply. Putting Molly in her highchair she dished up Tom's dinner then waited for him to sit down at the table. As soon as he did, she marched over and slammed down the plate. Arms folded, she stood and glared at him.

Tom glanced at the newspaper then, his breath catching, he looked more closely. He paled. *Damn that photographer*, he silently cursed. But he'd been sure Kitty never read the sports pages. He pushed the newspaper aside and pulled the plate forward. Then, grinning falsely and giving a nonchalant shrug, he said, 'It's not what it looks like. She was just some girl who got too excited and grabbed hold of me.' He forced a chuckle.

'Liar! Ye know damned well who she is. Ye spent a weekend with her. She's Nigel Hutchinson's daughter.' Tom looked abashed. 'Ye see, Tom, a good liar has to remember what he's said,' Kitty continued sarcastically. 'Did ye forget ye'd told me his name? I didn't, and I'm not stupid. The pair of ye look *very* friendly.'

Tom slammed down his knife and fork. 'Of course we're friendly,' he snapped. 'Her father's my business associate.'

'Aye, and what is she? Ye don't hold a girl like that an' have that look on your face if she means nothing to ye.' Kitty's lip curled as she stared him down. 'The Tom Conlon I married would never have dreamed of having an affair. But you're not that man. I don't know who ye are any more, an' I don't think I want to know.'

* * *

The next few days dragged by. The photograph haunted Kitty and she was finding it hard to hide her misery.

'There are days when you look as miserable as sin, an' this is one of them,' Maggie said as soon as she entered Kitty's kitchen.

'Comments like that do wonders for a girl's morale,' said Kitty, putting on the kettle then giving her full attention to Lily who was asking for a biscuit. 'Here ye are, love.' She handed her two custard creams. When Molly saw Lily, she gurgled with delight and crawled across the rug to meet her. Lily squatted down beside her.

'She's growing into a lovely girl,' Kitty exclaimed, beaming at Lily then at Maggie. But the smile didn't reach her eyes. 'Isn't it grand the way they get on?'

'Don't try changing the subject,' Maggie scorned. 'Like I said, you've a face like a slapped arse. Is everything all right between you an' Tom?'

Kitty flinched. 'Why would ye ask that?' she said sharply.

Maggie sat down at the table and lit a cigarette. 'For a start, he's never hardly here, an' for another you haven't been yourself this past while back.' She blew out a stream of smoke then said, 'Come on, Kitty. What's wrong?'

Turning her back on Maggie, Kitty bit down on her lip as she filled the teapot. She had deliberately kept her more recent marital problems secret from even her closest friends. She didn't want their sympathy. That wouldn't solve anything. And that, coupled with the sneaky feelings she had about being unable to keep her man might lead them to see her has someone to be pitied. She wanted to avoid that at all costs. If nothing else, she had her pride.

'Tom's busy,' she said, putting the teapot then the cups and milk on the table.

Maggie snorted. 'Tom's busy doing a lot o' things, Kitty! Don't pretend with me. I saw that picture in the paper – the one with that girl – Fred showed it to me.'

Kitty paled and her heart lurched painfully. It was what she had dreaded. She marched over to the cupboard and pulled out the newspaper. Back at the table she slapped it down, open at the photograph. 'Do ye mean this, Maggie?'

Maggie glanced at the paper. 'Yeah. Is it as bad as it looks?'

Kitty sat down at the table feeling utterly deflated. 'It's worse,' she said softly. 'He's forever going off to see her an' I'm at a loss what to do.'

'Kick him out. Tell him to pack his bags an' bugger off.'

'It's his house. I can't tell him to leave.' Kitty sounded woefully forlorn.

'I suppose not,' Maggie replied despondently. 'Bloody men! They always have the upper hand.' She swallowed a mouthful of tea. 'Take my Fred – not that you'd want him – I can't get rid of him no matter how nasty I am to him. He sticks to me like shit to a blanket, and it's not because he loves me. He stays because he has no rent to pay an' he gets free grub.'

'He's not running round with another woman though, is he?' Kitty said bitterly.

'I wish he was,' Maggie crowed. 'She might take him off my

hands.' She gave an ugly laugh. 'Do you know, when I first got to know you I was jealous of you and your Tom. He seemed like an angel compared to my Fred – an' Beth's Blair's too good to be true – but you wait an' see, they're all as bad as one another.'

'That's a bit of an overstatement,' Kitty said, feeling better now that Maggie knew the truth. Although why she should just didn't seem to make sense. Out of the blue she thought of John Sykes. 'There are some lovely men, Maggie. We just happened to marry two stinking rotten maggots.'

Maggie burst out laughing. 'Dead right, we did. Me an' you are a right pair.'

'We are,' Kitty said sadly. 'We're trying to hang on to the love, honour an' obey bit when there is no love an' no honour, an' as for the obey bit...' She threw up her hands in frustration.

'I never did go in for honouring an' obeying.' Maggie gave a dirty chuckle. 'And do you know what? All them promises are not worth a candle. Who needs 'em when we've got each other? So keep your chin up, Kitty, you've still got me.' Maggie smiled sweetly, satisfied with her philosophy.

'An' glad I am of it,' Kitty said, her voice wobbling with emotion. 'I never thought I'd say this Maggie, but it's ye that keeps me sane.' She gave a grateful grin. 'An' I've got that one over there to love me —' she nodded at Molly '—an' this one on the way—' she patted her belly '—an' I'll be damned if I let Tom Conlon make my life a misery.'

After Maggie had left, Kitty sat on at the table. Mixed emotions surged through her and she didn't know what to make of them. On the one hand, she felt broken, betrayed, but on the other, she felt a sense of relief. So what if everyone knew she had a rotten, cheating husband? She still had her good reputation, and she'd hold her head high, preserve her dignity, and let the world know she was beholden to nobody. She got to her feet, and lifting Molly into her arms, she danced slowly about the room whispering, 'It's just me, you an' the baby from now on, an' when we open the café we'll show 'em we're not beaten.'

* * *

'I'll be away for a few days,' Tom said on Friday morning as he strode into the kitchen with his overcoat on and a small suitcase in his hand.

'Give my regards to the Hutchinsons,' Kitty gushed without looking at him.

Tom's cheeks reddened. 'Aye, well, take care while I'm gone,' he mumbled.

Kitty chirped, 'We will, Tom,' and to Molly, 'We always do, don't we, darlin'?'

31

Tom had been away two days when Kitty visited the second-hand store in Broad Green. Holding Molly by the hand they wandered the narrow alleyways between sideboards and wardrobes in search of the owner. He appeared from behind a tall bookcase.

'Morning, Peter,' said Kitty. 'I was wondering where I'd find ye.'

'Hello, Kitty, what can I do for you?' He recognised her from the time she had bought the sewing machine and gave her a warm smile.

'I'd like to buy a single bed, nothing fancy, just one in good condition,' she said.

'The beds are in the back store. Come this way and I'll show you what I've got. Is it for Molly?'

Kitty was overcome with embarrassment. She could hardly tell him it was for her two-timing husband. Pasting on a smile, she pretended it was.

'Do you hear that, Molly? Your mammy's buying you a bed. She's turfing you out of your cot so that she can put the new baby in it.' Peter laughed.

Kitty blinked. The idea of buying the bed for Molly had never entered her head, but now she latched onto it. 'That's right. She's a big girl now, an' she'll have to make room for her brother or sister, won't ye, Molly.' Molly's eyes darkened and she stuck out her bottom lip.

Weaving down the alleys piled high with furniture they went to the back store, Peter leading the way. Kitty chose a bed, and Peter said, 'I can bring it round straight away. I'll set it up for you, an' all – unless you want Tom to do it.'

'No!' Kitty exclaimed. It was the last thing she wanted. Thanking Peter, she hurried back home. A short while later he arrived with the bed. 'I'm putting it in the back bedroom,' she said when she answered his knock on her front door. He heaved the bedspring off the back of his lorry. Three more trips brought up the bed ends and the mattress.

'It won't take me five minutes to put it together,' Peter said.

Kitty gave him a winning smile and said, 'Thanks, that'll be grand. I'll go an' put the kettle on.'

Back downstairs, Peter found a mug of tea and a jam scone waiting for him. 'Mmm,' he said, licking his lips as he sat at the table.

'It's just a wee thank you for being so kind,' Kitty said, having realised that she wouldn't have been able to assemble the bed without his help. She needed it to be ready for when Tom eventually arrived home.

'I've put it against the far wall for now,' Peter said. 'You'll no doubt be decorating the room before Miss Molly sleeps in it.' He winked over at Molly, sitting on the rug eating a crust of bread with jam.

Kitty thought of the drab, bare room. 'Of course,' she lied, giving Peter a smile.

After he'd gone, she lifted Molly and went upstairs to the front bedroom. She gazed at the bed she and Tom shared. *Not for much longer,* she thought, lifting Molly and putting her in her cot. 'Now, play with Teddy while I finish my jobs.'

Kitty went back and forth taking Tom's clothes into the back bedroom and piling them on the bed. She gazed with regret at the heap, and steeling herself not to relent, she nipped downstairs to get scissors and a length of stout cord.

Back in the bedroom, she tied the cord from one convenient nail in the wall to another and hung his suits and shirts on it. Then she placed his shoes underneath and stuffed his underwear and socks into the old chest of drawers. Finally, with sheets and blankets she'd taken from the airing cupboard, she made up the bed.

There, Mr Conlon. I hope you find your new accommodation to your satisfaction. She closed the bedroom door behind her and stood by the window on the landing, her eyes blurred with tears as she gazed over the allotments. Now that it was done she was assailed by a gamut of emotions, sadness fighting with defiance and self-righteous indignation. Feeling the need to do something nice to clear her head, she went and lifted Molly from her cot. Downstairs, she glanced at the clock. Twenty past eleven. She'd take Molly and go into town.

She was window shopping outside Blacklers when she heard John Sykes's voice. 'Hello, Kitty, and hello, Miss Molly. It's a glorious day, isn't it?'

'It is,' Kitty agreed. She found herself thinking she was glad she was wearing a pretty dress and had left her tawny curls unrolled.

John gazed into her eyes, hazel flecked with gold. They were beautiful yet they looked incredibly sad. He felt the urge to make them look happy. 'Listen,' he said, his lips curving in an eager smile. 'I've a delivery to make in New Brighton. Why don't you come with me? Molly can play on the sands.'

Taken aback, Kitty hesitated. In another mood she might have refused, but defiance reared up like a tidal wave. Her husband was dallying with his lady friend. Why shouldn't she enjoy herself – in an unromantic way of course.

'We'd love to,' she said, anticipation colouring her cheeks.

What a day they had, building sand castles, paddling and eating fish and chips on the promenade. On the way home, Kitty mused on how pleasurable she found John's company and that she and Tom never spent days like this.

* * *

Tom arrived back from York just after ten. Kitty was sitting waiting for him, her nerves jangling. She made a pot of tea, and as she sipped, her thoughts ran riot. Could she go through with putting him out of her bed and out of her life? She thought of where he had been and what he had been doing, and draining her cup, she stood defiantly. 'I'm going to bed,' she said.

Tom had barely spoken two words to her. He'd been musing on his glorious conquest of Priscilla, but now, his cup empty and his cigarette burned to a stub, he watched Kitty uneasily, sensing that something was afoot.

'I'm right behind you,' he said, following her upstairs, so close that she could smell tobacco and whiskey on his breath. Kitty's heart was drumming in her ears and she wondered if he could hear it. When she reached the landing and Tom the top step, she pushed open the back bedroom door.

'You're in here from now on, Tom,' she said, surprised by how confident she sounded and amazed by her own audacity. 'I've moved all your things.'

'What? What...' Tom reeled, and would have fallen back down the stairs had he not grabbed for the newel post with one hand and

Kitty's hand with the other. She felt the clasp of his fingers against her own and saw his mouth hanging loose; fingers that had traced every inch of her skin, and lips that had kissed and caressed every curve and crevice of her body. Her throat clogged with a sickly sweetness. She shook her hand free.

'I don't want to share my bed with ye any more, Tom.' A punch of fear hit her stomach as she said the words.

His eyes were wild, his expression one of utter disbelief. 'But... but...'

'But what, Tom?' she said wearily. 'Ye chose to destroy our marriage and I'm choosing the way things will be from now on.' She felt her confidence wilting, and drew a sharp breath. An immense wave of emotion roiled in her chest leaving her feeling bruised. 'I never wanted it to come to this,' she continued brokenly, as though she was swallowing stones. 'I truly believed ye'd always love me as much as I loved ye but—' she gave a sad, little shrug '—time an' again you've proved ye have neither love nor respect for me, and I won't sully myself by pretending it doesn't matter, because I think I deserve better.' She turned and walked to the front bedroom on feet that didn't feel as though they belonged to her.

'Have it your own way,' Tom snarled, stamping into the back bedroom and slamming the door.

Kitty couldn't sleep. She lay in confused silence, no tears. Had she raised a massive, impenetrable barrier that could never be breached? Was there no turning back? She pressed her eyes shut and clamped her lips together to stem the flood. She was afraid to feel. Numbness was far safer. It didn't hurt.

Next door, flat on his back in the narrow bed, gazing at the ceiling, Tom Conlon felt such a deep sense of loss and loneliness that sleep evaded him.

* * *

After that, the days dragged by in a spiral of ups and downs. The upside for Kitty was thinking about the new baby, and marvelling that this time round she wasn't plagued with swollen ankles and puffy feet. Then there was Molly; what a joy she was. She stood on her own two feet, wobbling as she took uncertain steps. She had her own language, each new word she uttered making Kitty exclaim, 'Who's a clever girl, Molly?' Every day brought something new to rejoice over, but at night Kitty often lay waken, afraid to rest in the darkness of the night.

She was never short of Maggie and Beth's company, and she had her baking lessons with Mavis. 'That's the lightest, tastiest Victoria sponge I've had in a long time,' Mavis had said at the end of Kitty's most recent lesson, Kitty's cheeks pink as much from her praise as the heat of the oven.

Best of all had been the two Saturday afternoons that she had met John while walking on the riverbank. Her spirits had lifted each time she saw the golden retriever plodding towards her, closely followed by her master. John and his dog then fell into step with her like old friends did, and not once had conversation run dry. 'I could listen to ye all day,' Kitty had told him at their last meeting, after John had described a trip he'd recently made to Wales.

He had replied, 'And I could talk to you all day given the chance.'

The downside of course was Kitty's relationship with Tom. They were barely speaking to one another and Kitty found it hard to even look at him. For his part, Tom stubbornly played the role of a lodger, coming and going as he pleased, and every now and then letting Kitty know that he thought she was being foolish. That her imagination had got the better of her, and before long she would relent and take him back into her bed. She, however, couldn't dismiss the incriminating photograph, and his frequent long weekends away from home convinced her that he was planning a future that did not include her and their children.

32

The day of Molly's first birthday, Tom announced that he had arranged to take them out for tea. 'It's a posh hotel, Kitty. You'll see how the other half live.' He began extolling its virtues, and was so sure that she'd accept that it made her blood boil.

'We're having a party here, Tom, an' I don't need to see what your wealthy friends get up to.'

'Cancel it,' he snapped. 'Have it another day.'

'No, Tom! Stick your posh hotels an' your fancy friends. I'm done dancing to your tune. We're having the party here.'

Tom glowered. 'Aye, Kitty. You stay where you belong,' he snarled, 'down with the dregs of society.' He grabbed his coat and stormed out.

* * *

'Tom wanted to take us to a swanky hotel,' Kitty said that afternoon as she laid the table with dishes of jelly and little buns. 'You know, the sort of place where they cut the crusts off the sandwiches.'

'What a bleedin' waste,' Maggie expostulated. 'Still, it was nice of him to ask you though, wasn't it?' She sounded envious.

Kitty surprised herself by replying, 'I suppose it was his way of trying to make up for things. Ye know we haven't been getting on lately.'

'Yeah, well, that's marriage for you,' Maggie said sagely.

'How's Fred behaving these days?'

'No better, an' drunk or sober he's horrible to Lily. I'll likely murder him afore long. I've been thinking about hammering a big darning needle through his heart then pulling it out so they can't accuse me,' Maggie said dryly.

Kitty gasped. 'Maggie Stubbs, you're the craziest woman alive.'

'Don't you mean craftiest?' said Maggie, smearing margarine on bread. At Kitty's suggestion they were having a joint birthday party for Molly and Lily as their birthdays were so close together.

Kitty nodded over to where the girls were having a dolls' tea party. As usual, Lily was bossing Molly into doing what she herself wanted, Molly placidly acquiescing. 'Lily looks lovely,' Kitty said.

In honour of her second birthday, Lily was wearing a shocking pink frock that clashed delightfully with her gleaming red curls. 'Yeah, she does, doesn't she?' Maggie agreed. 'She's a beauty like her ma.'

'It's plain to tell ye've not eaten any humble pie today,' Kitty retorted.

'Yoo-hoo! Anybody home?' Mavis trilled, coming in with Beth at her side. 'Now, where are the party girls?' Squishy packages were handed to the little girls. They tore at the wrappings: a fluffy stuffed dog and a spinning top for Molly, and a rag doll and pretty ribbons for Lily. The girls crowed with delight.

Just then, Vi walked in. She handed Lily a big, pink balloon. Maggie gave her a dirty look. 'You managed to find time to come then?'

Vi ignored the biting sarcasm and said, 'I can't stand bloody kids, but any road, it's her birthday, an' I am her grandmother.'

'Only when it suits you,' Maggie sneered.

Kitty clattered the hated, unused teaspoons that had been Tom's Christmas gift next to the dishes of jelly. *They'd come in handy for gouging out Miss Priscilla Hutchinson's eyeballs.*

The women sat round the table, and in between doling out buns and cake and spooning jelly and custard into little, hungry mouths, they gossiped.

'I asked May to join us, but she's working,' Kitty said as she refilled the teapot.

'Poor May. It's a pity she has to work so hard,' Mavis commented with a shake of her head. 'But then, with a husband like Bill...'

'Yeah, did you hear what she did to him?' Maggie crowed, the smile on her face letting them know she was pleased to be relating a tale about a woman other than herself who had a drunken husband. 'He came home rat-arsed and she clobbered him with the frying pan.'

'Yeah, he had a bump on his head as big as a duck egg when he came into the pub last night,' Vi chortled. She helped herself to a chocolate whirl. 'An' you'll never guess what happened to me last night,' she continued. 'I was giving 'em a song in the Weaver's when me elastic broke. I ended up wi' me britches round me ankles.'

How much more fun this is, Kitty thought, laughing uproariously as she recalled the idea of a stuffy, country house tea.

'I'm still laughing about Jack and his teeth,' Mavis said.

'Why? What happened to them?' Kitty and Beth chorused.

Mavis leaned forward, her beady eyes twinkling. 'When I saw him yesterday on his way to the allotment he was all gummy and embarrassed because he didn't have his dentures in. He told me he'd lost them, said he'd looked everywhere and couldn't find them.

Then, when he was walking away I saw them. They were stuck in the back of his jumper,' she hooted, 'all tangled up in the wool.'

'How... how did... they get.... there?' Kitty was choking with mirth.

Mavis rolled her eyes. 'He said they must have fallen out of his mouth when he was sleeping and he must have rolled on them.' By now, Mavis and the rest of the women were breathless with laughter. Kitty looked at their happy faces and thanked God for her friends. She could still find something to laugh about even if her husband was cheating on her.

After everyone else had gone, Maggie stayed behind to help clear up. Not that there was much to do because they'd all pitched in before they left. Stubbing out her cigarette, Maggie announced that she was going for a pee.

'Ye don't have to give the detail,' Kitty piped as Maggie went upstairs.

After using the bathroom, Maggie poked her head into the front bedroom. Unlike her own, it was neat and tidy and smelled of something pleasant. At the end of the landing she peered into the back bedroom and saw the single bed. Tom's clothes hung from a string across the room, his shoes underneath it.

'Why's Tom sleeping in the back bedroom?' she asked as she entered the kitchen.

Flustered, Kitty said, 'Oh... you know...' She patted her tiny bump, about to use the baby as an excuse. Then she changed her mind. 'He's sleeping there because I won't have him in my bed. He's definitely having an affair with that woman he met at the racetrack. It's been going on for ages.' The words came out quite firmly but she felt as though her heart was bleeding.

'Aw, Kitty! I didn't know things were as bad as that. You never said.' Maggie pulled Kitty up from her chair and hugged her. Kitty burst into tears. Maggie patted her back. 'Come on, love. Let it all out. You can tell me. You'll feel better for it.'

Kitty sobbed into Maggie's shoulder. 'That picture in the paper was for real. When he goes off for days sayin' he's workin', he's with her. Then he comes back like he's a lodger an' I'm his landlady, not caring that I can smell her on him.'

'The dirty, rotten swine!' Maggie's disgust was such that she let go of Kitty. 'That's worse than lying his head off,' she sneered. 'Playing that game's downright cruel. It's like he's messing with your head.'

'He is,' Kitty said, sitting down with a thud and clasping her hand to her forehead. 'He won't even talk about it. If I go on about it not bein' right he just walks out an' goes to the pub.' She wiped her cheeks with her hands and took a deep breath. 'So there ye have it.'

Her composure somewhat regained, she gave a wan smile. For some strange reason she felt lighter inside now that she had nothing to hide. She had unburdened herself to her dearest friend, and she knew that Maggie would support her every inch of the way ahead.

Maggie sat down, reaching across the table for Kitty's hands. 'Ne'er mind, Queen. You're not on your own,' said Maggie, gently squeezing Kitty's hands. 'There's dozens of women with rotten husbands.' She raised her eyes to the ceiling in despair. 'Your Tom thinks 'cos he's got a willy in his pants that it's all right for him to flash it around, but I'll bet if you so much as looked at another fella he'd give you a good hiding. I know my Fred would.'

'Ye did a bit more than look, Maggie. That's how you got your Lily.' Kitty sniffed, her lips twitching with wry amusement. Even though Tom's infidelity made her feel desperately sad, she always managed to see the funny side of the things that Maggie came out with. She gave a little shrug. 'I don't think Tom'd be that bothered if I did go off with another fella. In fact, I think he'd be glad to see the back of me. I don't expect him to be here much longer an' I'm not sure what'll happen when he goes.' The awfulness of what she had just admitted struck her with full force and she burst into tears again.

Maggie jumped to her feet and, going round the table, she cradled the friend she treasured most in the world against her breast, rocking her soothingly. 'Aw, Kitty love, don't cry.' Inwardly she cursed Tom Conlon. When she let go of Kitty she gave her a challenging look. 'So what if he does go? You'll not fall to pieces. You're too brave for that.'

Kitty gave a wobbly smile. 'Aye, I'll manage somehow. I'll not be beaten till they put me in a box an' carry me up to the church.'

'That's a bloody cheerful thought,' Maggie groaned, both of them laughing through their tears.

33

'Holy mother! Your head looks like it's on fire,' Kitty squealed as Maggie walked into the kitchen with Lily.

'Don't you start,' Maggie snorted, 'I've heard enough from Vi.' She patted her hair, now a mess of flaming red squiggles. 'It wan't meant to turn out like this. I only did it so it'd be more like Lily's.'

'Whatever do ye mean?' Kitty was mystified.

'Me mam says Fred's been puttin' it about in the Wagon an' Horses that I'm a slut an' that Lily's not his,' Maggie gabbled, 'an' Flo from the mill says they're all talkin' about it. He's been asking funny questions. You know. Like where did she get her red hair from, and why doesn't she look a bit like him? I told him I was ginger when I was younger.'

Kitty left off drying the dishes and looked askance. 'You daft ha'porth,' she crowed, throwing the tea towel at Maggie. 'He's known ye since ye were a wee blonde child. Makin' yourself look like a squirrel won't make him any the less suspicious.'

'I suppose you're right,' Maggie groaned. 'I just thought it'd put a stop to him slanderin' me. I don't really care what he thinks of me – I know what I think of him – but I don't want people pointing the finger at Lily an' saying she's a bastard. They will, you know, an' she'll have to grow up being called that.'

'Oh, Maggie,' Kitty said tenderly. 'I don't blame ye for tryin' to put things right for Lily but makin' yourself look a sight's not the answer.'

'Aw, shurrup! It'll wash out – eventually.'

Maggie slouched out of the house, back to her mending frame, leaving Kitty to wonder about the machinations of Maggie's logic. Whatever would she come up with next? Kitty didn't have long to wait to find out.

Later that same night Maggie barged into Kitty's as though the hounds of hell were chasing her. 'Didn't you hear me shoutin' for you?'

Kitty was sewing buttons on a coat she had altered for one of her customers and didn't immediately look up. When she did she gasped. 'Oh my jaysus, Maggie! What happened to ye? Did Fred do that?'

A huge, purple bruise blossomed on Maggie's left cheekbone and her bottom lip was swollen and split. Kitty leapt to her feet, the coat falling to the floor. Heedless of treading on it she led Maggie to a chair by the fire, shocked not only by her friend's injuries but the look of utter misery in her eyes.

'Sit ye down,' she urged, 'I'll make a cup of tea an' ye can tell me what happened. The kettle's not long boiled.'

'He's found out about Lily for definite,' Maggie mumbled, wincing as her teeth caught her torn lip. 'He was drinking in the Wagon an' Horses an' Lily's real dad came in. Some sneaky bugger told him I'd been messing about with him when Fred was in the army and when he saw his flaming red hair he put two an' two together.' She shrugged painfully. 'I suppose he was bound to find out in the end.'

'That's no excuse for doin' that on ye,' Kitty scorned as she made the tea.

Maggie sipped then groaned as the hot tea stung her lip. 'Any road,' she continued, 'I told him the truth. That's when the bugger went for me.' She put down her cup and pushed up her cardigan sleeves. 'Look at me bloody arms—' she lifted her skirt '—an' me legs.' Her limbs were mottled with dark yellow and blue-black patches criss-crossed with red lines. 'The bugger took his belt to me!' She poked at an ugly raised welt of broken skin.

Kitty's eyes bulged in disbelief when saw the full extent of the damage. 'That's downright wickedness.' She pushed her cardigan sleeves up to her elbows. 'Come on,' she said, heading for the door.

Maggie gaped. 'Where? What...'

'There's no way we're lettin' him get away with it this time,' Kitty cried as, with Maggie on her heels, she bounced down the steps and out into the lane, straight up to Maggie's door. She slammed it back on its hinges.

'Kitty! Kitty! Be careful. He...'

Fred was lying on the couch, a bottle of beer in his hand. He glanced round as Kitty barged in then took a swig from the bottle.

'Get up, ye bastard,' Kitty roared, waving a fist in his face.

Fred's jaw dropped. 'What the bloody hell...?' he slurred, shifting into a sitting position. He glared at Maggie. She glared back.

'Up with ye, ye black coward,' Kitty snapped, 'for if you're not out of this house in five minutes the police will have ye. I've already sent for them.'

'What's she on about, Maggie?' He got to his feet, swaying. He looked afraid.

Kitty gave him a push. 'Ye've beat her one last time an' I'm a witness to it. If ye don't want to end up in jail ye'll go now.'

Maggie, shocked by Kitty's bravery, found her own. 'Yeah, that's right, Fred,' she shouted, pulling on his arm and dragging him towards the door. Kitty pushed him from behind, Fred struggling to break free. Maggie yanked open the door and between them she and Kitty pushed him down the steps. Maggie grabbed his coat hanging behind the door and threw it after him. It landed on top of him as he sprawled at the foot of the steps.

Fred scrabbled to his feet. 'You can't throw—'

'We just have, Fred,' Kitty cackled. 'An' ye'd best get cracking. The police are on their way.'

'Yeah, and don't come back,' yelled Maggie. She slammed the door and locked it. Then she and Kitty went to the window, peering out to see what Fred would do next.

He put on his coat then stood on the path looking thoroughly confused. A few minutes later they heard him bawl, 'I wasn't staying any road. I'm not payin' to keep another fella's kid.' He shambled out into the dark lane.

'As if he ever paid a bloody penny,' Maggie sneered, rubbing at her arms as she flopped into a chair. 'I knew he'd be mad but I never thought he'd try to kill me.'

'Well, at least he's gone. Good riddance to bad rubbish, I'd say.'

The two women looked at one another and burst out laughing.

For the next half hour they relived what they had just done. 'Did you see his face when you told him you'd called the police?' Maggie chuckled. 'You're a crafty sod, and no mistake.' She frowned. 'He'll be back for his stuff though.'

'Don't let him in. Keep the door locked an' tell Vi to do the same. Put his stuff in a box an' leave it outside the door.'

When Kitty got up to go home, Maggie hugged her. 'You're a great mate. We make a smashing team, don't we?'

Back in her own house, in bed, Kitty pondered on what she would do if Tom were to beat her. He'd never once raised his hand to her but her coldness towards him and the fact that she denied him his conjugal rights might just drive him to violence, she thought. Then she gave a bitter laugh that ended in a flood of tears. Whatever was she thinking? Priscilla Hutchinson was doing her job for her. Tom didn't need her for that or for anything else.

* * *

Kitty's wasn't the only house in Weaver Street that was permeated with misery these days. Next door, in the Forsythes', things were almost as bad.

Beth lifted her tearstained face to Blair, begging him to understand. 'I don't mind taking him his dinner every day and doing his housework, Blair. He is my father,' she mumbled apologetically.

'I on the other hand, do mind,' said Blair. 'I hate seeing you come back home shaking with nerves at what that vile man has said to you. Isn't it enough that we have him to dinner every Sunday without you tending his daily needs?' He had spoken to Walter about his dominating behaviour but it had had no effect.

'We're quarrelling again and it's all because of my dad, but I don't know what else I can do,' Beth said tremulously.

'You could start by listening to me,' Blair snapped. 'You're my wife and we and our lives should come first. I'm sick of seeing you haring up and down the lane at his beck and call, but as long as you continue to comply with his demands there will never be an end to it.'

Beth gave a shuddering sob.

'I'm sorry for raising my voice,' Blair said contritely. 'I'm just trying to protect you. I love you so much I can't bear to see what he's doing to us.' He put his arms round her.

Beth leaned into his strong, warm body, searching for the protection she so badly needed. Her dreams of a happy marriage were crumbling and she knew that it was due to her own weakness.

Blair felt her body relax against his as they rocked together, each struggling to find a solution to their misery. 'Come on, Beth,' he said tenderly, 'don't cry. We'll come through this, I promise.' His lips found hers and he imbued every ounce of love into the kiss, but he couldn't help thinking that short of killing his father-in-law there was little he could do to free his wife from Walter's snare.

Later, as Beth soaked in a long, hot bath she knew that everything Blair had said was true. Marriage was much harder than she had imagined, and she knew that she was making a hash of hers. She had thought that once she was living in her own home she would be free from her father's cruel domination, but it had only worsened matters. When she called with a meal or to clean the house for him, the vitriol that spewed from his mouth tore her nerves to shreds. Each day she grew more and more tense. She had hoped to conceive by now. More than anything she wanted a baby: Blair's baby. But when she had confided in Renee Spivey, the midwife had told her she was lessening her chances, inner tension being one of the main reasons for not getting pregnant.

Beth slid deeper into the bath, and as the now tepid water lapped over her head she wished with all her heart that she could wash away her problems as easily as she washed her body.

34

The train chugged along the tracks from York to Leeds. Tom had been away for the weekend again and now he was lolling in the corner of the carriage with his eyes closed. He felt bone weary after the past few hectic days but it was a satisfying weariness. During the day he had gone with Nigel to the races, and at night he had partied with the cream of society, drinking and dancing with Priscilla on his arm.

At one riotous party he'd been dancing with a glamorous American woman. 'This is the life, dahling, make the most of it,' she'd drawled, shimmying against him. 'Let's go to my room for sex.'

Tom had resisted the temptation, but he loved the feeling of wild, crazy abandonment that Priscilla and her friends generated. It was the sort of life he'd always craved, where money spoke louder than words, and it wasn't what you knew but who you knew that counted. One night he'd been in the company of a Scottish laird who lived in a castle, and the next a millionaire racing magnate, and a well-known Member of Parliament.

As his head nodded gently against the windowpane, Tom told himself he had come a long way from a little village in the west of

Ireland. With the connections he'd made over the past few days he could go a lot further. He was still contemplating on this as the train pulled into Lime Street Station.

However, in the cab taking him to Weaver Street, his complacency evaporated. His future with Priscilla seemed pretty certain, but living in the elite society that was her world required money: a large amount of it. Shifting uncomfortably in his seat as the cab jounced along, he cogitated the problems facing him.

The money he made wouldn't go far in those circles, and if he wasn't to be found out for the small-time player and liar that he really was then he'd have to rely on worming his way in with the syndicate that made the big money. Nigel had promised to let him in on it, but as yet nothing was conclusive. Once that was settled, it should sustain his chosen lifestyle and keep Priscilla in hers. However, he still didn't have a solution as to how he was going to deal with the biggest problem of all. Kitty.

* * *

Kitty heard the front door open and close. It was after ten o'clock and she knew it was Tom, home at last. No one else would be calling at this time of night. She heard the thud of his suitcase hit the floor and the muffled sounds as he took off his overcoat, but she made no move to get up and greet him.

He stepped into the kitchen, surprised to see her sitting by the fire. 'I thought you'd be in bed,' he said, his smile forced.

Kitty set aside her copy of *Wuthering Heights* and got to her feet.

'Tea?' she said. Tom nodded. Kitty put the kettle on the hob then reached for her book, reading as she waited for it to boil.

Tom lit a cigarette, and through lowered lids he gazed at his wife. The green wool cloth of her skirt was stretched over her distended belly and the cream silk blouse enhanced the swell of her breasts. Her glorious tangle of red-gold hair caressed cheeks that were flushed from the heat of the fire. Her body didn't repulse him as it had during her first pregnancy, and he now felt a stirring in his loins. Kitty was still beautiful. Then he thought of Priscilla's slender, sensuous figure and the way her limbs entwined his as they engaged in mad, passionate sex, often fuelled by drink. His erection swelled. Kitty couldn't compete with Priscilla and the opportunities she provided for his entry into high society. Still, he couldn't take his eyes off his wife.

Kitty filled two mugs, and after handing one to Tom, she sat down again, her book in her lap. They sipped their tea in silence, until he couldn't bear it a moment longer. 'Was everything all right while I was away?' he asked.

'Aye, why wouldn't it be?' Kitty replied without raising her eyes from the page. *And if they hadn't been, would you care?* She drained her mug and closed her book. 'I'm going to bed.'

'I'll just finish this cigarette and be right behind you,' Tom said.

Kitty was coming out of the bathroom wearing only her petticoat when Tom appeared on the landing. He flashed her the smile that she had once thought was hers and hers alone. His blue eyes were dark with lust and longing. She knew that look. A swarm of butterflies invaded her tummy, and her mouth felt dry and her palms clammy. She hurried into her bedroom. From the doorway Tom watched her as she crossed the room, her hair bouncing. He eyed her neat, proud back and the tawny curls that he knew felt like silk against his fingers. Unable to resist he went closer and caressed her hips, his fingertips tingling as he stroked the satin petticoat. She whirled round.

'Don't you dare, Tom Conlon!'

Kitty's fists thumped into his chest so violently that he reeled backwards against the wardrobe. He saw the contempt in her eyes, eyes that had once laughed or gazed dreamily into his own. Fists still raised she stood quivering with rage and pent-up yearning for him. She swallowed the feeling.

'What? Is your racetrack whore not givin' ye enough, Tom, that ye have to come pesterin' me?'

Her venomous snarl cut him to the bone. She was his gentle, little Kitty.

Mixed emotions surged through him and he didn't know what to make of them. He hadn't prepared for the sick emptiness he now felt in the pit of his stomach or the coldness surrounding his heart. He stumbled out to the landing, and in the bleak back bedroom, devoid of the sweet scent of Kitty and sour with his own misery, he sat down heavily on the narrow bed. Was this what he really wanted?

Slowly, he undressed and lay on the bed, debating whether or not to fly down to the front bedroom and rant and rave – or plead and beg. Shivering in the emptiness of the lonely bed, he savagely dismissed the thought. He'd come too far to give up on his hopes and dreams of living the life he truly believed he deserved, he told himself, and now that he was on the cusp of it he would be foolish to let it go. His thoughts still churning he fell into a restless sleep, tossing and turning and searching for the feel of Kitty's soft warmth.

35

'I see Tom's back,' Maggie said the next day as she and Kitty were walking to the market with Molly and Lily in their pushchairs. Molly was sitting up and smiling at everyone she saw, but Lily was squawking and drumming her heels against the footplate.

'Aye,' Kitty replied tersely. She didn't want to think about Tom, let alone discuss him.

'Business must be booming if he has to stay away for so long,' Maggie slyly observed as she drew to a halt. 'I don't know why I bothered to buy this thing. She wants to walk all the time,' she grumbled, lifting Lily out of the pushchair and roughly planting her on her feet. Lily wobbled, then, grabbing hold of the footplate, she propelled the pram forwards, la-la-lahing happily as she toddled on.

'See!' Maggie expostulated. 'The little mare's only happy when she's getting her own way.'

Kitty gave Maggie a lopsided grin. 'I wonder who she gets that from?'

'I hope you're not referring to me. I never get me own way.'

'Come off it, Maggie,' Kitty laughed. 'You can be proper pig-headed when ye want to be.'

'Yeah, an' look where it got me,' Maggie groaned.

'Watch her! Get hold of her,' Kitty cried as Lily rammed the pushchair into the back of an elderly man's legs. Maggie dived and grabbed Lily, laughing as she apologised to the man. He laughed too.

'No harm done,' he said, ruffling Lily's red hair.

They continued ambling round the stalls, Lily back in the pushchair, tired out after her burst for freedom.

'Have you been talking to Beth lately?' Kitty asked Maggie.

'I had a word with her the other teatime when she was going down to her dad's with his dinner between two plates.' Maggie raised her eyebrows and pulled a face to show her opinion of such servitude.

'I'm worried about her. She's a bag of nerves.'

'She's always been a nervous little thing.' Maggie didn't sound in the least sympathetic, jealous as she was of Kitty and Beth's friendship. Immediately dismissing her she cried, 'Ooh! Look at that lovely cardigan.' She pointed out a garish woollen garment knitted in vivid purple and green stripes.

'It's awful,' Kitty said, catching hold of Maggie's arm. 'An' never mind the cardigan. I'm talking to you serious like about a friend.' Maggie reluctantly gave Kitty her attention.

'I said I'm worried about her,' Kitty continued, as they stopped by the grocery stall. 'These days she's so miserable and uptight she can barely get two words out without lookin' as though she's going to burst into tears. In fact, only yesterday when I was showing her the stuff I've made for the new baby, she suddenly started sobbing and ran out of the house.'

'What do you want me to do about it?' Maggie shrugged carelessly.

'I don't know,' Kitty said, paying for a tub of cinnamon and thinking, *Here am I worrying over Beth's problems as if I don't have enough of my own.*

'I'd best be getting back. I've loads of work on,' Maggie said.

'Aye,' Kitty agreed. 'An' I'm due at Mavis's so we'd best get a move on.'

Back in Weaver Street they parted, Maggie to her mending frame and Kitty to Mavis's kitchen.

'I see your hubby's back,' Mavis said when Kitty walked in. Groaning inwardly, Kitty did her best to hide her dismay. Why did everybody have to mention Tom? It didn't help at all, not when she was trying so hard to put him out of her mind.

'I'd like to try out that recipe for cinnamon biscuits,' Kitty said in an effort to deflect any further remarks, but she couldn't help but wonder what people would say if they knew the truth about her and her handsome husband. *They'll find out in good time,* she thought as she accepted the cup of tea Mavis handed her.

'Cinnamon biscuits it is then,' said Mavis, noting that Kitty looked weary.

'You haven't long to go now before the new baby arrives and I'm sure you get tired running round after this little madam.' Molly was pulling at Kitty's hand, wanting her to play then sulking when her mother said, 'Not now, darlin'.'

Kitty rubbed her belly. 'I must admit I'm feeling the weight of it, and I've still got three weeks to go. How I'll get through Christmas I just don't know. There'll be no parties this year.'

'But think what a wonderful gift you'll get in the New Year.' Mavis's tone was wistful. 'What better start to 1920 than a new life.'

Kitty pasted on a bright smile, but an inner voice whispered, *Was it just the baby that would be starting a new life, or was Tom also contemplating starting his?* If so then her life and Molly's would be irrevocably changed forever.

* * *

'Not long to go now,' May shouted as Kitty walked down the back lane feeling decidedly ungainly. Her belly bumped against the pushchair's handle as she turned and waved to May who was pegging out a line of shirts.

'Renee reckons it'll be early January,' Kitty called back. 'I had hoped it might be a Christmas baby.'

'Don't mention Christmas. It doesn't bear thinking about,' May grumbled, coming to the garden wall and leaning on her elbows. 'With three lads to buy for and my Bill celebrating the birth of our Lord by drinking his head off, there's not a lot of pleasure in it.'

'I love Christmas,' Kitty replied, thinking how different this next one might be, 'but I know what you mean. It's hard to find the extra money you feel obliged to spend.' She felt a twinge of guilt at what she had just said. May's circumstances were far different to her own: Tom never kept her short of housekeeping money.

'It's a bit easier this year now that our Ronnie's working, and our Joey leaves school next Easter, so I'll keep looking on the bright side.' May smiled stoically.

'You're lucky to have such lovely lads, May.'

May glowed. 'Well, I've allus brought 'em up to be kind an' respectful – and not to take after their father.' She chuckled wryly. 'Men, eh?'

Men indeed, thought Kitty as she carried on walking. She tried hard not to let the strained atmosphere in the house get her down, but Tom's sulky silences and the threat of what might happen next had cost her many a sleepless night. The distance between them was now so wide she felt as though she could never bridge it. If she didn't have Molly to love and cuddle and her neighbours to keep her smiling, she didn't know what she would do.

* * *

Tom slammed the telephone receiver back in its cradle then distractedly ran his fingers through his hair. It was the fifth time in as many days that his calls to Priscilla had been answered by one of Nigel Hutchinson's lackeys telling him Miss Priscilla was unavailable to take his call. That she had not bothered to return his messages angered him even further. However, the lackey who had answered the call he had just made had told him they were expecting her to return for dinner at seven that evening.

He glanced at the large clock he had installed on the wall in the betting shop. Like the telephone, it was a vital necessity to a bookmaker, but whereas the clock could be relied on to give accurate information the telephone sometimes played him foul. True, it kept him in touch with tipsters at the racetracks, and with the jockeys he sometimes advised to pull a race for his and their financial benefit, but at times like these, it left him feeling out of control.

He'd sent Rodney home soon after the last bets of the day had been taken, and the silence in the room was making him feel uneasy. He lit a cigarette and sat back in his chair gazing at the clock. It was seven minutes to seven. He thought about what he would say to Priscilla. He also thought about Kitty and what he would say to her. There had been a time when he had genuinely loved her and had wanted to take her with him in his pursuit of affluence and importance, but she didn't want that. She wasn't that sort of woman... whereas Priscilla...

It saddened him to think that his gentle, fun-loving, pretty little Kitty who had always been eager to please him had turned into a suspicious, acerbic shrew, but his self-belief in his own importance being such, he failed to see that he was the cause of this. He knew he couldn't stand the tension in the house for much longer and that he would move out once Christmas was over and the baby was born. It had never been his intention to hurt Kitty – in some ways he still loved her – but he was loath to let sentiment stand in the way of ambition. He had accepted that in order to achieve what he wanted it would inevitably distress them both when he made the final break.

Slowly, the hands of the clock ticked to seven. He lifted the telephone and asked for Priscilla. When she eventually came to the phone his heart leapt.

'Darling... yes... they told me you'd called. I did mean to get in touch but things have been such a whirl—' Priscilla trilled breathlessly.

'I'm coming down tomorrow,' he interrupted. He didn't want to hear about her whirl. Adopting a tone that he thought sounded both passionate and mysterious he said, 'I've something very important to ask you.' His smile wolfish, he sat back, hopeful that she'd be intrigued. Excitement building, he waited for her reply.

'Oh... but darling... you mustn't. We won't be here. We're going to Scotland for the last of the grouse shooting. Isn't it a wheeze?'

Tom felt as though he had been suddenly drenched in ice-cold water. 'When will you be back?' he snapped, a leaden feeling forming in his chest.

'Not until after New Year – or Hogmanay as the Scots call it,' Priscilla warbled. 'Brucie – you remember Bruce, darling? He's invited us to his castle to celebrate the festivities. How spiffing is that?' Her laughter tinkled down the telephone.

Bile filled Tom's throat. Oh yes, he remembered Brucie all right: the pale, undersized Scot with a freckled face and thinning red hair – the laird who, by the sound of it, owned half of Scotland. At the party he'd sniffed round Priscilla like a dog on heat, his tongue lolling out every time she looked at him.

'So I won't see you until sometime in January,' Tom said bleakly.

'It's looking that way, darling,' she trilled. 'Must dash. Have a lovely Christmas and be good. I'll be seeing you.' She hung up.

The silence in the betting shop swelled, and so did the veins in Tom's temples. The unfeeling, deceitful bitch; she was discarding him like last week's *Sporting Life*. The faint burring of the telephone in his hand reached his ears and he flung it across the room. It dragged the cradle with it and landed with a clatter. He clenched his fists, wanting to smash them into the face of the smug, rich Scot. He'd been pipped at the post, just when he'd been so near to winning. Tilting back his head, he felt tears seeping from the corners of his eyes and wetting his cheeks.

36

'Blair and I are going to Scotland to stay with his parents,' Beth said as she and Kitty huddled close to the fire one afternoon three days before Christmas Day. 'They celebrate New Year in a big way up there and he wants us to be there for it. Work in the mill's slack at the moment and Mr Holroyd's given us permission to take two weeks off. Blair says it will do me good.'

'An' I hope it does. You've certainly not been yourself lately. The change will do ye good.' Kitty re-threaded her needle to put the finishing touches to a blouse she had made for Connie. Her sewing kept her busy and it was something she could still do when she hadn't the energy for much else.

'I am looking forward to it,' Beth said, 'but—' she smiled, embarrassed '—I was wondering if you would do me a favour?' Her cheeks turned bright red. 'Do you think you could pop down with a bit of dinner for my dad on Christmas Day? I'll pay you for it,' she gabbled, 'I just don't like to think of him being all on his own and making do with a sandwich.'

Kitty didn't know whether to laugh or cry. The last thing she wanted to do was pander to Walter Garside, but she couldn't disappoint her friend. 'Ach, Beth! Will ye ever stop worrying about him? He'll not starve. I'll give him his dinner an' keep an eye on him,' she said, lumbering to her feet to prevent Molly from climbing up on a kitchen chair.

'Oh, Kitty, you're a treasure. Knowing that makes it all the easier for me to go.' Beth's relief was patent.

'Aye, off ye go, an' relax. I'll not be doing much celebrating meself in my condition. I think this Christmas will be a quiet one.'

* * *

On Christmas morning, Kitty carefully rolled out of bed. Even getting upright was an effort with all the extra weight she was carrying. Molly was still sleeping and Kitty stood for a moment to regain her breath, watching the rise and fall of her daughter's little chest and the put-put-putting of her rosebud lips. *She's a real Irish beauty*, thought Kitty, gently running the back of her finger over Molly's rosy cheek and up to her dark, finely arched eyebrows. *She'll break some hearts, just like her da.* She left her to sleep.

Downstairs, she put a piece of brisket into the oven along with a tray of roast potatoes she'd prepared the night before. She'd let them do slow until the meat was tender. Meat was still rationed, but Kitty had charmed the butcher into putting a piece to one side especially for her and she was pleased to have a decent joint to cook. Hearing Molly's cry, she fetched her downstairs, and in between making porridge and feeding Molly she peeled sprouts and made applesauce. Tom slept late, and when he came into the kitchen he looked the worse for wear.

'Merry Christmas,' Kitty sang out, desperate to bring some cheer into the house. Tom returned the greeting but his heart wasn't in it.

Shortly before they were due to sit down to eat Kitty filled a plate. Then, covering it over with another one, she said, 'I'm just popping down to Walter's. I won't be long. Keep an eye on Molly.' Tom gave a disconsolate nod.

Kitty hurried down the back lane, pausing briefly at number five's gate. May was putting peelings in the dustbin. 'Merry Christmas, May.'

'Merry Christmas, love.' May glanced curiously at the plates. 'What's that you've got there?'

'A dinner for Walter.'

May pulled a face. 'I hope you've laced it with arsenic,' she said, slamming the lid on the bin. 'I wouldn't give that miserable sod a crust.'

'I'm doin' it for Beth, not Walter.'

'She's lucky to have you,' May commented as Kitty hurried up Walter's path.

'Merry Christmas, Mr Garside,' she called out as she opened the door, 'I've brought ye your dinner.'

Walter jumped up from his chair by the fire looking sour. 'Put it on the table,' he growled. 'I don't know what things are coming to when I've to rely on strangers to cook me a meal. If my daughter had one ounce of love or respect for me she'd be here now.'

Kitty slammed down the plate, then, thinking better of it, she put it in Walter's side oven next to the blazing fire. 'It'll keep warm in there,' she snapped. Coming upright she put her hands on her hips and glared at him.

Walter started to bluster but Kitty overruled him. 'Love and respect, Mr Garside! Your Beth's terrified of ye. She's a bag of nerves what with your bullying ways.' Shocked, Walter plumped back into his chair.

'Look Mr Garside, Walter—' Kitty lowered her tone '—ye need to mend your ways. Ye should think yourself fortunate to have a daughter as willing as Beth. If ye take my advice ye'll start showing her some kindness for all she does for ye.' She paused meaning-fully. 'I know what it is to be bullied – my brothers tried it on me – an' ye know what I did? I beggared off to Dublin an' left them to do for themselves. Ye don't want Blair to take Beth to Scotland for good, do ye? He might if ye keep on the way ye are doing. Think about that!' she concluded.

Walter paled. His eyes stood out on stalks. Like a fish out of water he opened his mouth but no sound came out.

Kitty headed for the door. 'Enjoy your dinner, Mr Garside.'

Apart from her run-in with Walter, Kitty was right about Christmas being quiet. All over the festive season Tom was sullen and, for much of the time, silent. He'd barely touched his Christmas Day dinner, and after playing listlessly with Molly and her new toys he'd opened a bottle of whiskey and emptied it by bedtime. On Boxing Day he'd gone to the races.

However, for Kitty and Molly it wasn't all doom and gloom. They spent an enjoyable hour with Mavis, and Maggie popped in and out with Lily, the little girls happily playing and their mothers chatting over glasses of sweet sherry.

On New Year's Eve Tom got stinking drunk and slept all night in the chair.

So much for welcoming in 1920, Kitty thought as she climbed the stairs, humming the tune to 'Auld Lang Syne'.

37

Kitty had to get out of the house, couldn't stand it a moment longer. January was less than one week old and things were rather grim. Tom had been grumbling and grousing from the minute he'd come downstairs. He'd even shouted at Molly and made her cry. Now, he was slumped in an armchair with a surly look on his face. Earlier, Kitty had asked him, 'Why are you so prickly?' and the face he'd turned towards her was blank.

Outside it was bitterly cold, snow threatening. She was so big and ungainly now that everything was an effort and she leaned heavily on the pushchair as she made her way up Weaver Street. A flurry of light snow blew into her face. Maybe it had been a mistake to come out, but she was well wrapped up and Molly was snug in her pushchair under two blankets and with the hood up.

'Not a day to be out,' Connie remarked, her hair in curlers under a big woollen scarf. 'I've just been doing the flowers in the church and it was brass monkeys in there. You'll not want to be out too long.' Kitty agreed and plodded on.

At the top of the street she turned towards the towpath. A walk along the riverbank always raised her spirits. As she walked she chanted nursery rhymes to keep Molly entertained. Singing 'Pat-a-cake, pat-a-cake, baker's man' for the second time she approached the café. Bringing the pram to a halt she stood and gazed at the blue and white cabin. 'I haven't forgotten about ye,' she told it, her voice barely above a whisper. 'I've put enough money by to make a start, and as soon as this baby's here an' thriving, I'm coming to rescue ye.'

In her mind's eye, Kitty saw fresh paint on the outside, and blue and white checked cloths on the tables inside. She even imagined she could smell freshly baked rolls and the pungent scent of tea and coffee, and hear the sound of merry chatter at crowded tables. *Not long now,* she thought. *Come spring I'll be behind that counter serving the best of spreads to friends old and new.* A flurry of snowflakes blowing across the river and wetting her face broke her reverie. She turned back the way she had come, plodding as quickly as she was able.

The sky darkened, great, grey snow clouds massing above her head and the wind whipping at the hem of her coat. A sudden squall of thick, white flakes swirled along the towpath, reducing her visibility and slowing her progress. Snow clogged the pushchair's little wheels, the path treacherously slippery. Pristine white crystals coated the pushchair hood and apron. By the time she reached the steps up to the street they were blanketed in a drift of snow, Kitty unsure of where they began and ended. She stooped to brush the snow away.

Unbeknown to her, John had been hurrying to catch up with her. Now, with Goldie at his heels, he dashed up from behind, his footsteps muffled by the snow.

'Good God, Kitty, what are you doing out on a day like this?'

Startled, Kitty whirled round. When she saw John her breath whooshed out of her in a great gasp of relief. Blinking snow from ier eyelashes, she managed a wan smile. 'It took me by surprise,' she said.

John lifted the pushchair up to street level then helped Kitty up he steps. As she paused to catch her breath a sharp pain shot hrough her lower back and down into her thighs. She froze.

'What is it, Kitty? Are you hurt?' John caught hold of her arm.

'I think the baby's coming,' she gasped.

* * *

Patrick Joseph Conlon arrived in the middle of a blizzard less than an hour after his mother had been rescued on the riverbank.

'Where's Tom?' John had asked as he'd bundled Kitty and Molly and the pushchair indoors. But Tom wasn't at home. It had been John who fetched the midwife and minded Molly as her little brother made his way into the world with lusty cries. And it was John who made tea and sat at Kitty's bedside with Molly on his knee to admire the new baby.

'He looks like you, Kitty.' John was referring to Patrick's hazel eyes and at the fine red-gold hair clinging damply to his forehead. Then, before she left, Renee Spivey insisted on placing Patrick in the Moses basket, giving them a curt reminder that *'Mother needs to sleep.'*

Kitty smiled drowsily. 'Thank ye, John. You're a good, kind man. I'm lucky to have ye for a friend. I don't know what I'd have done without you.' Her eyelids drooped, and with Molly in his arms John crept quietly out of the room, wishing that the momentous occasion he'd just witnessed was his to celebrate.

When Tom eventually arrived back he found his daughter and John Sykes kneeling on the hearthrug building towers of coloured wooden blocks. Before Tom had to chance to question why he was there, John said, 'Congratulations, your wife and son are both doing well.'

Tom had the grace to look sheepish.

* * *

'He's gorgeous,' Maggie gushed, leaning over the Moses basket to take her first look at Patrick. 'I was knocked sideways when Tom told me you'd had him this afternoon. I thought you'd have given me a shout when you went into labour.'

'I didn't have time to shout for anybody.' Kitty then told Maggie what had happened on the riverbank. 'I don't know what would have happened if John hadn't come along. I'd have probably ended up giving birth at the church gate.'

She chuckled at the idea.

'Yeah, John Sykes's a lovely fella. He allus has been,' Maggie said, perching on the bottom of the bed. 'I've known him since we were kids. I'm surprised some woman hasn't snapped him up before now.'

'Maybe he hasn't met the right one.' Kitty recalled the loving look in John's eyes when he'd brought her a cup of tea and the way he had stayed to mind Molly. If only her husband had looked at her like that and been there for her. Tom had seemed pleased enough to have a son, but at the same time he seemed preoccupied, as though Patrick's birth had interrupted something more important. Had Kitty been able to read his mind she would have learned that he was more concerned with the news that Priscilla Hutchinson had left for Paris with the Right Honourable Bruce MacKenzie.

In the days that followed, friends popped in and out to see the new baby. One of them was Beth. When Maggie made one of her frequent daily visits Kitty asked, 'Have ye noticed the change in

Beth since she got back from Scotland? She's not half as nervy as she was. The holiday obviously did her good.'

'Yeah, I saw her coming out of her dad's today. She was proper perky, an' that old rat-bag was standing on the step with a grin on his face like a Cheshire cat. I couldn't believe it 'cos she usually comes away bawling her lamps out.'

'Walter must have turned over a new leaf.' Kitty smiled elusively.

'I find that hard to believe. Do you know something I don't?'

Kitty chuckled. 'I know no more than you, Maggie.'

'And I know sod all,' Maggie groused, 'except I'd best be going. Me mam'll be giving off for having to mind Lily. I'll be round first thing tomorrow to give you a hand, an' I can take Molly back to ours so you can take it easy.'

'That'd be grand.' Kitty smiled, inwardly quailing at the thought of Molly in Maggie's house with its dirty floors and overflowing ashtrays. Still, she did wonder how she'd manage with a new baby and a mischievous toddler to care for. It wasn't as though she could rely on their father to help out.

* * *

As things turned out, it was all so much easier than Kitty had anticipated. She couldn't believe how well she felt. She had none of the aches and pains she had suffered after Molly's birth, nor did she feel weary. Patrick was a dream baby. Once he was fed he slept peacefully, only waking to be fed again. Molly adored him. He was better than any teddy bear or dolly, and she lolled against Kitty's knee, fascinated as her brother latched on to his mother's breast and sucked. Kitty loved the tug on her nipple as Patrick took his fill. In the past few weeks she and her daughter had fallen into a steady routine.

'Pass me that nappy,' Kitty said, putting Patrick to her shoulder to burp him.

Molly gave her mother the nappy, then following her instructions she patiently handed over the jar of cream and the talcum powder from the little basket Kitty kept them in. 'Good girl, Molly. You're Mammy's little helper,' she praised. Kitty put Patrick in the pram then sat down with Molly on her knee. She didn't for a moment want Molly to feel rejected now that the baby was here.

'Hello-o-o,' Mavis trilled as she entered by the back door. 'And how are we today?' She waltzed over to the pram. 'He's certainly putting the weight on,' she said, beaming down at Patrick, now two months old.

'He has. Renee weighed him this morning. She says he's nearly doubled his birth weight.' Kitty lifted her son out of the pram for Mavis to hold. She readily took him in her arms, nuzzling her face in the folds of his neck.

Kitty put the kettle on, and as she set out cups and a plate of biscuits Molly stood at Mavis's knee making sure that she was holding her baby brother properly. 'She doesn't trust me,' Mavis chuckled.

'She's like a mother hen with a chick, an' I'll tell ye what, it makes life so much easier.' She lifted Molly up into her arms and hugged her. 'Who's my best girl an' Mammy's little helper?' Molly giggled. 'Let's put this little lad back in his pram so we can drink our tea in peace.'

With Patrick settled and Molly in her highchair enjoying a cup of milk and a biscuit, Kitty had just sat down to drink her tea when the door opened again.

Beth came in, her cheeks flushed and her smile wide.

'Ye look like somebody who lost a penny an' found a pound.' Kitty got to her feet to fetch another cup. To her surprise Beth hugged her.

'I'm pregnant, Kitty, I'm having a baby.' The words came out in a breathless rush.

'Holy mother! Did you hear that Mavis? Beth's expecting.' Kitty jigged Beth across the hearthrug, thrilled for her friend whom, she knew, so desperately wanted to become a mother.

'That's wonderful news, Beth. Congratulations.' Mavis's tone was sincere but Kitty couldn't help thinking that deep in her heart the kindly spinster must feel a twinge of regret.

'It must have happened while I was in Scotland,' Beth gasped excitedly as she plumped down into a chair at the table. 'Blair's like a dog with two tails.'

'What does your dad think?' Kitty asked warily.

Beth didn't answer immediately. Her expression flitted between bemusement then amazement to pure happiness. 'That's just it,' she marvelled, her voice high, 'I can't get over how pleasant he's been since I got back from Scotland. I expected him to be ranting and raving at my being away, but he didn't. I keep waiting for the bubble to burst. He seems thrilled about the baby, so much so that he told me he'd manage for himself during the week as he doesn't want to tire me out.' Her eyes widened. 'Can you believe that? It was like coming home to a different man.' Overwhelmed, she flapped her hand in front of her face.

'I'm glad he's seen sense.' Kitty gave a satisfied nod.

Beth gave her a searching look. 'Kitty Conlon, does this have something to do with you?' Her eyes had narrowed but her smiling face was alight with curiosity.

'I might have passed a few remarks when I took him Christmas dinner.' Kitty looked as though butter wouldn't melt in her mouth.

Beth and Mavis burst out laughing. 'We might have known it,' they chorused.

38

The weeks flew by, the cold, dark winter days drifting into a welcome early spring. At the first signs of crocuses and daffodils poking their green shoots through the damp earth in her back garden, Kitty felt her spirits rise. Even though things between her and Tom were no better, she counted her blessings: she was the mother of two beautiful children and her dreams for Kitty's Café were soon to be a reality.

One morning in April Kitty answered the rap on the front door; she could barely conceal her anticipation as the scraggy, young postman handed her a thick, brown envelope. 'It looks like some-one's sent you the key to his heart,' he chirped, having fingered the outline of the package.

'Sure, ye know my heart belongs only to ye, Cecil,' Kitty teased, her excitement mounting as she also felt the shape of the key through the paper. Cecil's pimply cheeks glowed. He loved Kitty's banter.

Waving him off, Kitty tore open the envelope. As promised, Gertie had sent the key to the café and a note wishing her every success. Minutes later, her cardigan on and Patrick in one end of he pram and Molly in the other, she dashed down the back lane, stopping off at number five to call for Joey Walker, who was always happy to help her carry her purchases. 'Good luck,' May called after them as her son and Kitty and her children went on their way.

'A large tin of paint in this colour of blue please.' Kitty placed a small bunch of bluebells on the counter in Jim Broadhead's hardware store.

Jim gave the bluebells then Kitty a withering look and growled, 'I'll see what I've got.' He stumped from behind the counter and went to the shelves at the rear of the shop. Kitty gave Joey Walker a mischievous grin. He grinned back.

'This is as near as damn it.' Jim banged a tin down on the counter then prised open the lid. It matched perfectly.

'That's grand, I'll take two,' said Kitty, barely able to keep from sounding like a child let loose in a sweet shop as she asked for two tins of white paint, some brushes and sandpaper.

'Doing a bit of decorating, are you?' Jim asked as he packaged up her order.

'Something like that,' Kitty chirped, paying for the goods then turning to Joey. 'You can carry two of the tins and I'll put the others and the brushes in the bag.' She lifted the tins of blue paint, one on top of the other, like a winner lifting a trophy, then handed them to Joey. Then she placed the others in the large bag hanging from the pram's handle. The pram tilted and Molly let out a little squeal.

Fully laden, Kitty and Joey walked up the back lane to Maggie's door. 'We've got the paint, Maggie,' she cried as they walked in.

'I'm all set,' Maggie replied, wheeling Lily in her pushchair to the door.

'What *are* you wearing?' Kitty hooted with laughter at Maggie's baggy, blue boiler suit and the turban covering her hair.

'I'm not getting covered in paint, not even for you,' Maggie retaliated. 'They gave this to Fred when he got that job in the scrapyard.'

She flicked the collar of the boiler suit. 'I'm putting it to good use – which is more than he ever did.'

'Very wise,' agreed Kitty. 'Right, let's go an' get Beth and Blair then we'll leave Molly an' Lily off with Mavis.'

'She's a good 'un is Mavis,' said Maggie as they left the little girls in the care of a beaming Mavis. 'She'll spoil 'em rotten.'

The motley troop of willing helpers made their way up Weaver Street. Kitty was pushing Patrick in his pram with the brushes tucked at the foot. Maggie flapped behind in her boiler suit, carrying two tins of blue paint, and Beth a bundle of cleaning cloths and a bag of sandwiches. Joey carried the other tins of paint and Blair brought up the rear, toting a small stepladder and a tool bag.

Maggie started to sing 'It's a Long Way to Tipperary' and they all joined in.

Kitty felt fit to burst. Everyone was pitching in to lend her a hand. As she descended the steps to the towpath she had to blink away tears of pure joy.

The sun was shining on the water and small birds flitted in and out of the hedgerows, chirruping a welcome as Kitty and her friends approached the café. She felt in the pocket of her overall for the keys, her fingers tingling as they closed round it and her tummy fluttering as she opened the door. A musty, dusty smell seeped into her nose but it didn't lower her spirits. Her helpers piled in behind, all talking at once.

'Right, let's get started,' Kitty cried, her eyes sparkling and her smile wide.

* * *

Scraping, scrubbing and brushing, the women stripped off peeling paint, and Blair and Joey took turns on the ladder to carry out necessary repairs. By midday they were ready to bring the café back to its former glory.

'You look as if you've been caught in a snowstorm.' Maggie sniggered at the flakes of old, dried paint clinging to Kitty's tawny hair as they sat eating sandwiches. 'And you'd the cheek to laugh at my turban.'

'An' you look like Fatty Arbuckle in that boiler suit.' Kitty riffled her fingers through her curls then turned to Blair. 'Are we ready to start painting?' she asked, deferring to Blair's superior knowledge. He had proved to be quite a handyman with his hammer as he secured loose boards and fixed the gutter that was hanging off.

'Ready when you are,' he said.

Wielding brushes slicked in paint they set to work, Kitty's heart lifting with every stroke as one wooden board after another sported its new coat.

'Oi! Mind who you're splattering.' A blob of white paint landed on Maggie's cheek. She flicked her brush, paint worming its way down Kitty's overall.

'Really, you two! You're worse than a couple of kids.' Beth, always the most circumspect of the three friends, gave Maggie and Kitty a despairing look.

Enjoying themselves immensely, Kitty and her good neighbours put their hearts and souls into giving the dilapidated building a new lease of life. By the end of the afternoon, the blue boards rivalled the bluebells on the riverbank, and the white boards gleamed like fresh fallen snow.

Kitty, her eyes glowing and brimming with tears, stood gazing at what they had achieved. 'We did it! We did it!' She danced up to each of her friends in turn, hugging and thanking them.

'What are friends for if they don't lend a hand when needed?' Beth said.

* * *

Tom strode through the crowd at Aintree, ignoring the horses galloping down the track and oblivious to acquaintances calling out greetings. His expression was grim and his thoughts black. He might have lost Priscilla, his first class ticket into racing's elite circle, but he'd be damned before he let them drop him from the syndicate. He'd invested too much time and money in the risky business. Seeing the person he was looking for coming towards him through the crowd, he quickened his pace until he stood foursquare in front of him.

'Nigel.' Tom stuck out his hand and forced a smile.

Nigel kept his hands in his pockets and glanced round shiftily.

'Not now, Tom,' he said, his expression not in the least friendly as he made to sidestep him. Tom blocked his way.

'What's happening with the syndicate? No one's answering my phone calls.'

'The syndicate's finished as far as you're concerned, Tom.' Nigel glanced nervously over his shoulder. 'And I'd rather not be seen talking to you.' He tried to push Tom out of his way, but Tom held his ground.

'What do you mean, finished?' Tom's lips twisted in a snarl and his blue eyes flashed dangerously.

'What I said,' growled Nigel. 'Certain people are asking awkward questions and I'll not have my reputation ruined by the likes of you and your shenanigans. Now, get out of my way!' He shouldered past Tom and hurried into the crowd. Tom paled. He knew exactly who the 'certain people' were. A shiver coursed down his spine. He'd been warned that the Jockey Club had their eye on him.

'Bastards,' he muttered under his breath.

Then he saw Winky Kelly, a has-been jockey he'd paid to pull a race or two. Winky spotted him and hurried in the opposite direction, his bowed legs thrashing like pistons, but not fast enough to escape Tom's long stride. 'Leave me be, Mr Conlon. Ye're bad news,' he hissed, twisting from Tom's grasp then vanishing into the crowd.

For a second Tom's brain refused to function. He was paralysed, couldn't breathe, as a glimpse of something dark and ominous flooded his mind. He'd been found out for what he really was. Suddenly, he needed a strong drink. He headed for the bar, his eyes barely focusing and his steps unsteady.

He sat in an alcove, a double whiskey in his hand.

'No, darling! He's a Scottish laird, the Right Honourable something or other,' a high-pitched, haughty voice in the next alcove squawked. 'Prissy's landed her catch at last, and Nigel's over the moon,'

Tom pricked his ears. Prissy... Scottish laird...

'And the wedding's in June, you say? What happened to the handsome Irishman? She was like a wasp round a jam pot the last time I saw her with him.'

Haughty voice gave a shrill laugh. 'Oh, darling, you know what Prissy's like. If it looks exciting and different, she wants it. He was just her bit of rough.'

Her companion gave a throaty chuckle.

Seething with rage, and the words 'her bit of rough' burning inside his head, Tom tossed his whiskey back in one gulp and went to the bar to order another.

* * *

Late that night, Kitty in bed, she heard Tom fumbling with his key at the front door and then the crash as the door swung on its hinges, hitting the wall. She sat up, her limbs tense as she listened to him stumble up the stairs into his bedroom, then the bathroom and back to the bedroom. In the silence that followed, she flopped back against the pillows, thankful that the noise hadn't wakened Patrick and Molly. Eyes wide open, she gazed up at the ceiling.

Only once since the night she had moved Tom into the back bedroom had he made an attempt to enter her room and demand his conjugal rights. For that she was grateful, but there were nights when she yearned for the feel of his hard body against hers, his lips seeking hers as they made sweet, passionate love. Nowadays, when he was standing close by, she had to steel herself to resist reaching out to touch him. Time and again she had searched for a solution that would take them back to the way things had once been when they had loved and laughed and faced the world together. But Tom had lied and cheated and they couldn't turn back the clock. She turned over and cuddled Molly's little, warm body tucked in beside her.

Tom looked wretched when he came downstairs the next morning, his face haggard and unshaven, and a wild, hunted look in his eyes.

'Should I get the children ready so we can go to twelve o'clock mass?' Kitty asked, trying desperately to bring an air of normality into their miserable lives. Tom ignored her. He slumped into his armchair and lit a cigarette. When Kitty handed him a mug of tea he said, 'You've got a smudge of blue paint on your arm.'

Kitty looked, and smiled. She must have missed it last night when she'd taken her bath and washed her hair. She told him why and then watched as his lips twisted into an ugly sneer. She waited for the angry words but none came. She carried on with her chores, and Tom sat lighting one cigarette off another. Kitty took a long look at him. He seemed diminished, his expression haunted.

* * *

The next day, Tom still in bed, Kitty paid another visit to the hardware shop. Patrick was sleeping, his tawny head resting on the pillow and Molly kneeling in the foot of the pram. Kitty parked it outside the shop door. 'Sit still, Molly, don't move an inch,' she warned before nipping inside.

'Another tin of bluebell paint, please,' she said, keeping one eye on the pram and willing Jim to hurry with the transaction.

She was putting the tin into a bag hanging from the pram handle when John arrived at her side. 'Good morning, Kitty. What are you up to today?'

'Painting chairs,' she replied, and then went on to tell him about painting the outside of the cabin.

'I'd have liked to be there. You should have let me know.'

Kitty grinned. 'There's still plenty of chairs to paint.'

'Give me half an hour. I'll meet you at the café.'

Kitty felt her cheeks redden. 'I... I wasn't hinting,' she stammered.

'Half an hour,' he said, smiling warmly and walking away.

* * *

Tom was up out of bed and washed and shaved when Kitty got back home.

'I'm going to work,' he grunted. When Kitty asked where he looked confused. 'The bookies. Where else?' His tone was hollow.

'Maybe a racetrack – or to meet your glamorous girlfriend,' she said perkily as she put clean nappies and some of Molly's toys into a bag.

Tom bit back the urge to say 'bitch'. He needed time to think then pick up where he'd left off; he couldn't bear the thought of losing all that he had gained. He wasn't prepared to stay a small town bookmaker for the rest of his life.

Kitty began to make sandwiches.

'What are you up to today?' Curious, Tom sounded as though he cared.

'I'm going to the café to paint chairs.' Kitty made it sound as though it was the most natural thing in the world.

Tom sighed. 'You're determined to make a go of this, aren't you?'

Kitty met his gaze directly. 'I have to, Tom. I have to take care of me and mine.'

'I'd never leave you without money, Kitty. You know that,' he said solemnly.

'I'm not sure what I know any more,' Kitty said sadly.

Tom almost ran from the kitchen and out of the front door.

Kitty concentrated on placing thinly sliced ham between slices of bread.

* * *

John was standing outside the café when Kitty arrived. 'You did a good job,' he said, admiring the fresh blue and white painted boards.

Kitty smiled. The café looked even better now that the paint had dried to a hard, gloss finish. 'I had plenty of good friends to help me,' she said, unlocking the door and feeling a thrill of anticipation as she stepped inside.

John helped her bring in the pram then watched as she made a playpen out of chairs in one corner and threw down a blanket for Molly to sit on. In went the toys, and then Molly.

'She's such a good, little thing,' Kitty remarked, as Molly began to play happily. 'Ye'd think she knows I have to work, and this is her way of helping. And this fella here,' she continued, wheeling the pram to the back door, 'is no bother as long as he's fed on time.' She parked the pram in the shade of a willow then went back into the café, leaving the door wide open.

John had already opened the tin of paint and laid out the brushes. They talked easily as they applied coats of blue paint, the shabby plain wooden chairs looking almost like new as Kitty and John shared interests and gossip. Kitty found it highly pleasurable to be working with someone who seemed to be enjoying himself as much as she was.

It was whilst they were sitting eating sandwiches that Kitty reached out to remove a buttery crumb clinging to the corner of John's mouth. She did it without thinking, but as she flicked her forefinger over his lips she wondered what they would feel like if she were kissing him. Her cheeks flamed at the thought.

She jumped up. *Whatever am I thinking?* Kitty chastised herself. And whatever had John made of her overly familiar gesture? To hide her embarrassment she rushed out on the pretence of attending to Patrick. He was sleeping peacefully, but Kitty's thoughts were in turmoil. *John Sykes is just a good, kind friend, isn't he?* she told herself, gazing up through the branches of the willow tree. *Yet he has a way of looking at me or saying something that makes me...*

Tossing aside the thought she went back inside. He couldn't possibly have notions about her, a married woman with two small children. *It's just that I miss that side of things,* she thought, and picking up her brush she resumed painting.

'You're quiet,' John said after a while, having noticed that Kitty was avoiding looking at him. He puzzled over what he might have said or done to offend her. He watched as she came upright to stretch her aching arms and back, wishing that he could place his own arms about her and stroke away her weariness.

* * *

'You know how John helped me paint the chairs? Well yesterday he reorganised the counter and tomorrow he's going to paint it and the inside walls white.' Kitty was giving Maggie an update. She was just as keen as Kitty was to see the café open.

'You an' him are spending a lot of time together,' Maggie said suggestively.

'He's just a good friend, and nothing more,' Kitty protested.

Maggie snorted and rolled her eyes.

'An' don't be lookin' at me like that,' Kitty snapped. 'I'm a married woman with children.'

'So what,' Maggie scoffed. 'It not as though you an' Tom...'

'That has nothing to do with it.' Kitty stamped her foot, her cheeks on fire.

'Methinks the lady protests too much,' Maggie jibed, laughing at Kitty's chagrin.

39

On Friday morning, Kitty walked up Weaver Street with alacrity. Tomorrow she was opening the café to the public. Molly, her chubby legs dangling over the front of the pram, drummed her heels and giggled at the speed they were travelling. Tucked under the hood, Patrick slept. At the church gate, Kitty paused and blessed herself. *Please God, let everything go all right.*

In the café, making last minute preparations, she told Molly, 'Tomorrow there'll be lots of people sat at these tables eating Mammy's buns and cakes.'

Molly, playing happily with her doll on the open doorstep, looked up and smiled. Suddenly, Kitty had the urge to dance, and lifting her daughter and humming the tune to 'If I Had My Way', she waltzed between the tables, casting a practised eye over the blue and white checked tablecloths, the gleaming cutlery and the shiny white cups, saucers and plates. 'Let's hope tomorrow's dry and sunny,' she said, twirling to a finish by the counter.

She was thinking of the flyers that Joey had delivered round the town. Good weather might encourage the people to come, as might the free bun with every cup of tea. She'd ordered her bread and sandwich fillings from Connie and now all she had to do was go home and bake, bake, bake.

Saturday dawned bright and dry. Kitty had been up since daybreak, and by ten o'clock she was pushing the pram, loaded with her babies and tins of cakes and biscuits, up Weaver Street. Alongside came Maggie with Lily in her pushchair, and behind them Mavis and Beth carrying bags filled with loaves, sliced ham and cheese. Scarce though these things were, the local shopkeepers had been more than fair. They all wanted to play a part for the grand opening at eleven.

'It's like a Sunday school outing,' Kitty remarked.

'You didn't think we were going to let you do it on your own, did you?' Maggie had one hand on the handle of Lily's pushchair and the other holding a cigarette.

'I'm just as excited as you, Kitty,' twittered Mavis. She had baked fancy pastries especially for the occasion.

Beth's coat hung open, revealing her little baby bump of which she was immensely proud. 'We're like the four musketeers,' she said.

Mavis frowned. 'I thought there were only three.'

'Yes, Athos, Porthos and Aramis,' Beth explained. 'D'Artagnan was the fourth.'

'Bloody hell!' Maggie groaned. 'Now we're getting history lessons. Which one are you gonna be, Kitty? Bags I be Arsehole.'

'It's Athos or Aramis,' Beth corrected primly.

Kitty flourished an imaginary sword. 'I'll be D'Artagnan.'

* * *

'Four cups of tea and four ham sandwiches, please.' The young woman sitting at a table by the window with a young man and an older couple smiled at Kitty.

The young man grinned. 'An' don't forget the free buns,' he said cheekily.

'I won't.' Kitty returned the grin then whisked between the crowded tables to fulfil the order.

Cora had been her first customer of the day, closely followed by May and Jack then several workers on holiday from the mill. Connie had dropped in during her lunch break. And it wasn't just neighbours who turned out to support Kitty. It being Easter weekend the inhabitants of Edge Hill, lured by glorious weather and curiosity for something new, had turned out in force. The café door was open wide, bright afternoon sun streaming in on the happy, chattering customers, and as Kitty served order after order, the lively scene warmed her heart, even though her feet were aching.

Beth and Mavis had left earlier, taking the children with them, but Maggie insisted on staying. Late in the afternoon, there was a lull. Behind the counter Kitty poured two cups of tea, and when Maggie approached carrying a tray of used cups and plates Kitty said, 'Here, take the weight off your feet an' drink this.' She lifted her own cup and drank thirstily. Maggie set down the tray and breathed a sigh of relief.

'An' there was you worrying it might not take off.' She swigged a mouthful of tea. 'This place'll be a gold mine.'

'It won't be like this every day, but if I get half the trade we've had today on a regular basis it'll suit me fine.' Kitty gave Maggie a rapturous smile then turned to wave at a party just leaving. 'Come again,' she called cheerily.

'We will,' they chorused, an elderly woman hanging back to say, 'It's been lovely. It's just what the towpath needs.'

Maggie rattled the tins that at the start of the day had contained the buns that Kitty had baked – six dozen in all. 'There's only one left. Can I have it?'

'Aye, help yourself.' Kitty was pleased to think there would be no leftovers.

'Are dogs allowed?' a voice called out.

Kitty hurried forward. 'She most certainly is,' she said, the very sight of John and Goldie adding pleasure to an already momentous day.

'How did it go?' He sat down at an empty table.

'Beyond all expectation,' she told him, her eyes dancing.

He gazed up at her, smiling warmly. 'I'm pleased for you, Kitty.'

Kitty knew he meant it.

* * *

Throughout the summer months the café thrived, regulars dropping in at specific times of day, and the mill workers from Holroyd's deserting the recently installed canteen for Kitty's tasty food and friendly banter. However, by late September, with the days drawing in and the weather uncertain, fewer people walked the towpath. Until now, Kitty had always been able to cover the rent and make a profit, but she couldn't help worrying about the future.

As she served a lively crowd of anglers and birdwatchers one day, she thought fondly of Mavis who sometimes helped by looking after Molly and Patrick, but such thoughts led to her thinking about Tom. It saddened her that he hadn't once bothered to visit the café. He was surly and withdrawn for much of the time, going about his business in that secretive way of his. Only two nights ago she had asked him why he continued to stay with her. He hadn't responded immediately, but when he had, he'd taken her by surprise.

'I never meant to hurt you, Kitty. I'd have let you stay on in the house, and I'd have seen you right for money,' he had said.

'So ye did intend to leave me.'

Tom's face had crumpled.

'Why didn't ye?' she'd asked gently, feeling an unexpected wave of pity for him. He hadn't answered.

No doubt he'll go when he's good and ready, she told herself as she cleared a table and welcomed new customers, *and until he does we'll continue to live together but apart, like ships that pass in the night.*

40

Kitty had just put Patrick and Molly upstairs for the night when she heard the knock on the front door. She hurried downstairs, wondering who it might be. It couldn't be Tom. He had a key. He'd been gone most of the day, to where she didn't know. She unlocked the door, clutching at the doorframe to steady herself as she looked at the tall man standing on the step. Her heart hammered and her mouth suddenly went dry. She gazed into his lean, handsome face and at his hair, as smooth and red as a fox's pelt. After all this time was it really...

'Shaun! Shaun!' She flung herself against his chest. 'Is it really you?'

Even as he returned her embrace, Shaun glanced nervously up and down the dark street. 'Steady on there, Kit, you nearly had me over. Let's get inside,' he urged, pushing her into the hallway. Tears of joy wetting her cheeks, Kitty held on to her brother as though she would never let him go.

'Oh, Shaun, I thought I'd never see ye again,' she cried, bringing her hands from behind his neck to cup his cheeks and look deeply into his eyes.

'Long runs the fox,' he said, giving Kitty his old, familiar smile. It was the code name he had used when he fought with the Irish Republican Army.

'Long runs the fox,' she echoed, almost dragging him down the hallway.

'Who's here?' he asked urgently. Kitty saw the nervous tic in his right cheek. He hadn't had that before. It pained her to see it and she wondered how he had come by it.

'Nobody but us – and the children,' she said, pulling him into the kitchen.

'Children?'

'Aye – just the two of 'em, upstairs sleeping.' She felt the tension leave his body, yet he still glanced round warily as she led him to the chair by the fire.

'How did you find me?' Amazed, she indicated for him to sit down. When he did she sat at his feet, her arms resting on his knees as she gazed up into his face.

'The brothers,' Shaun replied. 'Paddy wrote to me in jail telling me ye'd gone to live with your husband in England. When I knew that they were letting me go I wrote and asked him for your address.'

'Paddy wrote to ye? It's more than he ever did to me,' Kitty expostulated, furious to think that her older brother had known all this time where Shaun was and hadn't troubled to let her know. 'He never answered one of my letters, not even when I sent Christmas presents.'

'Aye, well, he's no great hand at letter writing, but the brothers were always sympathetic to the cause. I suppose they wanted to know how I was faring so they could pass the news on to the lads in the brigade.'

A door slammed in Maggie's house. Shaun reared up, only Kitty's weight on his knees preventing him from standing.

'Ye're awful jumpy.'

Shaun frowned. 'I have me reasons,' he muttered.

Tears gathered behind Kitty's eyes. 'Was it terrible bad in...?' The word stuck in her throat, her voice almost a whisper.

Shaun sighed. 'Bad enough, but I had friends along of me – and enemies.' He shrugged, his expression grim. 'An' now I've served me time they tell me I'm a free man fit to go wherever I choose.' His short, harsh laugh belittled the idea. 'But before I do I had to come and find ye,' he said, fondling her hair and pasting on a brave smile. 'I've missed ye, Kit.'

'And I've missed ye. Ye'll never know how much.'

'I think I do, Kit.' Shaun gave her a haunted look. Kitty wanted to say that he was still the same but his gaunt, nervous features belied that. She got to her feet.

'Ye must be tired and hungry. I'll put the kettle on an' do ye a fry.'

In a dream-like state she made her brother a meal, barely able to believe he was sitting by her fireside. Shaun sat at the table to eat and Kitty to drink her tea.

'Where were ye when they caught ye?'

'Dublin. There to do a job,' he said in between mouthfuls, shovelling in the food, 'but some cowardly bastard touted on us,' he added bitterly.

Dublin? Kitty thought how near to her he had been in the city and she not knowing he was there. She might have helped rescue him.

'What did they do to ye?' she asked, the words coming out in a strangled whisper as she reached for his hand.

The tic in Shaun's cheek jumped. 'They beat me senseless, and by the time I came to I was in shackles an' on me way to England. Wandsworth for a time then Birmingham.' He set aside his knife nd fork and shook his head as if to dispel the memories, his right ye and cheek twitching.

Kitty reached across the table and placed a soothing hand on ;haun's cheek. 'Ye must have suffered somethin' terrible.'

'Aye, ye could say that. The screws treated us like pigs, an' they eft us at the mercy of the bastards from the Black North,' growled ;haun, referring to the Protestant Unionists who detested the IRA and Catholicism. 'They hated us worse than the screws. We never had a minute's peace. I've them to thank for this,' he said, pushing up his sleeve to reveal a long, jagged scar on his forearm.

Kitty drew a sharp breath. 'Oh, my poor love.' She ran a gentle finger down the length of the scar. 'Had ye no one to protect ye?' She shivered, picturing him fighting for his life as the thugs took their revenge.

'Aye, but we were few in number, just wee Danny Og from Ballymacurly, remember him? An' two fellas from Kerry.' He gave a harsh laugh. 'When the Prods set about us the screws turned a blind eye. It was their way of killin' us without doin' it themselves.'

Kitty's heart bled for him as he told her of the danger and the indignities of life in prison. 'To think ye suffered all that, and for nothing.'

'Never say it was for nothing, Kitty. Things are changing. We'll win in the end.'

She wished she could believe him.

'Ah, my poor Shaun, my brave wee darlin',' she said through her tears. She lifted his hand, holding it to her cheek. 'Ye've paid the price, but you're here with me now an' that's all that matters.' They sat in silence for a moment as both of them tried to bury the past in the deepest, darkest corners of their minds.

'Well, what about this husband of yours?' Shaun's tone was forcedly cheery. 'How did ye meet him? Where is he from?'

'Clare. An' I met him in Dublin.' She glossed over how they had met, her hands growing clammy and her voice beginning to wobble as she delayed telling him that Tom had no love for the IRA, and had served in the British Navy.

When she did, Shaun looked askance. 'Ach, Kit! Whatever were ye thinking? Did what me an' the lads were fighting for mean nothing to ye?'

'I was in love, Shaun, head over heels. I thought I knew what I was doing. I loved him then.'

Shaun's eyes narrowed. 'Ye loved him then, but ye don't love him now? Is that what you're sayin', Kit?' His eyes darkened and his lips formed a thin, hard line. 'What has he done to ye?'

Choosing her words carefully, Kitty told him of why they had come to England, and about Tom's job. Then, like a tidal wave rushing to the shore, words gushed from her heart as she told him the whole sorry story.

'The bastard! The dirty bastard,' growled Shaun, clenching his fists.

They heard the front door open then slam shut. Kitty leapt to her feet, and so did Shaun. 'Don't ye be making any trouble now,' she pleaded. 'For my sake say nothing.' She wiped the tears from her cheeks and gave Shaun a threatening glare. He nodded grimly.

Tom stopped in his tracks as soon as he entered the kitchen. He'd never met his brother-in-law but one glance at the pelt of red hair told him that the man standing at the table was 'the fox', the man he had forbidden Kitty to talk about. He stared at Shaun, a gamut of emotions flitting across his face. Then he stretched his lips in a contentious smile.

'Look who's here, Tom,' Kitty said brightly, taking hold of Shaun's arm.

'So this is your brother Shaun.' Tom sounded far calmer than he felt.

'Hello, Tom. Kit's been telling me all about ye.' Shaun's words were weighted.

Tom flinched. Kitty tightened her grip on Shaun's arm. 'I'll make a fresh pot of tea and you two can get to know each other,' she said with false enthusiasm.

The two men stood eyeing one another warily. Kitty's eyes flitted from one man to the other. *How alike they are*, she thought, as she set the kettle to boil. It had never before occurred to her that Shaun's rangy physique and his facial features were so like Tom's.

The men sat down, Shaun asking about Tom's work, and Tom enquiring as to how Shaun had known where to come. The stilted conversation deteriorated into a tedious discussion about transport between Birmingham and Liverpool before petering out. Neither Tom nor Shaun mentioned his time in jail.

'Ah, that's grand, Kit,' said Shaun as she handed him a mug, the arrival of the tea as much a blessed relief to him as it was to Tom and Kitty. As they drank, Kitty talked about Molly and Patrick, Shaun delighted to be an uncle. He drained his mug. 'Where's your lavatory, Kit?'

The moment Shaun was out of earshot Tom said, 'He can't stop here.'

Kitty glared at him defiantly. 'An' where would ye have him go at this time of night? He's my brother, and if anyone should leave it's you, Tom. Shaun has done me no harm. I can't say the same for ye.' She walked to the door. 'I'll away an' make up the couch.'

Seething, Tom stood with his back to the dying fire, toying with the idea of throwing the fellow out into the street. But Tom wasn't a brawler; common sense told him he'd most likely lose the fight.

* * *

The next morning Tom had already left when Kitty came downstairs. Shaun was lying on the couch when Kitty popped her head round the front room door. Startled, he leapt up. He was still wearing his street clothes even though Kitty had given him a pair of Tom's pyjamas.

'It's only me,' she said, seeing fear in his eyes. She went to draw back the curtains.

'Don't!' Shaun snapped. 'Leave them be.'

Kitty let her arms fall to her sides. She turned and gave him a puzzled look. 'What has ye so nervous, Shaun? There's no one here will harm ye.'

'Ye don't know that, Kit.' His face contorted. 'They hunt ye down wherever ye go. Come nightfall, I'll be on me way.'

Kitty's face fell. 'Ye can't leave so soon,' she wailed. 'An' who is it that's after ye? What do they want?'

'Best ye don't know,' growled Shaun. His expression softened. 'I shouldn't a come, but I had to see ye one last time, Kit.' He pulled her close, kissing the top of her head. 'Now dry your eyes an' make me some breakfast.'

'But... but... tell me what the...' she stammered through her tears.

Shaun placed a gentle finger on her lips. 'The less ye know the better,' he said. 'Now off ye go.' He turned her towards the door, flicking her rump as she left. Kitty cried all the harder.

For the rest of the day, Shaun kept to the front room. Kitty introduced him to Molly and Patrick, and he played with Molly as he and Kitty reminisced about their own childhoods. In the late afternoon, Kitty had just nipped up to the bathroom when Maggie called round. Finding no one in the kitchen, and hearing Molly's laughter in the front room, she walked on in just as Kitty came downstairs. Making a hasty introduction, Kitty grabbed Maggie by the arm.

'He's as nervous as a bloody kitten,' Maggie said, when they were in the kitchen. 'He nearly jumped out of his skin when I walked in.'

'He's highly strung. An' if ye don't mind I've things to do. I'll explain later,' she said, shepherding Maggie to the back door. 'By the way, don't be telling anyone he's here.'

Burning with curiosity, Maggie went back home.

When Tom came back he ignored Shaun's presence, and as darkness fell Shaun prepared to leave. 'I'll be safe once I'm back in Ireland,' he said, holding Kitty in a tight embrace and wondering if he'd make it that far.

'God go with ye,' Kitty implored, her tears blinding her as she watched him disappear into the darkness of the cold November night. He didn't look back.

Kitty's heart was heavy as she made her way up Weaver Street the next morning. At the top she paused, and instead of carrying on to the towpath, she pushed the pram up to the church door. Lifting Molly down and letting her walk ahead, she scooped Patrick into her arms and went inside. Up at the altar Kitty knelt, and with Patrick in her arms and Molly kneeling at her side she said a fervent prayer for Shaun's safety. As she gazed up at the cross, the cloistral quiet calming her agitation, a sudden shaft of early morning sun pierced the stained glass window behind the altar. It lit on Patrick's red-gold hair. Kitty squinted her eyes and smiled. Taking it as a good omen, she got to her feet.

41

Tom was hunched in his chair in the bookies, showing no interest in what was going on around him. Rodney was busy taking the last bets of the day. Tom topped up his glass from the bottle of whiskey on his desk and drank deeply. He was done for. His trip to Sandown the day before had let him know without a doubt he was a pariah at the racetracks. Nigel had clearly done a good job in blackening his character with the owners and trainers; the rest he had done for himself. Even the no-marks had avoided him. His grand plans were all awry and he was at a loss what to do next.

Deep in thought, he drained his glass and replenished it.

* * *

In the Wagon and Horses, Vi lolled against the counter, not bothering to hide her yawns as old Sammy Brook, the town's busybody, wittered on about the state of the roads. Two strangers walked in. Vi perked up. They were burly, rough-looking fellows, the sort she fancied. The taller of the two had a scar running from below one eye to the corner of his mouth.

'What can I get you?' Her husky voice was most inviting. She pulled two pints of stout. 'I've not seen you before,' she said, fluttering her eyelashes.

'We're just passin' through, looking up an old friend,' Scar-face said. 'Mebbe ye can help us. We thought he might drink in here.' He gave her a brief description.

'Irish?' Vi thought of Tom then dismissed him. 'Red hair, you say? Sorry, love, I can't help you there.' Vi moved down the counter to serve a customer.

'He's Irish, him what takes bets in the Weaver's Arms,' Sammy said.

The men exchanged interested glances.

Scar-face frowned. 'Is he new to the place?'

'Aye,' replied Sammy. Anyone who had lived in the town for less than thirty years was a newcomer in his opinion.

'Where's the Weaver's Arms?'

Sammy furnished Scar-face with directions, and revelling in their attention, he added, 'You can either go in through the pub or the back door in the alley.'

'Ye've earned yourself a pint.' Scar-face rattled a handful of coins on the counter, and swigging his own in one gulp and his mate doing the same, they hurried off. Vi watched them go, disappointed.

* * *

Tom's drunkenness had made him maudlin. He staggered across the room to the cupboard and the safe he'd installed. He emptied its contents into his briefcase, every penny he owned: Tom didn't believe in banks. Tonight he'd give Kitty some of his savings, and tomorrow he'd leave and head south, maybe Newmarket or Cheltenham. They didn't know him there. Bleary-eyed, he let his gaze roam the little room that was his empire then struggled into his overcoat and rammed on his trilby hat. He didn't hear the footsteps outside the door or see the scarred face peering through the window. Neither could he hear the urgent whispers.

'Is it him, Clarry?'

'Aye, it's him all right. I'd know that long streak o' piss anywhere.'

Tom shambled to the door. The briefcase lay forgotten on his desk. He stepped out into the dark alley, closing the door behind him. He turned, fumbling for the key. His face smashed into the door and he slithered to his knees. He heard his ribs crack as a savage kick sent him sprawling. Before Tom hit the cobbles, Scar-face wielded his iron bar and Tom felt his head explode. His trilby hat flew off.

'Jaysus! It's not him,' Clarry gasped, staring down at Tom's thick, black hair.

42

Kitty closed the door behind the last of the mourners. Standing in the hallway, she recalled the first time she and Tom had entered the house in Weaver Street. *What hopes we had then, how fortunate we thought we were to have all this, and now look where we are,* she said silently to him, *you in the grave and me here alone with the children. Where did we go wrong, Tom?*

She wrapped her arms around her chest and rocked back and forth on her heels letting the tears that she had been holding back flow. Great gulping sobs tore from her throat, wracking her entire body. After a while, her tears spent, she went into the kitchen and sat in Tom's chair. Leaning her aching head against the cushion she smelled his cologne and the faint smell of tobacco. Tears flowed again. Deep in her heart she knew that she was crying for the Tom who had swept her off her feet in Dublin almost five years before, and not for the husband she had buried earlier that day. That their marriage had ended in such a devastating manner made it all the harder to bear.

A drayman making an early morning delivery of ale to the Weaver's Arms had found Tom's battered body in the alley. After that, everything had been a blur. Visits from the police – they were still looking for his attackers – and then the inquest, the coroner reporting the cause of death as a severe beating resulting in a bleed on the brain and a punctured lung from his broken ribs.

'I was lying in me bed an' he was across the street dying in the alley,' Kitty had wailed hysterically in Maggie's arms.

'You weren't to know, Kitty,' Maggie had consoled. 'He'd stayed out all night before when you didn't know where he was. Don't go blaming yourself.'

But Kitty was shrouded in guilt, haunted by the thought of him lying there with no one by to help or comfort him or send for the priest to give him the last rites. Not even when Sam and Cora had called with Tom's briefcase did she find any peace of mind. 'What does money matter at a time like this?' she'd screamed.

Yet, as she sat staring into the dying fire she knew that had things turned out differently for him Tom would eventually have left her, and that for some time now she had been preparing for the day when she would have to make a new life for herself and Molly and Patrick. She had to go on for their sakes.

And I won't be doing it alone, she told herself, thinking of the kindness her friends and neighbours had shown during the days leading up to the funeral. Maggie and Beth had been by her side almost constantly. Connie and May had helped with the children, and Mavis had provided a beautiful tea for the many friends and customers who had attended Tom's funeral. He would have been proud at the turnout, even though he would have preferred them to own or train racehorses, she mused wryly. Poor Tom.

Feeling in need of a strong cup of tea, she got to her feet and put the kettle on. She'd have one before she went to collect Molly from Connie's and Patrick from Mavis's. As she waited for the kettle to boil, she thought about the café. She'd reopen it next week; it would be a shame to let the business slide after all her hard work. Life must go on.

One thought led to another. She recalled the fear and the thrill of coming to live in Liverpool, and how she had then thought the world was her oyster. But life hadn't turned out quite like she'd expected. She found it hard to believe how, in a mere handful of years, her life had been filled with so many joys and sorrows. She had given birth to two beautiful children, formed wonderful friendships, was the owner of a successful business, and had endured the pain as her marriage to Tom had disintegrated only for it to end with his cruel death: so much grief and yet so much happiness.

She was standing in the middle of the room, lost in a plethora of memories, when there was a gentle knock at the back door. It opened and John came in, his face creased with concern. Two long strides and he faced her, taking both her hands in his and clasping them tenderly. His warm strength seeped through his palms and into her own and as they stood silently for a minute or two, Kitty felt that her world had just been coloured that little bit brighter.

'I just came to see if you were all right,' he said.

Kitty smiled a slow, sweet, gentle smile. 'I will be, John, I will be,' she said, her heart and her head telling her that his kindness and that of her friends and neighbours in Weaver Street would see her through the years to come.

ACKNOWLEDGMENTS

A novel springs from not from one idea but many. The main inspiration for this story came from the memories I have of living in a street in the north of England not unlike Weaver Street. Although it is a work of fiction I crafted it from stories my mother told me, and from real events in WWI, a period in history that fascinates me. To bring a novel like this to life involves many people – those we fondly remember who provided the heart of the story, and dedicated editors and publishers who then turn it into the finished copy: their expertise is invaluable.

I am indebted to my brilliant agent, Judith Murdoch, for her faith in me. She always has my best interests at heart.

My sincere gratitude to the talented team at Boldwood for their diligence, patience and friendly support. A special thank you Tara Loder and Candida Bradford. Your sharp eyes and attention to detail amaze me. Thanks also to Nia Benyon and the marketing team for producing such a beautiful cover, and promoting my book.

My love and sincere thanks to my son, Charles, and his wife, Martina, and to my nephew, Paul Downey and his wife, Annemarie. I can't thank them enough for the loving support they willingly give in countless other ways. Thanks also to my Downey/Oldroyd fan club in Yorkshire. And to the best grandsons in the world, Harry, Matthew and Jack. Thanks for making me a proud and happy Nana.

To my readers: I hope you enjoyed reading about the folks in

Weaver Street as much as I enjoyed writing about them. For some of you this may be the first of my books you've come across – for others it might be the latest. Either way, thank you for buying it and for reading it. You make the wonderful job of writing so much more worthwhile.

MORE FROM CHRISSIE WALSH

We hope you enjoyed reading *Welcome to Weaver Street*. If you did, please leave a review.

If you'd like to gift a copy, this book is also available as an ebook, digital audio download and audiobook CD.

Sign up to Chrissie Walsh's mailing list for news, competitions and updates on future books.

https://bit.ly/ChrissieWalshNewsletter

ABOUT THE AUTHOR

Chrissie Walsh was born and raised in West Yorkshire and is a retired schoolteacher with a passion for history. She has written several successful sagas documenting feisty women in challenging times for Aria. Welcome to Weaver Street was the first title in her new WWI saga series for Boldwood.

Follow Chrissie on social media:

 twitter.com/walshchrissie

Boldwood

Boldwood Books is an award-winning fiction publishing company seeking out the best stories from around the world.

Find out more at www.boldwoodbooks.com

Join our reader community for brilliant books, competitions and offers!

Follow us
@BoldwoodBooks
@BookandTonic

Sign up to our weekly deals newsletter

https://bit.ly/BoldwoodBNewsletter

Printed in Great Britain
by Amazon

24038291R00195